# CRITICS AND EXPERTS PRAISE HARRISON AND MINSKY'S
## **The Turing Option**

■

"High technology and deep psychology... a fast-paced thriller where the science isn't fiction."
—K. Eric Drexler, Ph.D., president, Foresight Institute, author of *Engines of Creation*

■

"A fine example of collaboration, in which a scientist and a writer craft a thriller around state-of-the-art intelligence."
—*Chicago Tribune*

■

"Undeniably fascinating."
—*West Coast Review of Books*

■

"This is an amazing novel written by two writers who are determined to take the 'fiction' out of science fiction."
—*New England Reviews of Books*

■

"The authors present, in a lucid and compelling manner, complex theories about how the brain stores and organizes information."
—*Washing...*

# THE
# TURING OPTION

# HARRY HARRISON
### AND
# MARVIN MINSKY

**WARNER BOOKS**

A Time Warner Company

WARNER BOOKS EDITION

Questar® is a registered trademark of Warner Books, Inc.

Book design by H. Roberts   |   Cover illustration by Bob Eggleton
Cover design by Don Puckey   |   Cover photo by The Image Bank

Warner Books, Inc.
1271 Avenue of the Americas
New York, NY 10020

 A Time Warner Company

Printed in the United States of America

Originally published in hardcover by Warner Books.
First Printed in Paperback October, 1993

10 9 8 7 6 5 4 3 2 1

*For Julie, Margaret and Henry: Moira and Todd—*
*A story of your tomorrow.*

# THE TURING TEST

In 1950, Alan M. Turing, one of the earliest pioneers of computer science, considered the question of whether a machine could ever think. But because it is so hard to define *thinking* he proposed to start with an ordinary digital computer and then asked whether, by increasing its memory and speed, and providing it with a suitable program, it might be made to play the part of a man? His answer:

*"The question, 'Can machines think?' I believe to be too meaningless to deserve discussion. Nevertheless I believe that at the end of the century the use of words and general, educated opinion will have altered so much that one will be able to speak of machines thinking without expecting to be contradicted."*

Alan Turing, 1950

# 1

## OCOTILLO WELLS, CALIFORNIA

### February 8, 2023

J. J. Beckworth, the Chairman of Megalobe Industries, was disturbed, though years of control prevented any outward display of his inner concern. He was not worried, not afraid; just disturbed. He turned about in his chair to look at the spectacular desert sunset. The red sky behind the San Ysidro mountain range to the west threw russet light upon the Santa Rosa Mountains that stretched along the northern horizon. The evening shadows of the ocotillo and cactus painted long lines on the gray sands of the desert before him. Normally the stark beauty of this soothed and relaxed him; not today. The gentle ping of the intercom cut through his thoughts.

"What is it?" he said. The machine recognized his voice and turned itself on. His secretary spoke.

*"Dr. McCrory is here and would like to speak with you."*

J. J. Beckworth hesitated, knowing what Bill McCrory wanted, and was tempted to keep him waiting. No, better to put him in the picture.

"Send him in."

The door hummed and McCrory entered, strode the length of the big room, soundlessly, his footsteps muffled by the deep-pile, pure wool Youghal carpet. He was a wiry, angular man, looking thin as a rail beside the stocky, solid form of the Chairman. He did not wear a jacket and his tie was loose around his neck; there was a good deal of informality at the upper levels of Megalobe. But he was wearing a vest, the pockets filled with the pens and pencils so essential for any engineer.

"Sorry to bother you, J.J." He twisted his fingers together nervously, not wanting to reprimand the Chairman of the company. "But the demonstration is ready."

"I know, Bill, and I'm sorry to keep you waiting. But something has come up and I can't get away for the moment."

"Any delay will cause difficulties with security."

"Of which I am well aware." J. J. Beckworth let none of his irritation show; he never did with those below him in the corporate pecking order. Perhaps McCrory did not realize that the Chairman had personally supervised the design and construction of all the security arrangements of this establishment. He smoothed his silk Sulka tie for a moment, his cold silence a reprimand in itself. "But we will just have to wait. There has been a sudden and exceedingly large spurt of buying on the New York exchange. Just before it closed."

"*Our* stock, sir?"

"Ours. Tokyo is still open, they have twenty-four-hour trading now, and the same thing seems to be happening there. It makes no financial sense at all. Five of the largest and most powerful electronic corporations in this country founded this company. They control Megalobe absolutely. By law a certain amount of stock must be traded, but there can be no possibility of a takeover bid."

"Then what could be happening?"

"I wish I knew. Reports from our brokers will be coming in soon. We can get down to your lab then. What is it that you want me to see?"

Bill McCrory smiled nervously. "I think we had better let Brian explain it to you. He says it is the important breakthrough he has been waiting for. I'm afraid that I don't understand what it is myself. A lot of this artificial intelligence stuff is beyond me. Communications is my field."

J. J. Beckworth nodded understandingly. Many things

were happening now in this research center that had not been allowed for in the original plan. Megalobe had originally been founded for a single purpose; to catch up and hopefully pass the Japanese with HDTV research. High-definition television, which started with a wider screen and well over a thousand scan lines. The United States had almost missed the boat on this one. Only the belated recognition of foreign dominance in the worldwide television market had brought the Megalobe founding corporations and the Pentagon together—but only after the Attorney General had looked the other way while Congress had changed the antitrust laws to make possible this new kind of industrial consortium. As early as the 1980s the Defense Department—or rather one of its very few technically competent departments, the Defense Advanced Research Projects Agency—had identified HDTV not only as an important tool in future warfare but as being vital for industrial progress in future technologies. So even after the years of reduced budgets DARPA had managed to come up with the needed research money.

Once the funding decisions had been made, with utmost speed all the forces of modern technology had been assembled on a barren site in the California Desert. Where before there had only been arid sand—and a few small fruit farms irrigated by subsurface water—there was now a large and modern research center. A number of new and exciting projects had been undertaken, J. J. Beckworth knew, but he was vague about the details of some of them. As Chairman he had other, more urgent responsibilities—with six different bosses to answer to. The red blink of his telephone light cut through his thoughts.

"Yes?"

*"Mr. Mura, our Japanese broker, is on the line."*

"Put him on." He turned to the image on the screen before him. "Good afternoon, Mura-san."

*"To you as well, Mr. J. J. Beckworth. I am sorry to disturb you at this late hour."*

"It is always my pleasure to hear from you." Beckworth controlled his impatience. This was the only way to deal with the Japanese. The formalities had to be covered first. "And surely you would not be calling me now if the matter was of no importance."

*"The importance must be assigned by your illustrious self. As a simple employee I can only report that the spate of buying of Megalobe shares has been reversed. The latest figures are on their way to me now. I expect them on my desk . . . momentarily."*

For the smallest instant the image on the screen stilled, the lips did not move. This was the first indication that Mura was actually speaking in Japanese, his words swiftly translated into English—while the movement of his face and lips were simulated by the computer to match the words. He turned and was handed a piece of paper, smiled as he read it.

*"The news is very good. It indicates that the price has fallen back to its previous level."*

J. J. Beckworth rubbed his jaw. "Any idea of what it was all about?"

*"I regretfully report complete ignorance. Other than the fact that the party or parties responsible have lost something close to a million dollars."*

"Interesting. My thanks for your help and I look forward to your report."

J. J. Beckworth touched the phone disconnect button and the voxfax machine behind him instantly sprang to life, humming lightly as it disgorged the printed record of their conversation. His words were in black, while Mura's were in red for instant identification. The translation system had been programmed well, and as he glanced through it he saw no more than the usual number of errors. His secretary would file this voxfax record for immediate use. The Megalobe staff translator would later verify the correctness of the translation the computer had made.

"What is it all about?" Bill McCrory asked, puzzled. He was a whiz at electronics, but found the arcane lore of the stock market a complete mystery.

J. J. Beckworth shrugged. "Don't know—may never know. Perhaps it was some high-flying broker out for a quick profit, or a big bank changing its mind. In any case it is not important—now. I think we can see what your resident genius has come up with. Brian, you said his name was?"

"Brian Delaney, sir. But I'll have to phone first, it's getting late." It was dark outside; the first stars were appearing and the office lights had automatically come on.

Beckworth nodded agreement and pointed to the telephone on the table across the room. While the engineer made his call, J. J. punched his appointment book up on the screen and cleared away his work for the day, then checked the engagements for tomorrow. It was going to be a busy one—just like every other day—and he pushed his memory watch against the terminal. The screen said WAIT and an instant later read FINISHED as it downloaded his next day's appointments into the watch. That was that.

Every evening at this time, before he left, he usually had a fifteen-year-old Glenmorangie Scotch malt whisky. He glanced in the direction of the hidden bar and smiled slightly. Not quite yet. It would wait.

Bill McCrory pressed the mute button on the phone before he spoke. "Excuse me, J. J., but the labs are closed. It's going to take a few minutes to set up our visit."

"That's perfectly fine," Beckworth said—and meant it. There had been a number of good reasons for building the research center here in the desert. Lack of pollution and low humidity had been two considerations—but the sheer emptiness of the desert had been much more important. Security had been a primary consideration. As far back as the 1940s, when industrial espionage had been in its infancy, unscrupulous corporations had discovered that it was far easier to steal another company's secrets than spend the time, energy—and money—developing something for oneself. With the growth of computer technology and electronic surveillance, industrial espionage had been one of the really big growth industries. The first and biggest problem that Megalobe had faced was the secure construction of this new facility. This meant that as soon as the few farms and empty desert had been purchased for the site, an impenetrable fence was built around the entire area. Not really a fence—and not really impenetrable, nothing could be. It was a series of fences and walls that were topped with razor wire and hung with detectors—detectors buried in the ground as well—and blanketed by holographic change detectors, the surface sprinkled with strain gauges, vibration sensors and other devices. It established a perimeter that said "No go!" Next to impossible to penetrate, but if any person or device did get through, why then lights, cameras, dogs—and armed guards were certain to be waiting.

Even after this had been completed, construction of the building had not begun until every existing wire, cable and drainpipe had been dug up, examined, then discarded. One surprising find was a prehistoric Yuman Indian burial site. Construction had been delayed while this had been carefully excavated by archaeologists and turned over to the Yuman and Shoshonean Indian museum in San Diego. Then, and only then, had the carefully supervised construction begun. Most of the buildings had been prefabricated on closely guarded and controlled locations. Sealed electronically, examined, then sealed again. After being trucked to the site in locked containers the entire inspection process had been done yet one more time. J. J. Beckworth had personally supervised this part of the construction. Without the absolutely best security the entire operation would have been rendered useless.

Bill McCrory looked up nervously from the phone. "I'm sorry, J.J., but the time locks have been activated. It's going to take a half an hour at least to arrange a visit. We could put it off until tomorrow."

"Not possible." He punched up the next day's appointments on his watch. "My schedule is full, including lunch in the office, and I have a flight out at four. It's now or never. Get Toth. Tell him to arrange it."

"He may be gone by now."

"Not him. First in and last out."

Arpad Toth was head of security. More than that, he had supervised the implementation of all the security measures; these seemed to be his only interest in life. While McCrory made the call J.J. decided that the time had come. He opened the drinks cabinet and poured out three fingers of the malt whisky. He added the same amount of uncarbonated

Malvern water—no ice of course!—sipped and sighed gratefully.

"Help yourself, Bill. Toth was in, wasn't he?"

"I will, thank you, just some Ballygowan water. Not only was he in but he will be supervising the visit personally."

"He has to do that. In fact, both he and I together have to encode an after-hours entry. And if either of us punches in a wrong number, accidentally or deliberately, all hell breaks loose."

"I never realized that security was so tight."

"That's good. You're not supposed to. Everyone who enters those labs is monitored ten ways from Sunday. Exactly at five o'clock the doors are sealed tighter than the bank vaults in Fort Knox. After that time it's still easy to get out, since scientists are prone to work late, or even all night. You must have done that yourself. Now you are going to find out that it is next to impossible to get back in. You'll see what I mean when Toth gets here."

This would be a good chance to catch the satellite news. J.J. touched the controls on his desk. The wallpaper—and the painting—on the far wall disappeared to be replaced by the news service logo. The sixteen-thousand-line high-resolution TV that had been developed in the laboratories here was sensationally realistic and so successful that it had captured a large share of the world TV, Virtual Reality and computer workstation market.

This screen contained tens of millions of microscopic mechanical shutters, a product of the developing science of nanotechnology. The definition and color of Beckworth's screen were so good that, to date, no one had noticed that the wallpaper and picture were just digital images—until he had turned them off. He sipped his drink and watched the news.

And that was all that he watched—and only those news items he was interested in. No sports, commercials, no cutesy animals or pop-singer scandals. The TV's computer sought out and recorded, in order of priority, just those reports that he wanted. International finance, stock market report, television shares, currency exchange rates, only news related to commercial relations. All of this done continuously, upgraded instantly, twenty-four hours a day.

When the head of security arrived the wallpaper and painting reappeared and they finished their drinks. Arpad Toth's iron-gray hair was still as close-cropped as it had been during all the years he had been a marine D.I. On that traumatic day when he had finally been forcefully retired from the Marine Corps he had gone right over to the CIA—who had welcomed him with open arms. A number of years had passed after that, as well as a number of covert operations, before he had a major difference of opinion with his new employers. It had taken all of J.J.'s industrial clout, helped by the firm's military connections, to find out what the ruckus had been about. The report had been destroyed as soon as J.J. had read it. But what had stuck in his memory was the fact that the CIA had felt that a plan presented to them by Toth was entirely too ruthless! And this was just before the operations arm of the CIA had been abandoned, when many of their activities had an air of desperation about them. Megalobe had quickly made him a most generous offer to head security for the planned project; he had been with them ever since. His face was wrinkled, his gray hair thinning—but he had not an ounce of fat on his hard-muscled body. It was unthinkable to ask his age or suggest retirement. He entered the office silently, then stood to attention. His face was set in a permanent scowl; no one had ever seen him smile.

"Ready when you are, sir."

"Good. Let's get started. I don't want this to take all night." J. J. Beckworth turned his back when he spoke—there was no need for anyone to know that he kept the security key in a special compartment in his belt buckle—then strode across the office to the steel panel set in the wall. It opened when he turned the key and a red light began blinking inside. He had five seconds to punch in his code. Only when the light had turned green did he wave Toth over. J.J. replaced the key in its hiding place while the security chief entered his own code, his fingers moving unseen inside the electronic control box. As soon as he had done this, and closed the panel again, the telephone rang.

J.J. verbally confirmed the arrangements with Security Control Central. He hung up and started for the door.

"The computer is processing the order," J.J. said. "In ten minutes it will make entry codes available at the outer laboratory terminal. We will then have a one-minute window of access before the entire operation is automatically canceled. Let's go."

If the security arrangements were invisible during the day this certainly was not true at night. In the short walk from the office block to the laboratory building they encountered two guards on patrol—both with vicious-looking dogs on strained leashes. The area was brilliantly lit, while TV cameras turned and followed them as they walked through the grounds. Another guard, his Uzi submachine gun ready, was waiting outside the lab doors. Although the guard knew them all, including his own boss, he had to see their personal IDs before he unlocked the security box. J.J. waited patiently until the light inside turned green. He entered the correct code, then pressed his thumb to the pressure plate. The computer checked his thumbprint as well. Toth repeated this procedure, then in response to the computer's query, punched in the number of visitors.

"Computer needs your thumbprint too, Dr. McCrory."

Only after this had been done did the motors hum in the frame and the door clicked open.

"I'll take you as far as the laboratory," Toth said, "but I'm not cleared for entry at this time. Call me on the red phone when you are ready to leave."

The laboratory was brilliantly lit. Visible through the armor-glass door was a thin, nervous man in his early twenties. He ran his fingers anxiously through his unruly red hair as he waited.

"He looks a little young for this level of responsibility," J. J. Beckworth said.

"He is young—but you must realize that he finished college before he was sixteen years old," Bill McCrory said. "And had his doctorate by the time he was nineteen. If you have never seen a genius before you are looking at one now. Our headhunters followed his career very closely, but he was a loner with no corporate interest, turned down all of our offers.''

''Then how come he is working for us now?''

''He overstretched himself. This kind of research is both expensive and time-consuming. When his personal assets began to run out we approached him with a contract that would benefit both parties. At first he refused—in the end he had no choice.''

Both visitors had to identify themselves at another security station before the last door opened. Toth stepped aside as they went in; the computer counted the visitors carefully. They entered and heard the door close and lock behind them. J. J. Beckworth took the lead, knowing that the easier he made this meeting, the faster he would get results. He extended his hand and shook Brian's firmly.

''This is a great pleasure, Brian. I just wish we could have met sooner. I have heard nothing but good news about the work you have been doing. You have my congratulations—and my thanks for taking the time to show me what you have done.''

Brian's white Irish skin turned red at his unexpected praise. He was not used to it. Nor was he versed enough in the world of business to realize that the Chairman was deliberately turning on the charm. Deliberate or not, it had the desired result. He was more at ease now, eager to answer and explain. J.J. nodded and smiled.

''I have been told that you have had an important breakthrough. Is that true?''

''Absolutely! You could say that this is it—the end of ten years' work. Or rather the beginning of the end. There will be plenty of development to come.''

''I was given to understand that it has something to do with artificial intelligence.''

''Yes, indeed. I think that we have some real AI, at last.''

''Hold your horses, young man. I thought that AI had been around for decades?''

''Certainly. There have been some pretty smart programs

written and used that have been called AI. But what I have here is something far more advanced—with abilities that promise to rival those of the human mind." He hesitated. "I'm sorry, sir, I don't mean to lecture. But how acquainted are you with the work in this field?"

"To be perfectly frank, I know nothing at all. And the name is J.J., if you don't mind."

"Yes, sir—J.J. Then if you will come with me I will bring you up to date a little bit."

He led the way to an impressive array of apparatus that filled an entire laboratory bench. "This is not my work, it's a project that Dr. Goldblum has under way. But it makes a perfect introduction to AI. The hardware isn't much, it's an old Macintosh SE/60 with a Motorola 68050 CPU and a data-base coprocessor that increases its execution speed by a factor of 100. The software itself is based on an updated version of a classic Self-Learning Expert System for renal analysis."

"Just hold it there, son! I don't know what a renal is. I know a little about Expert Systems, but what was it you said—a Self-Learning Expert System? You are going to have to go back and start at square A if you don't want to lose me."

Brian had to smile at this. "Sorry. You're right, I better go back to the beginning. Renal refers to kidney functions. And Expert Systems, as you know, are knowledge-based programs for computers. What we call computer hardware is the machinery that just sits there. Turn off the electricity switch and all you have are a lot of expensive paperweights. Turn it on and the computer has just enough built-in programming to test itself to see if it is working all right, then it prepares to load in its instructions. These computer' instructions are called software. These are the programs that you put in to tell the hardware what to do and how to do it. If you load in a word processing program you can then use the computer to write a book. Or if you load a bookkeeping program the same computer will do high-speed accountancy."

J.J. nodded. "I'm with you so far."

"The old, first-generation programs for Expert Systems

could each do only one sort of thing, and one thing only—such as to play chess, or diagnose kidney disease, or design a computer circuit. But each of those programs would do the same thing over and over again, even if the results of doing so were unsatisfactory. Expert Programs were the first step along the road to AI, artificial intelligence, because they do think—in a very simple and stereotyped manner. The self-learning programs were the next step. And I think my new learning-learning type of program will be the next big step, because it can do so much more without breaking down and getting confused.''

"Give me an example."

"Do you have a languaphone and a voxfax in your office?"

"Of course."

"Then there are two perfect examples of what I am talking about. Do you take calls from many foreign countries?"

"Yes, a good number. I talked with Japan quite recently."

"Did the person you were talking to hesitate at any time?"

"I think so, yes. His face sort of froze for an instant."

"That was because the languaphone was working in real time. Sometimes there is no way to instantly translate a word's meaning, because you can't tell what the word means until you have seen the next word—like the words 'to,' 'too,' and 'two.' It's the same with an adjective like 'bright,' which might mean shining or might mean intelligent. Sometimes you may have to wait for the end of a sentence—or even the next sentence. So the languaphone, which animates the face, may have to wait for a complete expression before it can translate the Japanese speaker's words into English—and animate the image to synchronize lip movements to the English words. The translator program works incredibly fast, but still it sometimes must freeze the image while it analyzes the sounds and the word order in your incoming call. Then it has to translate, again, into English. Only then can the voxfax start to transcribe and print out the translated version of the conversation. An ordinary fax machine just makes a print of whatever is fed into a fax machine at the other end of the connection. It takes the electronic signals that it receives from the other fax and reconstructs a copy of the original. But your voxfax is a different kind of bird. It is not intelligent—but it uses an analytical program to listen to the translated or English words of your incoming telephone calls. It analyzes them, then compares them with words in its memory and discovers what words they make up. Then it prints out the words.''

"Sounds simple enough."

Brian laughed. "It is one of the most complex things that we have ever taught computers to do. The system has to take each Japanese element of speech and compare it to stored networks of information about how each English word, phrase or expression is used. Thousands of man-hours of programming have been done to duplicate what our brains do in an instant of time. When I say 'dog' you know instantly what I mean, right?''

"Of course."

"Do you know how you did it?"

"No. I just did it."

"That *I just did it* is the first problem faced in the study of artificial intelligence. Now let's look at what the computer does when it hears 'dog.' Think of regional and foreign accents. The sound may be closer to *dawg*, or *daw-ug*, or any other countless variations. The computer breaks down the word into composite phonemes or sounds, then looks at other words you have recently said. It compares with sounds, relationships, and meanings it holds in memory, then uses a circuitry to see if its first guesses make sense; if not it starts over again. It remembers its successes and refers back to them when it confronts new problems. Luckily it works very, very fast. It may have to do thousands of millions of computations before it types out 'dog.' ''

"I'm with you so far. But I don't see what is expert about this voxfax system. It doesn't seem to be any different from a word processing system."

"But it is—and you have put your finger on the basic difference. When I type the letters D-O-G into an ordinary word processor, it simply records them in memory. It may move them around, from line to line, stretch them out to fit a justified line or type them out when so instructed—but it is really just inflexibly following unchanging instructions. However, your languaphone and your voxfax program are teaching themselves. When either of them makes a mistake it discards the mistake, then tries something else—and remembers what it has done. This is a first step in the right direction. It is a self-correcting learning program.''

''Then this is your new artificial intelligence?''

''No, this is only a small step that was made some years ago. The answer to developing true artificial intelligence is something completely different.''

''What is it?''

Brian smiled at the boldness of the question. ''It is not that easy to explain—but I can show you what I have done. My lab is right down here.''

He led the way through the connected laboratories. It all appeared very unimpressive to Beckworth, just a series of computers and terminals. Not for the first time he was more than glad to be at the business end to this enterprise. Much of the apparatus was turned on and running, though unattended. As they passed a bench mounted with a large TV screen he stopped dead.

''Good God! Is that a three-dimensional TV picture?''

''It is,'' McCrory said, turning his back on the screen and frowning unhappily. ''But I wouldn't look at it for too long if I were you.''

''Why not? This will revolutionize the TV business, give us a world lead . . .'' He rubbed his thumb along his forehead, realizing that one of his very rare headaches was coming on.

''If it worked perfectly, yes, it should certainly do just that. As you can see it apparently works like a dream. Except that no one can watch it for more than a minute or two without getting a headache. But we think we have a good way to fix this in the next model.''

J.J. turned away and sighed. ''What did they use to say? Back to the drawing board. Anyway, perfect this one and we own the world.'' J.J. shook his head and turned back to Brian. ''I hope you have something to show us that works better than that.''

"I do, sir. I'm going to show you the new robot that will overcome most of the limitations of the older AI machines."

"Is this the one that can learn new ways to learn?"

"That's it. It's right over there. Robin-1. Robot Intelligence number 1."

J.J. looked in the indicated direction and tried to control his disappointment.

"Where?"

All he could see was an electronic workbench with various items of some kind on it, along with a large monitor screen. It looked just like any other part of the lab. Brian pointed to an electronic instrumentation rack about the size of a filing cabinet.

"Most of the control circuitry and memory for Robin-1 is in there. It communicates by infrared with its mechanical interface, that telerobot over there."

The telerobot did not look like any robot J.J. had ever seen. It was on the floor, a sort of upside-down treelike thing that stood no higher than his waist. It was topped by two upward-reaching arms that ended in metallic globes. The two lower branches branched—and branched again and again until the smaller branches were as thin as spaghetti. J.J. was not impressed. "A couple of metal stalks stuck on two brooms. I don't get it."

"Hardly brooms. You are looking at the latest advance in microtechnology. This overcomes most of the mechanical limitations of the past generations of robots. Every branch is a feedback manipulator that enables the management program to receive input and—"

"What can it do?" J.J. said brusquely. "I'm very pressed for time."

Brian's knuckles whitened as he made hard fists. He tried to keep his anger from his voice. "For one thing, it can talk."

"Let's hear it." J.J. glanced obviously at his watch.

"Robin, who am I?" Brian said.

A metallic iris opened in both of the erect metal spheres. Tiny motors hummed as they turned to face Brian. They clicked shut.

"You are Brian," a buzzing voice said from the speakers also mounted on the spheres.

J.J.'s nostrils flared. "Who am I?" he asked. There was no response. Brian spoke quickly.

"It only responds when it hears its name, Robin. It also would probably not understand your voice, since it has only had verbal input from me. I'll ask. Robin. Who is this? Figure next to mine."

The diaphragms opened, the eyes moved again. Then there was a faint brushing sound as the countless metallic bristles moved in unison and the thing moved toward Beckworth. He stepped backward and the robot followed him.

"No need to move or be afraid," Brian said. "The current optic receptors only have a short focus. There, it has stopped."

"Object unknown. Ninety-seven percent possibility human. Name?"

"Correct. Name, last, Beckworth. Initial J."

"J. J. Beckworth, aged sixty-two. Blood type O. Social Security number 130-18-4523. Born in Chicago, Illinois. Married. Two children. Parents were..."

"Robin, terminate," Brian ordered, and the buzzing voice stopped, the diaphragms clicked shut. "I'm sorry about all that, sir. But it had access to personnel records when I was setting up some identification experiments here."

"These games are of no importance. And I am not impressed. What else does the damned thing do? Can it move?"

"In many ways better than you or I," Brian replied. "Robin, catch!"

Brian picked up a box of paper clips—and threw them all toward the telerobot. The thing whirred in a blur of motion as it smoothly unfolded and rearranged most of its tendrils into hundreds of little handlike claws. As they spread out they simultaneously caught every one of the paper clips. It put them all down in a neat pile.

At last J.J. was pleased. "That's good. I think there could be commercial applications. But what about its intelli-

gence? Does it think better than we think, solve problems
that we can't?''

''Yes and no. It is new and still has not learned very
much. Getting it to recognize objects—and figure out how
to handle them—has been a problem for almost fifty years,
and finally we have made a machine learn how to do it.
Getting it to think at all was the primary problem. Now it is
improving very rapidly. In fact, it appears that its learning
capacity is increasing exponentially. Let me show you.''

J.J. was interested—but dubious. But before he could
speak again there was the harsh ringing of a telephone, a
loud and demanding sound.

''It's the red phone!'' McCrory said, startled.

''I'll take it.'' Beckworth picked up the phone and an
unfamiliar voice rasped in his ear.

*''Mr. Beckworth, there is an emergency. You must come
at once.''*

''What is it?''

''This line is not secure.''

J.J. put down the phone, frowned with annoyance. ''There
is an emergency of some kind, I don't know what. You both
wait here. I'll attend to it as fast as I can. I'll phone you if it
looks like there will be any lengthy delays.''

His footsteps retreated and Brian stood in angry silence
glaring at the machine before him.

''He doesn't understand,'' McCrory said. ''He hasn't the
background to understand the importance of what you have
accomplished.''

He stopped when he heard the three coughing sounds
followed by a loud gasp, a crash of equipment falling to the
floor. ''What is it?'' he called out, turned and started back
into the other lab. The coughing sounded again and McCrory
spun around, his face a bloody mask, collapsed and fell.

Brian turned and ran. Not with logic or intelligence, but
spurred on by simple survival—painfully learned from a boy-
hood of bullying and assaults by older children. He went
through the door just before the frame exploded next to his
head.

Straight in front of him was the vault for the streamed

backup tapes. Lodged there every night, empty now. Fireproof and assault proof. A closet for a boy to hide, a dark place to flee to. As he threw the door open bright pain tore into his back, slammed him forward, spun him about. He gasped at what he saw. Raised his arm in impotent defense.

Brian pulled on the handle, fell backward. But the bullet was faster. At the close range through his arm and into his head. The door closed.

"Get him out!" a hoarse voice shouted.

"The door's locked itself—but he's dead. I saw the bullet smash into his head."

Rohart had just parked his car and was getting out and closing the door when his car phone buzzed. He picked it up and switched it on. He heard a voice but could not understand the words because of the overwhelming roar of a copter's rotor blades. He looked up in astonishment, blinking in the glare of its spotlight as the chopper settled out of the sky onto his front lawn. When the pilot slacked off the power he could make out some of what was being shouted into his ear.

"... at once ... incredible ... emergency!"

"I can't hear you—there's a damn chopper just landed and digging up my lawn!"

"Take it! Get in ... come at once."

The spotlight switched off and he saw the black and white markings of a police helicopter. The door opened and someone waved him over. Rohart had not become Managing Director of Megalobe by being dim or slow on the uptake. He threw the telephone back into his car, bent over and ran toward the waiting machine. He stumbled on the step and hard hands dragged him in. They were airborne even before the door was closed.

"What in blazes is happening here?"

"Don't know," the policeman said as he helped him to belt in. "All I know is that all hell broke loose over at your place. There is a three-state alarm out, the Feds have been called in. Every available unit and chopper we have is on the way there now."

"Explosion, fire—what?"

"No details. The pilot and I were monitoring traffic on Freeway 8 over by Pine Valley when I got the call to pick you up and take you to Megalobe."

"Can you call in and find out what is happening?"

"Negative—every circuit is tied up. But we're almost there, you can see the lights now. We'll have you on the ground inside sixty seconds."

As they dropped down toward the helipad Rohart looked for damage, could see none. But the normally empty grounds were now a seething ant's nest of activity. Police cars everywhere, helicopters on the ground and circling outside with their spotlights searching the area. A fire engine was pulled up before the main laboratory building but he could see no flames. A group of men were waiting by the helipad; as soon as they touched down he threw the door open and jumped to the ground, bent and ran toward them, the downdraft of the rotors flapping his clothing. There were uniformed police officers here, other men not in uniform but wearing badges. The only one he knew was Jesus Cordoba, the night supervisor.

"It's incredible, impossible!" Cordoba shouted over the receding roar of the chopper.

"What are you talking about?"

"I'll show you. Nobody knows how or what really happened yet. I'll show you."

Rohart had his next shock when they ran up the steps of the laboratory building. The lights were out, the security cameras dark, the always sealed doors gaping open. A policeman with a battery lamp waved them forward, led the way down the hall. "This is the way I found it when we got here," Cordoba said. "Nothing has been touched yet. I—I just don't know how it happened. Everything was quiet, nothing unusual that I could tell from where I was in Security Control Central. Guard reports were coming in on time. I was keeping my attention on the lab buildings because a late party was in there with Mr. Beckworth. That was all—just like normal. Then it changed." Cordoba's face was running with sweat and he brushed at it with his sleeve, scarcely aware of it. "It all blew at once. It seemed every alarm went off, the guards were gone, even the dogs. Not every alarm, not on the other buildings. Just the perimeter alarms and the lab building. One second it was quiet—the next it looked like that. I don't know."

"Have you talked to Benicoff?"

"He called me when the alarm went through to him. He's on the plane now from D.C."

Rohart went quickly down the hall, through the doors that should have been shut. "This was the way it was when we got here," one of the police officers said. "Lights out, all the doors open, no one here. It looks like some of this stuff has been broken. And more, in here, it looks like, and equipment, computers too, I imagine—there are a lot of disconnected cables. It looks like a lot of heavy stuff was dragged out of here in a big hurry."

The Managing Director looked around at the emptiness, remembered the last time he had been here, at this spot.

"Brian Delaney! This is the lab, where he works. His equipment, experiments—they're all gone! Get on your radio at once! Get some officers to his home. Make sure that they are heavily armed, or whatever you do, because the people who did this will be going there too."

"Sergeant! Over here!" one of the policemen shouted. "I've found something!"

"There," he said, pointing. "That's fresh blood on the tiles, right in front of the door."

"And on the jamb of the door as well," the Sergeant said. He turned to Rohart. "What is this thing? A safe of some kind?"

"Sort of. Backup records are stored in it." He pulled out his wallet. "I have the combination here."

His fingers shook as he worked the combination, turned and pulled the handles, threw open the door. Brian's body, soaked with blood, slumped forward at his feet.

"Get the medics!" the Sergeant roared, pushing his fingers into the sticky blood of the man's throat, feeling for a pulse, trying not to look at the ruined skull.

"I don't know, can't tell—yes!, he's still alive! Where's those paramedics?"

Rohart stepped aside to let them by, could only blink at the shouting organized confusion of the medical teams. He recognized the intravenous drips, the emergency aid, little else. He waited in silence until Brian had been hurried out to the waiting ambulance and the remaining medic was repacking his bag.

"Is he going to be—can you tell me anything?"

The man shook his head gloomily, snapped the bag shut and rose. "He's still alive, barely. Shot in the back, bounced off his ribs, nothing serious. But the second bullet, it went through his arm, then . . . there has been massive destruction in the brain, trauma, bone fragments. All I could do was add paravene to the IV solution. It reduces the extent of injury in brain trauma cases, reduces the cerebral metabolic rate so cells don't die quickly of anoxia. If he lives, well, he will probably never gain consciousness. It's too early to tell anything more than that. He's going by helicopter now to a hospital in San Diego."

"I'm looking for a Mr. Rohart," a policeman said, coming into the room.

"Over here."

"I was told to tell you that your tip was right. Only too late. The premises in question, the property of a Mr. Delaney. It was cleared out completely a couple of hours ago. A rental van was spotted at the scene. We're trying to track it. The investigating officer said to tell you all the computers, files and records were gone."

"Thank you, thank you for telling me." Rohart clamped his lips shut, aware of the tremor in his voice. Cordoba was still there, listening.

"Delaney was working on an artificial intelligence project," he said.

"*The* AI project. And he had it—we had it. A machine with almost human abilities."

"And now?"

"Someone else has it. Someone ruthless. Smart and

ruthless. To plan a thing like this and get away with it. They have it.''

"But they'll be found. They can't get away with it."

"Of course they can. They are not going to make the theft public. Or announce their new AI tomorrow. It will happen—but not right away. Don't forget that a number of research people are working on AI. You'll see, it will happen one day, apparently and logically, with no relation to what happened tonight, and there will be nothing that can be proved. Some other company will have AI. And as certain as that is—it is equally certain that it won't be Megalobe. As far as anyone will be able to tell, Brian died and his work died with him.''

Cordoba had a sudden, ghastly thought. "Why does it have to be another company? Who else is interested in artificial intelligence?''

"Who indeed! Only every other country on the face of the globe. Wouldn't the Japanese just love to get their hands on real, working AI? Or the Germans, Iranians—or anyone.''

"What about the Russians—or anyone else trying a power play? I don't think I would like to see an invading army of tanks driven by machine intelligences without fear or fatigue, attacking nonstop. Or torpedoes and mines with eyes and brains that just bob up and down in the ocean until our ships go by.''

Rohart shook his head. "That kind of worry is out of date. Tanks and torpedoes aren't what count anymore. The new name of the game is productivity. With real AI a country could run rings around us, put us in the economic poorhouse.''

He looked around with distaste at the ruined laboratory.

"They have it now, whoever they are.''

# 2

**February 9, 2023**

The Learjet was flying at 47,000 feet, well above the seething cumulus clouds. Even at this altitude there was still the occasional clear air turbulence, reminder of the storm below. There was only a single passenger, a solidly built man in his late forties, working steadily through a sheaf of reports.

Benicoff stopped reading long enough to take a swig from his glass of beer. He saw that the receive light on his E-fax was blinking as more messages poured in over the phone link and were stored in memory. Benicoff displayed them on the screen as fast as they arrived, until the exact extent of the disaster at the Megalobe laboratories was made all too clear. The light blinked as more messages arrived but he ignored them. The basic facts were fantastic and terrible beyond belief—and there was nothing he could do about the matter until he got to California. Therefore he went to sleep.

Anyone else in his position would have stayed up all night, worrying and working on possible solutions. That was not Alfred J. Benicoff's way. He was a man of immense practicality. Worrying now would just be a waste of time. Not only that, he could certainly use the rest, since the future promised to be an exceedingly busy one. He settled the pillow behind his head, let down the back of his seat, closed his eyes and was asleep at once. As the muscles in his tanned face relaxed, the lines of tension eased and he looked even younger than his fifty years. He was a tall, solid man just beginning to add a thickness to his waist that no amount of dieting could take away. He had played football when he was at Yale, line, and had managed to keep in condition ever since. He needed to be in this job where sleep was sometimes at a premium.

Benicoff's official title was Assistant to the Commissioner of DARPA, but this was a courtesy title with little real meaning, basically a front for his work. In practice he was the top scientific troubleshooter in the country—and reported directly to the President.

Benicoff was called on when research projects got into trouble. To prepare himself for the worst, he made it his job to check on work in progress whenever possible. He visited Megalobe as often as he could because of the extensive research being done there. But that was partly an excuse. Brian's research was what fascinated him the most and he had come to know and like the young scientist. That was why he took this attack personally.

He woke with the whining thud of the landing gear locking into place. It was just dawn and the rising sun sent red shafts of light through the windows when they turned in their final approach to the runway of the Megalobe airport. Benicoff quickly displayed and ran through the batch of E-fax messages that had come through while he slept; there were updates but no really new information.

Rohart was waiting for him as he came down the steps, haggard and unshaven; it had been a very long night. Benicoff shook his hand and smiled.

"You look like hell, Kyle."

"I feel a lot worse. Do you realize that we have no leads at all, all the AI research gone—"

"How is Brian?"

"Alive, that's all I know. Once he was stabilized and on life support the medevac chopper took him to San Diego. He's been in the operating room all night."

"Let's get some coffee while you tell me about it."

They went into the executive dining room and helped themselves to the black Mexican roast coffee; Rohart gulped some down before he spoke. "There was quite a flap at the hospital when they discovered the extent of Brian's injuries.

They even sent a copter out for a top surgeon, someone named Snaresbrook.''

"Dr. Erin Snaresbrook. The last I knew she was doing research at Scripps in La Jolla. Can you get a message through for her to contact me when she gets out of the O.R.?''

Rohart took the phone out of his pocket and passed the message to his office. "I'm afraid I don't know her.''

"You should. She's a Lasker Award laureate in medicine, neuropsychology, and perhaps the best brain surgeon in this country. And if you check the records you will find out that Brian has been working with her on some of his research. I don't know any of the details, I just saw it in the last report filed with my office.''

"If she's that good, then do you think that . . . ?''

"If anyone can save Brian then Snaresbrook can. I hope. Brian was a witness to what happened. If he lives, if he regains consciousness, he may be our only lead. Because as of this moment there are absolutely no other clues as to how this incredible affair was carried out.''

"We know part of what happened. I didn't want to E-fax you the security details on an open line.'' Rohart passed over a photograph. "That's all that is left of what must have been a computer. Melted down by thermite.''

"Where was it?''

"Buried behind the control building. The engineers say that it was wired into the alarm circuitry. The device was undoubtedly programmed to send false video and alarm circuitry information to Security Central.''

Benicoff nodded grimly. "Very neat. All that the operators at Central ever know is what is shown on the screen and readouts. The whole world could come to an end outside—but as long as the screen showed recordings of the moon and stars—along with sound recordings of coyotes—the watch officer wouldn't be aware of anything outside. But what about the foot patrols, the dogs?''

"We haven't a clue there either. They're gone—''

"Just like the equipment—and everyone, except Brian, who was in the lab. There has been one hell of an incredible breach of security here. Which we will go into but not now. The barn door is wide open and your AI is gone..."

The phone buzzed and he picked it up.

"Benicoff speaking. Tell me." He listened briefly. "All right. Call back every twenty minutes or so. I don't want her to leave without talking to me. That is urgent." He folded the phone. "Dr. Snaresbrook is still in the operating room. In a few minutes I want you to take me to the lab. I want to see the entire thing for myself. But first tell me about these stock purchases in Japan. How does this relate to the theft?"

"It's the timing. Those sales could have been arranged to keep J.J. in his office until the lab had shut for the night."

"A long shot—but I'll look into it. We'll get over there now—but before you do that, I want to know exactly who is in charge."

Rohart's eyebrows lifted. "I'm afraid that I don't understand."

"Think. Your Chairman, your top scientist and your head of security have all vanished. Either they have gone over to the enemy—whoever that is—or they are dead..."

"You don't think—"

"But I *do* think—and you had better too. This firm and all of its research have been badly compromised. We know that the AI is gone—but what else? I am going to initiate a complete security check of all the files and records. But before I do I ask the question again. Who is in charge?"

"I guess the buck stops with me," Rohart said with very little pleasure. "As Managing Director I appear to be the top official left."

"That is correct. Now, do you feel that you are able to keep Megalobe operating, manage the entire firm by yourself and at the same time conduct the in-depth investigation that is called for?"

Rohart sipped at his coffee before he answered, searching Benicoff's face for some clue and finding nothing there. "You want me to say it, don't you? That while I can keep Megalobe operational I have no experience in the kind of investigation that is called for here, that I am out of my depth."

"I don't want you to say a thing that you do not think is true." Benicoff's voice was flat, dispassionate. Rohart smiled grimly.

"Message received. You are more than a bit of a bastard—but you're right. Will you conduct the investigation? This is a formal request."

"Good. I wanted it to be completely clear where the line of demarcation lies."

"You're in charge, right? What do you want me to do next?"

"Run the company. Period. I'll take care of the rest."

Rohart sighed and slumped back in his chair. "I'm glad that you are here—and I mean that."

"Good. Now let's get over to the lab."

The door to the laboratory building was closed now—and protected by a large, grim man who wore a jacket despite the dry warmth of the morning. "ID," he said, unmoving in the entrance. He checked Rohart's identification, then glowered suspiciously at Benicoff when he reached into his pocket, grunted reluctant approval when he looked at the ID holograph and he saw who it was.

"Second door down there, sir. He's waiting for you. You're to be alone."

"Who?"

"That's all the message I have, sir," the FBI man said stolidly.

"You don't need me," Rohart said. "And I have plenty that needs doing in the office."

"Right." Benicoff walked quickly to the door, knocked then opened it and went in.

"No names while the door is open. Get in and close it," the man behind the desk said.

Benicoff did as he was told, then turned and resisted the impulse to come to attention. "I wasn't told that you would be here, General Schorcht." If Schorcht had a first name no one knew it. It was probably "General" in any case.

"No reason you should be, Benicoff. Let's just keep it like that for a while."

Benicoff had worked with the General before. He had

found him ruthless, unlikable—and efficient. His face was as wrinkled as a sea tortoise—and he was probably as old as one. At one time in the misty past he had been a cavalry officer and had lost his right arm in battle. In Korea, it was said, though Gettysburg and the Marne were mentioned as well. He had been in Military Intelligence ever since Benicoff had known him; something high up, very secret. He gave orders, never took them.

"You'll report to me once a day, minimum. Oftener if there is anything of importance. You have the secure number. Input all your data as well. Understood?"

"Understood. You know that this is a real bad one?"

"I know that, Ben." For a moment the General relaxed, looked almost human. Tired. Then the mask dropped back into place. "You're dismissed."

"Is there any point in my asking what your involvement is in this matter?"

"No." The General made himself an easy man to hate. "Report now to Agent Dave Manias. He heads the FBI sweep team."

"Right. I'll let you know what they have found out."

Manias was in his shirt sleeves and sweating generously despite the cool of the air-conditioning, fueled by some furious inner fire as he punched rapidly into his hand computer. He looked up as Benicoff approached, wiped his palm on his trouser leg and shook his hand firmly and quickly.

"Glad you're here. Told to hold my report until you showed."

"What have you found out?"

"This is a preliminary report, okay? Just what we have so far. Data still coming in." Benicoff nodded agreement and the FBI agent stabbed at his keyboard. "Starting right here in this room. We're still analyzing all the prints we've found. But the odds are ninety-nine to one there'll be no aliens. Just employees. Pros wear gloves. Now look there. Plenty of scratches, grooves in the lino. Hand truck wheel marks. Rough guess from the records what was taken. At least a ton and a half of stuff. Five, six men could easily move all that out in well under an hour."

"Where did you get that one hour figure from?"

"Records. The front door here was opened by Toth and Beckworth. With private codes. From that time until everything blew was one hour twelve minutes and eleven seconds. Let's go outside."

Manias led the way through the front door and pointed to black marks on the white concrete outside. "Tire marks. A truck. You can see where it went over into the grass a little bit, left a groove."

"Can you identify it?"

"Negative. But we're still working on it. And the recorder on the main gate says it opened and closed twice."

Benicoff looked around, then back at the building. "Let me see if I can put together what we know. Just after the visitors entered the building, security was compromised for over an hour. They were blind and deaf inside Security Central, watching and listening to piped pictures and Muzak. During this period all security ceased—so we can assume that all of the guards were part of the operation. Or are dead."

"Agree . . ." His computer bleeped and he looked down at the screen. "An ID just in on a drop of blood found in a crack on the floor. The lab did a rush DNA match and the identification is positive. J. J. Beckworth."

"He was a good friend," Benicoff said quietly after a moment's silence. "Now let's find his killers. Who we now know were let into this building by one or more accomplices already inside. They entered the lab, and if Brian's condition is any clue they shot everyone there—and carried out everything they found that related to AI. Loaded the truck and drove away. To where?"

"Nowhere." Manias wiped perspiration from his face with a sodden handkerchief and moved his finger in a quick circle. "Other than the guards there is no one normally here after dark. There is empty desert on all sides with no homes or farms close by. No witnesses. Also, there are only four roads out of this valley. All sealed by the police when the alarm blew. Nothing. Copters searched out beyond the roadblocks. Stopped a lot of campers, fruit trucks. Nothing more. We've been searching a hundred mile radius since dawn. Negative results so far.''

Benicoff kept his cool—but there was a sharp edge of anger to his voice. ''Are you telling me that a large truck loaded with heavy files, and at least five men in it as well, just vanished? Right out of a flat, empty valley with desert on one end and a first-gear grade on the other.''

''That's right, sir. If we do find out anything more, you'll be the first to know.''

''Thanks—'' His phone bleeped and he unhooked it from his belt. ''Benicoff. Tell me.''

''*I have a message for you, sir, from Dr. Snaresbrook—*''

''Put her on the line.''

''*I'm sorry, sir, but she disconnected. Message says meet me soonest San Diego Central Hospital.*''

Benicoff looked back at the lab building as he folded the phone away. ''I want copies of everything that you find— and that means everything. I want your evaluation—but I also want to see every bit of evidence as well.''

''Yes, sir.''

''Fastest way to San Diego Central Hospital?''

''Police chopper. I'll get one now.''

It was waiting on the pad when he reached it, rose up with a roar of blades as soon as he had buckled in. ''How long to San Diego?'' he asked.

''About fifteen minutes.''

''Do a circle around Borrego Springs before we go. Show me the roads out.''

''Sure thing. If you look over there, going straight east down the valley, past the badlands, you'll see the road to the Salton Sea and Brawley. If you look that way, in the foothills to the north, that's the Salton Seaway. Goes east too. Forty miles to the Salton Sea. Now, going south is that one, the SW5, with plenty of grades and switchbacks all the way up to Alpine. Pretty slow. So most folks use the Montezuma Grade there. We'll go west now, right over the top of it.''

Below them the desert ended abruptly at the wall of surrounding mountains. A two-lane road had been scratched up from the valley rising and twisting higher and higher until it reached the wooded plateau above. Benicoff looked back as they climbed—and shook his head. There was just no way out of the valley that the truck could have taken that was not watched, blocked.

Yet it was gone. He put the mystery from his mind, filed it away and thought instead about the wounded scientist. He took out the medical reports and read through them again. It was grim and depressing—and from the severity of the injuries Brian was probably dead by now.

The copter bounced as they hit the thermals over the rocky valleys at the top of the grade. The plateau beyond was flat, grazing lands and forests, with the white band of a major road far beyond. Towns, cities—and the freeway in the distance. A perfect escape for the truck. Except for the fact that it would probably still be grinding up the twelve miles of eight-degree grade. Forget it! Think about Brian.

Benicoff found Dr. Snaresbrook in her office. Her only concession to age was her iron-gray hair. She was a strong and alert woman, perhaps in her fifties, who radiated a feeling of confidence; she frowned slightly as she looked at the multicolored 3-D image before her. Her hands were inserted in the DataGloves of the machine to rotate and move the display—even peel away layers to see what was inside. She must have just come from the operating room because she was wearing a blue scrub suit and blue booties. When Snaresbrook turned around, Benicoff could see that the fabric of the sleeves and front was spattered and stained with blood.

"Erin Snaresbrook," she said as they shook hands. "We haven't met before—but I've heard about you. Alfred J. Benicoff. You're the one who beat down the opposition to the use of human embryonic tissue grafts. That's one of the things that made my work here possible."

"Thank you—but that was a long time ago. I'm in government now, which means that I spend most of my time looking at other people's research."

"A waste of talent."

"Would you prefer a lawyer in the job?"

"God forbid. Your point taken. Now let me tell you about

Brian. I have very little time. His skull is open and he is on life support. I'm waiting for the next V.I. records.''

"V.I.?''

"Volume Investigation. Infinitely better than looking at X rays or any other single type of image. It combines the results of every available type of scan—including the old tomograms and NMRs as well as the latest octopolar antibody fluorescence images. These are all churned up together in an ICAR-5367 spatial signal processing computer. This can display not only images from the patient's data, but can also highlight or exaggerate the differences between that patient and the typical person, or changes since earlier scans of the same patient. So when the new V.I. data is ready I will have to go. Up until now it has been emergency procedures just to save Brian's life. First total body hypothermia, then brain cooling to slow oxygen intake and all the other metabolic processes. I used anti-hemorrhage drugs, mainly RSCH, as well as anti-inflammatory hormones. With the first surgery I cleaned the wound and removed necrotic tissue and bone fragments. In order to restore the anatomy of the ventricles I was forced to sever part of the corpus callosum.''

"Isn't that part of the connection between the two halves of the brain?''

"It is—and it was a serious, and possibly dangerous, decision. But I had no choice. So at this time the patient is really two half-brained individuals. Were he conscious this would be a disaster. But, having severed the corpus callosum cleanly, I hope to be able to reconnect the two halves completely. Tell me—what do you know about the human brain?''

"Very little—and all probably out of date since my undergraduate days.''

"Then you are completely out of date. We are at the threshold of a new era, when we will be able to call ourselves mind surgeons as well as brain surgeons. Mind is the function of the brain and we are discovering how it operates.''

"Specifically, then, in Brian's case, how serious is the damage—and is it repairable?''

"Look here, at these earlier V.I. images, and you will

see.'' She pointed to the colored holograms that apparently floated in midair. The three-dimensional effect was startling—as though he was looking inside the skull itself. Snaresbrook touched a white patch, then another. ''This is where the bullet went into the skull. It exited here, on the right. It passed through the cortex of the brain from side to side. The good news is that the cerebral cortex of the brain seems mostly intact, as are the central organs of the middle brain. The amygdala here appears to be undamaged, as well as most important of all, the hippocampus, this roughly seahorse-shaped organ. This is one of the most critical agencies involved in forming memories, and retrieving them. It is the powerhouse of the mind—and it wasn't touched.''

''That's the good news. And the bad—''

''There is some cortical damage, though not enough to be very grave. But the bullet severed a large number of bundles of nerve fibers, the white matter that makes up the largest portion of the brain. These serve to interconnect different parts of the cortex to one another—and also to connect them to other midbrain organs. This means that parts of Brian's brain are disconnected from the data bases and other resources that they need for performing their functions. Therefore at this moment Brian has no memories at all.''

''You mean his memory is gone, destroyed?''

''No, not exactly. Look—the largest parts of his neocortex are still intact. But most of their connections are broken—see here, and here. To the rest of the brain they do not exist. The structures, the nerve connections that constitute his memories are still there—in various sections of his shattered brain. But they can't be reached by the other parts, so they are meaningless by themselves. Like a box full of memory disks without a computer. This is a disaster since we *are* our memories. Now Brian is essentially mindless.''

''Then he is a . . . vegetable.''

''Yes—in the sense that he cannot think. You might say that his memories have been largely disconnected from his brain computers, so that they cannot be retrieved or used. He cannot recognize things or words, faces, friends, anything. In short, so far as I can see, he no longer can think to any degree. Consider this. Other than size, one could say that there is little observable difference between most of the brain of a man and a mouse—except for those magnificent structures of our higher brain—the neocortex that evolved in the ancestors of the primates. In this present state, poor Brian, my friend and my collaborator, is little more than a selfless shell, a submammalian animal.''

''Is that it? The end?''

''No, not necessarily. Although Brian cannot actually think, he is definitely not brain-dead as the lawyers put it. A few years ago nothing more could have been done. This is no longer true. I am sure that you know that Brian has helped me in a practical application of his AI theories, the development of an experimental technique to rebuild severed brain connections. I have had a measure of success, but only on animals so far.''

''If there is a chance, any chance at all, you must take it. Can you do it, can you save Brian?''

''It is too early to say anything with any degree of certainty. The damage is extensive and I don't know how much I can repair. The trouble is that in addition to the general trauma the bullet has severed millions of nerve fibers. It will be impossible for me to match up all of them. But I hope to identify a few hundred thousand and join them.''

Benicoff shook his head. ''You just lost me, doctor. You are going into his open skull and identify something like a million different and severed nerve fibers? That will take years.''

''It would if I had to do them one by one. However, computer-controlled microsurgical technology can now operate on many sites at one time. Our parallel computer can identify several connections every second—and there are 86,400 seconds in each day. If everything goes as planned the memory-probe process should only take a few days to identify and label the nerve fibers we must reconnect.''

''Can this be done?''

''Not easily. When a nerve fiber is cut off from its mother cell it dies. It is fortunate that the empty tube of the dead cell remains in place and this makes regrowth of the nerve possible. I will be using implants of my own design that will control that regrowth." Snaresbrook sighed. "And after that, well, I fear that the nerve repair will just be the beginning. It is not simply a matter of connecting up all the severed nerves we can see."

"Why is that not enough?"

"Because we must restore the original connections. And the problem is that all nerve fibers look, and are, almost the same. Indistinguishable. But we have to match them up correctly to get the right connections inside the mind. Memory, you see, is neither in the brain cells nor in the nerve fibers. It is mostly in the layout of the connections between them. To get things right, we shall need a third stage—after we've finished the second stage today. After that, we shall have to find a way to access and examine his levels of memory—and rearrange the new connections accordingly. This has never been done before and I am not sure that I can do it now. Ah, here we are."

The technician hurried in with the multiscan cassette of the V.I. and inserted it into the projector; the three-dimensional hologram sprang into existence. Snaresbrook examined it closely, nodded grimly. "Now that I can see the extent of the damage, I can finish the debridement and prepare for the second and vital stage of this operation—the reconnection."

"Just what is it you plan to do?"

"I'm going to use some new techniques. I hope to be able to identify the role that each of his nerve fibers once played in his various mental activities—by finding out where each of them fit into his semantic neural networks. These are the webs of brain connections that make up our knowledge and mental processes. I must also take the radical step of severing the remaining portions of his corpus callosum. This will provide the unique opportunity of making connections to virtually every part of his cerebral cortex. This will be dangerous—but will provide the best chance to reconnect the two halves completely."

"I must know more about this," Benicoff said. "Is there any chance you will let me observe the operation?"

"Every chance in the world—I have had up to five residents in the O.R. breathing down my neck at one time.

It's fine with me as long as you stay out of my way. What's this sudden interest?"

"More than morbid curiosity, I assure you. You've described the machines you use and what they do. I want to see them in operation. I need to know more about them if I am going to ever know anything about AI."

"Understood. Come along, then."

# 3

## February 10, 2023

Benicoff, gowned and masked, stretchable boots pulled over his shoes, pressed his back to the green tiles of the wall of the operating room and tried to make himself invisible. There were two large lights on ceiling tracks that one of the nurses moved about and focused until the resident surgeon approved their positioning. On the table sterile blue sheets had been draped tentlike over Brian's still figure. Only his head was exposed, projecting beyond the end of the table and held immovably by the pointed steel spokes of the head holder. There were three of them, screwed through the skin of his scalp and anchored firmly in the bone below. The bandages that covered the two bullet wounds were stark white in contrast to his orange skull, shaved smooth and painted with disinfectant.

Snaresbrook looked relaxed, efficient. Discussing the approaching operation with the anesthesiologist and the nurses, then supervising the careful placement of the projector. "Here is where I am going to work," she said, tapping the hologram screen. "And this is where you are going to cut."

She touched the outlined area that she had inked onto the plate, checking once again that the opening would be large enough to reveal the entire area of injury, large enough for her to work within. Nodding with satisfaction, she projected the holograph onto Brian's skull and watched while the resident painted the lines on the skin, following those of the image, matching it exactly. When he was finished more drapes were attached to the surrounding skin until only the area of the operation remained. Snaresbrook went out to scrub: the resident began the hour-long procedure to open the skull.

Luckily Benicoff had seen enough other surgical procedures not to be put off. He was still amazed at all the force that is needed to penetrate the tough skin, muscle and bone that armor the brain. First a scalpel was used to cut through to the bone; the scalp, spreading apart as it was severed, was then sewn to the surrounding cloth. After the bleeding arteries were sealed shut with an electric cautery it was time to penetrate the bone.

The resident drilled holes by hand, with a polished metal brace and bit. Bits of skull, like wood shavings, were cleared away by the nurse. It was hard work and the surgeon was sweating, had to lean back so that the perspiration could be dabbed from his forehead. Once the holes were through the bone he enlarged them with a different tool. The final step was to use the motorized craniotome, fitted with a bone-cutting extension, to connect the holes. After this had been done he worked the flat metal flap elevator between skull and brain to slowly pry up and free the piece of skull; a nurse wrapped the piece of bone in cloth and put it into an antibiotic solution.

Now Snaresbrook could begin. She entered the O.R., her scrubbed-clean hands held up at eye level, poked her arms through the sleeves of the sterile gown, slipped on the rubber gloves. The instrument table was rolled into position, the tools on it carefully laid out by the scrub nurse. The scalpels, retractors, needles, nerve hook, dozens of scissors and tweezers, all the battery of equipment needed for the penetration of the brain itself.

"Dural scissors," Snaresbrook said, holding out her hand,

then bent to cut open the outer covering of the brain. Once it had been exposed to the air, automatic sprays kept it moist.

Benicoff, standing against the wall, could not see the details now; was just as glad. It was the final stage that mattered, when they rolled over the odd-looking machine that was now pushed back against the wall. A metal box, with a screen, controls and a keyboard, as well as two shining arms that rose from the top. These ended in multibranching fingers that grew smaller and smaller in diameter, each tipped with a glistening fuzziness. This was caused by the fact that the sixteen thousand microscopic fingertips at the branching ends of the instrument were actually too small to be seen by the human eye. The multibranching manipulator had been developing for only a decade. Unpowered now, the fingers hung in limp bundles like a metallic weeping willow.

It took the surgeon two hours, working with the large microscope, scalpels and cautery, to clean the track of destruction, a slow and precise debridement of the lesion left by the bullet.

"Now we repair," she said, straightening up and pointing to the manipulator. Like everything else in the O.R. it was on wheels; it was pushed into position. When it was switched on, the fingers stirred and rose, descended again under her control into the brain of its designer.

Snaresbrook's skin was gray and there were black smears of fatigue under her eyes. She sipped her coffee and sighed.

"I admire your stamina, Doctor," Benicoff said. "My feet hurt just from standing there and watching. Do all brain operations last that long?"

"Most of them. But this one was particularly difficult because I had to insert and fix those microchips into place. It was like combining surgery with solving a jigsaw puzzle, since every one of those PNEPs had a different shape in order to perfectly contact the surface of brain."

"I saw that. What do they do?"

"They are PNEP film chips—programmable neural electron pathway devices. I have applied them to every injured surface of his brain. They will make connections to the cutoff nerve fibers that end at those surfaces, that control the regrowth of Brian's nerves. They have been under development for years and have been thoroughly tested in animals. These chips have also been wonderfully effective in repairing human spinal injuries. But until now they have never been used inside human brains, except in a few small experiments. I would certainly not be using them if there were any good alternative."

"What will happen next?"

"The chips are coated with living embryonic human nerve cells. What they should do is grow and provide physical connections from the end of each of the severed nerves to at least one of the quantum transistor gates on the surface of the PNEP. That process of growth should already have started, and will continue for the next few days."

"As soon as those new nerve fibers grow in, I'll start to program the PNEP chips. Each chip has enough switching capacity to take every nerve signal that comes in from any part of the brain and route it out along an appropriate nerve fiber that goes to another location in the brain."

"But how could you know exactly where to send it?"

"That is precisely the problem. We will be dealing with several hundred million different nerves—and we don't know now where any of them should go. The first stage will be to follow Brian's brain's anatomy. This should give us a crudely approximate map of where most of those fibers should go. Not enough to support fine-grained thought but enough, I hope, to restore a minimal level of functional recovery, despite all the errors in wiring. For example, if the motor area of his brain sends a signal to move, then *some* muscle should move, if not the right one. So we'll have a response that later could be relearned or retrained. I have implanted a connector in Brian's skin, just about here." Erin touched the back of her neck just above her collar. "The computer communicates by inserting the microscopic ends of fiber-optic cables that communicate with each of the PNEP chips inside. Then we can use the external computer to do the search—to find opposite areas relating to the same memories or concepts. Once these are found, the computer can send signals to establish electronic pathways inside, between the appropriate PNEPs. Each separate chip is like an old-fashioned telephone exchange where one phone was plugged through a board to another phone. I'll start using the neural telephone exchange inside Brian's brain to reestablish the severed connections.''

Ben took a deep breath. ''That's it, then. You'll restore all of his memory!''

''Hardly. There will be memories, skills and abilities that will be lost forever. Really all I hope to do is restore enough so Brian may be able to relearn what is now gone. An incredible amount of work is needed. To understand the complexity of the brain, you must realize that there are many times more genes involved in growing the structure of the brain than in any other organ.''

''I appreciate that. Do you believe that the personality, the person we know as Brian, is still alive?''

''I believe so. During the operation I saw his limbs move through the drapes, a familiar movement that reminded me of the way we move when we are dreaming. A dream! What could that half-ruined brain possibly dream about?'' .

*Darkness* . . .

Timeless darkness, warm darkness.

Sensation. Memory.

Memory. Awareness. Presence. Around and around and around. Going nowhere, relating to nothing else, an endless loop.

Darkness. Where? The closet. Safety was in the darkness of the closet. Refuge of a child. No light. Just sound. The memory repeated itself, over and over.

Sound? Voices. Voices he knew. Voices he hated. And a new one. A strange one. An accent like on telly. Not Irish. American, he recognized that. Americans, they came to the village. To the pub. Took pictures. One took a picture of him. Gave him a golden twenty pence. Spent it on sweets. Ate them all. Americans.

Here? In this house. Curiosity took his hand to the knob

on the closet door. He held it, turned it and opened it slowly. The voices were louder now, clear. Shouting even, that would be his uncle Seamus.

"A bloody sodding nerve to come here! Nerves of brass, you blackguard. Come here right to the house where she died and all. Bloody nerve—"

"There is no need to shout, Mr. Ryan. I told you why I came. This."

That was the new voice. American. Not really American. As Irish as everyone, but sometimes American. This was too unusual to miss. Brian forgot his anger at being sent to his room so early, forgot his tantrum that had sent him to the closet, into the darkness to bite his knuckles and cry where no one could see or hear him.

On tiptoes he crossed the tiny room, the wood cold on his bare feet, warm on the rag rug by the door. Five years old, he could look out through the keyhole now without standing on a book. Pressed his eye close.

"This letter came a few weeks back." The man with the accent had red hair, freckles. He looked angry as he waved the piece of paper. "And there's the postmark on the envelope. Right here, Tara, this village. Do you want to know what it says?"

"Get out," the heavy, phlegmy voice rumbled, followed by a deep cough. His grandfather. Still smoked twenty a day. "Can you not understand the simple words—you're not wanted here."

The newcomer slumped back, sighed. "I know that, Mr. Ryan, and I don't wish to argue with you. I just want to know if these allegations are true. This person, whoever it was, has written that Eileen is dead—"

"True enough, by God—and you killed her!" Uncle Seamus was losing his temper. Brian wondered if he would hit this man the same way he hit him.

"That would be difficult since I haven't seen Eileen in over five years."

"But you saw her once too often, you twisting sonofabitch. Got her with child, ran out, left her here with her shame. And her bastard."

"That's not quite true—nor is it relevant."

"Get away with your fancy words!"

"No, not until I've seen the boy."

"I'll see you in hell first!"

There was a scrape and crash as a chair went over. Brian clutched the doorknob. He knew that word well enough. *Bastard.* That was him, that's what the boys called him. What had this to do with the man in the parlor? He did not know; he had to find out. He would be beaten if he did. It didn't matter. He turned the knob and pushed.

The door flew back and crashed against the wall and he stood in the doorway. Everything stopped. There was Grandfer on the couch, torn gray sweater, the cigarette end in his lips sending a curl of smoke into his half-closed eye. Uncle Seamus, fists clenched, the fallen chair behind him, his face red and exploding.

And the newcomer. Tall, well dressed, suit and tie. His shoes were black and shiny. He looked down at the boy, his face twisted with strong emotions.

"Hello, Brian," he said, ever so quietly.

"Watch out!" Brian shouted.

Too late. His uncle's fist, hard from years in the mine, caught the man high on the face, knocked him to the floor. Brian thought at first that it was going to be one of those fights, like on Saturday night outside the pub, but it wasn't going to be like that, not this time. The newcomer touched his hand to his cheek, looked at the blood, climbed to his feet.

"All right, Seamus, maybe I deserved that. But just that once. Put your fists down, man, and show some intelligence. I've seen the boy and he's seen me. What's done is done. It's his future I care about—not the past."

"Look at the two of them," Grandfer muttered, holding back a cough. "Alike as two pennies, the red hair and all." His temper changed abruptly and he waved his arms, sparks flying from his cigarette. "Get back into your room, boy! Nothing here for you to see—nothing here for you to hear. Inside before you feel my hand."

\* \* \*

*Incomplete, disjointed, adrift in time. Memories, long forgotten, disconnected. Surrounded and separated by blackness. Why was it still dark? Paddy Delaney. His father.*

Like slides in a cinema, flickering and quick, too quick to see what was happening. The blackness. The slides, suddenly clear again.

A loud roaring, the window before him bigger than any window he had seen before, bigger even than a shop window. He clutched tightly at the man's hand. Frightened, it was all so strange.

"That's our plane," Patrick Delaney said. "The big green one there with the bump on top."

"747-8100. I seen a pitcher in the paper. Can we go into it now?"

"Very soon—as soon as they call it. We'll be the first ones aboard."

"And I'm not gonna go back to Tara?"

"Only if you want to."

"No. I hate them." He sniffled and wiped his nose with the back of his hand. Looked up at the tall man at his side. "You knew my mother?"

"I knew her very well. I wanted to marry her but—there were reasons we couldn't get married. When you are older you will understand."

"But—you're my father?"

"Yes, Brian, I am your father."

He had asked the question many times before, never really sure that he would really get the right answer. Now, here, in the airport with the big green plane before them, he believed it at last. And with the belief something seemed to swell up and burst inside him and tears welled out and ran down his face.

"I never, never want to go back."

His father was on his knees, holding him so tightly that he could barely breathe—but that was all right. Everything was all right. He smiled and tasted the salt tears, smiling and crying at the same time and unable to stop.

# 4

## February 12, 2023

Erin Snaresbook was tired when she entered the operating room the next day. Yet when she saw Brian she forgot the fatigue. So much had been done; so much was left to do. The wrecked brain tissue, mostly white matter, had been removed.

"I am about to begin the implanting series," she said, almost in a whisper to herself. This was for the record, not for the edification of the others working in the O.R. The sensitive microphones would pick up her words, no matter how softly or loudly she spoke, and record everything. "All of the dead tissue has now been removed. I am looking at a severed section of white tissue. This is the area where the axons of many neurons have been severed. The proximal end of each cut nerve will still be alive because the cell body will be located there. But the distal end, the other part of the axon that goes on to join the synapses of other cells, all these will be dead. Cut off from food and energy supplies. This necessitates two different techniques. I have made molds of the surfaces of the cleanly cut and transected areas of white matter. Flexible PNEP microfilm chips have been fabricated from these molds. The computer remembers each mold so will know where each matching chip is to go. Connective tissue cells will anchor the chips into place. First the proximal fibers will be freed up to make contact with the connection chips as I insert them. Each axon stump will be coated with growth-stimulating protein. The chip film is coated with chemical spots that when electrically released will attract each growing axon to extend and then attach itself to the nearest film-chip connection pad. That is what I will begin doing now.''

As she talked she activated the connecting machine and instructed it to move over the open skull, told it to descend. When she did this the tiny, branching fingers slowly widened, spread apart, moved slowly downward. The computing capacity of the machine's computer was so great that every single one of the microscopically fine fingers was separately controlled. The fingertips themselves did not contain the lenses, which needed a larger number of wavelengths of light to form an image. So the lenses themselves were a few branches back. The image from the lens on each finger was relayed back to the computer, where it was compared with the other images to build an internal three-dimensional model of the severed brain. Down the tendrils went again, some moving slower than the others until they were close to the surface, spread out and obscuring the surgeon's view of the area.

Snaresbrook turned to the monitor screen, spoke to it.

''Lower. Stop. Lower. Tilt back. Stop.''

Now she had the same view as the computer. A close-up image of the severed surfaces that she could zoom in on—or move back to get an overall view.

''Begin the spray,'' she ordered.

One in ten of the tendrils was hollow; in reality they were tiny tubes with electronic valves at the tip. The spray—it had to be a microscopically fine spray so small were the orifices—began to coat the surface of the severed brain. It was an invisible electrofluorescent coating.

''Turn down the theater lights,'' she ordered, and the overall illumination dimmed.

The connection machine was satisfied with its work and had stopped spraying. After selecting the lowest area of the wound, Snaresbrook sent the tiniest amount of ultraviolet light down the hair-thin fiber optics.

On the screen a pattern of glowing pinpoints speckled the brain's surface.

''The electroluminescent coating has now been sprayed onto all the nerve endings. Under UV light it emits enough photons to be identified. Only those nerves that are still alive cause the reaction that is activated by the UV. Next I will put the implants into place.''

The implants, specially manufactured to conform to the contours of the raw surfaces of Brian's brain, were now in a tray in which they were immersed in a neutral solution. The tray was placed on the table next to Brain's head and the cover removed. With infinitely delicate touch the tendrils dropped down into it.

''These PNEP implants are custom-made. Each consists of layers of films, flexible organic-polymer semiconductor arrays. Flexible and stretchable because the severed tissues of the brain will have changed slightly since they were measured for the manufacture of these chips. That is what is going to happen next. The chips appear to look identical, but of course they are not. The computer measured and designed each of them to fit precisely to a selected area of the exposed brain. Now it is able to recognize and match each of them to the correct area. Each film has several optical-fiber connecting links that will be attached to adjoining chips multiplexing in-out cross-communication signals between parts of the brain. If attention is directed to the upper surface of the films it will be seen that there is also an I-O wire on each of them. The importance of this will be explained at the next operation. This particular session will be completed when all ten thousand of the implants are in place. The process will now begin.''

Although Snaresbrook was there to supervise, it was the computer that controlled the implants, the fingers moving so fast that they blurred into invisibility. In flashing procession the thin-film chips were guided one after the other into place, until the last one was secure. The fingers withdrew and Snaresbrook felt some of the tension drain away. She straightened and realized that the pain in her back was sharp as a knife point. She ignored it.

''The next stage, the connecting process, has now begun. The film surfaces are a modification of active matrix display technology. The object is for each semiconductor, when activated by the luminescence, to identify a live nerve. Then to make a physical connection with that nerve. The films are coated with the correct growth hormones to cause the incoming nerve fibers to form synapses with the input transistors. The importance of these connections will be made manifest at the next implant procedure. Each dead distal fiber must be replaced by a fetal cell that is genetically engineered to grow a new axon inside the sheath of the cell it is replacing—then grow new synapses to replace the old, dying distal ones. At the same time as the fetal cells, dendrites will grow to contact the output pad on the film chip.''

The operation took almost ten hours. Snaresbrook was present the entire time.

When the last connection had been made the fatigue hit like a locomotive. She stumbled and had to clutch the door frame as she left the room. Brian required constant monitoring and attention after the operation—but the nursing staff could handle this.

The procedures to mend Brian's brain were exhausting— yet she still had other patients and scheduled operations that had to be done. She rescheduled them, sought out and received the best assistance from the top surgeons, took only the most urgent cases. Yet she was still working a full twenty-four hours, had been for days. Her voice trembled as she made verbal notes on the procedure just finished. Her desk computer would record and transcribe them. Dexedrine would see her through the day. Not a good idea but she had little choice.

Finished, she yawned and stretched.

"End of report. Intercom on. Madeline." The desk computer accepted the new command and bleeped the secretary.

"Yes, Doctor."

"Send in Mrs. Delaney now."

She rubbed her hands together and straightened her back. "Switch on and record as file titled Dolly Delaney," she said, then checked to see that the tiny red indicator in the base of the desk light came on. The door opened and she smiled at the woman who hesitantly entered. "It was very good of you to come," Snaresbrook said, smiling, standing slowly and indicating the chair on the other side of the desk. "Please make yourself comfortable, Mrs. Delaney."

"Dolly, if you please, Doctor. Can you tell me how he

is?'' Her voice had a tight edge to it as though she was working hard to keep it under control as she spoke. A thin, sharp-eyed woman clutching her large handbag in her lap with both hands; a barrier before her.

''Absolutely no change, Dolly, not since I talked to you yesterday. He is alive and we must be grateful for that. But he has been gravely injured and it is going to be weeks, possibly months, before we will know the outcome of the procedures. That is why I need your help.''

''I'm not a nurse, Doctor. I don't see what I can possibly do.'' She straightened the purse on her lap, keeping the barrier in place. She was a good-looking woman—would have looked better if the corners of her mouth hadn't turned down sharply. She had the appearance of a person the world had not been kind to and who resented it. ''You say you need help— yet I don't have any idea at all what has happened to Brian. Whoever called me simply said that there had been an accident in the laboratory. I had hoped that you would be able to tell me more. When will I be able to see him?''

''Just as soon as possible. But you must realize that Brian has suffered extensive cranial damage. Severe trauma of the white matter of his brain. There is—memory impairment. But he can be helped if I find a way to evoke enough of his early memories. That is why I need more information about your son . . .''

''Stepson,'' she said firmly. ''Patrick and I adopted him.''

''I didn't know, I'm sorry.''

''Don't be, Doctor, there is certainly nothing to be sorry about. It is common knowledge. Brian is Patrick's natural son. Before we met, before he left Ireland, he had this . . . liaison with a local girl. That was Brian's mother.'' Dolly took a lace hanky from her bag, touched it to her palms, pushed it back into the bag, which closed with a loud snap.

''I would like to know more about that, Mrs. Delaney.''

''Why? It's past history, nobody's business now. My husband is dead, has been for nine years. We had . . . separated by that time. Divorced. I have been living with my family in Minnesota. He and I did not communicate. I didn't even know that Paddy was ill, no one ever told me anything. You can understand my being a little bitter. The first I knew that something was wrong with his health was when Brian called me about the funeral. So that is all in the past as you can see."

"I am very sorry to hear about the separation. But, tragic as this is, it does not alter in any way the earlier details about Brian's life. That is what you must tell me about. It is Brian's developing years that I want to understand. Now that your husband is dead, you are the only person in the world who can supply this information. Brian's brain has been severely injured, large areas have been destroyed. He needs your help in restoring his memories. I admit that much of what I am doing is experimental, never tried before. But it is the only chance he has. In order to succeed I must know where to look—and what to look for in his past.

"The problem is that in order to reconstruct Brian's memories I will have to retrace his mind's development from his infancy and childhood. The enormous structure of a human mind can be rebuilt only from the bottom up. The higher-level ideas and concepts cannot be activated until their earlier forms again become able to operate. We will have to reconstruct his mind—his mental societies of ideas—in much the way they were built in the first place, during Brian's childhood. Only you can guide me at this point. Will you help me give him back his past in the hopes that he will then have a future?"

Dolly's mouth was clamped tightly shut, her lips white with the strain. And she was shivering. Erin Snaresbrook waited in patient silence.

"It was a long time ago. Brian and I have grown apart since then. But I raised him, did my best, all that I could do. I haven't seen him since the funeral . . ." She took her handkerchief out again and touched it to the corners of her eyes, put it away, straightened up.

"I know that this is very difficult for you. Dolly. But it is essential that I get these facts, absolutely vital. Can I ask you where you and your husband first met?"

Dolly sighed, then nodded reluctant agreement. "It was at the University of Kansas. Paddy came there from Ireland, as you know. He taught at the university. In the School of Education. So did I, family planning. As I am sure you know, there is finally the growing awareness that all of our environment problems are basically caused by overpopulation, so the subject is no longer banned in the schools. Paddy was a mathematician, a very good one, overqualified for our college, really. That was because he had been recruited for the new university in Texas and was teaching in Kansas until they opened. That was part of the arrangement. They wanted him under contract and tied up. For their own sake—not his. He was a very lonely man, without any friends. I know he missed Dublin something fierce. That was what he used to say when he talked about it, something fierce. Not that he talked about himself that much. He was teaching undergraduates who were there just for the credits and didn't care at all about the subject. He really hated it. It was just about that time when we began going out together. He confided in me and I know that he found comfort in my companionship.

"I don't know why I'm telling you all this. Perhaps because you are a doctor. I've kept it inside, never talked about it to anyone before. Looking back now, now that he is dead, I can finally say it out loud. I don't . . . I don't think he ever loved me. I was just comfortable to have around. There is a lot of mathematics in demography, so I could follow him a bit when he talked about his work. He lost me rather quickly but he didn't seem to notice. I imagine that he saw me as a warming presence, to put it simply. This didn't matter to me, not at first. When he asked me to marry him I jumped at the chance. I was thirty-two then and not getting any younger. You know that they say that if a girl is not married by thirty that's the end of it. So I accepted his proposal. I tried to forget about all the schoolgirl ideas of romantic love. After all, people have made successes of arranged marriages. Thirty-two is a hard age for a single girl. As for him, if he loved anyone it was her. Dead, but that didn't matter."

"Then he did talk about this earlier relationship with the girl in Ireland?"

"Of course. Grown men aren't expected to be virgins. Even in Kansas. He was a very honest and forthright man. I knew he had been very, very close to this girl but the affair was long over. At first he didn't mention the boy. But before he proposed he told me what had happened in Ireland. Everything. I'm not saying I approved, but past is past and that's all there was to it."

"And how much did you know about Brian?"

"Just as much as Paddy did—which was precious little. Just his name, that he was living with his mother in some village in the country. She didn't want to hear from Paddy, not at all, and I knew that made him very upset. His letters were returned unopened. When he tried to send money, for the boy's sake, it was refused. He even sent money to the priest there, for the boy, but that didn't work either. Paddy didn't want it back, he donated it to the church. The priest remembered that, so when the girl died he wrote Paddy about it. He took it badly, though he tried not to show it. In the end he worked hard to put it all from his mind. That's when he proposed to me. As I said, I knew a lot of his reasons for what he did. If I minded I kept it to myself. She was dead and we were married and that was that. We didn't even talk about it anymore.

"That is why it was such a shock when that filthy letter came. He said he had to see what was happening and I didn't argue. After he came back from that first trip to Ireland, I have never seen anyone so upset. It was the boy that mattered now, past was past. When Paddy told me about his plans for the adoption I agreed at once. We had no children of our own, could have none, there were fertility problems. And the thought of this motherless little boy growing up in some filthy place at the end of the world, you see there was really no choice."

"You have been to Ireland?"

"I didn't have to go. I knew. We had been in Acapulco for our honeymoon. Filthy. People ought to realize that there is nothing wrong with the United States—and it is a lot better than all those foreign places. And by this time the new position had come through and Paddy was teaching at the University of Free Enterprise, double the Kansas salary. A good thing too, the amount we had to pay to those Irish relatives. But it was worth it to save the child from that kind of a life. Paddy did it all—nor was it very easy. Three trips to Ireland before it was settled. I fixed up the boy's room while Paddy went back that final time. He had a friend there, a Sean something he had been to school with. A lawyer now, a solicitor they call it over there. Paddy had to go to court, before a judge. Ours is a Catholic marriage, that was the first thing they wanted to know. No chance of adoption if we weren't. Then paternity tests, humiliating. But worth it in the end. The plane was four hours late getting in but I never left the airport. It seemed they were the last ones off. I'll never forget that moment. Paddy looked so tired—and the boy! Skin the color of paper, must have never been out in the sun for his entire life. Skinny, arms like matchsticks sticking out of that filthy jacket. I remember I looked around, almost ashamed to be seen with him dressed like that.''

Snaresbrook raised her hand to stop her, checked again that the recording light was on. ''Do you remember that moment well, Dolly?''

''I could never forget it.''

''Then you must tell me about it, every detail. For Brian's sake. His memory has been—shall we say injured. It is there but we have to remind him about it.''

''I don't understand.''

''Will you help me—even if you don't understand?''

''If you want me to, Doctor. If you tell me that it is that important. I am used to taking things on faith. Paddy was the brains in the family. And Brian of course, I think they both looked down on me, not that they ever said. But a person can tell.''

''Dolly, I give you my word that you are the only person in the world who can help Brian now, at this moment in time. No one can look down on you now. You must restore those memories. You must describe everything, just as you remember it. Every single detail.''

''Well, if you say it is that important, that it will help, I will do my best." She sat up straight, determined. "At that time, when he was young, the boy was very dear to me. Only when he was older did he grow so distant. But I think, I *know*, that he needed me then."

They both looked so tired as they came toward her, Paddy holding the boy's hand. Father and son—there was no mistaking that red hair with the gold highlights.

"I must get the bags," Paddy said. His unshaven cheek rough when he kissed her. "Look after him."

"How do you do, Brian? I'm Dolly."

He lowered his head, turned away, was silent. So small too for an eight-year-old. You would have guessed his age at six at the most. Scrawny and none too clean. A bad diet for certain, worse habits. She would take care of that.

"I've fixed your room up—you'll like it."

Without thinking she reached out to take him by the shoulder, felt him shiver and pull away. It was not going to be easy; she forced a smile, tried not to show how uncomfortable she felt. Thank God, there was Paddy now with the bags.

When the car started the boy fell asleep almost at once in the backseat. Paddy yawned widely then apologized.

"No need. Was it an awful trip?"

"Just long and wearisome. And, you know"—he glanced over his shoulder at Brian—"not easy in many ways. I'll tell you all about it tonight."

"What was the problem about the passport you mentioned on the phone?"

"Red tape nonsense. Something about me being born Irish and a nationalized American and Brian still being Irish, though the adoption papers should have taken care of that. But not according to the American consul in Dublin. They found some forms to fill out and in the end it was easier to get Brian an Irish passport and sort the rest out at this end."

"We'll do that at once. He is an American boy now and has no need for a strange foreign passport. And wait until you see. I fixed up the spare room like we agreed. A bunk bed, a little desk, some nice pictures. He's going to like it.''

Brian hated this strange place. He was too tired at first to think about it. Woke up when his father carried him into the house. He had some strange-tasting soup and must have fallen asleep at the table. When he woke in the morning he cried out in fear at the strangeness of everything. His bedroom, bigger than the parlor at home. His familiar world was gone—even his clothes. His shorts, shirt, vest, gone while he slept. New clothes in bright colors now replaced their grays and blacks. Long trousers. He shivered when the door opened, pulled up the covers. But it was his father; he smiled, ever so slightly.

''Did you have a good sleep?'' He nodded. ''Good. Take yourself a shower, right in there, it works just like the one in the Dublin hotel. And get dressed. After breakfast I'll show you around your new home.''

The shower still took some getting used to and he still wasn't sure that he liked it. Back home in Tara the big cast-iron bathtub had been good enough.

When they walked out he felt that it was all too strange, too different to take in at once. The sun was too hot, the air too damp. The houses were all the wrong shape, the motorcars were too big—and drove on the wrong side of the road. His new home was a strange place. The pavement was too smooth. And water all around, no hills or trees. Just the flat, muddy-looking ocean and all the black metal things in the water on all sides. Why did it have to be like that? Why weren't they on land? When they had arrived at the big airport they had changed to another plane, had flown across the state of Texas—that is what his father had called it—to get here, an apparently endless and empty place. Driven from the airport and parked the car.

''I don't like it here.'' He said it without thinking, softly to himself, but Paddy heard.

''It takes some getting used to.''

''Middle of the ocean!''

''Not quite.'' Paddy pointed to the thin brown line on the

distant horizon; it shimmered in the heat. "That's the coast, just over there."

"There ain't no trees," Brian said, looking around at this strange new environment.

"There are trees right in front of the shopping center," his father said.

Brian dismissed them. "Not real trees, not growing in barrels like that. It's not right. Why isn't this place properly on the land?"

They had walked the length of the metal campus and the adjoining housing area. Stopped now to rest on a shaded bench overlooking the sea. Paddy slowly filled his pipe and lit it before he spoke.

"It's not simple to explain, not unless you know a lot about this country and how things work here. What it comes down to is that it is all a matter of politics. We have laws in the United States about research money, research projects at the universities, who can and cannot invest. A lot of our big corporations felt we were falling behind Japan, where government and industry cooperate, share money and research. They couldn't change the laws—so they bent them a little bit. Here, outside the continental three-mile limit, we are theoretically exempt from state and federal law. This university, built on old oil rigs and dredged land, is ruthlessly product-orientated. They have spared no expense at headhunting teachers and students."

"Headhunters live in New Guinea and kill people and cut off their heads and smoke them and shrink them. You got them here too?"

Paddy smiled at the boy's worried look and reached out to ruffle his hair; Brian pulled away.

"Different kind of headhunters. That's slang for offering someone a lot of money to leave their old job. Or giving big grants to get the best students."

Brian digested this new information, squinting out at the glare of the sun upon the water. "Then if you was headhunted here, then you must be something special?"

Paddy smiled, liking the way Brian's brain worked. "Well, yes, I suppose I must be if I am here."

"What do you do?"

"I'm a mathematician."

"Twelve and seven is nineteen like in school?"

"You start there and then it gets more complicated and more interesting."

"Like what f'rinstance?"

"Like after arithmetic there's geometry. And after that comes algebra—and then calculus. There is also number theory, which is sort of out of the mainstream of mathematics."

"What's number theory?"

Paddy smiled at the serious expression on the little boy's face and started to dismiss the question. Then thought twice about it. Brian seemed to be always surprising him with odd bits of information. He appeared to be a bright lad who believed that everything could be understood if you asked the right questions. But how could he possibly begin to explain higher mathematics to an eight-year-old? Well, one step at a time.

"Do you know about multiplying?"

"Sure—it's fun. Like 14 times 15 is 210 because so is 6 times 35 and 5 times 42."

"Are you positive?"

"Ain't no mistake. Because they're both as 2 times 3 times 5 times 7. I like 210 because it's made up of four different chunky numbers."

"Chunky numbers? Is that an Irish term?"

"Nope. Made it up myself," the boy said proudly. "Chunkies are numbers with no parts. Like 5 and 7. And big ones like 821 and 823. Or 1721 and 1723. A lot of the big ones come in pairs like that."

Chunky numbers was Brian's term for prime numbers, Paddy realized. Should eight-year-olds know about primes? Were they taught at this age?—He couldn't remember.

It was after eleven that night when Dolly turned off the television. She found Paddy in the kitchen. His pipe had gone out and he was staring, unseeing, out into the darkness.

"I'm going to bed," she said.

"Do you now what Brian seems to have done! All by himself. At the age of eight. He has discovered prime numbers. Not only that—he seems to have worked out some pretty efficient ways to find primes.''

"He's a very serious little boy. Never smiles.''

"You're not listening. He's very bright. More than that—he has a basic understanding of mathematics, something almost all of my students are lacking.''

"If you think so then have them do an I.Q. test in school. I'm tired. We can talk about it in the morning.''

"I.Q. tests are too culturally orientated. Later maybe, when he has been here a while. I'll talk to his teachers about it when I take him to school.''

"Not the very first day you won't! He has to get used to things first, settle in. And it's about time you thought about your own classes, research. I'll take him to school tomorrow. You'll see, it's going to work out fine.''

Brian hated the school. From the very first moment he arrived. Hated the big fat black headmaster. He was called a principal here. Everything was different. Strange. And they laughed at him, from the very beginning. It was the teacher who started it.

"That will be your class seat,'' she said, pointing not too precisely at the row of desks.

"The terd one?''

"The third one, yes. But you must say it correctly. Third.'' She waited, smiling insincerely at his silence. "Say third, Brian.''

"Terd.''

"Not turd, that is a different word. Third.''

That was when the children laughed, whispered "Turd!'' at him as soon as the teacher's back was turned. When the bell rang and the class ended he went into the hall with the others, but kept going right out of the school, away from them all.

"And that was the very first day in school,'' Dolly said. "Ran away after his very first class. The principal phoned and I was worried sick. It was after dark before the police found him and brought him home.''

"Did he tell you why?" Snaresbrook asked.

"Never, not him. Either closemouthed or asking too many questions, nothing in between. Not sociable either. You might say that the only friend he had was his computer. You would think he would have had enough of that during school hours. All computerized now, you know. But no. As soon as he was home he would be right at it again. Not just games, but writing programs in LOGO, the language he had learned in school. Very good programs too, that's what Paddy said. The boy was writing learning programs that wrote their own programs. There was always something special between Brian and computers."

# 5

# February 18, 2023

Benicoff was waiting when Snaresbrook came out of the operating room.

"Do you have a moment to spare, Doctor?"

"Yes, of course. You can tell me what is happening at your end . . ."

"Can we continue this in your office?"

"Good idea. I have a new coffee machine that I want to try out. It just arrived and was installed this morning."

Benicoff closed the office door, then turned and raised his eyebrows at the brass machine. "I thought you said new?"

"New to me, that is. This gorgeous device must be ninety years old if it is a day. They just don't make them this way anymore."

"With good reason!"

It was six feet high, an impressive gleaming array of valves, pipes, riveted plates, cylinders—all of which was crowned by a bronze eagle with wide-spread wings. Steam hissed loudly from a protruding pipe when Dr. Snaresbrook twisted a knob. "Espresso or cappuccino?" she asked, loading fragrant black coffee into the black-handled holder.

"Espresso—with a twist of lemon."

"I can see that you have been around. That's the only way to drink it. Is there any news on the thieves?"

"Negative—but a hard-worked negative. The FBI, the police and a dozen agencies have kept this investigation going night and day. Every possible lead has been followed, every detail of that night's events investigated exhaustively. Yet there's not a thing discovered worth mentioning since I talked to you last. That's good coffee." He sipped again and waited until Snaresbrook had made one of her own. "And that, I am sorry to say, is all that I have to report. I hope you have better news about Brian."

Erin Snaresbrook stared into the steaming dark liquid; stirred in another spoonful of sugar. "Basically the good news is that he is still alive. But the severed nerves deteriorate more every day. I'm racing against time—and I don't know yet if I am winning or losing. As you know, after a nerve fiber dies, a sort of empty tube remains. That was why I have implanted fetal brain cells to grow and replace those fibers. The manipulating machine will also inject tiny amounts of the nerve growth drug gamma-NGF to induce the fetal cells' axons to grow down those tubes. This technique was discovered in the 1990s by researchers looking for a way to repair spinal-cord injuries—they used to always result in permanent paralysis. Now we repair brain injuries by using this and another drug, SRS, that overcomes the tendency of mature brain cells to resist invasion by other nerve fibers trying to make new connections."

Benicoff frowned. "Why would brains do such a thing, if it keeps them from repairing themselves?"

"An interesting question. Most other body tissues are very good at making repairs, or admitting other cells that offer help. But think for a moment about the nature of a memory. It is based on the precise relations of unbelievably tiny fiber connections. Once those connections are made, they have to persist, with almost no change, for twenty, or fifty, or even ninety years! Therefore the brain has evolved many peculiar defenses of its own, defenses found in no other tissue, to prevent most normal kinds of change. It appears that the advantage of having better memory outweighs the advantage of being able to repair injury.

"Brian's recovery is going to take some time. The slowest part of the process will be regrowing the severed nerve fibers. That will require at least a few months, even using NGF, since we don't dare to use it in large doses. NGF causes uninjured brain cells to grow as well—which if not monitored closely will disrupt the parts of the brain that still work! To say nothing of the risk of cancer. Because of this, Brian's progress will be very slow."

"Will you be proceeding with this process now?"

"Not at once, not until the new nerve fibers have grown. When that has happened we will have to find out what the brain cells do on each side of the injury. When we have sorted that out, we can think about reconnecting the correct pairs."

"But there must be millions of them!"

"There are—but I won't have to untangle them all. I'll start by finding the easiest ones. Bunches of nerve fibers that correspond to the most common ideas, ones that every child has. We'll display pictures of dogs, cats, chairs, windows, a thousand objects like that. And look for fibers that are active for each one." For the first time she forgot her chronic exhaustion, buoyed up by enthusiasm.

"Then we'll go on to words. The average educated person normally uses about twenty thousand. That's really not very many when you think about it. We can play a tape of them in less than a day—then go on to word relationships, groups, sentences."

"Excuse my stupidity, Doctor, but I don't see the sense of this. You've been trying to talk to Brian for days now—with absolutely no sign of response. He doesn't seem to hear anything."

"It looks like that—but Brian is not a *him* right now. He is only a shattered brain, a collection of nonconnecting parts. What we must discover is what these parts, these agencies are—and reconnect them. That is the entire point of what we are doing. If we are ever to rebuild his mind, we must first go back and retrieve its parts, so that we can integrate them and bridge between his memories. And this was a good day as far as input. About Brian's early school years, the important, formative time that shaped his life to come. It was fortunate that your people located his school psychiatrist, he's teaching now in Oregon, and flew in. Man by the name of Rene Gimelle. He met Brian the first day the boy arrived in the school, saw him regularly after that. In addition he had many interviews with the boy's father. He gave us some excellent input.''

"Is there anything wrong, Dr. Gimelle?'' Paddy asked, trying to keep the concern from his voice and failing badly. ''I came as soon as I got your message.'' Gimelle smiled and shook his head.

"Quite the opposite, very good news. When I talked to you and your wife last I remember telling you to be patient, that Brian was going to need time to adjust to this totally new life. Any child who is plucked from a small town—in a different country—and sent around the world is going to need time to get accustomed to all the changes. When I did my evaluation I was sure that Brian would have his troubles and I was prepared for the worst. It didn't take long to find out that he had been bullied and rejected by his peer group in Ireland, laughed at—if you will excuse the word—for being a bastard. Even worse, he felt rejected by all of his close relatives after his mother died. I have been seeing him once a week and doing what I can to help him to cope. The good news is that he seems to need less and less help. Admittedly, he's not very social with his classmates, but this should get better in time. As far as his classwork goes—it would be hard to improve upon it. With very little persuasion by his teachers he has gone from failing grades to straight A's in every subject.''

"Persuasion sounds ominous. What do you mean?''

"Perhaps that was the wrong word to use in this context. I think rewards-for-effort might express it better. As you well know, experienced teachers will make sure that good behavior, good classwork, is noticed and complimented. It is really a matter of positive reinforcement, a technique with proven efficacy. Doing the direct opposite, pointing out failures, accomplishes very little—other than instilling a sense of guilt, which is almost always counterproductive. In Brian's case the computer proved to be the key to any learning problems he had. I've seen the recordings—you can look at them as well if you wish—of just what he has accomplished in a very few weeks—"

"Recordings? I am afraid that I don't understand."

Gimelle looked uncomfortable, arranging and rearranging paper clips on the desk before him. "There is nothing unusual or illegal in this. It is common practice in most schools—in fact it is required here at UFE. You must have seen it in your employment contract when you signed it."

"Hardly. There were over fifty pages of fine print in the thing."

"What did your lawyer say about it?"

"Nothing—since I didn't consult one. At the time life for me was, shall we say, rather stressful. What you are saying is that all of the students in this school have taps on their computers, that everything they enter can be seen and recorded?"

"A common and accepted practice, a very useful diagnostic and educational tool. After all, in the days of written notebooks they were turned in to be graded. You might say that accessing a student's computer is very much the same thing."

"I don't think it is. We grade notebooks—but not personal diaries. All of which is beside the point. I'll consider the morality of this dubious practice some other time. Now we are thinking about Brian. What did these clandestine recordings reveal?"

"An exceedingly unusual and original mind. LOGO, as you know, is more than a first computer language that children learn. It is very flexible when implemented correctly. I was delighted to see that Brian not only solved the problems of the class assignments, but when he had a solution he tried to write a meta-program that incorporated all of his solutions. He invented data bases of IF-THEN rules for his own programming. For example if an answer was needed then he would insert some lines of code. And edit later. Very easy to do in LOGO—if you know how—because all the tools are there. For example, while other students were learning to draw pictures, graphics programs, using LOGO, Brian was way ahead of them. He saved and indexed each useful drawing fragment with changeable parameters, along with geometric constraints on where to draw it. His programs now draw recognizable caricatures of the other students, and myself as well. They can even change expression. That was last week—and he has improved the programs already. Now the figures can walk, and solve simple problems, right on the screen.''

Paddy had a good deal to think about when he went home that night.

Benicoff and the surgeon both looked up, startled, when the door slammed open and General Schorcht stamped in, the pinned-up empty sleeve of his jacket swinging as he stabbed the index finger of his left hand at Snaresbrook.

''You. If you are Dr. Snaresbrook you're coming with me.''

The surgeon turned about slowly to face the intruder. She had to lean back to look up at the tall General's face. She appeared not to be impressed.

''Who are you?'' she said coldly.

''Tell her,'' Schorcht snapped at Benicoff.

''This is General Schorcht who is with . . .''

''That's identification enough. This is a military emergency and I need your help. There is a patient here in intensive care, Brian Delaney, who is in great danger.''

''I am well aware of that.''

''Not medical danger—physical attack.'' Benicoff started to speak but the General waved him to silence. ''Later. We have very little time now. The hospital authorities inform me that the patient is too ill to be moved at this time.''

''That is correct.''

''Then the records must be altered. You will come with me to do this.''

Snaresbrook's skin grew livid; she was not used to being spoken to in this manner. Before she could explode Benicoff quickly intervened.

"Doctor, let me fill you in very quickly. We have firm reason to believe that when Brian was shot, that others were killed as well. There must be national security involved or the General would not be here. I am sure that explanations will be forthcoming—but for the moment would you please be of assistance?"

Brain surgeons are well used to instant, life-and-death decisions. Snaresbrook put down her coffee cup, turned at once and started toward the door.

"Yes, of course. Come with me to the nurse's station."

The General had certainly made no friends since he had entered the hospital. The angry head nurse was reluctantly pacified by Snaresbrook and finally convinced of the urgency of the matter. She dismissed the other nurses while Snaresbrook managed to do the same with the staff doctor. Only when they were gone did the General turn to the gray-haired head nurse, who matched him glare for glare.

"Where is the patient now?" he asked.

She turned to the indicator board and touched a lit number. "Here. Intensive care. Room 314."

"Are there any other rooms on this floor that are empty?"

"Just 330. But it is a double..."

"That doesn't matter. Now change the indicator board and the records to show Delaney in 330, and 314 as being empty."

"There will be trouble..."

"Do it."

She did—with great reluctance. As she punched in the changes another nurse hurried in, still pinning on her badge. Schorcht nodded grimly.

"About time, Lieutenant. Get into the station. The rest of us are leaving. If anyone asks, the patient Brian Delaney is in room 330." He silenced the staff nurse with a quick chop of his hand. "Lieutenant Drake is a military nurse with a great deal of hospital experience. There will be no trouble." His beeper sounded and he switched on his radio and listened to it. "Understood." He put it back on his belt and looked around him.

"We have about two minutes, possibly. Listen and don't ask questions. We will all leave this area—leave this floor in fact. Lieutenant Drake knows what to do. We have just learned that there will be an attempt on the patient's life. I not only want to prevent this crime but obtain information about the would-be perpetrators. You can all help by simply leaving now. Understood?"

The General led the way; there were no arguments. Nurse Drake stood almost at attention as they were hurried down the corridor to the stairwell and off the third floor. Only when they were gone did she take a deep breath and relax slightly. She pulled her uniform straight and turned to the mirror on the wall to make sure her cap was square and correct. When she turned back she controlled her start of surprise when she saw the young man standing at the counter.

"Can I help you . . . Doctor?" she said. He was dressed in hospital whites and had an electronic stethoscope hanging from his pocket.

"Nothing important. I just came on. Passed some worried visitors asking about a Brian Delaney. A new admittance?" He leaned over the counter and tapped the indicator. "Is that him?"

"Yes, Doctor. Intensive care, 330. Critical but stable."

"Thanks. I'll tell them when I go out."

The nurse smiled at him. Nice-looking, tanned, late twenties, carrying a black bag. Still smiling, she put her hand to her waist and as soon as he had turned his back pressed twice on the button of what appeared to be an ordinary pager.

Whistling softly through his teeth, the young man went down the corridor, turned a corner and past 330 without a glance. He stopped at the next cross corridor and looked both ways—then ran swiftly and silently back to the room. No one was in sight. With his hand in the black bag he threw open the door and saw the empty beds. Before he could react the two men inside the room, one to each side of the door, pushed automatic pistols into his midriff.

"Whatever you're thinking of doing—don't!" the taller one said.

"Hello there," the young man said and let the bag drop, swinging up the bulbous-tipped revolver at the same time.

They fired to wound, not kill. Quick shots into his arms and shoulder. He was still smiling as he fell face-forward. Before they could grab him and roll him over, there was a muffled *pop*.

They looked very uncomfortable when Schorcht came stalking in.

"He did it himself, sir, before we could stop him. Single shot into the chest with an explosive bullet. Blew a great damned hole in himself. Nothing left to patch up—even being right here in the hospital."

The General's nostrils flared and his glare, aimed first at one then the other of them like a swiveling cannon, was far worse than anything he could have said. It smoked with demotion, reprimand, blighted careers. He turned on his heel and stomped out to the waiting Benicoff.

"Get the FBI onto the body. Find out anything, *everything!*"

"Will do. Can you tell me now what this is all about?"

"No. This is a need-to-know situation—and you don't need to know anything further. Let us say only that this Megalobe business has become slotted into something much larger that we have been aware of for some time. And this sort of attack will not be permitted to happen again. There will be guards here right around the clock until the patient can be moved. When he can he is going to go right out of here and over there, across the bay to Idiot's Island. Coronado. I don't like the Navy—but at least they are part of the military. They should be able to guard one man inside their hospital inside the largest naval base in the world. I hope."

"I am sure that they can. But you are going to tell me the background to this assassination attempt. Or my own investigation will be compromised."

"When the time comes you will be informed." Icily. But Benicoff was not buying it; his voice was just as cold as the General's.

"Not satisfactory. If the people behind this are the same as the ones who shot Brian then I do need to know. Now tell me."

It was a standoff—until General Schorcht reluctantly made the decision.

"I can tell you the absolute minimum. We have an informant in a criminal organization. He discovered this assassination attempt, contacted us as soon as he could. He knows only that the killer was hired—but as yet he doesn't know who made the approach. If and when he acquires that information it will be passed on to you. Satisfactory?"

"Satisfactory. As long as you remember to tell me." Benicoff smiled cheerfully in response to General Schorcht's glare of hatred, turned and left. He found Snaresbrook in her office, closed and locked the door before he told her what had happened.

"And no one knows yet who is behind this attempt, or why they are doing it?" the surgeon asked.

"The why is pretty obvious. Whoever stole the artificial intelligence equipment and details wants a monopoly—and no witnesses. They wanted to be sure that Brian would never be able to talk."

"In that case—let us see what we can do to interfere with their plans. But the relocation to Coronado will not be easy—or soon. Brian's in no condition to be moved, nor am I willing to interrupt the healing process. As I have said, this is a battle against time. So you and your obnoxious General will just have to find a way to make this hospital secure."

"He is going to love that. I'll take another coffee before I even think about facing him."

"Help yourself. But I have to get back to the O.R."

"I'm going with you. I'm staying there until I see just what kind of security the General comes up with."

# 6

## February 19, 2023

The next morning Benicoff got to Dr. Snaresbrook's office just before she left for the operating room.

"Got a moment?"

"Just that and nothing more. This is going to be a difficult day."

"I thought you might want to know about the assassin. As was expected no identification, no labels in his clothes, no identification. His blood was more revealing. The report said that his blood type placed his origin in South America. Colombia in fact. I didn't know they could be that specific."

"Blood typing is getting more and more refined—and you will probably find that given enough time they will be able to pinpoint his origin exactly. Is that all?"

"Not quite. He had full-blown AIDS and was a three-bag-a-day heroin addict. He came down from his high just long enough to pull the job—but he had a hypodermic in his bag loaded with a dose that would kill a horse. Se we have a hired gun, more than ready to kill for his expensive fix. The trail gets cold there but the investigators are trying to work through the people who arranged the contract with him for the hit. I have not yet even been told who they are or how this information reached us. So you will appreciate that it is not very easy."

"I appreciate. Now if you will excuse me I have to go to work. Come with me." They scrubbed and dressed in silence, then went into the O.R. Once more the covering on Brian's open brain was pulled back.

"This operation will hopefully be the last," Erin Snaresbrook said. "This is a computer that will be implanted in his brain."

She was balancing an oddly shaped black plastic form on the palm of her gloved hand, holding it up so that the camera that was recording the operating procedure could get a clear view of it. "It is a million-processor CM-10 connection machine with a 1,000-megahertz router and then a thousand megabytes of RAM. It has the capacity to easily do 100 trillion operations per second. Even after the implantation of the connection chip films there is space in the brain left for this where the dead tissue was removed. The computer case was shaped to exactly fit into this space."

She laid the supercomputer on the sterile tray. The tendrils of the machine above dropped down over it, examined it, picked it and rotated it into the correct position for implantation. When the preparation was complete the computer was lifted, then lowered into the opening in Brian's skull.

"Before being finally positioned the connections are made between the computer and each of the films. There, the connections have been made, the case is being fitted into its permanent position. As soon as the last, external connection is complete we will begin closure. Even now the computer should be in operation. It has been programmed with reconnection-learning software. This recognizes similar or related signals and reroutes the nerve signals within the chips. Hopefully these memories will now be accessible."

"It's a strange kind of graduation present," Dolly said. "The boy needs clothes and a new jacket."

"He'll get them, just take him shopping after school," Paddy said, grunting as he bent to tie his shoes. "Anyway, clothes aren't any kind of real present for a boy. Especially on an occasion like this. He's finished high school in less than a year and is looking forward to the university. And he's only twelve years old."

"Have you ever thought that we are pushing him too fast?"

"Dolly—you know better than to say a thing like that. There's no pushing here. If anything we have to work hard not to hold him back. It was his idea to finish high school so quickly because there are courses he wants to take that aren't available in secondary education. That's why he wants to see where I work. The security regulations prevented him coming until now. So this is a very exciting moment in his life because he now has all the grounding that he needs to go ahead. To him the university is the horn of plenty, bursting with good things to consume.''

''Well that's all right. He really should eat more. He gets into that computer and forgets where he is.''

''A metaphor!'' Paddy laughed. ''Intellectual food to feed his curiosity.''

She was hurt, tried not to show it. ''Now you're laughing at me, just because I worry about his health.''

''I'm not laughing at you—and his health is fine. And his weight's fine, he grows like a weed and swims and works out just like every other kid. But his intellectual curiosity— that's what is different. You want to come with us? This is his big day.''

She shook her head. ''It's not for me. Just enjoy yourself and see that you are back by six. I'm making a turkey with all the trimmings and Milly and George are coming over later. I want to be cleaned up before they get here—''

The door crashed open and Brian thundered in.

''Aren't you ready, Dad? Time to go.''

''Ready when you are.'' Brian was at the front door, almost out of it; Paddy called after him. ''And say good-bye to Dolly.''

''Bye,'' and he was gone.

''An important day for him,'' Paddy said.

''Important, of course,'' Dolly said quietly to herself as the door closed. ''And I'm just the housekeeper around here.''

The artificial island and attendant oil platforms were home to Brian now; he was no longer aware of this unusual environment. When it all had been new to him he used to explore the rigs, sneaking down the gangways to the bottom level with the sea surging around the steel legs below. Or up to the helipads, even climbing around a locked barrier once to clamber up the ladder to the communication mast on the administration building, the highest point in UFE. But his curiosity about these mechanical constructs had long since been satisfied; he had much more important and interesting things to think about now as they walked across the bridge that led to the lab rig.

"All the electronic laboratories are here," Paddy explained. "That's our generator over there, the dome, since we need a clean and stable power supply."

"Pressurized water reactor from the submarine *Sailfish*. Junked in 1994 when the global agreement was signed."

"That's the one. We go in here, second floor."

Brian stared about in silence, tense with excitement. It was Saturday so they had the place entirely to themselves. Though an occasional sudden humming of drives and a glowing screen showed that at least one background program had been left running.

"Here is where I work," Paddy said, pointing to the terminal. A charred briar pipe was resting on top of the keyboard and he removed it before he pulled the chair out for Brian. "Sit down and hit any key to turn it on. I tell you I'm proud of this yoke, the new zed seventy-seven. It gives you an idea of the kind of work we're doing if they pop for something like this. Makes a Cray look like a beat-up Macintosh."

"Really?" Brian's eyes were wide as he ran his fingers along the edge of the keyboard.

"Well, not really." Paddy smiled as he rooted in his pocket for his tobacco. "But it is faster in certain kinds of calculation and I really need it for the development work on LAMA. That's a new language that we are developing here."

"What's it for?"

"A new, rapidly developing and special need. You write programs in LOGO, don't you?"

"Sure. And BASIC and FORTRAN—and I'm learning E out of a book. My teaching has been telling me something about Expert Systems."

"Then you will already know that different computer languages are used for different purposes. BASIC is a good first hands-on language for learning some of the simplest things computers can do—for describing procedures, step by step. FORTRAN has been used for fifty years because it is especially good for routine scientific calculations, though it now has been replaced by formula-understanding Symbolic Manipulation systems. LOGO is for beginners, particularly children, it is so graphical, making it easy to draw pictures.''

"And it lets you write programs that write and run other programs. The others don't let you do that. They just complain when you try."

"You'll discover that you can do that in LAMA, too. Because, like LOGO, it is based on the old language LISP. One of the oldest and still one of the best—because it is simple and yet can refer back to itself. Most of the first expert programs, in the early days of artificial intelligence, were developed by using the LISP language. But the new kinds of parallel processing in modern AI research need a different approach—and language—to do all those things and more. That's LAMA."

"Why is it named for an animal?"

"It isn't. LAMA is an acronym for Language for Logic and Metaphor. It is partially based on the CYC program developed in the 1980s. To understand artificial intelligence it is first vital that we understand our own intelligence."

"But if the brain is a computer, what is the mind? How are they connected?"

Paddy smiled. "A question that appears to be a complete mystery to most people, including some of the best scientists. Yet as far as I can see it's really no problem at all, just a wrong question. We shouldn't think of the mind and brain as two different things that have to be connected, since they are just two different ways of looking at the same thing. Minds are simply what brains do."

"How does our brain computer compute thoughts?"

"No one really knows exactly—but we have a pretty good idea. It isn't really just one big computer. It's made of millions of little bunches of interconnected nerve cells. Like a society. Each bunch of cells acts like a little agent that has learned to do some little job—either by itself or by knowing how to get some other agents to help. Thinking is the result of all those agents being connected in ways that make them help each other—or to get out of the way when they cannot help. So even though each one can do very little, each one can still carry a little fragment of knowledge to share with the others."

"So how does LAMA help them share?" Brian had listened with complete concentration, taking in every word, analyzing and understanding.

"It does this by combining an Expert System shell with a huge data base called CYC—for encyclopedia. All previous Expert Systems were based on highly specialized knowledge, but CYC provides LAMA with millions of fragments of common sense knowledge—the sorts of things that everyone knows."

"But if it has so many knowledge fragments, how does LAMA know which ones to use?"

"By using special connection agents called nemes, which associate each knowledge fragment with certain others. So that if you tell LAMA that a certain drinking-cup is made of glass, then the nemes automatically make it assume that the cup also is fragile and transparent—unless there is contrary evidence. In other words, CYC provides LAMA with the millions of associations between ideas that are needed in order to think."

When Paddy stopped talking to light his pipe the boy sat in silence for almost a minute.

"It's complex," Paddy said. "Not easy to pick up the first time around."

But he had misunderstood Brian's silence, misunderstood completely because the boy had followed what he had said to its logical conclusion.

"If the language works like that—then why can't it be used to make a real working artificial intelligence? One that can think for itself—like a person?"

"No reason at all, Brian, no reason at all. In fact that is just what we are hoping to do."

# 7

## February 22, 2023

Erin Snaresbrook felt logy with sleep—even though she had slept for only five hours. It had not been by choice but by necessity, since she hadn't been to bed at all for almost three days. She was beginning to hallucinate and more than once had found her eyes closing in the O.R. for lack of proper rest. It was too much. She had used one of the vacant intern's rooms, fallen into a black hole of fatigue and, what seemed like a moment later, had been dragged painfully awake by the clamor of alarm. A cold shower shocked her back to life; reddened eyes blinked back at her from the mirror as she put on a touch of lipstick.

"Erin, I have to tell you. You look rotten," she muttered, sticking out a furred and tired-looking tongue. "I prescribe coffee for your condition, Doctor. Preferably intravenously."

When Snaresbrook came into her waiting room she saw that Dolly was already there, turning the pages on a worn copy of *Time*. She looked at her watch.

"Patients steal all the new magazines, would you believe it? Rich patients, or they wouldn't be here, they even pinch the toilet paper and bars of soap. Sorry I'm late."

"No, that's fine, Doctor, it's all right."

"We'll have some coffee, then get to work. You go in, I'll be just a moment."

Madeline had the mail ready and she flipped quickly through it, glancing up when the door flew open. She smiled insincerely at the angry General.

"Why are you and the patient still in this hospital?

Why have my orders for moving him not been carried out?''

General Schorcht snapped the words like weapons. Erin Snaresbrook thought of many answers, most of them quite insulting, but she was too tired for a shouting match this early in the day.

''I will show you, General. Then maybe you will climb down off my back.'' She threw the correspondence onto the desk, then pushed by the General and out into the hall. She stamped toward the intensive-care unit where Brian was, heard the General's heavy footsteps behind her. ''Put this on,'' she snapped, and tossed General Schorcht a sterile mask. ''Sorry,'' she said, took the mask and fixed it into position over the other's nose and mouth; it's not easy to fit one of the things with only one hand. When her own mask was in place she opened the door to the ICU just enough so they could see in. ''Take a good look.''

The figure on the table was barely discernible behind the network of pipes, tubes, wires, apparatus. The two arms of the manipulator were positioned over him, the multibranching fingers dropping down into the opening in the cloth. The flexible tube of the oxygen mask wormed out from under the drapes and there were drips and tubes plugged into arms and legs and into almost every orifice of the unconscious body. Lights flickered on one of the complex machines; a nurse looked at a readout on the screen and made an adjustment. Snaresbrook let the door swing shut and pulled the mask from the General's face.

''You want me to move all *that?* While the connection apparatus is in place—and in operation? It is working with the internal computer now to reroute nerve signals.''

She turned on her heel and left: General Schorcht's continuing silence was answer enough.

She was humming cheerfully when she entered her office and turned on the hulking coffee machine. Dolly sat on the edge of her chair and Erin pointed a spoon at her.

''How about a nice strong espresso?''

''I don't drink coffee.''

"You should. It is certainly easier on the metabolism than alcohol."

"I can't sleep, it's the caffeine you see. Nor do I drink alcohol either."

Nodding sympathetically over the coffee, an answer to the unanswerable, Snaresbrook sat down at her desk and brought up on the screen the transcribed notes of their previous interview.

"You told me a lot of very vital things last time you were here, Dolly. You not only have a good memory but a deep understanding. You were a good and affectionate mother to Brian, that is obvious in the way you speak about him." She glanced up and saw that the other woman was blushing lightly at this casual compliment; life had not been that kind to Dolly and compliments very rare. "Do you remember when Brian reached puberty?" Erin asked, and the blush deepened.

"Well, you know, it's not as obvious as with girls. But he was young I think, around thirteen."

"This is most important. Up until now we have been tracking his emotional life as a small child, then going on to follow his learning patterns and intellectual history. That is all going very well. But major emotional and physiological changes take place with the onset of puberty. That time and area must be explored in depth, charted as well as we can. Do you remember him dating—or having any girlfriends?"

"No, nothing like that. Well there was a girl he saw for a bit, she would come around the house to use his computer sometimes. But it didn't seem to last very long. She was the only one. Then of course there was the matter of their age difference, she was much older than him. So the relationship could only have been platonic. I do remember that she was a pretty little thing. Name of Kim."

"Kim, I want you to take a look at your screen right now," Dr. Betser said. "You had trouble with this last week and until you know exactly what is happening you won't be able to move on to the next step. Now look at this."

The instructor had typed the equations into his own computer—which not only displayed them on the screen in front of the class but entered them into the desk computers of all the students at the same moment.

"Show us how to do it," he said and switched command to her. All eyes were on the screen as Kim reluctantly touched her keyboard.

All eyes except Brian's. He had worked out the solution within a minute after the problem had been entered. College was becoming as frustrating as high school had been. He spent almost all of his class time waiting for the others to catch up with him. They were a stupid and despicable lot who looked down on him like some kind of freak. All of them were four, five years older than he was—while most of them stood a head taller. At times he felt like a midget. And it wasn't just paranoia on his part—they really did hate him, he was sure of it. Disliked him because he was younger, out of place here. Plenty of jealousy too, since he did the work so much better and faster than they did. How had people who really knew how to think, like Turing or Einstein or Feynman, how had they managed to live through school?

He looked at his screen and tried not to groan as the girl made a hash of it. It was too awful to watch. He casually pushed his pocket calculator against the side of his terminal and punched in a quick code. A list of Italian verbs appeared in a window on the screen and he scrolled through them, memorizing the new ones.

Brian had discovered, very early on, that the school tapped into every student's computer and recorded all the data that was entered into it. This was made obvious by some of the questions they had asked him, knowledge they could only have obtained in this underhand way. Once he had discovered it, he made sure that the school computer was just used for schoolwork. He had observed that his teachers, Dr. Betser in particular, were quite certain that their words were golden—and would be quite upset if they discovered that during their lectures he had been running war games or accessing data bases instead of giving them a hundred percent attention. But there were ways around everything. If all of the computers in the schoolroom had been connected by cables it might have been easier—or harder to misdirect information. But now narrow-band infrared links, like ether-net systems, filled the room with invisible communication. Every computer had a digitally tunable LED, a light-emitting diode, that transmitted on low-noise channels. A photodetector picked up messages it was tuned to. Brian's solution to this was to build an intercepting device into what appeared to be a pocket calculator. When it was placed at the side of his computer it intercepted the incoming signal and rebroadcast it. So he could do whatever he wished without anyone being able to detect the operation. What was on the screen was for his eyes alone! *Allattare* to feed or to nurse . . . *allenare* to exercise, to train.

He was still keeping track of the class and became vaguely aware that Dr. Betser's voice was taking on that weary, nagging tone.

". . . a basic misunderstanding of how we make successive approximations. Unless you get this basic point, you'll never get any further. Brian—will you do this correctly so we can move on. And, Kim, I want to see you after class."

The Italian verbs vanished as Brian pushed the calculator aside. He looked at the screen and tracked her first error. "The misconception begins here," he said, moving the cursor and highlighting the equation. "After you find the first-order solution, you have to remove it—subtract it from the original equation—before you can apply the same method to find the next term. If you forget to do that, you'll keep getting the same term again. And then you have to divide out the independent variable, or you will just get zero the next time. And finally, you have to go backward again, adding the terms back in and multiplying back the variable again. I think the trouble is that everyone in the class believes that there are a lot of different ideas here, derivatives, approximations, second-order approximations, and so on. But there's only one idea, used over and over. I don't see why they make it out to be so complicated . . ."

An hour later Brian was eating his cheese and tomato sandwich and reading *Galaxy Warhounds of Procyon* when someone sat down heavily on the bench beside him. This was unusual enough since he was left strictly alone by the other students. More unusual were the tanned fingers that pulled the book from him and slammed it onto the table.

"Juvenile science fiction space crap that only kids read," Kim snapped at him.

He had had this argument often enough before. "Science fiction utilizes a vocabulary twice as large as that of all other popular fiction. While SF readers are in the top percentile . . ."

"Space balls! You made me look pretty dumb today."

"Well you were pretty dumb! I'm sorry."

Brian's worried expression got to her; she could never stay angry very long in any case. She laughed aloud and pushed his book back to him. Pushing it through a slice of tomato on the table. He smiled and wiped the cover with his napkin.

"In fact it wasn't even your fault anyway," he said. "Old Betser may be a wizard programming mathematician but he doesn't know a gnat's fart about explaining it to anyone."

"What do you mean?" She was interested now, reached out and broke off a corner of his sandwich. He noticed that her teeth were very white and neat, her lips red—and that was without lipstick. He pushed the remains of the sandwich over to her.

"He's always going off on tangents, getting sidetracked into explanations that have nothing to do with the material he should be teaching, things like that. I always stay a chapter ahead of him in the text so he won't confuse me when he starts to explain something."

"Amazing!" Kim said, meaning the thought of reading a text you didn't have to when there were so many other wonderful things to do. "Can you do better than him, Mr. Smartass?"

"Run circles around him, Miss Birdbrain. Using the heretofore totally secret Brian Delaney lightning instruction system all will be made clear! In the first place, it's not really so important to know exactly how to solve each problem."

"That sounds stupid. How can you solve a problem if you don't know how to solve it?"

"By doing just the opposite. You can learn a lot of ways

not to solve it. A lot of wrong methods not to try. Then, once you find the most common mistakes, you can hardly help doing the right thing without even trying."

He remembered exactly where she had gone wrong and knew at once what her misunderstanding was. He explained it patiently, two or three ways, until she finally caught on.

"Is *that* what my trouble was! Why didn't Beastly Betser explain it like that? It's obvious."

"Everything is obvious once you understand it. Why don't you work through the rest of those examples while this is clear in your head?"

"Maybe tomorrow. Got things to do, gotta run."

Run she did, or at least trotted out of the dining room, and he shook his head as he watched her go. Girls! They were a strange breed. He opened his book and winced at the red tomato stains. Sloppy. Sloppy thinking too, she should have worked this thing out while it was fresh in her head. Five will get you ten she would forget the whole thing by tomorrow.

She did. "You were right! It was gone, zip. I thought I remembered, but not exactly."

He sighed dramatically and rolled his eyes heavenward. Kim giggled.

"Look," he said, "there's really not much use spending the time to learn something unless you spend a little more time making sure that it stays learnt. First, you can't really understand anything if you only understand it one way. You have to think a little about each new idea—which old ones it is like, and which are really different. If you don't connect it to a few other things, it will evaporate the moment anything changes. That's what I meant yesterday, about the solution not being important. It's the differences and similarities." He could see that this was having no effect, so he played his ace. "Anyway, I worked out an auto-tutor program that simplifies the subject of successive approximations. I'll give you a copy. Then you can run it whenever the curtain starts to fall in your brain and all will be made instantly clear. At least it will get you through this part of the course."

"You really have a program like that?"

"Would I lie to you?"

"I don't know. I really don't know anything about you at all, Mister I.Q. Kid."

"Why did you call me that?" He was angry, hurt, both feelings mixed together. He had overheard the other students calling him that behind his back. Laughing.

"I'm sorry—I didn't mean it, I just never thought. Any moron that calls you that must be a moron. I apologized so you can't be angry."

"I'm not," he said, and realized that he meant it. "Give me your log-on ID and I'll zap a copy of that program to your modem."

"I always forget the ID, but I've written it down someplace."

Brian groaned. "You simply can't forget your ID. That's like forgetting your blood type."

"But I don't *know* my blood type!"

They both laughed at that and he found the only solution. "You better come over to my place and I'll give you a copy."

"You will? You're a great guy, Brian Delaney."

She shook his hand in gratitude. Her fingers were very, very warm.


# 8

## March 25, 2023

There were muttered complaints from people waiting in the line, but not from Benicoff. Not only didn't he mind—he enjoyed the security. When he finally reached the two M.P.s they coldly asked him for his ID—although they knew him very well. They examined this closely, then his hospital pass, before they let him approach the front door of the hospital. Another guard inside unlocked it for him.

"Any troubles, Sergeant?"

"None other than the usual with you-know-who."

Benicoff nodded in understanding. He had been present when General Schorcht had chewed the Sergeant out, him with hash marks up to his elbows, a Master Sergeant, not that the General cared. "I got my troubles with him too— which is why I'm here."

"It's a tough life," the Sergeant said with marked lack of sympathy. Benicoff found the internal phone and called Snaresbrook's secretary, discovered that the surgeon was in the library, got instructions how to find it.

Leather-bound medical books lined the walls; but all of them were years out of date and just there for decoration. The library was completely computerized, since all technical books were published in digital form. This had only become possible when conventions and standards were set for illustrations and graphics which were animated most of the time. So any medical book or journal was entered into the library's data base the instant that it was published. Erin Snaresbrook sat in front of a terminal speaking instructions.

"Can I interrupt?" Benicoff asked.

"In two seconds. I went to make a copy of this in my computer. There." She hit return and the item was instantly transferred to the data base in her own computer upstairs. The surgeon nodded and spun about in her chair. "I was talking to a friend in Russia this A.M., he told me about this. It's in St. Petersburg, a student of Luria. Some very original work on nerve regeneration. What can I do for you?"

"General Schorcht keeps bugging me for more detailed reports. So I bug you."

"*Niet prahblem*, as our Russian friends say. But what about your end? Progress there?"

"An absolute dead end. If there is a trail, and I doubt it, it gets colder every day. No hints, no clues, no idea of who did it or how they did it. I'm not supposed to know this, but the FBI has managed to get undercover data taps into every AI lab or department of every university, every major industry in the country, to report any sudden changes or input of new information. They are looking out for the AI data stolen from Brian. Of course the trouble is that they don't exactly know what to look for.''

"Sounds sort of illegal, snooping like that.''

"It is. But I'll put up with it for a short time before I blow the whistle on them. But that's not what worries me. The real question is whether the security agencies have enough experts to interpret any or all of that data. We must get a lead. Which of course is why the General is bugging me.''

"Because the possibility that Brian may remember something, recover, respond in any way—is the only chance we have? Fascinating. I've read in bad novels 'he nodded gloomily.' Now I know what it looks like because you just did it.''

"Gloomily, depressingly, suicidally—take your pick. And Brian?''

"Our progress has been good, but we are running out of time.''

"He's getting worse, regressing!''

"Not that, you misunderstood. Modern medicine can stabilize a body, keep it alive for years when the mind is not in control. Physically, I could leave Brian in the recovery unit until he died of old age. I don't think we want to do that. What I mean is that I have traced and reconnected nearly a million nerve fibers. I've tracked and accessed Brian's earliest memories, from birth right up until about age twelve. The film connectors and computer are in place and in the very near future they should have hopefully made all of the possible connections. I have gone about as far as I can go with this technique.''

"Why are you working on his childhood—when it is the adult we need to answer our questions?''

"Because the old expression about the child being the father of the man is quite true. There is no way we can restore the higher level brain connections until the lower levels begin to operate. This means that the enormous structure of the human mind can be rebuilt only from the bottom up—in much the same way it was built in the first place . . .''

"When you say building a mind—built of what?''

"The mind is made of many small parts, each mindless by itself. We call these basic parts *agents*. Each agent by itself can only do some simple thing that needs no mind or thought at all. But when the agents get connected up, in certain very social ways, they work together as societies—that's how intelligence emerges from non-intelligence.

"Fortunately, most of the agents themselves are okay, because their brain cells are located in the uninjured gray matter. But most of the connections between the agents thread their way through the brain's white matter—and too many of those connections have been severed. That is where I am now. Locating and reconnecting large numbers of the simplest agents, at the sensory and motor levels. If I can reconstruct enough of the society of agents formed during each stage of Brian's development, that will give me a foundation for repairing the structures that were formed in his next period. Stage after stage. Layer after layer. And the different kinds of cross-connections between them. While at the same time I have to restore the feedback loops between the agents at each level, as well as the systems in other parts of the brain that control reasoning and learning. These different kinds of loops and rings are crucial because they are what supports the thoughtful and reflective activity that distinguishes human from animal thinking. At the present time I am almost at the end of this first period of rebuilding. In a few days I will know if I have succeeded or not."

Benicoff shook his head in wonderment. "You are getting me used to thinking the unthinkable as a daily habit. What you are doing is so new, so different, that I find it basically—I'm sorry to say this—incomprehensible. That you can enter Brian's head, listen to his thoughts and repair the damage done! Better you than me. Does he feel anything while you are doing this?"

Snaresbrook shrugged. "There is really no way to tell. I suppose the experience will be indescribable because it is happening to a mind that is not yet human. My personal belief, however, is that while his brain is being reconstructed his mind might very well be retracing and reliving the important early events of his life."

* * *

Dolly could hear the clatter of computer keys as she came down the hall; she smiled. Brian was usually alone so much, it was nice to see him with a school friend.

"Anyone for a fresh-baked chocolate-chip cookie?" she said, holding out the plate. Kim squeaked with pleasure.

"Me for one, Mrs. Delaney. Thanks!"

"Brian?"

"Finish this first," he muttered. "Come on, Kim. It would be a lot better if you did this before you take a break. You are just beginning to understand what basis vectors are."

"We can finish it later. Take one."

Brian sighed and pushed one of the still-warm cookies into his mouth. "Good," he spluttered.

"I'll get some cold milk to go with that."

When Dolly brought the tray with the filled glasses she had her purse with her. "I've got to go to the market and it is going to be crowded. Which means I'll be late and your father will be upset if he gets in before I do. Tell him that dinner will be at six like always and it's ready for the microwave now. You won't forget?"

Brian shook his head and drained the glass as Dolly left. He put it down and turned back to the computer. "Now to pick up where we left off."

"No!" Kim said. "We're taking a break, remember?" She pushed the books aside and dropped onto the bed, punched his pillow into a mound and settled it behind her back. "A break is a break—and you have to learn that."

"Work is work and you have to learn *that*. Just look at your term paper, for instance." He spun his revolving chair about and punched the scroll button. The copy flipped by in the screen, most of it white letters against red blocks. "Do you see all the red copy? You know what it means?"

"You had a nosebleed?"

"You ought to take this seriously, Kim. You know that I've been helping you with this paper for Bastard Betser, adding bits and straightening it out when you get it wrong. Just for the heck of it I wanted to check up on my input and started marking off the blocks of what I was doing in red, all the corrections and changes that I had made. There is sure a lot more red than white here.''

"There is a lot more to the world than AI. Since you are standing up, bring me over a cookie.''

"You're going to flunk this course.'' He got up and passed her the plate.

"Big deal. So maybe I flunk out of school altogether and marry a millionaire and travel around the world on my own yacht.''

"You talk big for a Redneck from the Rigs. I bet you've never even been ashore.''

"I have been around, leetle man, I have been around.'' She licked the chocolate from her fingertips and half closed her eyes, spoke huskily in a fake French accent. "I have zeen zee world, have driven ziz prince mad with passion.''

"Mad with boredom! You've got a good mind, Kim. You just don't like to use it.''

"Mind! Enough zee mind. What about zee body?''

She pulled at the top of her blouse to disclose her cleavage. Pulled a little too enthusiastically and the blouse opened wide disclosing one bare breast, a sweet pink nipple. She giggled as she buttoned the blouse.

"I drive zee men mad . . .''

Her voice died away as she saw the effect the accident had had on Brian. His skin had gone pale, his eyes wide.

"Relax,'' she said. "You've seen lots of bare skin before down on flesh beach where all the kooks hang out.''

"I've never been there,'' he said, his voice hoarse.

"Well I don't blame you. Some pretty ugly guys and gals are naturists.'' She looked up at him and arched her eyebrows. "Hey, how old are you?''

"Thirteen.''

She bounced up onto her knees and looked him in the eye. "You're as tall as I am and not too bad looking. Ever kissed a girl?''

"Let's go to work,'' he said uncomfortably as he turned away. She took him by the shoulder and pulled him back. "That's no answer—and I know you know about girls because I found some old *Playboy*s under your bed—with scorch tracks that your eyes had left on all the centerfold nudes. Maybe you know what they look like—but I'll bet dollars to dongles that you are sweet thirteen and have never been kissed—so you're going to learn now.''

Brian did not pull away when she took his head gently in her hands and pulled his mouth down to hers. She made a happy humming sound and let her tongue drift inside his lips, felt his hands harden on his back. She moved her hand down; that wasn't the only thing that was hard.

She opened his belt.

What Brian could not understand was why everyone didn't know what had happened just by looking at him. It was so momentous, earth-shattering, that it must show on his face. Whenever he thought about it he could feel his skin glow with the strength of his memories. Kim was gone by the time Dolly came home; he heard his father arrive a few minutes later. He stayed in his room as long as he could, waiting until he was called a second time for dinner.

But neither of them noticed a thing. Brian ate in silence, face lowered over his plate. They were discussing a barbecue they had been invited to next weekend; neither wanted to go. But it was business not pleasure and in the end they made the obvious decision. They were barely aware that he had left the table and was back in his room.

The thing that bothered Brian most was that what had happened did not seem to have affected Kim in the slightest. The next morning she passed him in the hall with a ''Hi!'' and nothing else. He thought about it all day in school, muttered some incorrect answers which shocked his teachers, then cut all of his afternoon classes and went out on the rigs. Alone above the sea.

If he felt so strongly about what had happened—why didn't she? The answer was pretty obvious when he asked the question that way. Because she had done it before. She was eighteen, five years older than him, had had five years to get interested in boys. He was jealous of them—but who were they? He couldn't dare ask her. In the end he said the hell with it and tried to put it from his mind. And sought for an excuse to see her alone as soon as possible.

Brian was waiting in the hall next morning, caught her before class. "I stayed up late last night, finished your term paper."

"My hearing is going. Did you just say what I thought I heard you say?"

"Mm-hmm. Thought it would be easier to get it done all at once than take you through it step by step. Maybe that way you will remember what you wrote." He tried to be more casual than he felt. "Come over this afternoon and I'll give you a first run-through of how it works."

"You bet. See you there."

The day dragged by. It was Dolly's afternoon to play bridge and the house would be empty.

"This is the final surgery," Snaresbrook dictated quietly. "The implants are all in place. The CPU put into position. The regrowth of new nerve connections to the damaged portions of the cortex is almost completed. The replacements for the corpus callosum connections are being stimulated. The fiber-optic interfaces between the chips have been installed, the last of the intracranial procedures. The meningeal tissues have been repaired or replaced and I am now coating the edges of the section of bone that was removed to give access to the brain. This will grow and seal the section of skull into place. The procedure now begins."

She did not add her silent thoughts that this was just the end of the surgical procedures. But the new and untried procedures that would hopefully restore the connections inside Brian's brain were only in their opening stages. New, unproven—would they work?

Stop thinking about it. Complete this and move on.

It was a muggy and torrid July afternoon when Brian finally got away from the computer lab. He had worked out what he hoped would be an improvement on LAMA, and AI programming language that his father had helped to develop. If he was right the cross-linking nemes of the CYC information nets could be speeded up by a factor of 10. But his new technique had to be tested and this would have taken days to work through on his own computer—so he managed to borrow some time on the Cray 5 and if all went well he should get some results by morning. Which meant there wasn't much else he could do until then.

And there was a good chance Kim might be waiting for him at home. He walked faster now and his sweat-soaked shirt stuck to his skin. She had no classes this afternoon so she might come over for what she called tutoring. Yes, there would also be some tutoring because she really needed it. She was cutting classes now and ignoring lectures because she knew that he would be there to tell her what to do before the exams. She really hated the schoolwork and was always happy to find something better to do. Brian slowed down when he realized he was gasping for breath. Easy did it in this heat or he would get back dead.

The cool air puffed out and embraced when he opened the front door.

"Anyone home?" he called out, but silence was his answer. Then he heard the music playing, smiled and pushed open the half-closed door to his room.

"I called—you didn't hear me."

The stereo was on, switched to the Mississippi soul food station, but the room was empty. His bed was rumpled and his pillows pushed into a backrest the way she liked them. He looked around for a note, Kim still wrote them, never thinking to access the network, found nothing. He turned off the music and the only sound was the whir of the fan on the computer. It muttered to itself while it accessed a disk. The kitchen—that was it. Kim was the world's best nibbler. The glass and dirty dish in the sink proved it. But she wasn't there.

Nor did she answer her phone. He searched more carefully a second time; she had left him handwritten messages more than once, probably the only person in computer-happy UFE that did his anymore, but still couldn't find any note. Maybe she actually broke a long-standing dislike and actually left a message in the computer. He called up his communication program but there was nothing there.

Mysterious—and he was beginning to get worried. Could something have happened to her? The front door had been closed, but not locked. It usually wasn't locked except at night; the university was a cutoff and safe place. Except no place was really safe. Hadn't they just caught the drug smugglers a few miles down the coast? The isolated rigs of UFE might be the ideal spot for another try. A sudden sound caught his attention as the computer whirred and a drive light came on.

Of course! This program had been running for a couple of days and the machine was in verbal command mode, left that way most of the time even when he was entering data from the keyboard, programmed to record any words or sounds and respond if necessary. There would be a record of her voice.

It was easy enough to find. He jumped back, turned on the speakers—and heard himself snoring. Jumped forward and heard the morning news he had listened to while dressing. Forward and forward—and there she was! Humming along with the radio. Nothing wrong here; he skipped forward, the sound track making Donald Duck sounds—then stopped when he heard her voice. Talking on the phone.

"Sure, yes. If you insist. Soon. Right. Bye."

Only one side of the conversation: he had never considered putting a tap on his phone. He did a high-speed forward, heard something, backtracked. It was Kim laughing.

Then a male voice said, "Do that again and there's no stopping me."

Brian rested his head on his fingertips, bent over the computer, the speaker close to his ear. Listening to what could only have been sounds of lovemaking. In his bed. With someone else. Listening to every humiliating sound and gasp, to her mounting little cries of delight.

Listened until it was all over. They were talking quietly but he listened no longer. The voices were nothing, meant nothing.

Finished. Through. The blood hammered in his temples as he was possessed by a terrible sense of betrayal. He had meant absolutely nothing to her—except maybe as an unpaid tutor, or maybe that was how she paid for his lessons! She had never been serious about him, never felt what he felt. What he realized shamefully now was that his puppy love had been completely one-sided. She hadn't shared it—probably didn't even know his overwhelming and consuming feelings for her. His fingers were trembling with rage, mortification, as he wiped the program and the voices of betrayal, struck out the file, deleted it. Then formatted tracks over it so it could never be restored. More destruction. He sought out every piece of work he had done for her and wiped the disk clean. Wiped out a com file of messages from her. His hands were shaking and there were tears of rage in his eyes. Love turned to anger, attraction to betrayal. His hands shook as he seized the keyboard, began to lift it to throw at the screen.

This was crazy. He dropped it and rushed from the room banged down the hall into the kitchen, stood in the doorway, fists clenched, shaking with conflicting emotions. The rack of knives was before him on the counter and he pulled out the largest, tested the edge with his thumb, longed to plunge it into her. Again and again.

Kill her? What was he thinking about? Did simple, rutting emotions control his life? What had happened to logic and intelligence? His hands were still shaking as he slid the knife back into the slot. He stood at the sink staring unseeingly out of the window.

*You have a brain, Brian. Use it.* Or let your emotions run your life. Kill her, get revenge, go to jail for murder. Not the world's greatest idea, really. What is happening? How come emotion has taken the place of intelligent thought?

A subunit had taken control, that was what had happened. Think of the society of the mind and how it works. The mind is divided into many subunits, subunits with absolutely no intelligence of their own. What was the example his father had used when he explained it? Driving a car. A subunit of the mind can drive the car while the conscious mind is occupied with other things. Turning back control only when something unusual happened. The society of mind usually worked in a state of cooperation between all of its units. Now one stupid subunit had taken over and was controlling everything. One dumb, irrational subunit of infatuation—with gonads for brains and involved only with betrayal and jealousy and rage. Is this what he wanted to control his life?

"Hell, no!" He opened the refrigerator and took out a can of soda, popped the seal, drank half of it in one long chugalug. Much calmer and more rational now. He knew what was happening, one part of his brain had taken over and was calling all the shots and suppressing everything else. There was no such thing as a central *me*, though it was easy to believe that there was. The more he had studied the operation of intelligence, the more he had come to believe that each person was sort of a committee. The brain was made up of a lot of little subanimals—protospecialists, that's what they were called.

The hunger-animal took over when looking for food. Or the fear-animal when there was trouble looming. And every night the sleep-animal took its place. It was King Solomon's ring. All the machinery that Lorenz and Tinbergen had discovered. Those intricate networks of brain centers for hunger, sex, defense that had taken hundreds of millions of years to evolve. Not only in reptiles, birds and fish—but in parts of his own brain.

And now his own internal sex-animal was chomping and salivating and taking over. A primitive agency way down in the brain stem—and he had to fight it!

"That's not me!" he shouted out loud, slamming his fist onto the table so hard it hurt. "Not the whole me. Just a singularly stupid but powerful part. Balls galore!"

He was more than a rutting animal. He had intelligence—so why couldn't he use it? How could he let a stupid subunit take control? Where was the mental manager that should have evaluated it and put it into proper perspective and place?

He took the can of soda with him, sipping at it slowly. Sat in front of his computer and opened a new file labeled SELF CONTROL, then leaned back and thought about what came next.

Most mental processes work unconsciously, because most subunits of his mind had to become autonomous—as separate as his hands and feet—in order to work efficiently.

When he had learned to walk as a baby he must have done it badly at first, stumbling and falling, then gradually improving by learning from mistakes. The old subunits for not-good walking must slowly have been replaced or suppressed by new agents for good-walking agents that worked more automatically, with less need for reflective thinking. So many agents, he thought, to be controlled by what? Right now, they seemed to be quite out of control. It was time for him to take them in charge; he must exercise more self-control. It was time that he, himself, must decide which of those subunits should be engaged. That mysterious, separate *He*, must be the manager, the central control that would correspond to the essence of Brian's own consciousness.

"Those stupid AI programs could sure use a managing machine like that," he said, then choked on the soda.

Was it that simple? Was this the missing element that would pull together all the separate pieces? The AI research labs were filling up with so many interesting systems these days at universities like Amherst, Northwestern, and Kyushu Institute of Technology. Rule-based logic systems, story-based language understanders, neural-network learning systems, each solving its own kind of problem in its own way. Some could play chess, some could control mechanical arms and fingers, some could plan financial investments. All separate, all working by themselves—but none of them seemed to really think. Because nobody knew how to get all those useful parts to work together. What artificial intelligence needed was something like that internal *he*. Some sort of central Managing Machine to tie all the subunits into a single working unit.

It couldn't be that simple. There can't be any such *he* in charge—because the mind doesn't contain any real people, only a lot of subunits. Therefore, that *he* could not be any single thing—because no single thing could be smart enough. So that *he* must itself be some sort of illusion created by the activity of yet another society composed of subunits. Otherwise there would still be something missing, something to manage that Manager.

"Not good enough. I haven't got it quite right yet. It will need a lot more working out."

He saved the file with his thoughts—then noticed that there was one KIM file left on disk. The term paper for Betser. She had a copy of it—but she would never understand it, much less explain it when she was queried. Maybe he should save this one as well, after all she had been responsible for his idea about a managing program. No way! He hit delete and it vanished with all the rest.

The very last thing he did was put a lock on the computer so it would not accept calls from her phone. But this wasn't good enough—she could still call from a public phone. He added a program that would turn away all incoming calls, no calls now or forever from anyone.

In the end he sat there tired and dry-eyed. Betrayed in every way.

Nothing like this was ever going to happen to him again. No one was ever going to get close enough to him to hurt him. He was going to think about his AI managing program and see if he could get it to work and forget about her. Forget about girls. Something like this was never going to happen to him again. Ever.

# 9

# CORONADO

## April 2, 2023

The helicopter came in over the bay, past the bridge that connected the hooked peninsula of Coronado to San Diego. The roads below were sealed tight by security: the copter was not only the safest but was the fastest way in and out of the base. It swooped low over the gray shapes of the mothball fleet, quietly rusting into extinction since the end of the Second World War. They dropped down to the HQ helipad, dust clouds roiling out, and saw a stretched limo pull up.

"This seems like an awful lot of trouble to go to for a meeting," Erin Snaresbrook snapped. "Some of us have work to do. This is totally ridiculous—when we could have had a teleconference."

"All of us have work to do, Doctor, all of us," Benicoff said. "You have only yourself to blame—this meeting was your idea. You must have realized that this was the only way that we could guarantee security."

"A progress report, that was all that I said." She raised her hand before Benicoff could speak. "I know. I hear the arguments. It is far safer here. The disappearances, the thefts, assassination attempt. It's just that I hate these infernal awful choppers. They are the most dangerous form of transportation ever invented. One of them fell off the Pan Am Building, you're too young to remember, dropped right into Forty-second Street. They are death traps."

They drove into an underground entrance to the headquarters building. Past marine sentries, guards and locked gates, TV cameras and all the security apparatus so adored by the military. One last guarded door admitted them to a conference room with a panoramic view of the bay and Point Loma. An aircraft carrier was just coming in from the open sea. In front of the window at least a dozen dark-suited civilians and uniformed officers were gathered around the teak table.

"Is this room secure?" Snaresbrook whispered.

"You're being facetious, Doctor," Benicoff whispered back. "That window will stop a thirty-inch naval shell."

Erin turned to look at it, then caught Benicoff's smile. Like her, he was joking to relax the tension.

"Sit down," General Schorcht ordered, his usual charming self. His introductions were equally succinct. "Dr. Snaresbrook is on the left. With her is Mr. Benicoff, whom you have met before and who is in charge of the ongoing Megalobe investigation."

"And who are all these people?" Erin Snaresbrook asked sweetly. General Schorcht ignored her.

"You have a report to make, Doctor. Let's have it."

The silence lengthened, the General and the surgeon radiating cold hatred at each other. Benicoff broke in, not wanting the situation to decay any further.

"I called this meeting because it appears that the operations undertaken by Dr. Snaresbrook have now reached an important and most vital stage. Since the rest of our investigation is stalled, I feel that everything now depends on Dr. Snaresbrook. She had been a pillar of strength, our only hope in this disastrous matter. And she seems to have worked a miracle. She will now bring us up to date. If you please, Doctor." Slightly mollified, still very angry, the surgeon shrugged and decided that she had had enough of the petty feuding. She spoke calmly and quietly.

"I am now approaching the end of the basic surgery on the patient. The superficial damage caused by the bullet has had a satisfactory resolution. The more important and vital deep repairs of the nerve bundles in the cortex have been completed. The film implants were successful and the connections have been made by the inbuilt computer. Gross surgery is no longer called for. The skull has been closed."

"You have succeeded. The patient will talk . . ."

"I will have no interruptions. From *anyone*. When I have finished my description of what has been done and what my prognosis is I will then answer any questions."

Snaresbrook was silent for a moment. So was General Schorcht, radiating pure hatred. She smiled demurely, then went on.

"I may have failed completely. If I have, that is the end of it. I'll not open his head again. I want to tell you strongly that there is always a chance of this. Everything I have done is still experimental—which is why I make no promises. But I will tell you what I hope will happen. If I have succeeded the patient will regain consciousness and should be able to talk. But I doubt if I will be talking to the man who was shot. He will not remember any of his life as an adult. If my procedures succeed, if he regains consciousness, it will be as a child.''

She ignored the murmur of dismay, waited until it died down before she continued.

''If this is what happens I will be very pleased. It will mean that the procedure has succeeded. That will be the first step. If it goes as planned I must then proceed with additional input and communication in the hopes that his memories will be brought forward to the period in time when the assault occurred. Questions?''

Benicoff got in first with the question so vital to him. ''You hope to bring his memory right up to the day the assault occurred?''

''That may indeed be possible.''

''Will he remember what happened? Will he tell us who did it?''

''No, that is impossible.'' Snaresbrook waited until the reactions had died away before she spoke again. ''You must understand that there are two kinds of memory, long-term and short-term. Long-term memories last for years, usually for an entire lifetime. Short-term is what happens to us in real time, details of a conversation we might be hearing, a book that we are reading. Most short-term memories simply fade away in a few seconds, or minutes. But some parts of short-term memories, if they are important enough, will eventually become long-term memory. But only after about a half an hour. It takes the brain that much time to process and store it. This is demonstrated in what is known as posttrauma shock. Victims of car accidents, for instance, can remember nothing of the accident if they were rendered unconscious at the time. Their short-term memory never became long-term memory.''

General Schorcht's cold voice cut through the other voices and questions.

''If there is no chance of your succeeding in this dubious medical procedure why did you undertake it in the first place?''

Erin Snaresbrook had her fill of insults. Her cheeks flushed and she started to rise. Benicoff was on his feet first.

"May I remind everyone here that I am in charge of this ongoing investigation. At great personal sacrifice Dr. Snaresbrook volunteered to help us. Her work is all that we have. Though there have been deaths already, and the patient may very well die as well, it is the investigation that is of paramount importance. Brian Delaney may not reveal the killers—but he can show us how to build his artificial intelligence, which is what this entire matter is all about."

He sat down slowly and turned in his chair. "Dr. Snaresbrook, will you be kind enough to tell us what procedures are still to come?"

"Yes, of course. As you know I have left a number of surgical implants within the patient's brain. They consist of various kinds of computers connected by microscopic terminals to the brain's nerve fibers. Controlled measures of chemicals can be released through these. By combining this with a carefully monitored variety of stimuli, I hope he will soon learn how to access more of his later but now inaccessible memories. When these are integrated he should have a functional mind once again.

"There may be gaps—but he will not be aware of them. What I hope he will be aware of and remember is all of the work he did in developing his AI. So that he can rebuild it and make it function.

"I will of course use more than chemicals. I have also implanted computer film chips that will interface directly with nerve endings. On these chips are embryonic brain cells that can be induced to grow in various ways. They can be kept dormant as long as I want, waiting for an opportunity to make the correct connections. When they are activated each one will be tested. The ones that end up wrong will be disconnected so that only the successful will remain active. This can all be done by opening microscopic chemical holes implanted in the chips. Either a connection will be made—or a tiny package of neurotoxins will destroy the cell."

"I have a question," one of the men said.

"Of course."

"Are you telling us that you are installing a machine-mind interface inside that boy's skull?"

"I am—and I don't know why you sound so shocked. This kind of thing has been going on for many years now. Why, even in the last century we were hooking up neural connections in the ear to cure deafness. Many times in recent years we have been able to use nerve impulses from the spinal cord to activate prosthetic legs. Connecting to the brain itself was a logical next step."

"When will we be able to talk to Mr. Delaney?" Schorcht snapped.

"Perhaps never." Dr. Snaresbrook stood up. "You have my report. Make of it what you will. I am doing my very best, with still-experimental techniques, to rebuild that shattered mind. Trust me. If I succeed you will be the first to know."

She ignored the voices, the questions, turned and left the room.

# 10

## September 17, 2023

Brian came slowly back to consciousness, rising up from a deep and dreamless sleep. Awareness slipped away, came again, sank into darkness again. This happened a number of times over a period of days and each time he remembered nothing of the previous approach to consciousness.

Then, for the first time, he did remain on the borderline of full awareness. Though his eyes were still shut he gradually began to realize that he was awake. And dreadfully tired. Why was that? He did not know, did not really care. Cared about nothing.

"Brian..."

The voice came from a very great distance. At the edge of audibility. At first it was just there, something to be experienced and not considered. But it kept repeating. *Brian*, then *Brian* again.

Why? The word rolled around and around in his thoughts until memory returned. That was his name. He was Brian. Someone was speaking his name. His name was Brian and someone was speaking his name aloud.

*"Brian—open your eyes, Brian."*

Eyes. His eyes. His eyes were shut. Open your eyes, Brian. Light. Strong light. Then soothing darkness once again.

*"Open your eyes, Brian. Do not keep your eyes closed. Look at me, Brian."*

Glare again, blink, shut, open. Light. Vagueness. Something floating before him.

*"That's very good, Brian. Can you see me? If you can, say yes."*

This was not an easy thing to do. But it was a command. See. Light and something. See me. See the me. See me say yes. What was seeing? Was he seeing? What was he seeing?

It was hard, but each time he thought about it the process became easier. See—with the eyes. See a thing. What thing? The blur. What was a blur? A blur was a thing. What kind of a thing? And what was a thing?

Face.

*Face!* Yes, a face! He was very happy to discover that. He saw that this was a face. A face had two eyes, a nose, a mouth, hair. What about the hair?

*The hair was gray.*

Very good, Brian. He was doing so well. He felt very happy.

His eyes were open. He saw a face. The face had gray hair. He was very tired. His eyes closed and he slept.

"You saw that, didn't you!" Dr. Snaresbrook clasped her hands together with excitement. Benicoff nodded, puzzled but agreeing.

"I saw his eyes open, yes. But, well—"

"It was terribly important. Did you notice that he looked at my face after I spoke?"

"Yes—but is that a good response?"

"Not just good, but immensely significant. Think for a

moment. You are looking at a young man's body that for a long time had a disconnected mind—broken into disconnected fragments. But you see what happened now—he heard my voice and turned to look at my face. The important thing is that the brain centers for auditory recognition are in the back half of the brain—but the eye-motion controls are in the front part of the brain. So we must have got the new connections at least partly correct. And there was more. He was trying to obey—to understand my command. This means that a good many mental agencies must have been engaged. And note that he labored very hard, made mental connections, rewarded himself with a feeling of happiness—you saw the smile. This is tremendous.''

''Yes, I did see him smile a little. It's good that he is not depressed, considering his injuries.''

''No. That's not the important point at all. If I were concerned about his attitude, I'd prefer for him to be depressed. No, my point is that regardless of whether he's pleased or annoyed, at least he isn't apathetic. And if his systems can still assign values to experiences, then he can use those values for self-reinforcement—that is, for learning. And if his systems can learn properly, he'll be able to help us repair more of the damage.''

''When you put it that way—then I see why it is important. What next?''

''The process continues. I will let him sleep, then try again.''

''But won't he lose his short-term memories? The memories that you have restored? Won't they fade away if he sleeps?'

''No—because these are not short-term memories but reconnected K-lines or functions that existed before. K-lines are nerve fibers connected to sets of memories, sets of agents, that reactivate previous partial mental states. Think of them as reconnected circuits. Not reconnected in fragile human synapses, but in tough computer-memory units.''

''If you are right—that means that everything you have done is working out,'' Benicoff said, hoping that his lack of enthusiasm did not show in his voice. Was the doctor reading an awful lot into one little flicker of a smile? Perhaps wanting to believe so much that she might be deceiving herself. He had been expecting something more dramatic.

Erin Snaresbrook had not. She had not known what to expect in this totally new procedure, but was immensely satisfied with the results now. Let Brian rest, then she would talk to him again.

A room. He was in a room. The room had a window because he knew what a window looked like. There was someone else in the room. Someone with gray hair and a white thing on her body.

Body? Her? The white thing was a *dress* and only *hers* wore dresses.

That was good. He smiled widely. But not completely right. The smile slowly slipped away. It was almost right, he had done well. The smile returned and he slept.

What had happened the night before? He stirred with fear; he couldn't remember, why was that? And why couldn't he roll over? He was being held down. Something was very wrong, he didn't know what. It took an effort of will to open his eyes—then quickly clamp them shut since the light burned them painfully. He had to blink away the tears when he hesitantly opened them again, looked up at the face of the stranger looming close above him.

"Can you hear me, Brian?" the woman said. But when he tried to answer, his throat was so dry that he started coughing. "Water!" A cool, hard tube pushed between his lips and he sucked in gratefully. Choked on it, coughed and a wave of pain swept through his head. He moaned in agony.

"Head . . . hurts," he managed to say.

Nor would the pain go away. He moaned and twisted under the assault, pain so great that it overwhelmed all other sensations. He was not aware of the tiny slice of pain when the needle went into his arm, but did sigh with relief when the all-encompassing agony began to ebb.

When he opened his eyes again it was with great hesitation. Blinked tears as he fought to see.

"What . . . ?" His voice sounded funny but he did not understand why. What was it? Wrong? Too deep, too rasping. Listened as the other voice came from a great distance.

"There's been an accident, Brian. But you are all right now—you are going to be all right. Do you have any pain? Do you hurt anywhere?"

Hurt? The pain in his head was lessening, was being muffled somehow. Other pain? His back, yes his back—his arm too. He thought about that. Looked down and could not see his body. Covered. What did he feel? Pain?

"Head . . . my back."

"You've been hurt, Brian. Your head, your arm and back too. I've given you something to take away the pain. You'll feel better soon," Erin said, looking down at him with grave concern at the white face on the pillow, framed by the crown of bandages. His eyes were open, reddened and black-rimmed, blinking away the tears. But he was looking at her, questioning, following her when she moved. And the voice, the words clear enough. Though wasn't there a marked Irish accent to what he said? Brian's accent had changed after all his years in America. But an earlier Brian would certainly have more of the brogue he had brought to this country. This was Brian all right.

"You have been very ill, Brian. But you are better now—and will get better."

But which Brian was she talking to? She knew that as we grow we learn new things all of the time. But we do not burden our minds with remembering every detail of *how* we learned a new process, how to tie a shoe or hold a pencil. The details of remembering belong to the personality that remembered. But this personality is left behind, buried when the new personality develops. How this was done was still unclear—perhaps all the old personalities still existed at some level. If so—which one was she talking to now?

"Listen, Brian. I am going to ask you a very important question. How old are you? Can you hear me? Can you remember your age—how old are you?"

This was much harder than anything he had ever thought about before. Time to go to sleep.

"Open your eyes. Sleep later, Brian. Tell me—how old are you?"

This was a bad question. Old? Years. Time. Date. Months. Places. School. People. He did not know. His thoughts were muddled and this confused him. Better to go back to sleep. He wanted to—but sudden fear chilled him, made his heart hammer.

"How old—am I? I can't—tell!" He began to cry, tears oozing from his tight-clamped lids. She caressed his sweat-damp forehead.

"You can sleep now. That's right. Close your eyes. Sleep." She had come along too fast, pushed him too hard. Made a mistake—cursed her own impatience. It was too early yet to integrate his personality into time. It had to integrate into itself first. But it was coming. Each day there was that much more of a personality present, rather than a collection of lightly linked memories. It was going to work. The process was slow—but she was succeeding. Brian's personality had been brought as far forward in his own personality time line as was possible. How far that was she still did not know; she had to be patient. The day would come when he would be able to tell her.

More than a month went by before Dr. Snaresbrook asked the question again.

"How old are you, Brian?"

"Hurts," he muttered, rolling his head on the pillow, eyes closed. She sighed. It was not going to be easy.

As often as she dared she tried the question. There were good days and bad—mostly bad. Time passed and she was beginning to despair. Brian's body was healing, but the mind-body link was still a fragile one. Hopefully, still hopefully, she asked the question again.

"How old are you, Brian?"

He opened his eyes, looked at her, frowned. "You asked me that before—I remember..."

"That is very good. Do you think you can answer the question now?"

"I don't know. I know you have asked me that before."

"I have. It is very smart of you to remember that."

"It's my head—isn't it? Something has happened to my head."

"That is perfectly correct. Your head has been hurt. It is much better now."

"I think with my head."

"Correct again. You are getting much better, Brian."

"I'm not thinking right. And my back, my arm. They hurt. My head—?"

"That's right. You have had head injuries, your back and arm were injured as well—but they are mending very well. But your head injuries were not good, which will give you some confusing memories. Don't let that worry you because it will come right in time. I am here to help you. So when I ask you a question you must help me. Try to answer—as well as you can. Now—do you remember how old you were at your last birthday?"

There had been a party, candles on the cake. How many of them? He closed his eyes, saw the table, the candles.

"Birthday party. Cake—a pink cake."

"With candles?"

"Plenty candles."

"Can you count them, Brian? Try to count the candles."

His lips moved, his eyes still closed, working at the memory, stirring in the bed with effort.

"Lit. Burning. I can see them. One, two—more of them. All together, I think, yes, there are fourteen."

The gray-haired woman smiled, reached out and patted him on the shoulder. Smiled down at him when his eyes fluttered open and he looked at her.

"That is good, very, very good, Brian. I am Dr. Snaresbrook. I have been taking care of you since the accident. So you can believe me when I say that your situation is greatly improved—and will improve steadily now. I will tell you about that later. I want you to sleep now—"

It wasn't easy. At times it seemed to be two steps backward for every one ahead. The pain appeared to be lessening but it still bothered him; at times that was all he wanted to talk about. He had little appetite, but wanted the intravenous drip removed. For one day he just sobbed with fear; about what, she never discovered.

Yet, bit by bit, with dogged insistence, she helped the boy put his memories together. Slowly the tangled and cut skeins of his past were gathered up, rejoined. There were still large sections of memory missing. She was aware of that even if he wasn't. After all—how can one miss something one does not remember? The personality of Brian was slowly and surely emerging, stronger each day. Until one day he asked:

"My father—Dolly, are they all right? I haven't seen them. It has been a long time."

The surgeon had been expecting the question, had prepared a carefully worded answer.

"When you were wounded there were other casualties— but none of them were people you know. Now the best thing for you to do is get some rest." She nodded to a nurse and out of the corner of his eye Brian could see her inject something into the drip that led to his arm. He wanted to talk, ask more questions, tried to move his lips but plunged down into darkness instead.

When Dr. Snaresbrook next visited Brian she was accompanied by her neurosurgical resident, Richard Foster, who had closely followed the Delaney case.

"I've never seen so much recovery from such a grave injury." Foster said. "Unprecedented. This kind of gross brain damage always leads to major deficiencies. Serious muscle weaknesses and paralyses. Massive sensory deficits. Yet all of his systems seem to be operating. It's amazing that he's recovered any mental function at all, with such an extensive injury. Normally such a patient would be permanently comatose. He ought to be a vegetable."

"I think you're using the wrong concept," Snaresbrook explained patiently. "Brian has not, in fact, 'recovered' in the usual sense of the word. No natural healing process has repaired those connections of his. The only reason that his brain acts like more than a bunch of disconnected fragments is that we have provided all those substitute connections."

"I understand that. But I can't believe that we got enough of them right."

"I suspect you're completely correct about that. We were only able to approximate. So now, when an agent in one part of his brain sends a signal to some other place—for example, to move the arm and hand—that signal may not be precisely the same as it was before his injury. However, if we got things nearly right, then at least some of those signals will arrive in the right general area, somewhere they can have roughly the right effect. And that is the important thing. Give the brain just half a chance, and it will do the rest for you. The same as in any surgery. All the surgeon can do is approximate. One can never restore exactly what was there before—but that usually doesn't matter that much because of how much the body can do."

She looked at the monitors: blood pressure, temperature, respiration, carbon dioxide—and most important of all, the brain wave scan. The characteristic patterns of normal, deep sleep. Without realizing it she let out a deep breath. There were real and positive results now. Everything she had seen in the past weeks that suggested that her unorthodox, new, unproven plan might work after all.

Benicoff was waiting in the room outside, started to stand and Erin waved him back, sat down slowly in the armchair across from him.

"I've done it!" she said. "The words bubbled out, finally released. "When you saw him last—it was a very early stage. I have been working with him, helping him to access those memories and thoughts that are the periphery of his mind. He is still confused about a lot of things of course, has to be. But he speaks well now, has told me his age, that he is fourteen years old. And now he is asking about his father and stepmother. Do you realize what that means?"

"Very much so—and I'm happy to be the first to congratulate you. You have taken what was essentially a dead man with a dead brain—and have restored enough of his earlier memories to bring him to a mental age of fourteen."

"Not really. Much of that is illusory. It certainly is true

that Brian has now recovered many of his own memories of himself up to the age of fourteen. But very far from all of them. Some parts are missing, will remain missing, leaving gaps in his memory that may interfere with a lot of his abilities and attitudes. Furthermore, the age of that cutoff is far from sharp. A lot of threads that we've repaired do not go all the way up to that date—while others go well past that time. But the important thing is that we're starting to see signs of a reasonably well integrated personality. Not a very complete one yet—but one that is learning all of the time. Much of the original Brian has returned—but in my opinion not yet enough."

She was frowning as she said it, then forced a smile.

"In any case, none of that need concern us now. The important thing is that now we can enlist his active, thinking cooperation. And that means that we can proceed to the next stage."

"Which is—?"

Snaresbrook looked at him grimly. "We have done just about as much reconstruction as we can do 'passively.' But there still are many concepts that we simply have not reached. For example, Brian seems to have lost virtually all his knowledge about animals, a particular form of aphasia that has been seen before in cerebral accidents. We seem to be at the point of diminishing returns in trying to reconnect all of Brian's old nemes. So although I plan to continue that, I shall now also begin the new phase. It might be called knowledge transfusion. What I plan to do is to try to identify those missing domains—those domains of knowledge that virtually every child knows, yet Brian still does not—and upload the corresponding structures from the CYC-9 commonsense data base."

Benicoff weighed the significance of this, started to speak—but she raised her hand to stop him.

"We had better discuss this at another time." She shook her head, felt herself fading, felt the onslaught of exhaustion too long held at bay.

"Now let's get a sandwich and some coffee. Then, while Brian is sleeping I'll get my notes up to date. He is going to need guidance every step of the way. Which means that I—and the computer—will have to know more about him than he knows himself."

The restraints had been removed and only the raised sides of the bed remained in place. The end of the bed had been lifted up so that Brian was no longer lying flat. The bandages that encased his skull covered the connecting fiber-optic cable that led to the back of his skull. All of the drips and other invasive devices and monitors had been removed; the few remaining ones were small and noninvasive and fixed to his skin. Other than his bruised and bloodshot eyes and pallid skin he looked to be in adequate health.

"Brian," Erin Snaresbrook said, looking at the brain-wave monitor as the wavelength changed to consciousness. Brian opened his eyes.

"Do you remember talking to me before?"

"Yes. You're Dr. Snaresbrook."

"That's very good. Do you know how old you are?"

"Fourteen. My last birthday. What happened to me, Doctor? Don't you want to tell me?"

"Of course I do. But will you let me set the pace, explain things one step at a time in what I think is the best order?"

Brian thought for a moment before he spoke. "I guess so—you're the doctor, Doctor."

She felt a sudden spurt of enthusiasm when he said this. A small verbal joke. But immense in significance, since it indicated that his mind was alert and functioning.

"Good. If you let me do it that way I promise to tell you the complete truth—to hold nothing back from you. So first—what do you know about the structure of the brain?"

"You mean physically? It's the mass of nerve tissue inside the skull. It includes the cerebrum, cerebellum, pons and oblongata."

"That's pretty specific. You have had brain trauma and have been operated on. In addition—"

"There is something wrong with my memory."

Snaresbrook was startled. "How do you know that?"

There was a weak grin on Brian's lips at this small

victory. "Obvious. You wanted to know my age. I have been looking at my hands while you talked. How old am I, Doctor?"

"A few years older."

"You promised that you would tell me only the complete truth."

She had planned to hold this information back as long as possible; the knowledge might be traumatic. But Brian was way ahead of her. The truth and only the complete truth from now on.

"You are almost twenty-four years old."

Brian ingested the information slowly, then nodded his head. "That's okay then. If I was fifty or sixty or something really old like that, it would be lousy because I would have lived most of life and wouldn't remember it. Twenty-four is okay. Will I get my memories back?"

"I don't see why not. Your progress to this point has been exceedingly good. I will explain the techniques in detail if you are interested, but first let me put it as simply as I can. I want to stimulate your memories, then restore your neural access to them. When this happens your memory will be complete and you will be whole again. I can't promise that all of your memories will be restored. There was injury, but—"

"If I don't know they're missing I won't miss them."

"That's perfectly correct." Brian was sharp. He might only have the memories of his first fourteen years now, but the thinking processes of his conscious brain appeared to be much older. He had been a child prodigy, she knew. Graduate school at fourteen. So he was not just any fourteen-year-old. "But not missing a memory is only a small part of it. You must realize that human memory is not like a tape recorder with everything stored in chronological order. It is very different, far more like a badly maintained file system organized by messy and confusing maps. Not only messy to begin with, but we reclassify things from time to time. When I say that I have memories of my childhood—that is not true. I really have *memories* of memories. Things that have been thought about over and over, simplified, reduced."

"I think I understand what you mean. But please, before we get started, there are a few things you will have to tell me. Ten years is a long time. Things happen. My family . . ."

"Dolly has been here and wants to see you."

"I want to see her too. And Dad?"

*The truth only,* Snaresbrook thought, although it would hurt something terrible.

"I'm sorry, Brian, but your father—passed away."

There was silence as slow tears ran down the man's—the boy's—face. It was long moments before he could speak again.

"I don't want to hear about that now. And me, what about me, what have I done in those years?"

"You've gotten your degrees, done original research."

"In artificial intelligence? That's what Dad does, what I want to do."

"What you have *done*, Brian. You have succeeded in everything that you tackled. In fact you made the breakthrough to actually construct the first AI. Before you were injured you were at the threshold of success." Brian noticed the juxtaposition of the terms, made the snap logical leap.

"You have told me everything so far, Doctor, I don't think that you have held back."

"I haven't. It would be unfair."

"Then tell me now. Does my injury have anything to do with AI? Was it the machine that did it? I always thought the stories of evil AIs were dumb."

"They are. But men are still evil. You were injured in the laboratory by men wanting to steal your AI. And reality has turned out to be quite the opposite of myth. Far from being evil, your work with AI-assisted micromanipulators has aided me greatly—and has enabled me to bring you here and speak with you like this."

"You must tell me all about AI!"

"No, Brian. We must rebuild your memories step by step until you can tell *me* how AI works. You were the inventor—now you are going to be the rediscoverer."

# 11

## October 1, 2023

The blinds had been pulled up by the nurse when she had brought Brian his breakfast. He had been awake since dawn, unable to sleep with the whir of thoughts in his head. Bandages covered it, he could feel them with his fingertips. What had happened to him that had made him lose all those years? Selective amnesia? It just wasn't possible. He should ask the doctor to physically describe the damage—though maybe he better not. He really didn't want to think about that now. Not yet. The same way he didn't want to think about Dad being dead.

The TV controller—where was it? He was still amazed at the quality of the picture—if not the contents. Programs were just as bad as ever. Should he watch the news again? No, it was too confusing, full of references he did not understand. It depressed him when he tried to figure it out, since he was mixed up too much as it was. There, that was better—kiddie cartoons. They had some really fantastic computer animation now. But despite the incredible quality the animation was still being used to sell breakfast cereal drenched in sugar. Ten years was a long time. He ought to forget about that too. Or look forward to getting the years back. Or did he want to? Why live the same life twice? What's done is done. Though it might be nice not to make the same mistakes twice. But he wasn't going to relive those years, just get back his memories of them. It was a very strange situation and he wasn't sure that he liked it. Not that he had any choice.

Breakfast was a welcome intrusion. A lot of the chemical taste was gone from his mouth now and he was hungry. The orange juice was cold—but so were the poached eggs. Still he finished them and used a bit of toast to wipe up the last bits. The nurse had just cleared the dishes away when Dr. Snaresbrook came in. There was a woman with her—and it took a long moment to recognize Dolly. If she noticed his startled expression she did not let on.

"You're looking good, Brian," she said. "I'm so happy that you are getting better."

"Then you have seen me here before, here in the hospital?"

"*Seen* is the wrong word. You were hidden behind all those bandages, pipes and tubes. But that's all in the past."

So was he. In the past. This thin woman with the wrinkles at the corners of her eyes, and graying hair, was not the maternal Dolly he remembered. Memory had taken on a new meaning for him now, something to be raked over, examined, rebuilt. Remembrance of things past, that was what old Proust had written about in such a long-winded way. He would see if he could do a better job of it than the Frenchman had done.

"Dolly has been of immense help," the surgeon said. "We've talked about you and your recovery and she knows that your memories stop some years back. When you were fourteen."

"Do you remember me, when I was fourteen years old?" Brian asked.

"A little hard to forget." She smiled for the first time, looking far more attractive with the worry lines gone from around her eyes, the tension from her mouth. "You were going into graduate school the next year. We were very proud of you."

"I'm really looking forward to it. Though I guess that is kind of stupid to say now. I've gone and graduated already, the doctor has told me. But I remember all too clearly the trouble I'm having—had!—with the registrars. They know I have all the credits that I need and it is just the administration still standing in the way. Because I'm too young. But that's all in the past, isn't it? I guess it all worked out well in the end."

It was odd hearing him talk like this. Dr. Snaresbrook had

explained to her that Brian could remember nothing of the years since he had been fourteen, that it was her job to help him recover those years. She did not understand it—but the doctor had been right so far.

"They didn't cause trouble for very long. Your father and some of the others got in touch with the companies funding the university. They couldn't have cared less if you were five years old—or fifty. It was the search for talents like yours that had caused them to start the school in the first place. The word came down from on high and you were admitted. I'm sure that you made a success of it, but of course I wouldn't know."

"I don't understand."

Dolly took a deep breath and glanced at the doctor. Her face was expressionless; there was no help there. Going through it the first time had been bad enough; reliving it for Brian's benefit was not easy.

"Well, you know that your father and I had—have—our difficulties. Or maybe you didn't—don't—know."

"I do. Adults think kids, even teenagers, are dim when it comes to family matters. You keep your voices down but there have been a lot of fights. I don't like it."

"Neither did I."

"Then why do you—why did you—fight with Dad? I have never understood."

"I'm sorry it caused you pain, Brian. But we were two different kinds of people. Our marriage was as sound as most, sounder maybe since we didn't expect too much of each other. But we had little in common intellectually. And once you joined us I began to feel a little like a fifth wheel."

"Are you blaming me for something, Dolly?"

"No. Quite the opposite. I'm blaming me for not making everything work out for the best. Maybe I was jealous of all the attention he lavished on you, how close you two were and how left out I felt."

"Dolly! I've always—loved you. You are the closest thing to a real mother I have ever had. I don't remember my mother at all. They told me I was only a year old when she died."

"Thanks for saying that, Brian," she said with a slight smile. "It really is a little too late to assign blame. In any case I and your father separated, had a very amicable divorce a few years later. I went back to live with my family, got a new job and that is where I am now." Sudden anger flared and she turned on Snaresbrook.

"There it is, Doctor. Is that what you want? Or a bit more guts spilled on the floor."

"Brian has the physical age of twenty-four," she said calmly. "But his memories stop at age fourteen."

"Oh, Brian—I am so sorry. I didn't mean—"

"Of course you didn't, Dolly. I suppose that everything you have just told me about was in the wind and I should have seen it coming. I don't know. I guess kids think that nothing basic will ever change. It's just that school is so busy, the AI work so exciting—" He broke off and turned to Dr. Snaresbrook. "Am I at least fifteen by now, Doctor? I've certainly learned a lot in the past few minutes."

"It doesn't quite work that way, Brian. You heard a lot—but you don't have your own memories of the events. That's what we must restore next."

"How?"

"By using this machine. Which I am very proud to say you helped to develop. I am going to stimulate memories which you will identify. The computer will keep track of everything. When other memories have been matched on both sides of the lesion they will be reconnected."

"There can't be enough wires in the world to reconnect all the nerves in the brain. Aren't there something like ten-to-the-twelfth hookups?"

"There are—but there are plenty of redundancies as well. Associations with one sector of memory will permit compatible reinforcement. The brain is very much like a computer and the opposite is true as well. But it is important to always be aware of the differences. Memory is static in a computer—but not in the human mind. Recalled memories get stronger, untouched memories weaken and vanish. My hope is that when enough pathways have been reconnected, other interconnections will be reestablished as well. We will be looking for nemes.''

''What are nemes?''

''A neme is a bundle of nerve fibers that is connected to a variety of agents, each of whose output represents a fragment of an idea or a state of mind. For example, what is red and round, with a sweet taste and a crunchy texture, a fruit about the size of your fist and . . .''

''Apple!'' Brian said happily.

''That's exactly what I had in mind, but notice I never used that word.''

''But it's the only thing that fits.''

''Yes, indeed—but you'd only know that if you had an 'apple-agent' that was connected so that it would automatically get activated when enough of the right other nemes are activated—like the ones for red, round, sweet and fruit.''

''And also cherries. I must have nemes for cherries too.''

''You do. That's why I added 'fist-sized.' But you didn't have those nemes two months ago. Or, rather, you certainly had some apple-nemes, but their inputs weren't wired up right. So you didn't recognize that description before, until we connected them up during therapy.''

''Strange. I don't remember that at all. Wait. Of course I can't remember that. It happened before you restored my memory. You can't remember anything until you have some memory.''

Snaresbrook was becoming accustomed to that startling sharpness, but it still kept taking her by surprise. But she continued in the same manner. ''So that is how nemes hook up. By making the right kinds of input and output connections. So far, we've been able to do this for the most common nemes—the ones that every child learns. But now we'll be looking for more and more complex nemes and discover how they connect as well. I want to find higher and higher levels of your ideas, concepts and relationships. These will be increasingly harder to locate and describe, because we'll be getting into more areas that are unique to your own development, ideas that were known to you and you alone, for which there are no common words. When we find them, it may be impossible for me—or anyone else—to understand what they mean to you. But that won't matter because you will be learning more every day. Every time the correlation machine discovers ten new nemes, it will have to consider a thousand other possible agents to connect them to. And every twenty nemes could trigger a million such possibilities.''

"Exponential, that's what you mean?''

"Perfectly correct.'' She smiled with pleasure. "It would seem that we're well on our way to restoring your mathematical ability.''

"What will I have to do?''

"Nothing for now, you've had a long enough day for the first session.''

"No, I haven't. I feel fine. And don't you want to work with my new information in case it slides away when I go to sleep? You were the one who told me that a given period of time must pass before my short-term memory becomes long-term memory.''

Erin Snaresbrook chewed her lip, chewed at this idea. Brian was right. They ought to get on with the process as soon as possible. She turned to Dolly.

"Can you be here tomorrow? Same time?''

"If you want me.'' Her voice was very cold.

"I do, Dolly. Not only do I want you but I need you. I know you must feel upset about this—but I hope that you won't forget the boy Brian once was. Brian the man is still Brian the child whom you took into your home. You can help me make him whole again.''

"Of course, Doctor, I'm sorry. I shouldn't think of myself, should I? Until tomorrow, then.''

They were both silent until the door closed behind her.

"Guilt,'' Brian said. "The priest was always talking about it, the nuns in school too. Expiation as well. You know, I don't think that I ever called her Mother. Or Mom like the other kids—or even Mammy the way we do in Ireland.''

"No blame or remorse, Brian. You are not living in your

past but are re-creating it. What's done is done. Cold logic, as you always told me.''

"Did I say that?"

"All the time when we were working together on the machine—when my thought processes got woolly. You were very firm about it.''

"I should have been. It saved my life once."

"Want to tell me about it?"

"Nope. It's part of my past, remembered in all too clear embarrassment. The time when I let a bit of stupid emotion get a hold of me. Can we move on, please? What's next?''

"I'm going to plug you into the computer again. Ask you questions, establish connections, stimulate areas of your brain near the trauma and record your reactions."

"Then let's go then—hook them up."

"Not at once, not until we have established a bigger data base.''

"Get things rolling then, Doctor. Please. I am looking forward to growing up again. You said we worked together before?''

"For almost three years. You told me that my brain research helped you with your AI. You certainly helped me develop the machine. I couldn't have done it without you.''

"Three years. Since I was twenty-one. What did I call you then?''

"Erin. That's my first name."

"A little too presumptuous for a teenager. I think I'll settle for Doc.''

Snaresbrook's beeper signaled and she looked at the message on its screen. "You rest for a few minutes, Brian. I'll be right back.''

Benicoff was waiting for her outside—and looking most unhappy.

"I have just been informed that General Schorcht is on his way over here. He wants to talk to Brian.''

"No, that's impossible. It would interfere too much with what we are doing. How could he have known that Brian is conscious? You didn't tell him—"

"No way! But he has his spies everywhere. Maybe even

your office bugged. I should have thought of that—no, a complete waste of time. What he wants to know, he finds out. As soon as I heard he was coming here I got on the phone, went right to the top. No answer yet so you will have to help me. If he gets this far we need a holding action."

"I'll get my scalpels!"

"Nothing quite that drastic. I want you to stall. Keep him talking as long as possible."

"I'll do better than that," Erin Snaresbrook said, reaching for the phone. "I'll use the same trick he pulled, send him to the wrong room . . ."

"No you won't. I'm in the right room now."

General Schorcht stood in the open doorway. The slightest smile touched his grim features, then instantly vanished. A Colonel was holding the door open and there was another Colonel at the General's side. Snaresbrook spoke without emotion, the tone of the surgeon in the operating room.

"I'll ask you to leave, General. This is a hospital and I have a severely ill patient close by. Kindly get out."

General Schorcht marched up to the woman and stared down at her coldly. "This has long ceased to be humorous. Stand aside or I will have you removed."

"You have no authority in this hospital. None whatsoever. Mr. Benicoff, use that phone, get the nurse's station. This is an emergency. I want six orderlies."

But when Benicoff reached for the phone the Colonel placed his hand over it. "No phone calls," he said.

Dr. Snaresbrook stood firmly with her back against the door. "I will place criminal charges against you for these actions, General. You are in a civilian hospital now, not on a military base—"

"Move her aside," General Schorcht ordered. "Use force if you have to."

The second Colonel stepped forward. "That would be unwise," Benicoff said.

"I'm removing you from this investigation as well, Benicoff," the General said. "You have been uncooperative and disruptive. Get them both out of here."

Benicoff made no attempt to stop the officer when he stepped by him and reached for the doctor. Only then did he clasp his hands together into a joined fist—that he swung hard into the small of the Colonel's back over his kidneys, knocking him gasping to the floor.

In the silence that followed this sudden action the sound of the telephone ringing was sharp and clear. The Colonel who had his hand over it started to pick it up—then turned to General Schorcht for instructions.

"This is still a hospital," Dr. Snaresbrook said. "Where telephones are *always* answered."

The General, radiating cold menace, stood motionless for long seconds—then nodded his head.

"Yes," the Colonel said into the phone, then stiffened, almost coming to attention.

"For you, General," he said, and held out the phone.

"Who is it?" General Schorcht asked, but the Colonel did not answer. After an even briefer hesitation the General took it.

"General Schorcht here. Who?" There was a long silence as he listened, before he spoke again. "Yes, sir, but this is a military emergency and I must decide that. Yes I do remember General Douglas MacArthur. And I do remember that he overstepped his orders and was removed from command. The message is clear. Yes, Mr. President, I understand."

He handed the phone back, turned and walked from the room. The officer on the floor climbed painfully to his feet, shook his fist at Benicoff, who smiled back happily, before he went after the others.

Only when the door had closed behind them did Erin Snaresbrook permit herself to speak.

"You pulled some long strings, Mr. Benicoff."

"The President's Commission is making this investigation— not that military fossil. I think he had to be reminded who was his commander in chief. I liked that reference to MacArthur and the expression on General Schorcht's face when he remembered that President Truman fired the General."

"You have made an enemy for life."

"That happened a long time ago. So now—can you tell me what is happening? How is Brian progressing?"

"I will in just a moment. If you will wait in my office, I'll finish up with him. I won't be long."

Brian looked up when the door opened and the doctor came in.

"I heard voices. Something important?"

"Nothing, my boy, nothing important at all."

# 12

## October 27, 2023

"Feeling fine today, are we?" Dr. Snaresbrook asked as she opened the door, then stood aside as a nurse and an orderly rolled in the heavily laden trolleys.

"I was—until I saw that hardware and that double-ended broom with the bulging glass eyes. What is it?"

"It's a commercially manufactured micromanipulator. Very few have been made."

Snaresbrook kept smiling, gave Brian no hint that this was part of the machine that Brian had helped her develop. "At the heart of the machine is a parallel computer with octree architecture. This enables it to fit it on a single and rather large planar surface. Wafer-scale integration. This interfaces with a full computer in each joint of the tree-robot."

"Each joint—you're putting me on!"

"You'll soon discover how much computers have changed— particularly the one that controls this actuating unit. The basic research was done at MIT and CMU to build those brooms, as you call them. It is a lot more complex than it looks at a distance. You will notice that it starts out with two arms—but they bifurcate very quickly. Each arm then becomes two—"

"And both of them smaller, by half it seems."

"Just about. Then they split again—and again." She tapped one of the branching arms. "Just about here the arms become too small to manufacture, tools get too gross—and assembly would have to have been done under a microscope. So . . ."

"Don't tell me. Each part is standardized, exactly the same in every way—except size. Just smaller. So the manipulators on one side make the next stage on down for the other."

"Exactly right. Although the construction materials have to change because of structural strength and the volume-to-size ratio. But there is still only a single model stored in the computer's memory, along with manufacture and assembly programs. All that changes with each stage is the size. Piezoelectric stepping motors are built into each joint."

"The manufacturing techniques at the lower end must really be something."

"Indeed they are—but we can go into that some other time. What is important now is that sensors in the small tips are very fine and controlled by feedback from the computer. They can be used for microsurgery at a cellular level, but now they will be used for the very simple job of positioning this connection precisely."

Brian looked at the projecting, almost invisible, length of optic fiber. "Like using a pile driver to push in a pin. So this gets plugged into a socket in my neck, as you told me—and the messages start zipping in and out?"

"That's it. You won't feel a thing. Now—if you will just roll over onto your side, that's fine."

Dr. Snaresbrook went to the controls and when she switched the unit on, the multibranching arms stirred to life. She guided them to a position close behind Brian, then turned over control to the computer. There was a silken rustle as the tiny fingers stirred and separated, dropped slowly down, touched his neck.

"Tickles," Brian said. "Like a lot of little spider legs. What is it doing?"

"It is now positioning the fiberoptic to contact the receptor unit under your skin. It will go through your skin, though you won't feel it. The point is sharper than my smallest hypodermic needle. Plus the fact that it is looking for a path that avoids all nerves and small blood vessels. The tickling will stop as soon as the contact is in place—there."

The computer bleeped and the fingers held the metal pad that held the fiber optic firmly in place against his skin. They rustled again as a strip of adhesive tape was picked up from the bench and passed along swiftly to the site on his neck, where it was pressed down firmly to secure the pad in place. Only then did the arms contract and move away. Snaresbrook nodded to the nurse and orderly, who withdrew.

"Now it begins. I want you to tell me anything you see or hear. Or smell."

"Or think about or imagine or remember, right?"

"Perfectly correct. I'll start here . . ." She made a slight adjustment and Brian shouted hoarsely.

"I can't move! Turn it off! I'm paralyzed—!"

"There, it's all right now. Did it clear up instantly?"

"Yes, ma'am, but I sure hope you won't have to do that again."

"I won't—or rather the computer won't. We have been trying to locate, identify and establish controls over the major low-level agencies in the brain stem. The system apparently shut off the whole cerebellum. Now that the computer knows—it won't happen again. Are you ready to go on?"

"I guess so."

At times there was warmth, then darkness. A chill that filled his entire body in an instant, vanished as quickly as it had come. Other sensations were impossible to describe, the functions of the mind and body at the completely subconscious level.

Once he shouted aloud.

"Are you in pain?" she asked, worried.

"No, really—the direct opposite. Don't stop, please, you

mustn't.'' His eyes were wide, staring at nothing, his body rigid. She did not hesitate to interrupt. He relaxed with a profound sigh. "Almost . . . hard, impossible to describe. Like pleasure squared, cubed. Please note the site.''

"It's in the computer's memory. But do you think it wise to repeat—"

"Quite the opposite. Stay away from there. Something like that, like a rat pressing a button to stimulate its pleasure centers until it dies of thirst and hunger. Stay away.''

Erin Snaresbrook was keeping track of the time and when an hour was up she stopped the session.

"I think that is enough for the first day. Tired?''

"Now that you mention it—the answer is yes. Are we getting anyplace?''

"I believe so. There is certainly a lot of data recorded.''

"Any matchups?''

"Some . . .'' Snaresbrook hesitated. "Brian, if you're not too tired I would like to go on a few minutes longer.''

"I bet you want to try some new way to locate higher-level nemes?''

"Precisely.''

"Well I do too. Fire it up.''

If anything was happening Brian was certainly not aware of it. The answer was obvious when he thought about it. If the machine really was connecting bundles of nerves, reestablishing memories, there was really no reason for him to be aware of the process. Only when he made an attempt to recover those memories would it be obvious that they were there. Yet he was aware of *something* happening at a very remote level of consciousness. It was a transient thought that slipped away like an eel when he tried to approach it. This was annoying. Something was happening that he couldn't quite grasp. And he was tired. Plus the fact that now he had noticed, it was like an itch he couldn't quite grasp.

*That's enough*, he thought.

"I think that we'll stop for the day,'' the doctor suddenly said. "It's been a long session.''

"Sure." Brian hesitated, but then decided why not. "Dr. Snaresbrook—can I ask you a question?"

"Of course. But just a second until I finish here—now, what is it?"

"Why did you decide to end the session at that moment?"

"Just a little difficulty. The control is very fine and this is all still experimental. There was an abort signal on one of the connections being established. I must admit this was the first time something like this has happened. I want to rerun the program to that point and find out why."

"You won't have to—I can tell you."

Erin Snaresbrook looked up, startled, then smiled. "I doubt if you can. This wasn't in your brain but in the CPU, or rather in the interaction of the implanted central processor and the one in the computer."

"I know. I told it to shut down."

The surgeon fought to keep her voice calm. "That's hardly possible."

"Why not? The CPU is on the chip implanted in my brain—and is interrelating with my brain. Is there any reason why there can't be feedback?"

"None whatsoever—except to my knowledge it has never been done before!"

"There's a first time for everything, Doc."

"You must be right. It appears that while the computer was learning some of the connections in your brain, parts of your brain were learning some of the computer's control signals."

Snaresbrook was beginning to feel dizzy. She walked to the window then back, rubbing her hands together—then laughed. "Brian, do you realize what you are saying? That you have interfaced your thought processes directly with a machine. Without pressing buttons or giving voice commands or any other kind of physical action. It was not planned, it just happened. Before this all communication has been at the level of a motor action, from a nerve to a muscle. This is the first time that communication has been effected directly from the brain to a machine. Nothing of this kind has ever happened before. It's ... breathtaking. Opens up all sorts of incredible possibilities!"

Brian's answer was a low snore. He had fallen asleep.

Erin Snaresbrook unplugged the neural link from the computer and coiled it under his pillow, not wanting to wake him by attempting to remove it now. Then she quietly shut down the machine, closed the curtain and left the room. Benicoff was waiting for her outside, radiating gloom. Erin raised her hand before the other man could speak.

"Before you deliver the bad news I prescribe a cup of coffee in my office. It has been a busy day for both of us."

"It shows that much?"

"I'm a great diagnostician. Let's go."

The surgeon had a lot to think about as she led the way. Should she tell Benicoff about Brian's newfound ability? Not yet, later perhaps. She must run some controls first to make sure that it had not been an accident, a coincidence. The possibilities it opened were so large as to be frightening. Tomorrow, she would think about it tomorrow. She sipped the coffee and smacked her lips, passed Benicoff his coffee— then dropped into a very welcome chair.

"Bad news time?" she asked.

"Not really bad news, Doctor, just pressure. General Schorcht is not going away that easily. He insists that every day Brian remains here in the hospital the security worsens. In a way he has a point. And it is sure wracking hell with normal day-to-day hospital management. I know—I get the complaints. The General has been on to the Pentagon, who has been on to the President—who has been on to me. Is it possible that Brian can be moved now that he is conscious and off all the life support equipment?"

"Yes, but—"

"It had better be a world-buster of a but."

Erin Snaresbrook finished her coffee, then shook her head. "I'm afraid that it isn't. As long as very prudent medical precautions are taken."

"That's why the long face. General Schorcht, a small army and a medevac copter are standing by right outside—at this very moment. If that's your answer they are going to do it now. I'll try a holding action, but only if you have some really strong medical reasons."

"No. In fact, if he has to be moved eventually, it might be best to move him at the present time. Before I get too involved in the memory reconstruction. And I am sure that we will all be a bit more relaxed once security is tightened."

Brian was quite excited when he heard what was going to happen.

"Wow—a copter ride! I've never been up in one before. Where are we going?"

"To the naval hospital on Coronado."

"Why there?"

"I'll tell you after we arrive." Dr. Snaresbrook glanced at the nurses who were preparing Brian for the short trip. "In fact, I think I better answer a lot of your questions when we get there. I'm afraid we can't keep this a private party much longer. Are we ready?"

"Yes, Doctor," the nurse said.

"All right. Inform Mr. Benicoff. You will find him waiting outside."

The orderlies were navy medical corpsmen—and were backed up by a squad of heavily armed marines. The entire hospital floor had been cleared and there were more marines in front of and behind the party that surrounded the gurney. The first squad double-timed up the stairs to the roof when Brian was rolled into the elevator, were waiting there outside the door when it arrived. Nor were they alone. Sharpshooters looked down from the parapets, while at every corner of the roof there were soldiers with bulky surface-to-air missiles at the ready.

"You are right, Doctor, you do have a lot of explaining to do!" Brian called out above the roar of the copter's blades.

During the short hop across the city and bay they were boxed in by attack choppers, while a flight of jets circled higher above. After landing on the helipad of the naval hospital the same procedure was done in reverse. When the last marine had stamped out, there were still three people left in the room.

"Will you wait outside, General," Benicoff asked, "while I explain to Brian what this is all about?"

"Negative."

"Thanks. Dr. Snaresbrook, will you please introduce me?"

"Brian, this is Mr. Benicoff. The military officer next to him is General Schorcht, who has some questions to ask you. I wouldn't have him here now but I have been informed that this interview was expressly asked for by the President. Of the United States."

"For real, Doctor?" They may have been twenty-four years old but the eyes had the wide-eyed stare of a fourteen-year-old. Erin Snaresbrook nodded.

"Mr. Benicoff is a presidential appointee as well. He is in charge of an ongoing investigation—well, he'll explain that himself."

"Hi, Brian. Feeling okay?"

"Great. That was quite a ride."

"You have been seriously ill. If you want to postpone this . . ."

"No thanks. I'm a little tired, but other than that I feel fine now. And I really would like to know what happened to me, what is going on around here."

"Well, you do know that you succeeded in developing an operating artificial intelligence?"

"The doctor told me that—I have no memory of it at all."

"Yes, of course. Well then, without being too detailed, you were demonstrating the AI when the lab you were in was attacked. We have reason to believe that everyone there with you was killed, while you were badly wounded in the head. By a bullet. We assume that you were left for dead. All of your notes, records, equipment, everything to do with the AI was removed. You were taken to the hospital and operated on by Dr. Snaresbrook. You recovered consciousness in the hospital and of course everything that has happened since then you know about. But I must add that the thieves were never caught, the records never recovered."

"Who did it?"

"I am afraid to say that we have absolutely no idea."

"Then—why the military maneuvers?"

"There has already been one other attempt on your life, when you were in the hospital that you just left."

Brian gaped around at their blank faces. "So what you are telling me is that the AI has been pinched. And whoever has it wants to keep it their secret. So much so that they are ready to bump me off to *keep* it a secret. Even though I don't remember a thing about it."

"That's right."

"This takes some getting used to."

"For all of us."

Brian looked over at the General. "How does the Army fit into this?"

"I will tell you." General Schorcht stamped forward. Benicoff started to interfere, then hesitated. Best to get it over with. Snaresbrook was of the same mind and nodded agreement when she saw Benicoff draw back. The General raised his single hand and held out a recorder.

"You will identify yourself. Name, date of birth, place of birth."

"Why, your honor?" Brian asked in a wondering voice, his Irish brogue suddenly thick.

"Because you have been ordered to. Statements have been made about your health and sanity that need corroboration. You will answer the question."

"Must I do that? I know why. I'll bet it's because these people here been telling lies about me. Have they told you wild stories about me being only fourteen years old when with your own fine blue eyes you can see that is not true?"

"Perhaps something of that nature." The General's eyes sparkled as he leaned forward. "You are speaking for the record."

Benicoff moved away so the General could not see his face. He had spent time in Ireland. He knew what "putting the mickey to someone" meant—even if the General did not.

Brian hesitated and looked about him, licking his lips.

"Am I safe now, General?"

"I can guarantee that one hundred percent. As of this moment the United States Army is in charge."

"That's nice to know. I feel a great relief as I tell you that I woke up in me hospital bed, sore in the head. And with not a memory I could find after my fourteenth year. I may not look it, General, but as far as I know I am fourteen years old. And very tired. Feeling suddenly ill. I have something of medical importance to discuss with my attending physician."

"Mr. Benicoff," Dr. Snaresbrook said, right on cue, "would you and General Schorcht please leave. You may wait outside."

Whatever the General had to say never came out. His face was bright red, his jaw working. In the end he spun about so sharply on his heel that the pinned-up arm of his uniform jacket flew up. Benicoff was holding the door open for the General and closed it behind them as they left. Worried, Dr. Snaresbrook hurried to Brian's side.

"What's the trouble, Brian?"

"Don't worry, Doc, nothing terminal. I just had enough of that one. But, yes, there is one thing."

"Pain?"

"Not quite. If you will excuse the expression—I just have to pee."

# 13

## November 9, 2023

Almost two weeks passed before Benicoff saw Brian again. But he did get daily progress reports from Dr. Snaresbrook, which he passed on instantly to the President's office. He did not hurry the second report that he had to file every day.

Out of sheer malice at three in the morning, his E-fax was programmed to send a copy of the progress report to General Schorcht's unlisted security number. In the hope that some excitable staff officer might find an item in the report that was interesting enough to wake up the General. This thought sent Benicoff to sleep with a smile every night.

He also E-faxed a daily case report of the Megalobe investigation at the same time. These were getting shorter and emptier of any progress with every passing day. There had been a flurry of activity when a series of caves had been discovered not too far from Megalobe; a result of one of the more way-out theories that had been developed. This theory expanded on the supposition that maybe the truck that had been at the laboratory that night *had* left the valley after all. But had left empty. The stolen items might then have been buried at a prepared site, to be dug up later when things had cooled down. Therefore all the excitement about the cave discovery. But the caves contained only fossilized bat guano which, Benicoff thought to himself, described just about everything else about the case that they had uncovered so far.

He had jogged through Balboa Park for an hour just after dawn then, showered and dressed, he had scowled through a low-cal breakfast and black coffee. At nine he had phoned the electronic company to check the delivery time of the items he had arranged for. Then, after returning the calls from the East Coast that had been recorded while he was out, he sealed his computer and took the rear elevator that connected with MegaHertz car rental in the subbasement of the hotel. The yellow electric runabout he had reserved was waiting for him. He checked that it had a spare tire, that there were no obvious dents in the body and that it had a full charge in the battery. Traffic was light until he reached the Coronado Bridge where the tail-back from security reached back halfway along it. He switched to the VIP lane and stopped only at the far end when the marine guard flagged him down.

"I'm afraid you can't use this lane, sir."

"I'm afraid I can."

His pass and documents earned him a salute and another inspection at the VIP entrance. There were more salutes here—along with a complete search of the car. And all this just to get into the public part of Coronado. The searches became even more enthusiastic when he reached the gates of the military base.

Brian was standing at the window when Benicoff came in, turned around with a smile.

"Mr. Benicoff, it's good to see you. We're kind of short of visitors here."

"Even better to see you—and you look great."

"And that's just about how I feel. They took the bandages off my back and arm yesterday. I've got a couple of nice scars. And I'm going to get a cap instead of these bandages tomorrow. Everyone keeps peeking at my skull but won't let me see it yet."

"Which is probably not such a bad idea. And I can give you some more good news. Dr. Snaresbrook and I, after a frontal assault on the naval authorities, have obtained reluctant agreement to have a computer terminal plugged into the room here for you."

"That's great!"

"But you'll notice that I said terminal and not computer. A dumb terminal to the hospital's mainframe. So you can be sure that every keystroke you enter will simultaneously appear on General Schorcht's screen."

"That's even better! I'll see to it that the good man has plenty to read to keep his blood pressure up."

"Love at first sight. I appreciate the way you put the mickey to him."

"I had to. He looks and sounds just like one of the nuns at school back in Tara, the one who used to break her ruler over my knuckles. And speaking of breaks—any chance of breaking out of here? Getting some fresh air?"

Benicoff dropped into the armchair, which squeaked under his weight. "I have been fighting with the authorities on this one as well. When the doc says that your health is up to it you can use the balcony to the tenth floor."

"With ropes attached so I don't jump off?"

"Not that bad—I took a look at it on the way up. Some Admiral's personal little perk, I imagine. It's pretty big, with lounges, trees—even a fishpond. And well guarded."

"That's another thing I wanted to ask you about, Mr. Benicoff—"

"Just Ben, if you please, which is what my friends call me."

"Sure. It's about these guards, really, and what's going to happen to me when I get better. Doc said to ask you."

Benicoff climbed to his feet and began to pace. "I've thought about that a lot—without finding a good answer. When you leave this hospital I'm afraid that you'll have to go to someplace equally secure."

"You mean until you find out who it was that stole the AI and shot me—the same people who then came back later on and tried to finish the job."

"I'm afraid that's it."

"Then—can I see a printout of everything that has happened since the attack and theft in the lab, and everything you have discovered since?"

"It's classified Top Secret. But since it is all about you, and you're not going to do much traveling for a while—I don't see why not. I'll bring you a copy tomorrow."

A nurse poked her head in the door. "Some equipment here to be installed. Dr. Snaresbrook has approved it."

"Bring it in."

Two white-coated attendants pushed in the trolley, followed by a Yeoman with electronic patches on his uniform.

"Delivered a little while ago, sirs. Taken apart and searched, put back together again and operating A-OK. Who's going to sign for it?"

"Here," Benicoff said.

"That's not a terminal," Brian said, tapping the square metal machine.

"No, sir. That's a new-model printer for eternitree paper. Terminal is on its way up now. And initial here, please. Paper is in the box here."

"Eternitree? That's a new one to me."

"It shouldn't be," Benicoff said when the printer and

terminal had been plugged in and connected and they were alone again. He took out a sheet of paper and passed it to Brian. "It was developed at the University of Free Enterprise for the daily newspaper published there. In fact your father's name—as well as yours—is on the original patent applications. I understand you both helped in developing the process."

"Looks and feels like ordinary white paper."

"Try folding or tearing it—see what I mean? It is tough plastic that has been textured to feel like paper, with a bonded thin-film surface. Which means it is almost indestructible and completely reusable. The perfect thing for the daily newspaper—also developed by one of the brightest boys at your university."

"If I can sit down, with a glass of water—will you tell me about it?"

"I'll get the water. Here. You know about selective TV news programming?"

"Sure. You punch in your own program, things that you are interested in. Baseball, stock market reports, beauty contests, whatever. Labeled news reports go out twenty-four hours a day. Your TV records those that interest you the most so when you come home and turn on the news, whammo, it's only the stuff you care about."

Benicoff nodded. "Well, your university newspaper is a high-powered version of the same thing. The editor there has signed up scientists right around the world as reporters. They send in reports all the time about every kind of scientific and technical news. These are tagged and stored in a data bank, along with all the news items from standard services. The subscription system has a learning scheme. When you touch the advance button to reject something, the computer notes this and avoids future related items. More important is the fact that it follows your eye movements with a tracking device. Then it does a content analysis and records descriptions of the subjects that interest you. It is a true learning process and the system gets better and better at profiling your interests. It is so good that unless there is a cutoff you would find yourself doing nothing else but watching news and views that you agree with and approve of.''

"Sort of turn you into an info junky. But what about browsing?"

"Built into the system. The retrieval operation is so efficient that there are always plenty of sidetracks even in the documents that are relevant to your subject."

"Great! So it works out that every subscriber gets his own special newspaper. The hydraulics prof has nothing but pipes, pumps and splashes from around the world, along with Topeka, Kansas, obituaries, where he comes from, and chess news if he is into that as well. What a great idea."

"Thousands think so. The subscriber pays a fixed fee, while the computer keeps track of how many times any single item is used and automatically pays the contributor."

Brian rolled up the sheet of eternitree paper, real tight, but it instantly flattened out when he let go.

"A personalized newspaper waiting in the bin every morning. But still a tree's worth of paper to be dumped every week."

Benicoff nodded. "That's what you and your father thought. The thin-film lab at the school was working on flat computer screens. Your father helped with the math and this was the end result. The layered film is changed internally and electronically from white to black. Any font or size of type is apparently printed on it—even large size for those with weak eyes. After reading it the sheets are dropped back into the printer. As the new newspaper is printed it clears away the old one. And even this technology is going to be redundant soon. There is a hyperbook coming onto the market that is about three-eighths of an inch thick and contains only ten pages. The edge binder contains a really powerful computer that controls a detailed display on each page, one that is even more detailed than the pages of printed books. When you finish reading page ten you turn back to the first page, which already contains new copy. With a hundred megabytes of memory this ten-page book will really contain a quite substantial library."

"I'll settle for this one for now—it's really neat. I'll set up a newspaper for myself."

"You can—but that's not why I brought the printer. You've been trying to order some books, the request got passed on to me. With the printer you can only store them in memory, but with eternitree you can print the book you want, slip the sheet into a spring binder and sit in the sun while you read."

"And reuse the sheets again when I'm through! A lot has happened that I forgot about. Say, can't you print out that report I asked for on this? I could have it right now."

Benicoff turned to the terminal. "I don't know. If this hospital has a cleared high-security network it might be possible. Only one way to find out."

He punched in his own code, accessed base security and found the right menu. But before he had gone very much further the screen cleared and the lines of print were replaced by General Schorcht's scowling image.

"What is the meaning of this breach of security?" His rasping voice rasping even worse through the terminal's tiny speaker.

"Good morning, General. Just trying to get a copy of the classified Megalobe report for Brian."

"Are you crazy?"

"No more than usual. Think, General. Brian was there. He is our only witness. We need his help. If I can't get a copy now I will bring him one tomorrow. Does any of this make sense to you?"

General Schorcht stared in cold silence while he thought it through. "The hospital circuits are not secure. I'll have the Pentagon transfer a one-off copy to CNBSC, the Security Central there. A messenger will deliver the copy." The screen went blank as soon as he finished.

"Well good-bye then, sir, nice to chat with you. You heard."

Brian nodded. "I don't know if I can help—but at least I can find out what happened to me out there. Early on, Dr. Snaresbrook said that others had been killed. Very many?"

"We just don't know—that is one of the infuriating things

about this case. One man we can be fairly certain of, the Megalobe Chairman, J. J. Beckworth. We found a drop of his blood. But seventeen men in all are missing. How many were killed—and how many were in on the crime, we just have no idea. You'll read it in the report."

"What was taken?"

"Every record and every item of equipment relating to your work on artificial intelligence. They also moved out every piece of electronic equipment and record, every book and piece of paper from your home. The neighbors reported that a moving van was there for at least a half a day."

"You've traced the van?"

"The plates were forgeries and the company doesn't exist. Oh yes, the moving men were of oriental appearance."

"Chinese, Japanese, Thai, Siamese, Vietnamese or any specific country?"

"The elderly witnesses can only identify them as oriental."

"And the trail gets colder every day."

Benicoff nodded reluctant agreement.

"I wish I could be of help—but as far as my memory goes I'm still living back in UFE. Maybe if I saw the house I might get some clues. Maybe they missed my computer backup. I lost two important files when I first started programming seriously and I swore it would never happen again. I wrote an automatic program that saved to an external disk drive as I worked."

"Not a bad idea—but they got every disk in the house."

"But my program did more than just backup disks. When I was fourteen years old my program also backed the backup disk through the telephone modem to the mainframe in my father's lab. I wonder what setup I had here?"

Benicoff was on his feet, fists clenched. "Do you realize what you have just said?"

"Sure. There is a good chance that there is a copy of my AI work in a memory bank somewhere. That would help, wouldn't it?"

"Help! My boy, we might be able to rebuild your AI with it! It wouldn't solve the problem of who pulled this thing off—but they wouldn't be the only ones with artificial intelligence." He grabbed up the phone and punched in a number. "Dr. Snaresbrook, please. When? Have her contact me as soon as she gets back. Benicoff, right. Tell her that it is urgent to know just how soon her patient will be able to leave the hospital. That is a gold-placed top priority question."

# 14

---

## November 10, 2023

The nurse came bustling into the room, leaving the door open.

"You will have to leave now, Mr. Benicoff." She pulled back the bedclothes and plumped the pillows as she spoke. "Time to get into bed, Brian."

"Do I have to? I feel okay."

"Please do as I say. Your pulse, blood pressure, both are elevated."

"I'm just excited about something, that's all."

"Bed. Did you hear me, Mr. Benicoff?"

"Yes, great, sure. I'll talk to you later, Brian, after I've seen the doctor."

Despite the months of rest and treatment, the trauma of the shooting and the surgery that had followed was still taking its toll. Brian fell asleep almost at once and didn't wake until he heard voices, opened his eyes to see Ben and the doctor at his bedside.

"A little too much excitement," Dr. Snaresbrook said. "But nothing to worry about. Ben tells me that you are rarin' to go for a ride in the country."

"Could I?"

"Not for a while yet, not after the surgery you have undergone. But it may not be necessary."

"Why?"

"Ben will explain."

"My blood pressure must have gone as high as yours," Benicoff said. "In the heat of the moment I just wasn't thinking. There is no physical need to go to the house yet. I'll have it searched again, but I doubt if they will come up with anything new. You said, Brian, that you used to store your backup files in your father's computer."

"That's right."

"Well, there have been major changes in communication technology that you can't remember. For one thing everything is digital now and fiber optics have replaced copper wire in all but the most remote areas. Every telephone has a built-in modem—and they are already old-fashioned. All of the large cities have cellphone networks and they are expanding." He tapped the telephone on his belt. "I have my own number for this. About most of the time it rings wherever I am in the continental United States."

"Is it a satellite link?"

"No, satellite connections are too slow for most uses— particularly telepresence. Everything is fiber optics now— even the undersea cables. Cheap and fast. With plenty of room for communication with eight thousand megahertz band-width capacity available everywhere—and all of it two-way."

Brian nodded. "I get your drift, Ben. What you're saying is that there is very little chance that I had a local mechanical backup. It was undoubtedly an electronic one. Which will mean an electronic search."

"Right. There are countless mailboxes, data base and communication programs now. You could have used one or more of these. But computer privacy laws are very strict these days. Even the FBI has to go to court to get permission for a search."

"What about the CIA?"

"You'll be happy to hear that they pulled one murderous trick too many and legislation has just been passed to put them out of the dirty tricks business. Another victim of glasnost—and they won't be missed. Particularly by the taxpayers who, it turned out, had been shelling out billions for a government department that produced nothing but inaccurate reports, started revolutions in friendly countries, mined harbors and managed to kill thousands of people along the way. They've been cut back to the original meaning of their name, a central intelligence agency, and are restricted to monitoring the peace instead of starting new wars. Now, if you will sign an agreement we can start the search at once.''

''Of course.''

It was not only papers that had to be signed, but there were numerous circuitry searches and phone-backs, as well as identity checks by three different government agencies. Benicoff sent everything off by registered fax, yawned and stretched.

''Now we wait,'' he said.

''How long?''

''If it takes an hour that will be a long time. Before electronic transfers this would have taken days—even weeks.''

''A lot has changed in the ten years since—since I have been away,'' Brian said. ''I look at the news and some things haven't changed at all. Others I look at, I miss a lot of the references.''

But it was done within the hour—and brought results less than ten minutes later. The printer hummed and rustled out the sheets of eternitree. Benicoff brought them over to Brian.

''You have accounts with six different firms.''

''That many?''

''That few. This one is a scientific data base, one of the ones that are updated hourly. They replace technical libraries— and work a lot faster. Access time is usually under a second. This one is a mailbox, this gets tickets for everything from baseball games to plane flights. These four here are the best bets. Would you try them first?''

''What do I do? Can I get out of bed, Doc?''

''I would prefer it if you didn't.''

''No need to,'' Benicoff said, going to the terminal and

unplugging the keyboard. "This has an infrared link, you don't need wires. And I'll phone down for holospecs."

Brian really enjoyed the holospecs. They were lightweight eyeglasses with a tiny bulge of circuitry in each earpiece. The lenses seemed to be just windowpane, though he guessed that they could have been ground with a prescription if he wore glasses. When they were turned on the image of a computer screen floated in space in front of him.

"Right. What do I do next?"

"Call up the data base, identify yourself and give them your code number. Then guess."

"What do you mean?"

"Every account has a security code known only to the owner. Try any old ones that you remember. If that doesn't work guess at new ones. These companies have been told what is happening and have switched off the alarm software. Usually, after the third attempt, the connection is cut and the police are given the number of the calling phone that is making the attempt to break in."

"And if that doesn't work?"

"A court order is needed to crack in. Which will take a couple of days at the fastest."

Brian found that old habits die hard. Three of the four opened at once to some of his favorite Irish code words. Nothing as gross as SHAMROCK, but ANLAR opened the first and LEITHRAS the other two.

"*An Lar* means city center, it's on the front of all the buses. *Leithras* is the Gaelic word for toilet," he explained. "Bathroom humor is greatly enjoyed by kids. But I have no idea what will open this last one. Can we save it for a bit and see what's in the other three? It's a little like getting my memory back, isn't it?"

"Sure is," Benicoff agreed. "I'll tell you what—I'll start the proceedings for a court order on the last one, just in case. More papers for you to sign."

The first account turned out to be a letter box, only a little over two years old. Brian went to the oldest letters and read through them. It gave him an uneasy feeling. None of the correspondents was familiar—and his own letters had an alien ring to them. Yes, he had signed them—but, no, it did not sound like him at all. It was very much like reading someone else's correspondence. There were occasional mentions of AI, but only in passing—and never in detail.

He pushed all of it into the computer's memory for his attention at some other time, then looked at the other two. One held his financial statements and IRS reports and was fascinating in a depressing sort of way. He had started earning money from royalties when he was quite young, he remembered that, from software for the most part. Then there was a large deposit, from the sale of their house—then more from his father's estate. He hurried on. So did the money. In a few years it was all gone—just before he went to work for Megalobe. The correspondence with the corporation made fascinating reading, particularly the details of his contract. There was much food for thought here. He stored this one as well and turned to the last account.

Flipped through a few screens, read very closely for a while—then wiped it. The doctor had gone out and Benicoff was bent over the phone, punching in a number. It was almost sunset and the room was growing dark.

"Ben—got a moment?"

"Sure thing."

"I'm really getting tired. I'll look at these in the morning."

"Let me put the keyboard away. Find anything about AI?"

"Nothing in these."

"Then I'll accelerate the court order. After you get a night's sleep try to think of more passwords, okay?"

"Sure thing. See you in the morning."

"You *are* beginning to look tired. Get some rest."

Brian nodded and watched the big man leave. Not tired. Totally depressed.

He had read just enough of the contents to know that he did not like it. The opening was familiar enough, the notes he had made after the disastrous end of his affair with Kim. Once the depression and hatred had ebbed a bit he had made more notes on his Managing Machine theory. This he remembered developing into his AI work—but he also remembered noting that it could be a means of personal control. Apparently he had carried this idea even further, developing it into a new mind science, more theory than fact from what he had seen in the file, called Zenome Therapy. It didn't sound so way-out and nutty as Dianetics but there were, to put it kindly, large undercurrents of megalomania running through it. It had not made nice reading—and he was pretty sure that he did not like the person who had written it.

Some decisions are easy to make once the facts are in front of you. He had been thinking about this for the last week and the so-called science of Zenome Therapy made his mind up. One of the paging buttons was on the bedside table and he pressed it. The nurse entered a moment later.

"Do you know if Doc Snaresbrook is still here?"

"I believe that she is, supervising the equipment installation. The doctor is moving into a new office that has been assigned to her here."

"Could I see her, please."

"Of course."

The last colors of twilight were fading and Brian overrode the lighting controls to watch them. When the sky was dark he allowed the blinking warning button to have its way. The curtains closed as the lights came on. The doctor came in a moment later.

"Well, Brian, you have had a busy day. Feeling the worst for it?"

"Not really. I was tired earlier but a nap fixed that. How about my vital readouts?"

"Couldn't be better."

"Good. Then you would say that I am on the road to recovery, reasonably sane other than suffering from the delusion that I am only fourteen years old—though I am really over twenty-one."

"Take out the word 'delusion' and I would agree."

"Have I ever thanked you for what you have done for me?"

"You have now and I'm grateful—and tremendously happy at the way things are turning out."

"I don't want to make you unhappy, Doc. But would you be terribly put out if we stopped the memory restoration sessions pretty soon?"

"I don't understand—"

"Put it another way. I'm satisfied with the way I am. I think that I would like to grow up on my own from now on. Become an older me, if you see what I mean. If the truth be known I don't really care about the other me, the one that was wiped out by the bullet. I don't mind going on with the sessions to find out how badly my memory has been affected, if there are things I should know—that I don't. I want my past restored as much as possible. Then as soon as you are satisfied with that, maybe you will consider stopping there. Though I would like to go on with the experiments you suggested to see if I really can interface with the internal CPU. Is that okay with you?"

Erin Snaresbrook was shocked, tried not show it. "Well, of course you can't be forced. But sleep on it, please. We can talk about it tomorrow. It is rather a big decision to make."

"I know. That's why I am making it. Oh yes, one other thing. But we can take care of that tomorrow as well."

"What is that?"

"I want to see a lawyer."

# 15

## November 11, 2023

Benicoff waited until Brian had finished his breakfast before he went in to see him. Made small talk about his health, the weather, told him that he was trying to get a court order to unlock the computer file which might be in later in the day, waited for Brian to open the topic. Waited in vain. Had to do it himself in the end.

"I got a pretty disturbed call from Dr. Snaresbrook. She tells me that you want to stop the memory sessions. Want to tell me about it?"

"It's, well, a kind of personal matter, Ben."

"If it's personal—then I'm not asking. But if it bears upon my investigation, or AI, then I'm interested. They are all really tied up together, aren't they?"

"I guess so—which doesn't make it any easier. Can I talk to you as a friend, then? Which I think you are."

"I take that as a compliment. And we were pretty good friends before all this happened. What you have gone through was damned rough—I can tell you truthfully that a lot of people wouldn't have made it. You're a tough mick and I like you."

Brian smiled. "Thanks."

"No thanks needed or expected. And I'll be happy to be taken into your confidence. With the qualifier that you shouldn't forget that I am still in charge of the Megalobe investigation. Anything that you say that has to do with the case will have to be for the record."

"I know that—and I still want to help with that as much as I can. For my own sake as well. When I grow up—or when I grew up—past tense—I invented AI, then had it stolen from me along with my memory. So now that I know that AI can be built, I'm going to reinvent it if I have to. But *I* am going to do it, not another guy with my name. Am I making any sense?"

"In a word—no."

They both laughed at that. Brian threw back the covers and put on his robe, kicked into his slippers. The window was open and he went and stood before it, breathing in the clean ocean air. "A lot better here than the Gulf. Too humid there, too hot, I never did get used to it." He dropped into the armchair.

"I'll say it another way. Let's imagine that what happened to me, the shooting and everything, let us say that this thing happened to you. There you sit, thirty-seven years of age . . .''

''Many thanks. Fifty is closer to it.''

''Right. So how do you feel if I told you that you got knocked on the head and that you are really seventy years old? But that's okay because I've got an invention that will jiggle around with your mind and make you seventy again.''

And Benicoff frowned into the distance. ''I'm beginning to get to what you mean. I don't really want to be that old without having *lived* to be that old. Bringing back those memories would be like letting a stranger into my head.''

''You said it better than I could. That's exactly how I feel. If I find out that there are holes in my past memory, things that I need to know but have forgotten, sure I would like to fill the holes, so we are keeping on with the brain sessions. But I'm going to *grow* into the future, not have it pumped into my head.''

''What about your education? You can't very well say that you have a degree in something that you can't remember.''

''Point taken. If I can't remember something then I'll just have to relearn it. I have a transcript from graduate school, lists all the courses and lectures—and I've a copy of my reading list. And the doc says that if those memories are still there we might be able to find them. I'm willing to do that. If not—I'll just learn them again. In fact a lot of the texts are completely outdated and I'll need help on my reading list.''

''Let me see your list for Expert Systems. I still try to keep up with the literature.''

Brian looked up, startled. ''But I thought you were . . .''

''A civil service drudge! I just grew into that role—and not by choice. I started out writing Expert Systems and went from that into troubleshooting others. I got so good at it that I ended up here. The sad story of my life.''

''Not too sad. Not everyone can phone up the President and have a chat—''

As if on cue the telephone rang and Brian picked it up, listened then nodded. ''Right. Tell him to come up.''

''And I'll be going,'' Ben said. ''I already made that

lawyer you had on the phone just now wait an hour until I was through.'' Ben laughed at Brian's shocked expression. ''The President's investigator is all-seeing—never forget that. Part of that job is seeing that you stay alive. All visitors are screened. For the time being privacy is out.''

As he said this Ben put his finger to his lips, then pointed upward and shaped his mouth to silently say *General Schorcht*. Brian nodded understanding and Ben left.

He should have thought of that for himself. His terminal led right to the General and here, on a military base, it stood to reason that the room was probably bugged as well. That was something else that he had to keep in mind.

''Come in,'' he called out when he heard the knock. His eyes widened when the uniformed Army officer opened the door. His name tag read *Major Mike Sloane*.

''You asked to see me.''

''Not knowingly. But I did want to see a lawyer.''

''Then that's me.'' He smiled, an easy grin on his lean, tanned face. ''Adjutant General's office. Cleared for Top Secret, which is how I got to read your file. So tell me, Brian—what can I do to help?''

''Are you, well, sort of cleared for civilian law as well?''

Mike laughed. ''There is only one kind of law. I slaved in the legal snake pits of Wall Street before I opted for travel, education and career.''

''How are you on contracts?''

''A whiz kid. That was one of the reasons I enlisted—to get away from corporate law.''

''An important question then. Will you be helping me—or the Army?''

''A good question. If there is an overlap the military comes first. If this is strictly a civilian matter it is confidential between us, or until you hire civil counsel. Going to tell me what it's about?''

''Sure. As soon as I know that it is confidential. I know that my terminal is bugged—is there a chance that this room is bugged as well?''

''Now that is what I call an equally good question. Give

me a few minutes to make a call and I'll see if I can give you an answer.''

It was more than a few minutes, closer to an hour before the Major returned.

"Right, Brian, what can I do for you?"

"Was the room bugged?"

"Naturally I cannot answer that. But I can assure you that our talk is confidential."

"Good. Then tell me—can I sue Megalobe for not protecting me, for putting me in a situation that was hazardous to my health?"

"My first reaction is to say 'Not easily.' The government owns a good share of the company and no one ever got rich suing city hall. Then I'll have to see a copy of your employment contract."

"It's on the table, right over there. That is what got me upset. And I don't really want to sue them, the threat will do. Any threat to get a better contract than that one. Do you know all about me—about my memory?"

"Affirmative. I read the complete file."

"Then you will know that I have no memory of the past few years. So I was reading some of my correspondence and I discovered that far from being a benefactor, Megalobe put the financial squeeze on me when I ran out of money to finish developing my AI. I discovered, unhappily, that I was almost completely bereft of any financial sense. But I wanted to finish the work so much that I let myself be bullied into signing that contract. Which appears to give the company a lot more than it gives me."

"Then reading it takes top priority."

"Go to it. I'm getting an orange juice. You too? Or something stronger."

"Not on duty. Juice will do fine."

The Major read slowly and carefully. Brian read as well, a copy he had printed out of a tutorial article by Carbonell about the new mathematical field of excluor geometry. It was a subject of psychology, concerned basically with the question of why people begin to use diagrams whenever verbal explanations get too complicated. This was because language is still fundamentally serial and one-dimensional. We can say former or latter—but there is no easy way to refer to four or five things at the same time. With AI always in the front of his mind he realized that just because human intelligence worked this way did not put any limitations on artificial intelligence. Instead of three or four pronoun-like ideas, an AI could handle dozens of "pronomes" at the same time. He blinked and looked up when he heard the lawyer laugh as he put the contract down. He shook his head and drained the glass of juice before he spoke.

"As we used to say back in law school—you been screwed without the benefit of being laid. This contract is worse than you said. I really think you wouldn't profit at all from your work if you left their employment. And as long as you worked for them the profit would be all theirs."

"Can you write me a better contract?"

"With pleasure. Since the Army wants to see AI developed as much as anyone does, it would be very much in our favor to sort this matter out at once. But there are some strange precedents here. The contract is legal and binding—but you didn't sign it?"

"No, the older me did. The me sitting here never saw it until yesterday."

Mike rubbed his hands together happily as he walked back and forth the length of the room. "Oh, would I love the fees for arguing this one in court! You have them by the short and curlies because, stop me if I'm wrong, you are still far ahead of everyone else in developing a really smart AI."

"I hope I am. Apparently I was on the right track before my . . . accident, and Dr. Snaresbrook thinks there is a good chance I can get back to where I was. But right now, I'm still studying the basics and there's no guarantee that I can get back in front. But I have all the notes, and I'll do my best."

"Of course you will—and you are Megalobe's only hope. Nothing wins in this world like having a monopoly. I am going to suggest to my superiors that they suggest to

Megalobe that this contract be tossed out and a new one written. Does that satisfy you? Would you still sue?"

"A new contract and no lawsuit. What should I ask for?"

"Something simple and sweet. They put up the readies to develop AI. You put up the AI. Any net profit from future development of AI will be split fifty-fifty between the parties concerned."

Brian was shocked. "You mean I should ask for *half* of all profit from AI? That could be millions, maybe billions of dollars!"

"Yup. Nothing wrong with being a billionaire, is there?"

"No—but it is kind of a new idea."

"Want me to start on this?"

"Yes, please."

Mike stood and looked at the contract and sighed dramatically. "This is the first time since I enlisted that I have had the slightest desire to be back in private practice. If I was the shyster handling this new contract would I really make a bundle!"

"Someone once told me that lawyers eat their young."

"Brian my boy—it's true! I'll get back to you as soon as I have any news."

Brian napped after lunch and was feeling much better when the nurse opened the door and the hospital orderly pushed in the wheelchair at four in the afternoon.

"Ready for your session with the doctor?" the nurse asked.

"I sure am. Can't I walk down there?"

"Sit. Doctor's orders."

Brian grabbed the bound sheaf of papers he had been reading and took it with him. He remained sitting in the wheelchair as the tendrils brushed his neck and slid the thin fiber-optic link into place.

"Doc, can I ask a favor for this session?"

"Of course, Brian. What is it?"

"This." He held up the papers. "I did a graduate course in topology and this is an article about it that I just printed out. I started to read it and found that I am really out of my depth. If I read it now is there any chance you can access my earlier memories of the field? Will anything show up on your dials to show you've hit the right spot? Then you can press the button and give me my memories back.''

"I wish it were that easy—but we can certainly try. I was going to suggest input like this in any case—so am more than willing to have a go at it now."

The material was pretty intractable and Brian had to reread a lot for it to make any sense. He worked his way almost halfway through the article before he put it down.

"Any contacts, Doc?"

"Lots of activity, though it is so widespread that it is obvious that a very large number of K-lines are involved. My machine is not set up to handle networking like this. This is the kind of cross-connecting that only the human brain is so good at."

Brian pinched the bridge of his nose. "Bit tired. Can we call it a day?"

"Of course. We agreed to always pull the plug at the first hint of fatigue."

"Thanks. I wish I could access the inbuilt CPU with commands more complex than 'Turn Off.'"

"Well, you can always try."

"Wouldn't it be great if I could? Just issue the order to the CPU. You there, CPU, open the file on topology."

Brian's smile turned suddenly to one of surprise. He stared into space, then focused his eyes on Dr. Snaresbrook.

"Now that is what I call very interesting. Didn't I say when I came in that I knew little or nothing about the mathematical field of topology? Well I must have been very tired or something, just not concentrating. But now I remember my thesis very well. It had a lot of what was new stuff at the time. It started simply by using an algebraic theory of knots based on the old Vaughn Jones polynomial to classify chaotically invariant trajectories, then applied this to various physics problems. Nothing very inspired and I'm sure that it must be pretty old hat now. I'm beginning to understand why I quit pure math and went into AI."

Brian seemed to take his uploaded, transplanted memories for granted—but not Snaresbrook. Her hands were shaking so hard that she had to bring them together. Brian *had* used the CPU implant to interface with his own memories. There really was an internal man-machine interface in operation.

# 16

## November 14, 2023

The rest area of the tenth floor of the hospital was more like a roof garden than a balcony. A marine guard at the door checked Benicoff's ID before he let him proceed between the potted palms. Brian was sitting with his head in the shade of the beach umbrella; he had managed to sunburn his face by falling asleep in the sun the previous day and didn't want a rerun. He looked up from his book and waved.

"Good to see you, Ben."

"Likewise—though you are not going to like the news. There won't be any court order for those data bases of yours. In recent years the tightening up of the secrecy laws has ruled out access of this kind. If you were dead it would be different."

"I don't understand."

"Every once in a while someone gets killed in a car accident and leaves no record of his access codes. There has to be hearings, proof of relationship, a lot of work is needed to get a court order, let me tell you. And there are no exceptions to this."

"Then what can I do?"

"Go physically to the data base. Prove that you are you and then it is up to the company to decide if they will release the material or not. And that is going to be tricky."

"Why?"

"Because—and I am deadly serious—the company with your files is not in the country. It's in Mexico."

"You're having me on!"

"I wish I were. The company is in Tijuana. Salaries are still cheaper there. That's just across the border, about twelve miles from here. Lots of American electronic assembly plants there. This company was probably founded to service them. Should we start thinking about a trip down there?"

"No, not for the moment."

"That's what I thought you would say." Benicoff smiled at Brian's look of surprise. "Because I understood that your military legal eagle has the Megalobe lawyers running in circles and screaming in pain. They'll come around in the end. I've gone upstairs about this. So now there is pressure on the military to pressure the company to come up with a new contract."

"Upstairs—talking to God?"

"Almost. And I figured you weren't going to look at those files until your future was set."

"You're one step ahead of me."

"Not hard to outwit a fourteen-year-old!"

"Brag, brag. This is one fourteen-year-old that has developed a taste for beer. Join me?"

"Sure. As long as it's Bohemia ale."

"I don't know that one."

"From Mexico, since we are talking about that country. I think that you'll like it."

Brian phoned down and a mess attendant brought the beers. He smacked his lips and drank deep.

"Good stuff. Have you talked to Doc Snaresbrook lately?"

"This morning. She says that you are going stir-crazy here and want to crack out. But she wants you in the hospital for another week at least."

"That's what she told me. No problem—I guess."

"I suppose you are going to ask me next if you can go to Mexico."

"Ben—is this your mind-reading day?"

"Not hard to do. You want security for those files—and

so do we. Phone lines can be tapped, data copied. And GRAMs can go astray in the mail.''

"GRAM? Don't you mean DRAM?''

"A thing of the past. Dynamic random-access memory is now as dead as the dodo. These gigabyte ERAMs are static, no need for batteries, and have so much memory that they are replacing CDs and digital audiotape. With the new semantic compression techniques they'll soon replace videotapes as well.''

"I want to see one of them.''

"You will as soon as the trip can be arranged. And I am also not going to embarrass you, force you to say no, by offering to go there in your place. I've talked to various security people about this already.''

"I'm sure that it made them deliriously happy to even think about me leaving the country.''

"You better believe it! But when the shouting died down it turned out that the FBI has an ongoing agreement with the Mexican government about this kind of thing. There is a regular trade in going down there after drug money and computer records—usually in banks. Special armed Secret Service officers will accompany us all of the way. Mexican police will join us at the border and will bring us back to the States afterwards.''

"So I can go there and retrieve my files?''

Benicoff nodded. "Just as soon as the doctor says you're fit. And it will be more like an invasion than you strolling across the border on your own. You'll be escorted all the way there and home again.''

"And the files—will they be taken away from me?''

"You have a nasty and suspicious mind, Brian Delaney. What's yours is yours. But—and I'm just guessing now—this trip will probably be difficult, it not impossible, to set up until you have signed a new contract with Megalobe. The government does have an investment to protect.''

"And if I don't agree to the contract—I don't go?''

"You said it—not me.''

Brian had to think about this. He finished his beer and shook his head *no* when Ben offered another one. Once before in his life he had tried to develop AI on his own; the records he had gone through showed that. Showed that he went broke too and had to sign that Mickey Mouse contract with Megalobe. If you can't learn by experience you can't learn. If he was fated to relive this part of his life he was certainly going to do a better job of it the second time around.

"It all depends on my new employment contract," he finally said. "If it is fair then we retrieve the file and I go back to work for Megalobe. Okay?"

"Sounds like a winner. I'll start setting things up."

Benicoff was scarcely out the door when Brian's phone rang; he picked it up.

"Who? Of course. Yes, she has clearance, check with Dr. Snaresbrook if there is any doubt. She has been here before. Right. Then please send her up."

A marine guard brought Dolly in. Brian climbed to his feet and gave her a peck on the cheek.

"You're looking a lot better, filling out," she said, looking at him with the exacting eye of maternal scrutiny, then holding out a package. "I hope you still like these—I baked them this morning."

"Not chocolate-chip cookies!" Brian tore open the wrapper and bit into one. "Always my favorite, Dolly, many thanks."

"And how are things going?"

"Couldn't be better. I'll be able to get out of the hospital in a week. And the chances are I'll be getting back to work as soon after that as I can manage."

"Work? I thought that your memory, that was the trouble."

"It shouldn't be a hindrance. If I find any gaps when I start on the research—well, I'll face that if and when it comes up. When I actually start working again I'll quickly find out how much I have forgotten."

"You're not going to do that artificial intelligence thing anymore?"

"Of course. Why do you ask?"

Dolly leaned back in her chair, twisting her fingers together. "You don't have to. Please, Brian. You tried once and look where it got you. Perhaps you're not destined to succeed.''

He couldn't tell her that he had succeeded once, that his AI was out there somewhere. This information was still classified. But he wanted to make her understand the importance of his work. And ''destiny'' had nothing to do with it.

''You know I can't go along with that, Dolly. It's free will that makes the world go round. And I'm not superstitious.''

''I'm not talking about superstition!'' she said warmly. ''I'm talking about the Holy Spirit, about souls. A machine can't have a soul. What you are trying to do is a blasphemy. Dealing with the devil.''

''I have never been a great believer in souls,'' he said softly, knowing she would be hurt whatever he said. Her mouth pursed angrily.

''You are your father's son all right. Never went to mass at all, didn't want to talk about it. We have God-given souls, Brian—and He is not giving them out to machines!''

''Dolly, please. I know how you feel and what you believe, remember that I was raised as a Catholic. But my work has given me some insight into the brain and what might be called the human condition. Try to understand that I am no longer satisfied with what I was taught to believe. Can machines have souls? You ask me that and I ask you if souls can learn. If they can't—then of what importance is this concept? Sterile and empty and unchangeable for eternity. How much more preferable it is to understand that we create ourselves. Slowly and painfully, shaped basically by our genes, modified steadily by everything we see and hear and attempt to understand. That is the reality and that is how we function, learn and develop. That is where intelligence came from. I am just trying to discover how this process works and apply it to a machine. Is there anything wrong with that?''

''Everything! You deny God and you deny the Holy Spirit and the soul itself. You will die and burn in hell forever . . .''

''No, I won't, Dolly. That kind of destructive theory is where religion sinks into pure superstition. But what really hurts is that I know you believe that and suffer and worry for me. I wish you wouldn't. I don't really want to argue religion with you, Dolly. No one wins. But you're an intelligent woman, you know that the world changes, even religions change. You've had a divorce. And if the new Pope hadn't ruled that family planning wasn't a sin you wouldn't be teaching birth control—"

"That's different."

"No, it's not. You say that artificial intelligence is unnatural—but it's not. The growth of intelligence is part of the process of evolution. When we learn how the mind works there is nothing evil or wrong with making machine models of our work. Dad was one of the pioneers in this field and I'm proud to continue with it. Machines today can think in many ways, perceive—even understand. They'll soon be able to think better, understand, feel emotions . . ."

"That's close to blasphemy, Brian."

"Yes, it might be on your terms. I'm sorry. But it is the truth. But if you think about it you'll realize that emotions must have come before brains and intelligence. An amoeba, about the simplest animal you can get, will pull a pseudo-pod back when it detects something painful. Pain leads to fear, which leads to survival. You can't deny that animals, dogs, have emotions."

"They're not machines!"

"You're arguing in circles, Dolly. And there is no point to it either. When I build the first AI we'll see if it has emotions or not."

"I hope you enjoy the cookies," she said, standing abruptly. "But I think I have to go now."

"Dolly, stay a bit, please."

"No. I see that there is no way to stop you."

"It's not just me. Ideas have a strength of their own. If I don't put the pieces together correctly, why then someone else will."

She didn't answer him, even when he changed the subject, made a feeble attempt at small talk.

"I'll have to say good-bye now, Brian. And it's going to be a while before I see you again. I've had a lot of calls from the clinic back home. They were nice about giving me emergency leave at such short notice, but they really are short-staffed."

"I appreciate what you did to help me."

"That's all right," she said, already distant.

"Can I phone you?"

"If you think it necessary. You have my number."

Clouds had come up and the balcony was getting chilly. He walked slowly back to his room, no longer needing the wheelchair, and turned on the lights. Took off the knitted cap and ran his fingers over the growing stubble on his scalp, went and looked in the mirror. The scars on his skull were still obvious, although not as red as they had been. The hair was beginning to conceal them. He picked up the hospital cap—then threw it aside. He was beginning to hate this place. Benicoff had brought him a baseball cap that advertised the virtues of the San Diego Padres in large letters; he pulled that on, nodded approvingly at his mirrored image. Poor Dolly, life had not been that nice to her. Well it had not been nice to him either! As least she didn't get a bullet through the brain. His watch buzzed and the tiny voice spoke.

*"Four P.M. Time for your appointment with Dr. Snaresbrook. Four P.M. Time for yo . . ."*

"Belt up!" he said, and it went silent.

Erin Snaresbrook looked up and smiled when Brian came in. "I love your taste in hats. It sure beats that hospital-issue beanie that you have been wearing. Ready to go to work? I want to try something new today."

"What's that?" Brian took off the cap and settled back in the dentist's chair, felt the spidery touch of the metal fingers.

"If you don't mind I would like to hold off on the memory work for this session and see if we can't do more with your new talent of accessing your inbuilt CPU."

"Sure. I never thought to ask—but what kind of a central processor is it?"

"It's a CM-9 parallel processing unit that contains 128 million simple but fast computers. It has a very small current drain and runs very cool—imperceptibly above your body temperature. Uses hardly any current at all. In fact, this computer uses less energy than the equivalent brain cells. And plenty of memory. In addition to sixteen 64-billion-byte GRAMs, your implant contains four thousand million words of B-CRAM as well."

"B-CRAM. That must be something new I don't know."

"Yes, they are new. A B-CRAM is a best-matching content-accessed memory. These were developed for database applications and are perfect for use here, since they can almost instantly find records that match inputs. The B-CRAM automatically does pattern matching of every data entry, in parallel, against a vector of matching 'weights' provided to its input. These are the components that store your input-output nerve-reconnection information."

"Some setup! But even running cool it will still need *some* electricity. Don't tell me you will have to open my head again to change batteries?"

"Hardly! Electronic implants, like pacemakers, no longer depend on tricky power supplies that have to be recharged from the outside of the body. That's all a thing of the past. They are now powered by metabolic batteries that get their energy from blood sugar."

"Sweet batteries—technology run rampant. So what is it that you want to do now?"

"Run a benchmark sequence. This will take about ten minutes. I want you to see if you are aware of the central processing unit, can tap into it or hear it—or whatever we might call it. You remember that you were aware of the CPU when it was connecting memories. I want to see if you can re-create that awareness."

"Sounds good to me."

After a few minutes Brian yawned loudly.

"Anything yet?" the surgeon asked.

"Absolutely nothing. Is it really running?"

"Perfectly. Just started the benchmark run again."

"Don't look so depressed, Doc. Early days yet. Why don't you rerun the session where I did contact it, see if we can re-create the conditions."

"That's a good idea—we'll try it tomorrow."

"Will I really be able to get out of stir in a week?"

"Physically, yes, as long you do nothing strenuous. No stairs or fast walking, just about the same amount you do here in a normal day. After a while we can increase that. That is the physical side of the trip; your security is another matter. You'll have to ask Ben about that."

Would the memory bank in Mexico have the records of his AI work? A lot was riding on that.

# 17

## November 20, 2023

"This is it! I bring you Mr. Good News," Benicoff said, bursting enthusiastically through the door. Brian closed the book he was reading, *Introduction to Applied Excluor Geometry*, and looked up, at first not recognizing the other man who came in behind Ben. Three piece dark suit, Sulka tie, gleaming black boots.

"Major Mike Sloane!"

"The same. A necessary disguise, since the high-powered Megalobe lawyers sneer with contempt at our country's uniform—but look with humble respect at this sartorial souvenir of my civilian years. They've come around." He opened his hand-tooled leather Porsche attaché case and took out a thick wad of paper. "This is it. And it is my positive belief that it is just the contract that you wanted."

"How can I be sure?"

"Because I checked it," Benicoff said. "Not personally, but I sent it on down the line to Washington. We've got attorneys there that could eat Megalobe for breakfast. They assure me it's brassbound, you got the terms you asked for, a better salary than expected. And after overhead, development costs and all the usual deductions, you'll have something very close to a fifty-fifty split on profits. Ready for a little trip south of the border?"

"You bet. After I read through this."

"Good luck. It's tough going."

Mike guided him through the less coherent and densest legalese clauses, explained everything. By the time the lawyer left two hours later the contract was signed, registered and duly filed in the legal data bank. Along with an archaic paper copy locked away in the hospital's safe.

"Satisfied?" Benicoff asked as they watched the Yeoman seal the safe. Brian looked at his receipt and nodded.

"It's a lot better than the first contract."

"Which means that you have a job—when you're able to go back to work. You did notice the clause about how if you can't recover your backup files, which are hopefully in TJ, the company reserves the right to employ you or not? Or if they choose to employ you without your backup files, they can fire you whenever they feel like it and you get bupkas."

"Mike Sloane pointed that out to me in very great detail while you were on the phone. It seems fair. So let's open that Mexican file and see what's in it. I suppose you have been thinking about how I'm going to do that?"

"Not just me—Naval Intelligence, the Army and the FBI. Not to mention Customs and Excise. A plan has been produced which has the approval of everyone. Simple instead of complex, but hopefully foolproof."

"So tell."

"Let's go talk in your room."

"At least tell me when all this is going to happen."

Ben touched his finger to his lips and pointed to the exit. Only when the door to Brian's room had closed behind them did he answer the question.

"Tomorrow morning, eight A.M., height of the navy rush hour here in Coronado. And your doctor has approved all arrangements."

"I'm being sprung! How is it going to work?"

"You'll find out in the morning," Benicoff said with sadistic relish. "As of now only a handful of us know all the details. We want no slipups and no leaks. The best plan becomes no plan at all if someone talks."

"Come on, Ben, give me a clue at least."

"All right. Your instructions are to eat your breakfast at seven and to remain in bed after that."

"Some instructions!"

"Patience is a virtue. See you in the morning."

It was a slow day for Brian, and when he forced himself to retire he had trouble going to sleep. He was worried now. He had always assumed that his backups were in the files in Mexico. But what if they weren't? How could he rediscover his work on AI without them? Would it mean more sessions with Snaresbrook and her machine in an attempt to get back memories of the future, his past, that he did not really want? The clock said midnight when he called the nurse for something to make him sleep. He would need all the rest he could get for the day to come.

At eight the next morning he was sitting up in bed staring at the morning news and not seeing it. Precisely on the hour there was a quick knocking and two navy corpsmen came in wheeling a gurney. Behind them was the floor nurse and what could have been two doctors, except for the fact that they stood with their backs to the closed door, fingers brushing the fronts of their white jackets. They were both big men and, for some reason, strangely familiar. And were those bulges in the armpits? Brian thought. Or do they do it different these days.

"Good morning, Brian," the nurse said, laying a roll of bandages on the bedside table. "If you will sit up this won't take a moment."

She opened the roll and swiftly and expertly swathed his head completely, leaving just an opening for him to breathe through and a slit for his eyes. Then cut off the end of the bandage and secured it in place with plastic clips.

"Do you want help getting onto the stretcher?" she asked.

"No way."

He climbed onto the gurney and the blankets were tucked in around him, right up to the neck. They pushed him out into the corridor, an unidentifiable patient in a busy hospital. There were other passengers in the big elevator who carefully looked away. Whoever had dreamed this one up had produced a really good idea.

The ambulance was waiting and Brian was carried inside. He couldn't see out but knew that traffic was heavy by the frequent stops and slow progress. When the back doors were finally opened and he was gently lifted out, he found himself looking up at the aircraft carrier *Nimitz*. A moment later he was being carried aboard. Even before they reached the wardroom he heard muffled commands and a distant whistle as the vessel started away from the wharf. Still without a word, the navy personnel left and Benicoff came in, closing and locking the door behind him.

"Let me take that thing off your head," he said.

"Did you lay on this aircraft carrier just for me?" Brian asked, his voice muffled by the cloth.

"Not really." Benicoff threw the bandage into a wastebasket. "It was leaving harbor this morning in any case. But you have to admit that it's a beautiful cover."

"It certainly is. Now can you tell me what comes next?"

"Yup. But get off that cart first and put these clothes on. We are heading west into the Pacific and carrying on until the ship is out of sight of land. Then we turn south. We will pass west of the Islas Madres, small uninhabited islands that are just below the Mexican border. A boat went out after dark last night and will be waiting for us there."

Brian pulled on the trousers and sport shirt. They were unfamiliar but fit perfectly. The moccasins were scuffed and worn and very comfortable. "Mine?"

Benicoff nodded. "We picked them up last time we searched your place. How are you feeling?"

"Excited, but otherwise in great shape."

"Doc Snaresbrook ordered me to make you lie down, or barring that at least sit down during any lulls in this voyage—like this one. But first I want you to put on this rug and matching mustache."

The wig fitted his head perfectly, just as the clothes had. Well, after all the operations they should know the size and shape of his head by this time. The curling handlebar mustache had some kind of adhesive on its backing; he looked into the mirror and pressed it into place.

"Howdy, pardner," he said to his image. "I look like some kind of western gunslinger."

"You don't look like yourself—which is what counts. Sit, doctor's orders."

"I'll sit. How long will our cruise take?"

"Once we're out of the harbor and at sea, less than an hour." He looked up when he heard the light knock on the door. "Who is it?"

*"Dermod here. Ray is with me."*

Benicoff unlocked the door and admitted the two doctors from the hospital, now looking very touristy in plaid slacks and sport jackets.

"Brian, let me introduce you. The big guy here is Dermod, the even bigger one is Ray."

"I didn't think you were doctors," Brian said. When they shook hands he realized that the bulk was solid muscle on both of them.

"Our pleasure to be here," Dermod said. "Before we left Washington our boss said to wish you the best of luck and a speedy recovery."

"Boss?" Brian had a sudden insight. "Your boss isn't by any chance Ben's employer as well?"

Dermod smiled. "None other."

No wonder they looked familiar. Brian had seen them on the news, in a parade. Big solid men walking next to the President and looking everywhere but at him. Big because they were there to stay between him and any bullets or bomb fragments. Their presence was more revealing than any amount of words about the importance attached to his safety.

"Well—thank him for me," Brian said weakly. "Don't think I don't appreciate it."

"Doctor's orders!" Ben snapped. Brian dropped into the deep lounge chair.

"Do you have any idea how long we will be in Mexico?" Ray asked. "We were given no details at all. What we were told about was just the instructions about the hospital and the transferral to the carrier and the boat. And that we were being met onshore. I'm only asking because we have a plane ready to take us back to Foggy Bottom tonight. We leave early tomorrow morning for Vienna.''

"I would say that the operation will take two hours at most. We're going back a different way of course. Vienna? That must be the conference on AIDS treatment and control?"

"It is—and about time as well. Treatment is improving— but even with the new vaccine there are still over a hundred million cases in the world. The sums involved in just containing the disease are so large that the richer countries have to contribute—for selfish reasons alone.''

Brian found his eyes closing; even with the pills he had not slept well the night before. He woke when Ben shook him lightly by the shoulder.

"Time to get moving," he said.

Dermod led the way and Ray fell in behind them when they went on deck. The water was smooth, the day sunny. The aircraft carrier was barely slipping through the water when Brian made his way carefully down the steps behind Dermod. The boat waiting for them turned out to be a thirty-foot deep sea cruiser with its fishing poles secured vertically. As soon as he was helped aboard, and the others jumped down behind him, the motors burbled and roared and they swung away around the island, leaving the Nimitz behind. The Mexican coast came into view and they cut around two other fishing boats as they headed toward the marina. Brian found that the palms of his hands were suddenly moist.

"What happens next?''

"Two unmarked police cruisers will be waiting for us, driven by the Mexican plainclothesmen I told you about. We drive directly to Telebásico—who are expecting us.'' Ben dug into his pocket and handed over two black plastic boxes, about the size and weight of dominoes. Brian turned them over, noticed the socket each had in its base.

"Memory," Ben said. "These are GRAMs I told you about.''

Brian looked dubious. "There may be a lot of records in those files, years' worth maybe. Is there enough memory space in these two to hold it?"

"I should hope so. You don't really need both—the second one is for backup. Each of them holds a thousand megabytes. Should be more than enough."

"I should say so!"

The cars were long and black, the windows so heavily tinted that very little could be seen of the insides. The two Mexican plainclothesmen who were waiting by the cars had natural mustaches that were even more impressive than Brian's fake one.

"The guy in front is Daniel Saldana," Ben said. "He and I have worked together before. He's a good man. *Buenos días, caballeros. ¿Todos son buenos?*"

"No sweat, Ben. Easy as falling off a log. Good to see you again."

"The same. Ready for a little drive?"

"You betcha. We have been instructed to take you and your friends to a business premise here, and after that safely to the border. I will be pleased to drive you there." He opened the door of the first car. Ray stepped forward.

"No problem getting three in the back of this, is there?" he asked.

"If that's the way you want it."

Ben traveled with the other plainclothesman in the second car. Brian, sitting in the middle of the backseat, felt like the filling in a sandwich. Both big men kept their eyes on the street outside. Dermod, sitting on Brian's left, unbuttoned his jacket with his right hand—and kept his hand at his waist after that. When they swayed around a turn the jacket gaped open and Brian had a quick glimpse of leather and metal. So it *had* been a bulge he had seen in his armpit.

It was a brief drive to the industrial area, the typical low and windowless factories of high-tech manufacturing. The two cars drove into the complex and parked behind one of the buildings, entered it through the loading bay. The detectives had obviously been here before and led the way to a small, wood-paneled office. There were two men already there, sitting before a computer terminal. It was uncomfortably crowded when all of them except Ray, who stayed behind in the hall, pushed in and closed the door.

"Which of you is the gentleman with the account?" one of the technicians said, taking up a sheaf of papers.

"I am."

"I understand that you have forgotten your identification number and password, Mr. Delaney?"

"You might say that."

"This has happened to us before, but you will understand we must still take every precaution."

"Of course."

"Good. Could I please have your signature here—and here. This is your agreement not to bring charges against us if you cannot access your files. It also says that you guarantee you are who you say you are. Now—all that is left is to make the final verification. Could I have your hand, please."

He held out an electronic instrument about the size of a portable radio, touched it to the back of Brian's hand.

"It will take a few moments," he said, carrying it across the room and plugging it into a larger machine there.

"What is it?" Brian asked.

"Portable DNA matching," Benicoff said. "Just coming into commercial use. The adhesive on the handpiece picked off a few of your epidermal cells, the ones that flake off all the time. Now it's matching up your MHC complex with the one on file."

"Never heard of that."

"Major histocompatability complex. These are the so-called self recognizing antigens and are completely different for every person. The best part is that they are on the surface of the skin so DNA doesn't have to be extracted from the cell nucleus."

"Would you come over here, Mr. Delaney? Please use this terminal. Did you bring some memory—I see, fine. Everything checks out perfectly and we are satisfied re your identity. We have unlocked the security files and obtained your identification number and password."

The operator plugged in the GRAMs as Brian sat in front of the screen that faced away from the rest of the room. He also passed over a piece of paper. "This is your access number. After you have entered it you will be asked for a code—this is it."

PADRAIG COLUMBA, Brian read. The two most important saints in Ireland—no wonder he hadn't guessed it.

"After you enter that you will be in your files. After you have verified that they are yours, control key F12 will download to memory. Verification during loading is automatic. Do you want to enter a new code word—or are you closing this account?"

"I'm closing it."

"There is a balance due of..."

"I'll pay that," Benicoff said, taking out a roll of bills. "I'll need a receipt."

Brian entered the number, then the code, then hit return. He scrolled through quickly, then leaned back in the chair and sighed.

"What's wrong?" Benicoff asked, worried. "Isn't it what we were expecting, what we were looking for?"

Brian looked up and smiled.

"Bingo," he said, and stabbed his finger down on F12.

# 18

## November 21, 2023

Dermod led the way back down the hall, but stopped when he reached the outside door.

"Mr. Saldana—could I ask you a question?" he said.

"Of course."

"Did you have other cars tailing us, keeping an eye on our rear?"

"No. I did not think it was needed." The Mexican detective frowned. "Why? Did you see one?"

"I thought I did for a while, but it turned off when we crossed Independencia."

"And another car might have picked up the trail?"

"Always a possibility."

None of them were smiling now. Brian looked from face to strained face, his hands plunged deep into his pockets—with one of the GRAMs clutched tightly in each. "What's up?" he asked.

"Nothing—we hope," Daniel said, then snapped a quick command in Spanish to his companion, who eased out the door and closed it behind him.

"Do you want to shout for help?" Ben asked.

Daniel shook his head *no*. "The uniforms here are tourist police. I can get trained people—but not quickly. If there is anyone out there and we wait for reinforcements—they might be doing the same thing. We are to take you to the border at San Ysidro—is that correct?"

"That's the plan."

"Then I say do it and do it fast. Your Mr. Doe here will be in the second car with you driving, Ben. My associate and I will lead the way. What do you say?"

"We go," Dermod said. "But I'll be driving the second car, since I know TJ, Tijuana, very well. If there's trouble we are not stopping for you."

Daniel flashed a large toothy grin. "It would be unprofessional to do anything else."

The outside door opened an inch—then stopped. Brian blinked and realized that all three of the men were now holding healthy-sized pistols in their hands. Pointed at the door. There was a quick whisper in Spanish from outside and Daniel pushed his gun into his waistband.

"*Venga*. Tell us in English, what did you see?"

"Nothing in the street in either direction."

"We're going out fast," Daniel said. "There may be something out there—or nothing. We don't take chances—we act like there is something. Stay thirty meters behind me all the way. No closer—or any further back. All the glass is bulletproof. Open the window if you have to fire. Let's go."

Ben sat on Brian's left now. As soon as the door was closed Ray took out his heavy-barreled revolver and held it on his lap. Dermod started the engine and backed and turned until he was facing the exit, just behind the other car. He blinked his lights. The first car jumped forward and they were out of the drive and into the street.

Brian was looking at the lead car when it suddenly swerved; what appeared to be white dots appeared on the rear window. *"Down!"* Ray shouted, his hand on Brian's shoulder pushing him painfully to the floor. Their own car swerved and the tires shrieked as they accelerated around the corner. There were two loud crashing sounds and a thud in the seat behind him. Followed by an ear-destroying series of explosions as the handgun fired through the open window. They shrieked a turn in the opposite direction and Dermod shouted back over his shoulder.

"Anyone in trouble back there?"

Ray glanced quickly at the other two. "We're okay. What happened to the other car?"

"Rammed into a lamp pole. Did you hit anything?"

"Probably not. Just wanted to keep his head down. I saw someone leaning out of a window. Firing a rifle of some kind. High-velocity, the sort of a gun that can punch right through this kind of glass."

He pointed to the rear window of the car, to the neatly drilled hole there. Brian looked on, horrified, as Ray poked his finger into a hole in the seat cushion. Where he had been sitting.

They rocketed around another corner, accelerated down the boulevard beyond. "Any tails?" Dermod called out.

"Negative. I think they had just enough time to set up the trap. Counted on that. Close too."

"Then we change the route here," Dermod said, braking hard and heading into a side street. Turning corners apparently at random through the quiet suburb.

"Sorry to push you, Brian—but you see why." Ray's gun

was back in the holster and he gave Brian a tug back into the seat.

"There's been a leak," Benicoff said with cold anger. "They were waiting, followed us from the marina."

"That's the way I read it," Ray agreed. "How many people know about our return plans?"

"Myself. You two. And the two FBI men who will be meeting us at the border."

"Then we should be all right. How long, Dermod?"

"Five minutes more. I don't think Saldana walked away from that one. Must have been two guns shooting at us at least."

"I only saw the one."

"One for the backseat passenger, one for the driver. I've got a nice little hole up here as well. Would have been centered if I hadn't pulled the wheel when I saw the lead car hit. That Daniel Saldana was a good man."

There was nothing that could be added to that. They drove in silence the rest of the brief trip. Some alarm must have gone out because when they came closer to the border they passed a motorcycle policeman who waved them on, then spoke into his radio when they had passed.

A few blocks further on they were picked up by a motorcycle escort which, with flashing lights and loud sirens, cleared a path through the traffic waiting to cross into the United States. Behind the customs buildings was a parking lot with an open gate through the fence, the entire area overlooked only by blank walls.

"Wait here," Ray said. He and Dermod exited the car quickly, weapons drawn and pointed, looking slowly and carefully in all directions. "You can cross the lot now—and we'll be right behind you."

And they were, bodies between Brian and any possible threat.

"There's our transportation," Benicoff said. The only vehicle in the lot was an armored Brinks delivery truck; the back door opened when they approached and a uniformed guard got out.

"Get yourselves safely away from here," Dermod said.

"You're supposed to come with us," Benicoff said.

"You won't need us now. The President will want a complete report on this. Would you call our office, tell them what has happened? Tell them to let the plane know that we will be there by six at the latest."

"It'll be done."

The two guardians did not wait around for thanks, were in the car and gone before anything more could be said. They turned and walked toward the armored truck.

"Afternoon, gentlemen," the guard said. "It's all yours." He hadn't seen the bullet holes in the car, did not know anything had happened. Benicoff started to explain, then realized there was no point to it.

"Good to see you," he said. "We would like to get out of here."

"On the way now." After they had climbed in, the guard closed the door behind them, then went to the cab and took a seat next to the driver.

"That was pretty close," Brian said.

"Too close," Benicoff said grimly. "There must be a leak from the base, that's all I can think of. The FBI had really better get cracking on this one. I'm sorry this happened, Brian. I can only blame myself."

"You shouldn't. You did everything you could. I'm sorry about your friend back there."

"He was doing his job. A very good man. And we accomplished what we came here to do. You did find what you were looking for? Those GRAMs, are they copies of your work?"

Brian nodded his head slowly, finding it hard to forget what had just happened. "Yes, I'm pretty sure of it. They looked like it when I flipped through, but there wasn't enough time to be completely certain."

Ben pulled out his phone. "Can I call this through? I can't begin to tell you how many people are chewing their fingernails and waiting for the news." He tapped in a number and waited for the electronic bleep that told him he was connected. "Statue of Liberty," he said, and hung up.

"The code for success?" Ben nodded. "What would you have said if the records hadn't been there?"

"Grant's Tomb. The computer is now making seventeen simultaneous calls to pass on the good news. You're making an awful lot of people happy today. I can't say that I was positive it would turn out like this—just very hopeful." He reached under the seat and took out a parcel. "So I had this loaded aboard, just in case."

The black plastic case inside was about the size of a large wallet. Ben touched the latch and the screen flipped open and glowed whitely, illuminating the keyboard below it.

"A computer," Brian said admiringly. "And I suppose you are going to tell me this little thing will handle all my notes, spreadsheets, maths and graphics?"

"I am. Holographics too. Fifteen years ago you wouldn't have imagined how much could be put in a gadget like this. It also contains a phone-net transceiver and a satellite-based location system, so that you can always tell where it is. The entire surface of this black case is an extremely efficient photovoltaic coating for recharging itself—and...watch this!"

Benicoff pulled firmly on the latch-button, which came out with a whining sound on a length of cord.

"You can also charge it by hand with this built-in generator. It will do anything you want. And before we left I made sure to turn on its phone-net cutoff so that no one, not even General Schorcht, could track where you are, or take a look at what you are doing. Why don't you plug in one of the GRAMs and see what you have there?"

Brian had no problem at all in getting access to the records. Pretty soon he looked up at Ben. "No doubt about it. The earliest stuff there I can recognize, remember it well. It is the LAMA development I worked on with my father. Then, look here, we can jump ahead to some later developmental work. It seems sort of familiar, but I certainly don't remember it clearly. And all this later stuff, I feel sure that I've never seen it before. This last entry, made some months ago. It is only a few days before the raid on the lab!"

"That's fantastic. Better than we could have hoped for. Now let's go. Snaresbrook wants you right back in a hospital bed after this day's excursion. She didn't think that you would mind. I agreed—particularly if you had this computer in the room with you. And I also want you under guard where I won't have to worry about you while I turn over everyone in security."

"This has been the kind of day I could have lived without. I'm actually looking forward to getting back inside the hospital now. Peace and quiet and the chance to read my way through these files."

"That's fine by me. After I get the security investigation started I'll confer with Megalobe, then get back to you. Then we'll decide what happens next."

The armored truck slowed and left Freeway 5 at the Imperial Beach exit. Once they had passed through the city they saw that Shore Patrol vehicles were waiting for them at the causeway. They picked up speed then as they were escorted right through the center of Coronado—with all the red lights turning to green at their approach—and through a waiting open gate onto the base once more. Only when he was back in his room did Brian realize how very tired he was. He dropped onto the bed as Dr. Snaresbrook came in.

"Overdid it, I am sure—but there was no way of preventing it." She slapped a telemeter onto Brian's wrist and nodded at the readout. "Nothing life-threatening. Get some food and rest. No," she added when Brian reached for the computer. "Get into bed first. Eat something. Then we'll think about work."

Brian must have dozed off over the chocolate pudding. He awoke with a start and saw that it was almost dark. The bedside table was empty and he had a quick burst of fear before he felt the bumps under his pillow and pulled out the computer and the GRAMs. He may have fallen asleep—but not before stowing everything away. The door opened and the nurse looked in.

"You just had to be awake," she said. "You don't get a pulse jump like that in your sleep. Can I get you anything?"

"I'm doing fine, thanks. Wait, you can lift the head of the bed, if you don't mind."

He read through the files until they brought in his dinner.

Ate without noticing what he ate, was barely aware that the tray was removed. Was startled when the night nurse came and pointed to the time.

"Firm orders from Dr. Snaresbrook. Lights out at eleven at the latest—no excuses accepted."

He didn't protest, realizing how tired he had become. It was probably foolish to put the computer under his pillow—but it drained away the tension.

Benicoff was there when he woke up in the morning, his face grim and set.

"What's the news about the shooting?" Brian asked.

"Bad. Both detectives are dead. No sign of the killers. This is one that got away from us."

"I'm sorry about this, Ben. I know the one detective was a friend of yours."

"He did his job. Now—back to work. Got any news for me?" he asked. Pretending to be relaxed; tight as a wound-up spring.

"Some good—some troublesome. But don't get so pale, Ben! I suppose that being in the hospital is a good place to have a coronary, but you're still better off without one. I've been through the files, skipping a lot, but not missing anything important."

"For my heart's sake, then—the good news first."

"With what I have here I am ninety-nine percent sure I can design an AI that will work. I guess that's what you wanted to hear."

"Definitely. Now the troublesome part."

"What I have in memory is not plans or designs. There are specific bits and pieces that have been worked out, and there are detailed queries and notes. But for the most part these are my steps along the path to AI—not the path itself."

"Can you do it?"

"I'm sure I can. The assurance that each problem was solved, along with the notes of possible solutions, should keep me on the right track. The dead ends are pretty carefully marked out. I can do it, Ben, I'm sure that I can. So what comes next?"

"We check with Dr. Snaresbrook. See when you will be fit enough to be completely discharged from this hospital."

"What happens then? We've had some pretty gruesome evidence that the nasties are still gunning for me."

Benicoff stood and began to pace the length of the room. "We know now for sure that they are still waiting out there. They know that you lived through the two earlier attacks—or they would not have tried again. We live in a free society and secrets are hard to keep. If they really want to work at it, they are going to find your whereabouts, no matter where you go. So we must see to it that wherever you are, wherever you are working, you will be as inaccessible as possible. There has been a lot of hard thought about this one, believe me."

"Build me a laboratory in Fort Knox, down among the gold bars?"

"Don't laugh—that was one of the possibilities that was actually considered. Before all this happened you were just one more guy working away on a research project. I checked the records at Megalobe and believe it or not there was little or no commercial or development interest in your work. All that is changed now. The fact that party or parties unknown went to all that trouble to lay their paws on your invention has drawn the attention of every government department. Everyone wants to get into the act and they are all rushing through planning programs on how they can use AI in their departments. Which cheers Megalobe very much—and should cheer you as well. All the research funds are there for the grabbing. So grab."

"I would dearly like to. But where will all this grabbing take place?"

Benicoff rubbed his hands together and smiled wickedly. "Promise not to laugh when I tell you. As soon as you are up to it you are going back to your old Megalobe lab in Ocotillo Wells."

"After what happened there I should think it would be the last place to go!"

"Not really, not when it is barn-door-locking time. The security there was top class except for one small thing."

*"Quis custodiet ipsos custodes?"*

"Exactly right. Who is going to watch the watchmen? One or more of the watchmen betrayed their trust. The attack and robbery was a well-planned inside job. That won't happen again. We've got some new watchmen, professionals."

"Don't keep it a secret!"

"The United States Army, that's who. They have a one-sixth share in Megalobe and they are not pleased at what happened. The Marines also volunteered for the job. Felt they had a stake in the operation after guarding you here. There was even some talk of letting the Army and the Marines alternate months and see who did the better job— that plan was quickly abandoned, as you might imagine. Right now barracks are being put up in the parking lots. Which won't be needed, since there will be very limited access for vehicles in the future. I think that you will be able to finish your work this time."

"I don't like it. The constant threat doesn't make for easy concentration. But I can't think of anything better. I imagine you are still looking for these criminals?"

"After yesterday the case is back on the front burner."

Brian thought about this, then reached under his pillow and took out the duplicate GRAM. "Here, you better hold on to this. It's the backup of all my notes. Just in case."

"I'll never need it." Ben tried to sound sincere, didn't quite make it. "But as you say—just in case."

# 19

## January 28, 2024

"Today is knowledge base day," Dr. Snaresbrook said, checking the controls to be sure that the connection between

Brian's brain and the machine was complete. "Might I suggest that we begin with the latest edition of the *Encyclopedia Britannica?* The nineteenth is really a doozy. Almost all the illustrations involve animations and all the text is hypertext."

"Too general for me. I want specifics." He punched up a data-base menu and pointed to the screen. "Here is the sort of thing I mean. Technical handbooks. I want everything on this list from material science to geology and astrophysics. Hard facts. That is if my implant has the RAM for it?"

"More than enough. Just download the ones you want me to work with."

It took a long time and Brian almost dozed off in the comfortable chair. Did close his eyes and started when Snaresbrook spoke.

"More than enough for today," she said.

"If you say so. Can we see how things went?"

"Run a benchmark, you mean? Why not? Wait a moment while I load one of the texts at random into my machine, then I'll hit it with a random page number. Everything here looks medical—"

"*Dorland's Medical Dictionary,* forty-fifth edition."

"That's it. Have you ever heard of parendomyces?"

"That's a genus of yeastlike fungi species of which some have been isolated from various lesions of man."

"And kikekunemalo?"

"An easy one. It's a resin, like copal."

"You have it, Brian. Everything we downloaded, it's all there. And you can tap into it at will."

"Just as if they were real memories."

"They *are* real memories as far as you are concerned. Just filed away in a different manner. Now—I'm sorry, but we'll have to break off here. I have an appointment that I must keep."

When he got back to his room there was a message from Benicoff waiting for Brian; he dialed the number at once.

"I got your call . . ."

"*Got a moment to speak with me, Brian?*"

"Of course. You want to come up to my room?"

*"I would prefer the tenth-floor hanging garden."*

"Fine by me. I'm on my way now."

Brian arrived first, was halfway through his beer, a Pilsner Urquell, when Ben arrived, dropped heavily into a chair.

"You look beat," Brian said. "Want one of these?"

"Thanks, but I'll take a rain check. Now the news. You'll be pleased to hear that a company of the Eighty-second Airborne has moved into the Megalobe barracks. Their commanding officer, Major Wood, is a combat veteran who takes a very dim view of research scientists being shot. He doesn't want you to get there until he has his security arrangements and rosters set—and has run a few tests. After that the choice of a move is yours. And Dr. Snaresbrook's of course."

"Has everything been ordered that I asked for?"

"Ordered and shipped and in the lab. Which leads us to the next item. Your assistant."

"I've never had one."

"In this brave new world you will. Make your work that much easier."

Brian finished his beer and put it down, looking closely at Ben's expressionless face.

"I know that look. It means that there is more—but I should be able to figure it out for myself. And I can. They have made three attempts to kill me. I might not live through the fourth. So everyone would be very much happier if there was at least one other person who knew what was going on with the AI research."

"Security—you figured it out. The tricky part that comes next is getting someone who can do the work—but who can be trusted as well. Industrial espionage is a graduate course in most universities now, a major growth industry as well. Something like AI can be very tempting—as you have unhappily found out. I have narrowed my short list down to an even shorter list—two. I am off in the morning for a meet with a very promising lead, a graduate student at MIT. But until I get to see him I won't know. So let us run with the other possibility. How do you feel about the military?''

"Outside of our friend the General I don't have much feeling one way or the other. Certainly the Navy and the Marines have done a good job here. And I assume the Army will do the same at Megalobe. Why do you ask?''

"Because I've tracked down a Captain Kahn who is in the Air Force and has a very responsible job in the Expert Program section at the academy in Boulder, Colorado. Second-generation Yemenite greenie—slang term for a greenhorn, an immigrant. Kahn is working on programs for aircraft control. Interested?''

"Why not? Contact Boulder and . . .''

Ben shook his head. "No need. In the hopes you would say yes I had the Captain flown here.''

"Well wheel him in and let's hope.''

Ben smiled and made the call. The officer must have been waiting close by because the marine guard appeared a moment later.

"Your visitor, sir.''

Ben climbed to his feet; Brian turned and saw why. He stood as well.

"Captain Kahn, this is Brian Delaney.''

"Very pleased to meet you, sir,'' she said. Her hand was cool, her grip good. One quick shake and back to her side. She was a firmly built and attractive woman, dark-haired and dark-skinned. And very serious. She stood straight, silent, her face set and unsmiling—as was Brian's. Benicoff realized that the interview was not going that well.

"Please sit down, Captain,'' he said, pulling over a chair. "Can I get you something to drink?''

"No, thank you.''

"I'm going to have a beer. You too, Brian?'' A quick shake of the head *no* was his only answer. He dropped into his own chair. "Well then, Captain—that can't be your first name?''

"It is Shelly, sir. At least that is the name most people use. Shulamid is my name in Hebrew, which is not that easy to pronounce.''

"Well then—Shelly—thanks for coming. I'm afraid I didn't tell you much about the work, since security is tight. But now that you are here I know that Brian will be able to explain much better. Brian?"

Memories were getting in the way. Benicoff should have told him that the Captain was female. Not that this was bad. Or was it? Memories of Kim were too recent. But recent only to parts of him now. To the adult Brian those unfortunate events were long gone, part of his past, best forgotten. He realized that the silence had lengthened and that they were both looking at him.

"I'm sorry. My mind was wandering—it does that a bit. I think I will have a beer, Ben, join you."

While Ben was ordering, Brian tried to get his thoughts and emotions straightened out. The Captain was not Kim— who by this time was probably fat and old and married and with five kids. Forget her. He smiled at the idea and took a deep breath. Start over, forget the past. He turned to Shelly.

"I'm not sure where to begin—except to tell you that I could use some help on a research project that I will be launching soon. Could you tell me what you are doing now, about your work?"

"I can't tell you about it in detail because everything that I do is classified. But the overall program is public knowledge and easy enough to explain. It was originated because modern military planes are entirely too fast for the pilot's reflexes, the instrumentation too complex as well. If a pilot had to personally monitor all of the electronic systems, there would really be no time left to fly the plane. In order to assist the pilot, Expert Systems are always being developed and improved that assume as many as possible of his responsibilities. It is very interesting work." Her voice was low-pitched and ever so slightly hoarse and she spoke with self-assurance, sitting straight-backed on the front edge of the chair, her hands clasped in her lap. Brian was the one who felt a little unsure; she certainly wasn't. Not exactly what he had imagined he would get as an assistant.

"Have you ever worked with artificial intelligence?" he asked.

"Not really. Unless you consider that Expert System development is a part of AI. But I keep up with the developments since some of it is applicable to my own work."

"That's all for the good. I would rather have you learn than unlearn. Have you been told what the work is to be?"

"No. Only that it is important and relates to AI. Mr. Benicoff also explained to me about the violent industrial espionage that has been involved. His main concern was that I should know what I was getting involved with physically. He let me read a copy of his report on the unsolved crime. He also said there had been other attacks on your life since that time. If I work on the project I might be at risk myself. He wanted to be sure I knew all about this before I was even offered the job."

"I'm glad he did that. Because there is a real chance that there might be physical danger."

For the first time there was a change in her stern expression as she smiled. "An Air Force officer is assumed to be ready for combat at any time. When I was born Israel was still an armed camp. My father and mother, like everyone else, fought in the Army. When I was six years old my family emigrated to America so I was lucky to grow up in a country at peace. But I still like to think that some of their strength and ability to survive was passed on to me."

"I'm sure it was," Brian said, almost smiling in return. He was beginning to like Shelly, liked her air of self-assurance. But he was not sure that he really wanted to work with a woman—no matter how qualified she was. Memories of Kim still got in the way. But if Shelly was good enough to do Expert System work for the Air Force she might be qualified enough to help him. And the fact that she had never done AI research was an asset. Some scientists developed tunnel vision after a while and believed that their approach to the problem was the only one—even after they were proven wrong. He would just have to try to forget her sex; he turned to Ben with a question.

"Is there any reason I can't give Shelly some information

about what I'm doing? She deserves to know what she will be involved in before she makes her mind up.''

''The Captain has an absolutely top security clearance,'' Ben said. ''I'll take the responsibility. You can tell her whatever you think she needs to know.''

''Okay then. Shelly, I am in the process of developing an artificial intelligence. Not the sort of program that we call AI now. I mean a really complete, efficient, freestanding and articulate artificial intelligence that really works.''

''But how can you make an intelligent machine until you know precisely what intelligence is?''

''By making one that can pass the Turing Test. I'm sure that you know how it works. You put a human being at one terminal, talking to a human being on another terminal, and there are numberless questions that can be asked—and answered—to convince the human at one end that there is another human at the other terminal. And as you know the history of AI is filled with programs that failed this test.''

''But that's only a trick to convince someone that the machine is a person. It still doesn't give us a definition of intelligence.''

''True enough, but that was precisely Turing's point. There's really no need to have a definition and, in fact, we really don't want one. You can't define things, but only words. We tend to call someone intelligent if we think that they're good at solving problems, or learning new skills, or doing what other people do. After all, the only reason we consider other people to be intelligent is that they behave *intellectually* like human beings.''

''But couldn't something be intelligent and yet think completely different from a person? Like maybe a porpoise or an elephant?''

''Certainly—and you can call them intelligent if you want to. But for me, the word *intelligence* is just a handle to describe all the things I wish I were better at—and everything I'd like our future AI to do. The trouble is that I don't know just what those are yet. The reason for using those terminals is simply that it shouldn't matter what the thing looks like, so long as it responds to all questions asked, with answers that cannot be told from those of another person. Sorry about the lecture, for telling you what you already know. But I am developing an AI to pass that test. So my question is—would you like to help?''

For the first time since they had been talking Shelly lost her composure, was more woman than military officer. Her eyes had widened while Brian spoke and she touched her fingertips to her chin, shaking her head slightly with disbelief. ''I hear what you are saying—though it sounds both completely impossible—and incredibly exciting. Do you mean to say that you are working on a machine that I would recognize as intelligent?''

''He is,'' Ben said firmly. ''I can assure you that a real AI has been designed and that it will be built.''

''If that is the case, then I do want to be part of it! This is such a momentous and important development that there is no question in my mind.'' She frowned. ''Are there many others applying for the post?''

''I'm seeing someone else tomorrow,'' Ben said. ''That's the entire list.''

''I am sure that I can control my impatience for a while. But if you will let me help, there is something I can do to be of assistance right now.''

''We won't be able to get into the lab for some time yet,'' Brian said.

''That's not what I mean. I'm talking about the overall security matter.'' She turned to Ben. ''That report you showed me of the theft—is it complete?''

''I took out all the references to artificial intelligence. Other than that, yes, it's complete.''

''I don't mean that. I'm referring to the investigation of the crime. Do you know who was in charge of it?''

''I certainly do. Me. I can guarantee that that part of the report is complete.''

''And since the theft and Brian's being shot—there have been two other threats on his life?''

''That is correct.''

''Then it seems to me that solving the crime should take top priority.''

Benicoff did not know whether to laugh—or be insulted. "You do realize that I am in charge of the investigation? That I have been working on it full-time for some months?"

"Sir, please don't misunderstand! I was not denigrating your efforts—just offering to help."

"And how will you do that?"

"By writing an Expert Program with only one aim in mind. To solve this crime."

Benicoff dropped back into his chair and rubbed his jaw in silence for a moment—then nodded happily. "Captain—my thanks. I have been very, very dumb about this. I don't intend to be in the future. How soon can you transfer here?"

"I'm part of a team. They are very good and I know that they'll be able to carry on without me. I could be here in a day or two. I'll first have to make some notes of developments that I am working on so they'll have that input. Then, as long as they can contact me in the future, I could transfer here almost immediately. The end of this week if you want. The work there is important—but not as important as this. If you would let me I would like to develop this Expert Program for you. And keep myself available for further work on the AI. Is that agreeable?"

"Perfect. I'll organize all the material so you can access it at once. And I'm going to kick myself around the block for not thinking of it myself. An investigation like this one is mostly a dumb, boring, sorting of facts and running down endless leads. Which is a job for a computer—not for a human being."

"I couldn't agree more. I'll be back as soon as I can. And thank you again for asking me."

They stood when she did, shook hands, watched her leave—as did the marine guard who allowed only his eyes to follow her.

"She is one hundred percent right about that program to solve the Megalobe crime," Brian said. "If we can get my first AI back it will make my job an awful lot easier."

"Your job will be a lot easier if you stay alive. I want to stop the attacks—and solve the case."

"When you put it that way—I agree."

# 20

## February 15, 2024

Benicoff looked at his watch. "The good news is that as of today you're out of this hospital. Dr. Snaresbrook says that you are fit as a fiddle. You ready to make the move?"

"I'm ready whenever you are—and rarin' to go," Brian said, closing and locking the suitcase and putting it on the floor next to his computer. "How about this case! Looks like leather—but it's made of cross-linked teflar and boron nitride filaments. Can't rip or tear and will last forever. A present from Dr. Snaresbrook . . ."

Ben sighed. "I know. She curled her lip with scorn when she discovered that I had brought your clothes here in a plastic bag. And that you were happy enough to carry them away again in the same bag." He glanced at his watch. "We have some time yet. That's the good news."

"Now what's the bad news?"

"About your assistant. The MIT post-doc lead didn't work out. He was qualified all right—except he was married with three kids and no way was he going to leave Boston."

Brian rubbed at his jaw and frowned. "Then—that means that the Captain gets the job?"

"On paper she is equally good. If you want her and think that she's qualified. The decision is yours. I'll go on looking for more candidates if you want me to."

"I don't know, Ben—I guess that I am just being stupid. If the Captain, Shelly, were a man I wouldn't hesitate for a second. It's a gut feeling, nothing else." Ben was silent, leaving the decision up to Brian. Who paced the length of the room, came back and dropped into the chair.

"She's good?"

"None better."

"I'm being sexist?"

"I didn't say that. The decision is still yours."

"She stays then. How is she coming with the Expert Detection Program?"

"Very well. You want her to tell you about it?"

"Sure—as soon as it gets rolling. And it will give me a chance to see how she works."

Ben looked at his watch again. "It's time. I'll phone down and let them know we're ready. And I want you to meet the man who will be in charge of your security. Name of Wood. Very experienced, very reliable. I don't say that lightly because your life might very well depend upon him. I think—no, I know that he is the best."

Major Wood knocked and entered. A big man, built like a boxer with a narrow waist and wide shoulders. The scar on his right cheek made a ridge on his black-brown skin, ran down to his mouth and tucked up the corner of it to give him a tiny perpetual grin.

"Brian, this is Major Wood, who is in charge of security now at Megalobe."

"Pleased to meet you, Brian. If it is going to be first names my friends call me Woody. But not in front of the troops. We're going to take good care of you. Better than the last bunch." His nostrils flared slightly with anger. "The only thing good about the security that they used to have at Megalobe is that we can learn from their mistakes. Their one *big* mistake."

"Tell me," Benicoff said. "I'm still investigating what happened."

"Security is people—not machines. Anything one man can build another man can trick. Of course I'm going to use all the security apparatus that has been built in and installed there—plus some additions of my own. Machines and wire fences help. But it will be my men who will be guarding you and the others, Brian. *That* is security."

"I feel better already," Brian said—truthfully.

"Then stay that way," Dr. Snaresbrook said as she entered. "This is going to be a stressful day whether you realize it or not. Five hours maximum—then you lie down. Understood?"

"Do I have a choice?"

"No." Her smile softened the imperiousness of her command. "I'll give you a few days to get into your work. I'll need that time to move my equipment to the Megalobe infirmary. Since you won't be coming to this hospital anymore we'll do the machine sessions there. See if we can give you access to all those technical memories you are going to need. Now—take care of yourself."

"I will, Doc—don't worry."

"Are you ready?" Major Wood asked as soon as she had gone.

"Just waiting for orders."

"That's the correct attitude. Do what I say and you'll get there safely—and will stay safe. *Sergeant.*"

The soldier entered the room an instant after the sharp-barked command and handed the Major one of the two stubby, ugly automatic weapons he was carrying. Benicoff grabbed up Brian's bag and computer and they all left together.

Although this trip lacked the showiness of the Marine transfer that had brought Brian to the hospital, everything still proceeded with professional efficiency. A squad of soldiers moved into place, surrounding them when they walked down the hall; others kept pace before and behind. The officers' parking lot had been cleared of all vehicles—despite a lot of high-level protests—and a large transport copter now sat in the middle of it with its rotors turning. It lifted off as soon as they had all climbed in. Fast attack choppers circled them as they rose, getting altitude before they headed across the bay and over the sweep of streets and homes of San Diego. They followed the freeway west, then turned and went even higher to get over the mountains. It was a beautiful, sunny day with visibility apparently unlimited.

Away from the hospital at last, Brian felt elated and confident. He liked the view, first the craggy and bare mountains, then the parched colors of the desert beyond. They passed over the buildings and golf courses of Borrego Springs, then on to the desert. The slashed and desolate badlands drifted by below, then greenery appeared ahead. The squared-off area of low buildings and grassy plots grew larger as they dropped down toward it, settling easily onto the helipad. The attack copters dipped in one last protecting circle, then hurtled away—tracked automatically by the SAM radar. A soldier opened the copter's door.

Brian climbed out with no qualms, no fear. He would never remember what had happened to him here, was confident that it would not happen in this place again. What he wanted to do most was to get to work.

"Want to see your quarters?" the Major asked. Brian shook his head.

"Later if you don't mind. The lab first."

"You're the man. Your personal gear will be in your room. I'll walk you about today so the troops can see you."

"No ID needed?"

"Everyone else is going to be heavy with it. You don't need it. All the security is designed with one end in mind—keeping you safe. I hope that you will get to know the men. They're a good team. But right now it is more important that they know you. If you will just wait here for a minute I'll be right back and we will get started."

He moved quickly away toward the buildings. Ben pointed.

"That's the lab building," he said. "The big one with the gold-sputtered windows. Your own lab entrance is around the back, a special wing."

"It looks great! You know—I really can't wait to get my hands on more computer power, to debug the new systems described in the notes. I have already worked up some opening programs on the portable—but it simply isn't adequate for the kind of debugging I need to do. I need much more speed than that old portable laptop has. And much more memory. I am using some extremely large knowledge bases—which must be maintained in memory. Without memory, there can be no knowledge. And without knowledge, there can be no intelligence—I should know!"

"Are you saying that intelligence is just memory?" Ben said. "I can't believe that."

"Well, something like that, but without the 'just.' As far as I'm concerned, you need two kinds of things for thought to proceed—and both are based on memory. I don't care if it's a man or machine. First you need your processes—the programs to do the actual work. And you need the stuff that those programs will work on—that's your knowledge, your records of your experiences. And both the programs themselves and the knowledge they use must be embodied in memory."

"I can't argue with that," Benicoff said. "But surely, you'd also need something else, beyond the purely mechanical. The *me* that is me must still be around even when I'm not using my memory."

"What use would a *me* be if it doesn't actually do anything?"

"Because without it, we'd just have a computer. Working, but not feeling. Speaking, without understanding. Surely thinking must involve more than the simple processing of memory. There must also be something to initiate the wanting and intending—and then there must be something to appreciate whatever is accomplished and then to want something more. You know, the central spirit-thing that seems to sit in the center of my head, that understands what things really mean, that's aware of itself and of what it can do."

Dolly is not the only superstitious person, Brian thought. "Spirit my eye! I don't believe we need any such thing. A machine doesn't need any magic force to make it do whatever it does. Because each present state is sufficient cause to carry it into its subsequent state. If there were that spirit inside your head, it would only be getting in your way. Minds are simply what brains do. The hard part is that, as good as technology is, we cannot make an exact duplicate of the human brain."

"Why not? I thought that was exactly what you were doing."

"Then you thought wrong. We only have to get parts that have similar functions, not exact copies."

"But if you don't duplicate all the details, it won't think the same way, will it?"

"Not exactly—but why should that matter as long as it does the right *sorts* of things? My research is only to discover the general principles, the general patterns of function. Once the machine is able to learn the right sorts of things, it will fill in the small details itself."

"It sounds awfully hard. I'm with you—and don't envy your job."

The Major returned, then led them toward the building. The guard at the door snapped to attention when they approached. But instead of staring directly ahead of him in the approved manner, he turned as they passed, watching Brian closely, remembering.

"I'll take you inside," Major Wood said. He handed Brian an identification bracelet. "But first—I would appreciate it if you would put this on and wear it all the time. It's waterproof and pretty indestructible. I hope you won't mind—but once I lock it on, it will have to be sawn off. It doesn't unlock."

Brian turned it over, saw that his name was engraved on it. "Any particular reason for this?"

"A big one. Squeeze it once and you will get me—twenty-four hours a day. But if you squeeze it for more than one second the alarms go off everywhere and all hell breaks loose. Can do?"

"Can do. Seal it on."

Woody put it on Brian's wrist and joined the open ends together; it closed with a metallic clack. "Give it a try," he said, stepping back. "Be enthusiastic, a little push like that could happen accidentally. That's it." A rapid bleeping sounded from his own communicator; he thumbed it off. "That will do just fine. Now I'll show you the new laboratory—and I hope that you are not claustrophobic."

"Not that I know of—why?"

"I saw the lab where you used to work. It's a disaster—a security shambles. Too accessible in every way. You've got a brand-new one now. Only one entrance. Completely self-contained power supply, air-conditioning, the works. And belowground for the most part. That's the door you're looking at. Most of the equipment has been installed.''

"We were in luck there," Ben said. "We located a Russian technical exchange student who has never been out of Russia—or even out of Siberia—before. He never even considered studying here until we approached him. There is absolutely no chance that he could have been compromised by any industrial espionage agency.''

"I'll get him," the Major said. "If you would wait here a moment.''

He pulled open the unlocked door and went in, returning a moment later accompanied by a tall young man with a full blond beard.

"This is Evgeni Belonenko, who installed all the stuff in there. Evgeni, Brian Delaney—your boss.''

"A great pleasure," he said, speaking with a thick Russian accent. "Fine machines you got here, the best. May I assume that you are prepared to begin operations now?''

"That's the idea.''

*"Koroshow!* Good. I have installed this MHC matching machine here. Wonderful machine! Never saw one before but specs seem clear and complete. Adjust for input first—''

Evgeni had the metal plate in the wall swung open and worked the controls inside it. When he was satisfied he closed the door to the lab and pointed to a black-ringed indentation in the plate.

"Be so kind, Mr. Brian Delaney, to touch your fingertip here. Fine!''

The green light above the opening flashed for a few seconds, then turned red.

"Locked!" Evgeni said, closing the access plate, then pushed on the unyielding door. "Locked—and only you can open it, since it is coded to your DNA. The same goes for this access plate—only you can unlock it to change the DNA." He pushed his own finger into the opening and the light blinked but stayed red. However, when Brian touched it the green indicator flashed and there was a clack as the door unlocked. He pushed it open and they followed him in.

With great enthusiasm Evgeni pointed out all of the equipment that he had installed, the latest computers. Brian looked about but did not recognize most of the machines—finding out about them would be the first order of business. There was a good view from the large window that looked out onto the desert.

"I thought the lab was underground," he said—pointing at the roadrunner that scuttled by.

"It is," Ben said. "That is a five-thousand line high resolution TV screen. The camera is mounted on the wall outside. This screen used to be in the Chairman's office but I thought that it had more practical value here."

"It does, many thanks."

"I'll leave you to it," Major Wood said. "Will you let me out, please, Brian? You are also the only one who can ever open that door. It may be a pain—but it is damn good security."

"No complaints. And thanks for what you have done."

"That's my job. You'll be safe here."

"Okay. Then I better get started working on my old AI ideas. I mean not my ideas, the ideas the old Brian was working on." Many of the sketches were bits of code in a language he did not recognize. It must have been written in some computer language that his earlier self, the old Brian, had designed for the purpose.

Brian walked over to the computer, took the GRAM from his pocket and plugged it in. The screen came to life and the computer spoke with a clear contralto voice.

"Good morning. Will you be operating this machine?"

"Yes. My name is Brian. Speak in a deeper voice."

"Is this satisfactory?" it said, now a deep baritone.

"Yes. Keep it at that." He turned to Evgeni. "Looks good."

"*Is* good. Latest model. Costs millions in Russia except not available there. Boy will I have stories for the hackers in Tomsk when I get home. I got other work to do if you don't need me."

"No, I'm fine. I'll give a shout if I have any questions."

"The same goes for me," Ben said, looking at his watch. "I make it over four hours since we started this trip—which is deadline time."

"What do you mean?"

"Your orders from Dr. Snaresbrook. This is when you stop working for the day and lie down. No excuses accepted, she said—but there is no reason you can't lie down with your portable computer."

Brian knew better than to protest. He gave one last long, lingering look at the laboratory—then led the way to the door and locked them all out. Major Wood was waiting outside.

"Just coming to get you," he said. "I had a call from Dr. Snaresbrook that if you were not yet in your quarters that you were to be taken there immediately."

"We're on the way," Brian said, putting up his hands in surrender. "The long arm of the doctor reaches everywhere."

"You better believe it," Ben agreed. "I'll see you tomorrow."

Brian was not surprised to discover that he was quartered in the barracks with the troops. "Right in the middle of the building," Woody said. "You've got dogfaces on all sides, not to mention the guard stations. Here we are."

The apartment was small but comfortable; sitting room, bedroom, kitchen and bath. His computer was on the worktable and his bag had been unpacked.

"Just pick up the phone when you want dinner—it will be brought up to you. Tonight's meat loaf," the Major added as he closed the door.

# 21

## February 16, 2024

Brian could not fall asleep. It was the excitement of the move, the new bed perhaps, all of the things that had happened that day conspired to keep him awake. At midnight he decided to stop twisting and turning and do something about it. He threw back the covers and got out of bed. The room circuitry detected this, checked the time, then turned on the dimmed lights that were just enough to enable him to walk without stumbling. The medicine chest was not as kind to him. It had been programmed not to let anyone take medicine in the dark—and he blinked in the sudden glare when he opened the door. *If you can't sleep take two with a glass of water,* the doctor had printed on the label. He did as instructed and made his way back to bed.

The dreams began as soon as he fell asleep. Confused happenings, bits of school, Paddy appeared in one of them, Texas sunshine, the glare of the sun on the Gulf. Blinking into its glare. Rising in the morning, setting in the evening. How beautiful, how wrong. Just an illusion. The sun stays where it is. The earth goes around the sun, around and around.

Darkness and stars. And the moon. Moving moon, spinning around the earth. Rising and setting like the sun. But not like the sun. Moon, sun, earth. Sometimes all three lined up and there was an eclipse. Moon in front of sun.

Brian had never seen a total eclipse. His father had, told him about it. Eclipse: La Paz, Mexico, in 1991. On July 11 the day became dark, moon in front of sun.

Brian stirred in his sleep, frowning into the darkness. He

had never seen an eclipse. Would he ever? Would there ever be an eclipse here in the Anza-Borrego desert?

The equation to answer this should be a simple one. Just a basic application of Newton's laws. The acceleration is inverse to the square of the distance.

Each object pulled by the other two.

Sun, earth, moon. A simple differential equation.

With just eighteen variables.

Set up the coordinates.

Distances.

The earth was how far from the sun?

The *Handbook of Astronautics*, figures swimming before him, glowing in the dark.

The distance from the earth to the sun at its nearest point.

The axes and degrees of inclinations of the earth and the moon's orbits . . .

The precise elements of these orbits—their perihelions, velocities and eccentricities.

Figures and numbers clicked into place—and then it happened.

The differential equation began working itself out before him. Within him? Was he watching, living, experiencing? He murmured and twisted but it would not go away or stop.

Streaming by, number by number.

"November 14, 2031," he shouted hoarsely.

Brian found himself shouting, sitting up in bed and soaked with sweat, blinking as the lights came on. He fumbled for the glass of water on the night table, drained most of it and dropped back onto the crumpled bed. What had happened? The experience had been so strong, the racing figures so clear that he could still see them. Too strong to be a dream—

"The IPMC. The implant processors!" he said aloud.

Had that been it? Had he in the dreaming state somehow accessed the computer that had been planted in his brain? Could he possibly have commanded it to run some procedure? Some program for solving the problem? This seemed to be what had happened. It had apparently solved the problem, then fed the solution back to him. Is this what had happened? Why not? It was the most logical, plausible, least frightening explanation. He called out to his computer to turn on, then spoke a description of what had happened into its memory, adding his theory as well. After this he fell into a deep and apparently dreamless sleep. It was well after eight before he woke again. He turned the coffeemaker on, then phoned Dr. Snaresbrook. Her phone answered him and said that she would ring him back. Her call came as he was crunching into a second slice of toast.

"Morning, Doc. I have some interesting news for you." After he finished describing what had happened there was a long silence on the line. "You still there?"

*"Yes, sorry, Brian, just thinking about what you said— and I believe you might very well be right."*

"Then it is good news?"

*"Incredibly good. Look—I'm going to shift some appointments around and see if I can't get out there by noon. Is that all right with you?"*

"Sounds great. I'll be in the lab."

He spent the morning skimming through his recovered backup notes, trying to get a feel for the work he had done, the research and construction—all of the memories the bullet had destroyed. It was a strange sensation reading what he had written, almost a message from the grave. Because the Brian who had written these notes was dead and would remain dead forever. He knew that there was no way that he at the age of fourteen would ever grow into the very same man of twenty who had written this first report, based on several years of research. In the end to build the world's first humanlike intelligence.

Nor could he understand any of the shorthand notes and bits of program that his twenty-year-old self had written. He smiled ruefully at this and turned back to the first page. The only way to proceed was to follow everything, step by step. He would read ahead, whenever he could, to avoid dead ends and false starts. But basically he would have to recreate everything that he had done, do it all over again.

Dr. Snaresbrook phoned him at twelve-thirty when she

arrived: he shut down his work and joined her in the Megalobe clinic.

"Come in, Brian," she said, looking him up and down with a critical eye. "You're looking remarkably fit."

"I'm feeling that way as well. An hour or two reading in the sun every day—and a short walk like you said."

"Eating well?"

"You bet—the army rations are very good. And look at this . . ." He took off his cap and rubbed the fuzz growing there. "A mini crew cut. It'll be real hair one day soon."

"Any pain from the incisions?"

"None."

"Dizziness? Shortness of breath? Fatigue?"

"No, no and no."

"I'm immensely pleased. Now—I want you to tell me exactly what happened, every detail."

"Listen to this first," he said, passing over a disk. "I recorded this just after I had the dream. If I sound sort of stoned it's because I took that sleeping potion you gave me."

"That fact alone is interesting. It was a tranquilizer and that might have been one of the contributing factors to the incident."

Snaresbrook listened to the recording three times, making notes each time. Then she questioneded Brian closely, going over the same ground again and again until she saw that he was tiring.

"Enough. Let's have a cup of coffee and I'll let you go."

"Aren't you going to see if I can do it again—but consciously this time?"

"Not today. Get some rest first—"

"I'm not tired! I was just falling asleep from saying the same things over and over again. Come on, Doc, be a sport. Let's try it now while the whole thing is fresh in my mind."

"You're right—strike while the iron is hot! All right— let's start with something simple. What would be the square of . . . of 123456?"

Brian visualized the number, tried to find somewhere to put it. He pulled and pushed mentally, twisting his thoughts about it. Tried harder, grunted aloud with the effort.

"15522411383936! That's the square, I'm sure of it!"

"Do you know how you did it?" she asked excitedly.

"Not really. It was sort of like groping for a memory, something like a word almost on the tip of one's tongue. Reaching and finding it."

"Can you do it again?"

"I hope so—yes, why not? I don't know how it worked in the dream, but I think that I can do it again. But I have no idea how I do it."

"I think I know what is happening. But in order to verify my diagnosis I'll have to hook you up to the connection machine again. See what is going on in your brain. Will that be all right?"

"Of course. I must find out how this is happening."

She turned on the connection machine while he settled into the chair. The delicate fingers made their adjustments and he leaned back, ordered his thoughts.

"Then here is what we will do." She moved the cursor through the menu on her screen. "Here is an article I downloaded into my computer yesterday from a journal. It's titled 'Protospecialist Intensities in Juvenile Development.' Do you know anything about the subject?"

"I know a bit about what protospecialists are. The nerve centers located in the brain stem that are responsible for most of our basic instincts. Hunger, rage, sex, sleep—things like that. But I don't think that I ever read any article like that."

"You couldn't have, it was only published a few months ago. Then I am going to load it into your implant CPU's memory—under that title." She quickly touched the keys, then turned back to him. "It should be there now. See if you are aware of it. Are you?"

"No, not really. I mean I can remember the title because I just heard it."

"Then try to do what you did a little while ago, what you did in the dream. Tell me about the article."

Brian's lip tightened as he frowned, struggling inside his brain with invisible effort.

"Something—I can't tell. I mean there is something there if I can only get close to it. Get a handle on it . . ." His eyes opened wide and he began to speak, the words tumbling from his lips.

"...as the child grows, each primitive protospecialist grows level after level of new memory and management machinery and, at the same time, each of them tends to find new ways to influence and exploit what the others can do. The result of this process is to make the older versions of those specialists less separate and distinct. Thus, as those different systems learn to share their cognitive attachments, the resulting cross-connections lead to the more complex mixtures of feelings characteristic of more adult emotions. And by the time we're adults, these systems have become too complicated even for ourselves to understand. By the time we've passed through all those stages of development, our grown-up minds have been rebuilt too many times to remember or understand much of how it felt to be an infant."

Brian clamped his lips shut, then spoke again, slowly and hesitantly. "Is that . . . it? What the article was about?"

Dr. Snaresbrook looked at her screen and nodded. "That is not what it was about—that is it word for word. You've done it, Brian! What sensations are connected with it?"

He frowned in concentration. "It's like a real memory, though not exactly. It's there but I don't know all about it. I sort of have to read through it in my thoughts before it is complete, understandable."

"Of course. That's because it is in the computer's memory, not yours. You can access it but you won't understand it until you have gone through it, paying attention to and thinking about what each sentence means. Making the proper sort of links with other things you already know. Only then will you have made the cross-connections that are true understanding."

"No instant plug-in knowledge in the head?"

"I'm afraid not. Memory is made of so many cross-connections, that can be accessed in so many ways, that it is not linear at all like a computer's memory. But once you have gone through it once or twice it will be part of your own memory, accessible at any time."

"It's fun," he said, then smiled. "My goodness, I even

know the page numbers and footnotes! Do you think we could do it with a whole book—or an encyclopedia?''

"I don't see why not, since there is still plenty of memory available in the implant CPU. It would certainly speed up the process of relearning. But—this is such a wonderful thing! Direct access to a computer by thought alone. It is such a wide-open concept with such endless possibilities.''

"And it could help my work. Is there any reason why I couldn't load in all my earlier research notes so I could access them just by thinking about it?''

"No reason that I can think of.''

"Good. It would be nice to have everything there to digest. I'll do it now, upload all of the retrieved notes from my backup GRAM here—'' He yawned. "No, I won't. Tomorrow will be soon enough. I want to think about this a bit in any case. It all takes some getting used to.''

"I agree completely. But this is more than enough for one day. If you are thinking of going back to the lab—don't. You are now through with work.''

Brian nodded agreement. "In all truth I had planned to take a walk, think this new thing out.''

"A good idea—as long as you don't tire yourself.''

He put on his sunglasses before he stepped out in the midday desert glare. An armed corporal opened the door for him, fell in a few paces behind as he spoke softly into his lapel microphone. Other soldiers were out on both flanks, another walking ahead. Brian was getting used to their constant presence, barely noticed it now as he strolled along the path to his favorite bench by the ornamental pool. The Megalobe executive buildings were on the other side of the water, but shielded from sight by the trees and shrubbery. He was the only one who ever seemed to come here and he enjoyed the silence and privacy. He scowled when his phone buzzed. He thought of not answering it, then sighed and unclipped it from his belt.

"Delaney.''

"*Major Wood at reception. Captain Kahn is here. Says you weren't expecting her today but would it be okay to talk to you?*''

"Yes, of course. Tell her I'm at . . ."

*"I know where you are, sir."* There was more than a hint of firmness in the Major's voice at the suggestion that he didn't know Brian's location down to the nearest millimeter. *"I'll escort her to you."*

They came down the path from the main entrance, the wide-shouldered bulk of the Major dwarfing Shelly's small but shapely figure. She wasn't in uniform today and was wearing a short white dress more suitable to the desert climate. Brian stood up when she came close; Woody turned sharply on his heel and left them alone.

"I'm not disturbing your work, am I?" There was a thin line of worry between her eyes.

"Not at all. Just taking a break as you see."

"I should have called first. But I just got back from L.A. and wanted to put you in the picture about progress. I have been working with some of the best investigators in the

CONTOUR MAP OF BORREGO, FROM USGS

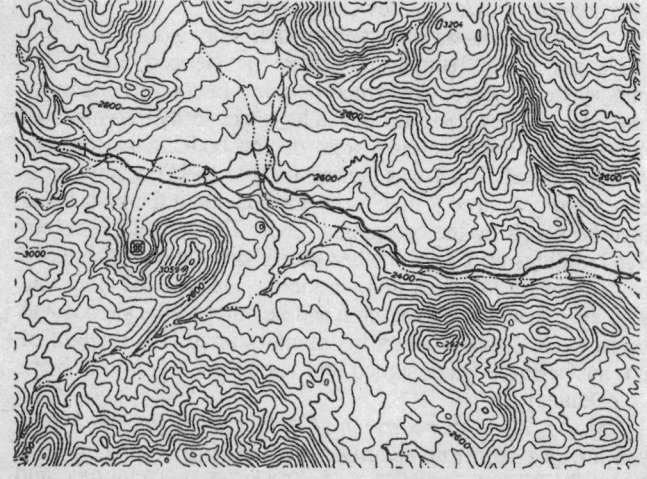

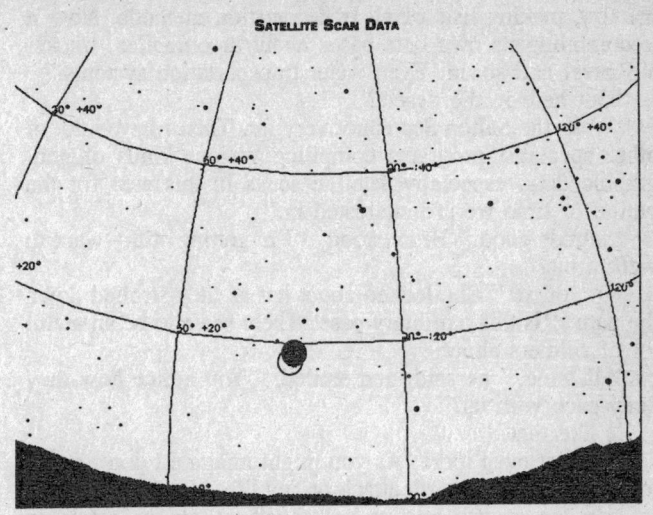

**SATELLITE SCAN DATA**

LAPD. With the kind of work you are doing I'm sure you know all about Expert Systems?''

"I wouldn't say *all*—and I am surely out of touch with work done in the last years. But tell me, what language do you write your programs in?"

"LAMA 3.5."

He smiled. "That's good news. My father was one of the team that developed LAMA, Language for Logic and Metaphor. Is your machine detective up and running?"

"Yes, it is in a working prototype stage. Works well enough to be interesting. I call it 'Dick Tracy.' "

"How does it work?"

"Basically, it is pretty straightforward. Three main sections. The first is a bunch of different Expert Systems, each with a specific job to do. These specialists are controlled by a fairly simple manager that looks for correlations and notices whenever several of them agree on anything. One of them has already searched through data bases all over the country, making lists of all transportation methods. Now it is compiling its own data bases about automobiles, trucks, air travel and so on. Even water transportation systems.''

"Out here in the desert?"

"Well, the Salton Sea is not very far. Then I have a lot of other specialist programs compiling various kinds of geographic data, especially satellite scans in this area for the period of time we are interested in.''

"Sounds good." Brian stood. "I'm getting stiff—want to walk a bit?"

"Of course." She looked about her as they strolled down the path. "Is this a military base? There seem to be an awful lot of soldiers about."

"All mine," he said, and smiled. "You notice how they keep pace with us?"

"I like that."

"I like it even more. As you might imagine I don't really look forward to a fourth attack on my life. Now the question is, can the system you've put together help us catch up with those crooks? Has Dick Tracy come up with hot leads yet?"

"Not really. It is still processing data."

"Then throw it onto a GRAM and bring it here. The big computer that I'm using will give you all the computational power that you could ever need."

"That would really speed things up. I'll need a day or two to pull all the loose ends together." She glanced up at the sun. "I think that I better go now. I am sure that I can get everything finalized by Wednesday, copy all my notes, and bring the GRAM out Thursday morning."

"Perfect. I'll walk you back to the guardhouse—I'm not allowed near the gate—and let Woody know what is happening."

After she had gone he realized that he should have asked her for a copy of LAMA 3.5—then laughed at his stupidity. The days of carrying programs around on disks, other than those that needed top security, were long gone. He headed for the lab. He probably had a copy of the program there on CD ROM. If not he could download from a data base.

This new-old world of 2024 still took some getting used to.

# 22

## February 21, 2024

Benicoff and Evgeni were waiting in front of Brian's lab when he got there in the morning.

"This is Evgeni's last day here and we want to check you out on the whole system before he leaves."

"Back to Siberia, Evgeni?"

"Soon I hope—you got too hot a place here. But first I go to do a bunch of tutorials in Silicon Valley, finish technical instruction on latest hardware. USA make them, Russia buy them, I fix them. Help design next version. Plenty of rubles in Evgeni's future, bet my arse."

"Good luck—and plenty of rubles. What's the program, Ben?" He touched his thumb to the plate and the door clicked open.

"Troubleshooting. All the equipment has been set up and is operating—Evgeni is a great technician."

"Write that out on paper—recommendation worth plenty more rubles!"

"I will, don't worry. But when you go we don't want to have any more technicians around this place."

"Sounds a winner. But what if a massive crash knocks out the whole system?"

"There not one system—is network of couple systems. Each got copy of network program that contains all diagnostic material from every machine. On top of this every memory and diagnostic report is copied from each machine to a couple of others every few minutes.''

''So whatever goes wrong, we should usually be able to recover all the functions. At the worst, we might only lose what was computed in the past few minutes.''

''*Da*. And in most cases, lose nothing at all. ''You got trouble, E-mail to me in . . .''

''*Visitors at the front entrance,*'' the security computer said.

Brian touched an ikon on the screen, and it displayed a view from the outside video pickup. Two soldiers were standing at attention, one on each side of Captain Kahn.

''Back in a minute,'' he said, then walked the length of the lab to the entrance and thumbed open the door for her.

''I hope I'm not too early? The Major told me that you were already here.''

''No, perfect timing. Let me show you your terminal and get you set up. I guess you'll want to download your program and files first.''

She took a GRAM out of her purse. ''All in here. I didn't want to send them through public lines. This is now the only copy—the rest has been wiped from the police computer. There is an awful lot of classified material that we don't want anyone else looking at.''

He led the way through the lab to a partitioned office at the far end.

''Just the terminal, desk and chair here now,'' he said. ''Let me know if there is anything else you might need.''

''This will be fine.''

''Done,'' Ben said, standing and stretching. ''I double-checked and Evgeni has done a great job. All the instructions for accessing and using the programs are right here in RAM.''

''I want to see that—but can you wait half a mo'? Shelly just came in and we can talk to her as soon as she has downloaded her Expert Program. This is a good chance for us to find out how far she has gotten.''

They walked Evgeni to the entrance, where he pumped their hands strenuously.

''Good equipment, good fun working here!''

"Good luck—and plenty rubles."

"*Da!*"

Shelly turned around in her chair when they came in and pointed to the empty office.

"Sorry about the hospitality."

"I'll get a couple of chairs," Ben said. "And some coffee. Anyone else interested? No? Two chairs then and one coffee."

"Any results to tell us about?" Brian said.

"Some. I have written the program to link the data-base manager with the discovery program and the human interface. It is mostly—I hope—debugged. I started it up with the goal of solving the Megalobe robbery. It has been running now for a couple of days. By now it might be ready to answer some questions. I held off until you were both here at the same time. This is your investigation, Ben. Do you want to go ahead?"

"Sure. How do I get into the program?"

"I started out using a working label of 'Dick Tracy'—and it stuck, I'm afraid. That and your name are all you need."

"All right." Ben turned to the terminal. "My name is Benicoff and I am looking for Dick Tracy."

"Program on line," the computer said.

"What is your objective?"

"To locate the criminals who committed the crime in the laboratory of Megalobe Industries on February 8, 2023."

"Have you located the criminals?"

"Negative. I have still not determined how exit was accomplished and how the stolen material was removed."

Brian listened in awe. "Are you sure that this is only a program? It sounds like a winner of the Turing test."

"Plug-in speech program," Shelly said. "Right off the shelf. Verbalizes and parses from the natural language section of the CYC system. These speech programs always seem more intelligent than they are because their grammar and intonation are so precise. But they don't really know that much about what the words mean." She turned back to Ben. "Keep querying it, Ben, see if it has come up with any answers. You can use ordinary language because it has a large lexicon of criminal justice idioms.''

''Right. Tell me, Dick Tracy, what leads are you exploring?''

''I have reduced the search to three possibilities. One, that the stolen material was hidden nearby for later retrieval. Two, that is was removed by surface transportation. Three, that it was removed by air.''

''Results?''

''Hidden nearby, very unlikely. Surface transportation more probable. However removal by air is the most likely when all factors are considered.''

Benicoff shook his head and turned to Shelly. ''What does it mean by most likely? Surely a computer can do better than that, give us a percentage or something.''

''Why don't you ask it?''

''I will. Dick Tracy—be more precise. What is the probability of removal by air?''

''I prefer not to assign an unconditional probability to a situation with so many contingencies. For this kind of situation it is more appropriate to estimate by using fuzzy distributions rather than deceptively precise-seeming numbers. But plausibility summaries on a scale of one to one hundred can be provided if you insist.''

''I insist.''

''Hidden nearby—three. Removed by surface transportation— twenty-one. Removed by air—seventy-six.''

Ben's jaw dropped. ''But—suspend program.'' He turned to the others, who were as astonished as he was. ''We've investigated the air theory very thoroughly and there is just no way they could have flown the stuff out of here.''

''That's not what Dick Tracy says.''

''Then it must know something that we don't know.'' He turned back to the computer. ''Resume operation. What is basis for estimate of removed-by-air estimate?''

The computer was silent for a moment. Then, ''No summary of basis is available. Conclusion based on weighted sum of twelve thousand intermediate units in discovery program's connectionist evaluation subsystem.''

''That's a common deficiency of this type of program,''

Shelly explained. "It's almost impossible to find how it reaches its conclusions—because it adds up millions of small correlations between fragments of data. It's almost impossible to relate that to anything we might call reasoning."

"It doesn't matter—because the answer is wrong." Benicoff was irritated. "Remember—I was in charge of the investigation. The airport here at the plant is completely automated. Most of the traffic is copters, though we get executive jets as well as cargo VTOLs and STOLs."

"How does an automatic airport work?" Brian asked. "Is it safe?"

"Safer than human control, I can assure you. It was finally realized back in the 1980s that more accidents were being caused by human error than were being prevented by human intervention. All aircraft must file flight plans before takeoff. The data goes right into the computer network so every airport knows just what traffic is going out or coming in—or even passing close by. When an aircraft is within radar range a signal identifies them by transponder and they are given clearance or instructions. Here at Megalobe all of the aircraft movements are of course monitored and recorded by security."

"But security was compromised for that vital hour."

"Doesn't matter—everything was also recorded at the Borrego airport control tower, as well as the regional FAA radar station. All three sets of records agree and the technical investigation proved that it would have been impossible to alter all of them. What we saw were true records of all aircraft movements that night."

"Were there any flights in or out of the airport during that hour?"

"Not one. The last flight was at least an hour before the blank period, a copter to La Jolla."

"How big an area does the radar cover?" Brian asked.

"A lot. It's a standard tower unit with a range of about one hundred and fifty miles. From Borrego it reaches out right to the Salton Sea to the east and across it to the hills beyond. Forty, fifty miles at least. Not as far in the other directions with all the hills and mountains that surround this valley."

"Dick Tracy, activate," Shelly said. "During the day in question, twenty-four hours, how many flights were recorded by the Megalobe radar?"

"Megalobe flights, eighteen. Borrego Springs Airport, twenty-seven. Passing flights, one hundred and thirty-one."

"Borrego Springs is just eight miles away," Shelly said, "but they had no flights in or out during the period in question, none that night at all. All three sets of radar records were identical, except for inconsequential minor differences, on all the passing flights. These are flights that are detected at the radar fringes that don't originate or end in the valley."

"There seems to be a lot of air traffic out here in the desert," Brian said. "One hundred and seventy-six in one day. Why?"

"Business flights to Megalobe we know about," Ben said. "Borrego Springs has a few commercial flights, the rest are private planes. The passing stuff is the same, plus some military. So we are back to zero again. Dick Tracy says that the stuff left by air. Yet there were no flights out of the valley. So how could it have got out of the valley? Answer that and you have the answer to the whole thing."

Ben had phrased the question clearly. *How could it have got out of the valley?* There was a paradox here; it had to go out by air, nothing went out by air. Brian heard the question.

His implanted CPU heard the question as well.

"Out of the valley by truck. Out of the area by air," Brian said.

"What do you mean?" Shelly asked.

"I don't know," he admitted. "I didn't say that, the CPU did." He tried not to smile at their blank expressions. "Look, we'll go into that some other time. Right now let's analyze this. How far could the truck have gone?"

"We worked out a computer model early in the investigation," Ben said. "The maximum number of men to have loaded the truck, without getting in each other's way, is eight. The variables are driving time from the gate to the lab, loading time, back to the gate. Once out of the gate the best figure we could come up with was twenty-five miles distance at fifty-five miles an hour. There were roadblocks up on every road out of here as soon as the crime was reported, well outside that twenty-mile zone. Radar covered the area as well, from copters and ground units, and after dawn the visual searches began. The truck could not have escaped.''

"But it did," Shelly said. "Is there any way a truck *and* cargo could have been airlifted out? We don't know—but we are sure going to find out. Let me at the computer, Ben. I am going to have this program check every flight recorded that day within a hundred- then a two-hundred-mile radius."

"Couldn't the criminals have gotten records of that flight erased? So there would be no traces at the time of the crime?"

"No way. All the radar signals are maintained for a year in FAA archives, as well as screen-dumps from each air traffic controller's terminal. A good computer hacker can do many wonderful things, but the air traffic system is simply too complex and redundant. There are hundreds, maybe thousands, of different kinds of records of every detected flight."

Shelly did not look up, was hard at work, oblivious of them as they left.

"Shelly doesn't know about the implant CPU," Ben said. "Was that what you were talking about?"

"Yes. I haven't had a chance to tell you, but Dr. Snaresbrook and I have had some success in my accessing the CPU by thought alone."

"That is—what can I say—incredible!"

"That's what we think. But it is early times yet. I have instructed it to do some math—that's how it started, in a dream, would you believe it? And I read data from its memory files. It is all exciting and a little frightening. Takes some getting used to. I have a strange head and I'm not sure I like it."

"But you're alive and well, Brian," Ben said grimly. "I saw what that bullet did to you . . ."

"Don't tell me about it! Someday, maybe. In fact I would like to forget this for a while, get on with AI. And you and Shelly get on with your Dick Tracy program. I don't like hiding—or the perpetual threat to my life. I'm beginning to feel like Salman Rushdie—and you remember what happened to him! I would like to, what can I say, rebuild my life. Be as normal as the rest of you. I'm beginning to feel like some kind of freak—''

''No, Brian—don't ever think that. You are a tough kid that has been through too much. Everyone who has worked with you admires your guts. We're on your side.''

There was little more that could be said. Ben mumbled an excuse and left. Brian punched up yesterday's work where he had been transcribing his notes in more complete and readable form but it made no sense to him. He realized that he was both depressed and tired and could hear Dr. Snaresbrook's voice giving the obvious order. Right, message received, lie down. He told Shelly that he would be back later and went to his rooms.

He must have fallen asleep because the technical journal was lying on his chest and the sun was just dropping behind the mountains to the west. The black depression still possessed him and he wondered if he should call the doctor and report it. But it just didn't seem serious enough. Maybe it was the room that was getting him down—he was spending more time alone here than he had in the hospital. At least there someone was always popping in and out. Here he even had to eat his meals alone; the novelty of this had worn off quickly.

Shelly had finished for the day and she mumbled goodbye when she left, her thoughts involved in her work. He locked her out and went in the opposite direction. Maybe some fresh air would help. Or some food, since it was getting dark and he had forgotten to eat lunch again. He left the building and walked around the lake and toward the orderly room. He asked if the Major was in—and was taken at once to his office.

''Any complaints—or recommendations?'' Woody asked as soon as they were alone.

''No complaints, and I think your troops are doing a tremendous job. They never seem to get in the way, but when I am out of the lab there always seem to be a few in sight.''

''There are a lot more than a few, I assure you! But I'll tell them what you said. They are trying hard and doing damn well at this assignment.''

"Tell the cooks that I like the food too."

"The chow hall will be delighted."

"Chow hall?"

"That's another name for the mess hall."

"Mess?"

Woody smiled. "You're a civilian at heart. We've got to teach you to talk like a dogface."

"Bark you mean?" They both laughed. "Woody, even though I'm not in the Army—is there a chance that a civilian dogface could have a meal in your chow hall?"

"You're more than welcome. Have all your meals there with the grunts if you like."

"But I'm not in the Army."

The Major's perpetual twisted grin widened at the thought. "Mister, you *are* the Army. You are the only reason that we are here and not jumping out of planes every day. And I know that a lot of the troops would like to meet you and talk to you." He glanced up at the time readout on the wall. "Do you drink beer?"

"Is there a Pope in Rome?"

"Come along, then. We'll have a brew in the club until the chow hall opens at six."

"There's a club here? That's the first I heard."

Woody stood and led the way. "A military secret which, I would appreciate, you didn't word about among the Megalobe civilian types. As far as I can find out the entire establishment is dry outside these walls. But this building right now is a military base for my paratroop unit. All army bases have an officer's club, separate ones for the NCOs and E.M. as well—" He saw Brian's eyes widen. "The military probably invented acronyms, they love them so much. Noncommissioned officers and enlisted men. This unit is too small for all that boozing discrimination—so we got this all-ranks club."

He opened the door marked SECURITY AREA—MILITARY PERSONNEL ONLY and led the way inside. It wasn't a big room, but in the few weeks that the paratroopers had been here they had managed to add some personal touches. A dart board on one wall, some flags, guidons and photographs—a nude girl on a poster with impossibly large breasts—tables and chairs. And the bottle-filled, beer-pump-sporting bar at the far end.

"How about Tiger beer from Singapore?" Woody asked. "Just tapped a fresh keg."

"Never heard of it, much less tasted it. Draw away!"

The beer was cold and delicious, the bar itself fascinating. "Some of the troops will be coming in soon, they'll be happy to meet you," Woody said, drawing two more glasses. "There is only one thing that I'll ask of you—don't talk about your work. None of them will speak to you about what goes on in the laboratory—that order is out—so please don't volunteer. Hell, even I don't know what you are doing in there—nor do I want to know. Top Secret, we've been told, and that's all the orders we need. Other than that, shoot the breeze."

"Shoot the breeze! My vocabulary grows apace!"

Soldiers, some of whom he recognized from their guard duties, came in one by one. They seemed please to meet him personally at last, to shake his hand. He was their age, in fact older than most, and he listened with pleasure to their coarse military camaraderie—heard heroic bragging about sexual prowess and learned some fascinating vulgarities that he had never dreamed existed. And all the time he was listening he never let on that he was only fourteen years old. He was growing up faster every moment!

They told stories and old, familiar jokes. He was included in the talk and was asked what part of the States he came from, phrased politely but with the implication that they were puzzled about his brogue. The soldiers of Irish descent were full of questions and they all listened eagerly when he told them about growing up in Ireland. Later they went into dinner together—getting him a line tray and supplying him with plenty of advice on what to eat and what to avoid.

All in all it was an enjoyable evening and he resolved to eat in the mess hall again, whenever he could. What with all the talk and friendliness, what the Irish called good crack— not to forget all the beers either, he had pulled completely out of the glooms. The grunts were a great bunch of government-issue dogfaces. He would still start the day alone with coffee and toast, since he hated to talk to anyone first thing in the morning. And he had got into the habit of making himself a sandwich to take to the lab for lunch.

But he was going to join the human race for dinner just as often as he could. Or at least that portion of it represented by the 82d Airborne. Come to think of it the human race really was well represented there. White and black, Asian and Latin. They were all good guys.

He went to sleep smiling. The dreams did not bother him this night.

# 23

---

## February 22, 2024

Brian was sitting on the edge of the decorative planter when Shelly came out of the Megalobe visitors' quarters the next morning.

"How is it in there?" he asked as they started toward the lab, the attendant bodyguards walking before and behind.

"Spartan but comfortable. The place was obviously designed for visiting salesmen and executives who manage to miss the last plane of the day. Fine for overnight—but a little grim by the second evening. Still, not too different from the first air force barracks I ever stayed in. I can stick it out for a few days at least."

"Have they found you a better place to stay?"

"Megalobe Housing Advisors is on the job. They are taking me to see an apartment right down the road. Three this afternoon."

"Good luck. How is Dick Tracy doing?"

"Keeping me busy. I had no idea before I started running this program that there were so many data bases in the country. I suppose it is Murphy's Law of computers. The more memory you have the more you fill it up."

"You'll have quite a job filling up this mini-mainframe here."

"I'm sure of that!"

He unlocked the lab door and held it so she could go by. "Will you have some time to work with me today?" he asked.

"Yes—if an hour from now is okay. I have to get permission to access some classified data bases that Dick Tracy wants to look at. Which will probably lead me to even more classified information."

"Right." He turned away and hadn't gone a dozen steps before she called after him.

"Brian! Come see this." She was studying the screen closely, touched a key and a copy emerged from the printer. She handed it to him. "Dick Tracy has been working all night. I found this displayed when I came in just now."

"What is it?"

"A construction site in Guatay. Someone was building prefabricated luxury apartments there. Dick T. has pointed out the interesting fact that this construction is taking place almost directly under the flight path for the planes landing at the San Diego Airport in Miramar."

"Am I being dumb? I don't see the connection . . ."

"You will in a second. First off, with that much air traffic, people in the area tend to treat aircraft sounds as if they were some kind of constant background noise—like surf breaking on the beach. After a while you just don't hear it. Secondly, because of the difficulty of getting to the building site—it's very scenic but is halfway up a cliff—the prefab sections were brought in by freight copter. One of those monster TS-69s. They can lift twenty tons."

"Or a loaded truck! Where's your contour map?"

"The program has access to a complete set of satellite and geodetic survey topographic data bases." She turned back to the terminal. "Dick Tracy—show me composite contour map and suspected route."

The color graphics were clear and crisp and so realistic they might have been filmed from the air. The program displayed an animation of a vehicle traversing the route, as seen from above, complete with compass headings and altitude. The dotted trace stretched across the screen and ended with a flickering Maltese cross in a flat field next to Highway S3.

"Let's have the radar view from Borrego Springs Airport." Another beautiful graphic, as good as a photograph, but this time seen from the ground. "Now superimpose the landing site."

The Maltese cross reappeared—apparently, deep inside the mountain.

"That is the suggested landing site. Anything further east would be detected by the Borrego Springs radar. This site is on the other side of the hills—in radar shadow. Now superimpose the flight path." The dotted line stretched out across the screen.

"And all of the suggested flight path is behind the mountains and hills!" Shelly said triumphantly. "The chopper could have left the building site and flown to that field, could have been waiting there when the truck arrived— picked it up and flown back along the same track with it."

"What about the radar at the airport here at Megalobe?"

The view of the mountains was slightly different on this display—but the computed track was the same; completely out of sight.

"The next and important question—how long would it take to drive from here to that pickup spot?"

"The program should be able to tell us—it has a data base of all the delivery vehicles in the area."

She touched the graphic image of the vehicle with her finger and a display window appeared beneath it. "Sixteen to twenty minutes driving time from here, the variable being the speed of the truck. Let's call it sixteen, then, because they would move as fast as they could without drawing attention."

"This could be it! I must call Benicoff."

"Done already. I had the computer get a call out with instructions to tell him that he is wanted here at once. Now let us find out how far the copter could have gone with the truck in those vital twenty minutes.''

"You are going to have to check all the radar units on the other side of the mountains that might cover that area."

Shelly shook her head. "No need—Dick T. did that already. It is on the fringe of San Diego Miramar. There is a chance that their peripheral radar records would not be kept this long—but as you said about computer memory. Until it fills up no one seems to notice. The programs now never erase memory drastically. Instead, when a memory or data bank is nearly full the lowest-priority data is overwritten. So there is always a chance that some of the old stuff is retained."

Ben arrived forty minutes later; Brian let him in. "I think we may have found it, Ben. A way for the truck to get out of the valley inside that vital hour. Come look."

They ran the graphics again for him, all of them wrapped in silence while the possibilities were explored on the screen. Ben slammed his fist into his palm when they were done, jumped up and paced the room. "Yes, of course. This could certainly be the way that was done. The truck left here and went to that spot to meet the copter—which probably didn't even land. Shackles would have been mounted on the truck to fit the lifting gear. Drive up, click on—and lift off. Then a flight through these passes and out of the valley to a remote landing site on the other side of the mountains. Someplace where they wouldn't be seen—but close enough to a road of some kind that would lead them to a highway. Which means that instead of moving at road speed the truck would be doing a hundred forty miles an hour and they would be long gone from the search well before the roadblocks went down. Trundling along the freeway with thousands of other trucks. The ice-cold trail has suddenly warmed up."

"What do you do next?" Brian asked.

"There can't be too many places to set down so we should be able to find the one they used. Then we do two things—and both at the same time. The police will search along the entire area under the flight path, finger-search any possible landing sites. They will look for marks, tracks, witnesses who may have seen or heard something that night.

They will search for any kind of evidence at all that this is what really happened. I'll supervise that myself."

"But this is a careful bunch of crooks. Surely, they would hide all the evidence, cover all the tracks."

"I don't think there'd be much chance of that. We're talking desert here, not well-developed real estate, and it's very fragile ecology. Even a scratch on the desert floor can take several decades to disappear. While that's being done, the FBI will be going through the building company records and those of the copter rental firm. Now that we know where to look—and if we are correct—we will be able to find signs, find a trail, and find *something*. Let me out, Brian."

"You betcha. Going to keep us informed—?"

"The instant we uncover anything at all your phone is going to ring. Both your phones." He patted the computer terminal. "You're a great dick, Dick Tracy."

"I'll leave the program running," Shelly said when Brian had locked Ben out and had returned. "It has taken us this far—but it probably can't go any further until we have some new input. You said earlier you had some work you wanted me to do with you today."

"I did, but it can wait. I am really going to have trouble concentrating until Ben calls back. What I can do is show you the basic setup that we will be assembling. I have most of the AI body here, but it's as brainless as a Second Lieutenant."

"Brian! Where on earth did you pick up a phrase like that?"

"Oh, television I guess. Come along." He turned quickly away so she would not see his face redden. He was going to have to be a bit more careful with his new G.I. expressions. In the excitement of the moment he had completely forgotten that Shelly was an Air Force officer. They went into Brian's lab.

"My goodness—what's that?" she said, pointing to the strange object standing on the workbench. "I've never seen anything like it before."

"It's easy to understand why. There can't be more than a

half dozen in existence. The latest advance in microtechnology."

"Looks more like a tree pulled out of the ground—roots and all." It was a good description. The upper part really did resemble a bifurcated tree trunk with its two multiply jointed metal stalks, each about a foot long, sticking up into the air. Each stalk was tipped with a metal globe that looked very much like a Christmas tree ornament. The two lower stalks were far different. They each divided in two—and each half split in two again. Almost endlessly because with each division the branches became smaller until they were as thin as broom straws.

"Metal brooms?" Shelly asked.

"They do look like that, in a way, but it is something far more complex than that. This is the body that our AI will use. But I'm not too concerned about the AI's physical shape now. Robot technology is pretty modular, almost a matter of taking parts off the shelf. Even computer components are modular."

"Then software is your main concern."

"Exactly. And it's not like conventional programming but more like inventing the anatomy of a brain: which sections of cortex and midbrain are interconnected by which kinds and what size bundles. Truthfully, very much the same sorts of bundles that had to be restored in my own brain operation."

Shelly was aware of the pain behind his words, changed the subject quickly. "I don't see any wires. Does that mean you're sending the information directly to each joint?"

"Yup. All modules are linked into a wireless communication network. Plenty of channels and plenty of speed. The trick is that each joint is almost autonomous. Has its own motors and sensors. So each of them needs only a single power wire."

"I love it. Mechanically it looks amazingly simple. If any joint malfunctions, just replace that section—and nothing else has to be changed. But the software operating system must be awfully complicated."

"Well, yes and no. The code itself is truly horrible, but most of it is constructed automatically by the LAMA operating system. Watch this. I have a good part of that working already.''

Brian went to the terminal on the bench and brought up the control program, then touched the keys. On the bench the telerobot stirred and hummed. There was a rustle as the circuitry activated the joints, causing them to straighten. Irises opened on the two metal spheres, revealing the lenses behind them. They moved back and forth in a test pattern, then were still. Shelly walked over and looked closely at the charge coupled pickups.

''It's just a suggestion—but I think that three eyes would be better than two.''

''Why?''

''There are errors that two-eye stereo can make. The third eye adds error-checking ability. And it can see more of a subject, making it easier to locate and identify things.'' She walked around the machine. ''Looks like you gave it everything here except a brain.''

''Right—and that's what comes next.''

''Great. Then where do we start?''

''At the very beginning. My plan is to follow the original notes. First we provide the system with a huge reservoir of preprogrammed commonsense knowledge. Then we'll add in all the additional programs it will need to do all its various jobs. And enough extra alternative units—including the managers—so that the system will continue to work even if some units fail. Designing an artificial mind is like evolving an animal—so my plan is to use the principles that evolved to manage the brain. That way, we'll end up with a system that is neither too centralized nor too diffusely distributed. In fact I'm already using some of those ideas right here with Robin-1.''

''Why did you give it that name?''

''That's what it was called in the notes—apparently an acronym for 'robot intelligence.' ''

''You said you already had some of your society-of-managers system on line. Could you show me more of how it works? Because the sub-programs in my Dick Tracy system have managers too—but never more than one manager for each program. With more than one manager I wouldn't know where to put the blame when anything fails. Won't it be almost impossible to make such a system work reliably?"

"On the contrary, it should make that easier to do, because each of the managers works closely with other alternative managers, so that when any one of them starts to fail another one can take over. It will be easier to explain after I finish repairing this connector. Would you please hand me that clipper?"

Shelly went over to the workbench and brought Brian the tool.

"What did you just do?" Brian asked her.

"I handed you the clipper. Why do you ask?"

"Because I want you to explain how you got it."

"What do you mean? I simply walked over to the workbench and brought it back to you."

"Simply, yes—but how did you know how far away it was?"

"Brian—are you trying to be difficult? I looked over and saw it on the bench."

"I'm not being difficult. I'm only making a point. How did you decide to walk, instead of simply reaching for it?"

"It was too far out of reach, that's why."

"And how did you know that?"

"Now you're being stupid. I could see how far it was. About two meters. Much too far to reach."

"Sorry, I didn't mean to seem obtuse. I meant to ask you for a theory of how you did it. That is, I'm asking what mechanism in your brain figured out the distance from your hand to the clipper."

"Well, I don't know, really. It was entirely unconscious. But I suppose I used both of my eyes for distance perception."

"Okay, but how does that actually work?"

"Stereoscopic distance perception."

"Are you sure that's how you judged the distance?"

"Not really. It could have been by its apparent size. And I know how far away the bench is as well."

"Exactly. So there are really lots of ways to judge

distance. Robin's brain must work like yours, with managers and submanagers choosing the correct subsystems that apply."

"And you're using the system that's sketched in the notes."

"Yes, and I've managed to make some of it work."

"Have you actually got the agent-modules in your system to learn for themselves?"

"I have. Right now, most of the agents are just small rule-based systems, each with a few dozen rules for invoking the UCSD range-finding processes. The agents learn simply by adding new rules. And whenever agents disagree, the system tries to find a different way that produces less conflict."

The bleep of the telephone interrupted Brian and he put it to his ear.

"Brian here."

*"Benicoff speaking, Mr. Delaney. If you are not busy could you join a meeting here in the executive building? Major Kahn as well. It is a matter of some importance."*

Ben's voice was cold and impersonal. Someone was with him—and something was up.

"We'll be there." He hung up. "It was Ben, a meeting that he says is important. Sounded that way too the way he spoke. He wants us both there."

"Now?"

"Now. Let me power Robin down and we'll see what is going on."

Considering Ben's tone of voice, Brian was not surprised to see the silent figure, flanked by two high-ranking Army officers, sitting at the end of the conference table. When Brian spoke it was with the darkest Wicklow brogue.

"Is that yourself, General Schorcht? Sure and it is? What is a grand man like you wasting his time with the likes of us?"

The General had not forgotten their last meeting in the hospital room, for there was a mean glitter in his cold eyes. He turned back to Benicoff before he spoke.

"How secure is this room?"

"One hundred percent. It has all the built-in safeguards—plus it was swept by the security officer just before we came in."

"You will now explain why you are withholding information from me—and why you refused to explain yourself before these people were present."

"General Schorcht, every situation is not a confrontation," Ben said with studied calm. "We are both on the same side—rather all of us are on the same side. I regret that we have had differences in the past, but let us leave that in the past. You have met Brian before. This is Major Kahn, who is assisting me in my investigation. She wrote the Expert Program that produced the new information, the first breakthrough that we have had in this case. The Major has top security clearance, as I'm sure you will know, since you would have had her investigated as soon as she was attached to the work here. She will outline in detail all of the new developments—as soon as you have told us what you know about the attempts on Brian's life."

"I have told you all you need to know. Major—your report."

Shelly was sitting at attention, starting to speak, when Benicoff raised his hand.

"Just hold that report for a moment, Major. General, as I said before, this is not a confrontational situation. May I remind you of some highly relevant facts. The President himself has put me in charge of this investigation. I am sure that you don't want me to consult him about this—a second time."

General Schorcht remained silent—but his face was a mask of cold hatred.

"Good. I am glad that is clear. If you will check you will discover that Brian has also been cleared for all and any information relating to this case. He—and I—would like to know all of the facts that you have about the two recent attempts on his life. Would you please?" Ben sat back and smiled.

The General was a man of action and knew when he was outflanked and outfought. "Colonel—a full report on those aspects of Operation Touchstone as it relates to this investigation."

"Yes, General." The Colonel picked up the sheaf of papers that rested before him. "Operation Touchstone is a joint operation between the armed forces and the narcotic investigation divisions of a number of countries. It is the culmination of years of work. As you undoubtedly know, due to the reconstruction and development of the inner cities in the last decade, the lower and violent end of the international drug market has effectively been reduced if not eliminated. All of the smaller drug barons have been wiped out, which leaves only two of the largest international drug cartels, virtually governments of their own in their home countries. They have been investigated and penetrated by cooperating agents. We are in the final stages of finally eliminating them. However, completely incidental to this operation, we learned of an approach by a third party with great resources enlisting aid for what I believe is referred to as a 'hit.'"

"The attack on me in the hospital?" Brian said.

"That is correct, sir. Our agent put himself at great risk to warn us. He himself did not know who contacted the organization, he was just aware of the hit contract. Since that time nothing more has been learned relating to this particular situation."

"What do you know about the attack on us in Mexico?" Ben broke in.

"We are sure that the only connection between the two attacks was Mr. Delaney. Since the attackers were never found this is of course supposition. Also, the second attack is not within my jurisdiction . . ."

"I am in charge of that investigation," the second officer said, a grizzled and menacing-looking Colonel. "My name is Davis, Military Intelligence. This concerns us greatly because the leak appears to have originated from inside a military base. A Navy establishment." There was no doubt from his tone of voice how he felt about naval establishments.

"What has your progress been?" Benicoff asked.

"We have some leads that we are following up. However we have found no trace of any connection between the individuals who were in the first and second attacks."

"Let me sum up then," Ben said. "If you add up what the theft at Megalobe and the attacks on Brian have cost—it must be up in the millions. So we know that some very well heeled source hired the hopheads to kill Brian at the hospital. When they did not succeed there, this same source, we assume, tried again in Mexico. Is that correct, Colonel?''

"It conforms to our own estimates of the situation."

"So in reality all we know is that someone with a lot of money has tried to kill Brian twice and has failed both times. Can we assume that this source is also the same one that committed the original attack and theft?''

He waited in silence until he obtained two reluctant and brisk military nods; the General was as stolid as ever.

"Then it would appear that we are all investigating the same people. Therefore I will keep you appraised in the future of our progress—firm in the knowledge that you will be doing the same. Is that agreed, General?''

"Agreed." The word could not have been more reluctantly produced had it been squeezed from a rock. Ben smiled around the table.

"I am glad that we are all on the same side. Major Kahn, will you explain about your Expert Program and the results that it has produced?'' Her report was succinct, clear and brief. When she was done they turned back to Benicoff.

"I took the investigation from there. The results so far are good. Firstly there *was* a flight at that time in that place. It was recorded by San Diego Miramar. The investigators found a cattle rancher who lives under the calculated flight path. He was disturbed by a low-flying chopper—he remembers it because it interfered with the end of a film he was watching on television at the time. We have a perfect time match from the program.''

"You have located the helicopter?'' the General snapped.

"Once we put all the bits and pieces together that was the easiest part. It had to be the TS-69 that was working on the construction site. Any machine from outside the area would have to have filed a flight plan and there was no record of one. The copter rental company's records reveal that on the afternoon of the evening in question there had been an electrical malfunction that temporarily grounded it. The machine did not return to Brown Field where it was based, but remained at the site in Guatay. The following morning mechanics were flown there and the fault, a minor electrical one, was repaired. So minor, I must add, that the pilot himself could have repaired it. A loose connection on one of the instruments."

"Was the machine flown that night?" the General asked.

"According to the records—no," Ben said. "That is the interesting part. Flight records are kept from the pilot's logbook since, unlike an automobile, there is no odometer on an aircraft, nothing to indicate how many miles the thing has flown. But every engine has an hour meter that records how many hours it has been on. And here we did find a discrepancy. The pilot reported no flight that night, that the machine was on the ground and never flew until the next day. That does not match the engine's records. So now we come to the interesting part. The FBI were into the company's records as soon as I reported this possibility to them. They had the pilot in custody within two hours—and this is a recording of an interview I had with him just before I came here."

There was absolute silence as Ben slipped the cassette into the built-in player in the desk. The screen slid down into position on the far wall and the room lights dimmed as he turned it on. The camera had been located behind his head, which could be seen in silhouette. Harsh lights revealed every detail of expression on the face of the man he was talking to.

"Your name is Orville Rhodes?" they heard Ben's voice ask.

"Sure. But nobody calls me that. Dusty, as in Dusty Rhodes, get it? And also, PS, I've told you all this a couple of times already—so how's about you telling me just what the hell I am doing here? Or even who you are. All I know is the FBI dragged me here without a word of explanation. I have my rights."

Dusty was young, strong, angry—good-looking. And he knew it too, a girl's dream the way he brushed his big blond mustache with the back of his hand, tossed his hair back with a quick motion of his head.

"I'll explain it all in a moment, Dusty. A few simple questions first. You are the helicopter pilot employed by SkyHigh Ltd.?"

"You've asked me that too."

"And in January and February of this year you were aiding in the construction of some buildings in Guatay, California."

"About that time, yes, I was working there."

"Good. Tell me about one specific day, Wednesday February 8. You remember that day?"

"Come on mister, whatever the hell your name is, how could I remember any one day in particular all these months later?" Dusty said it with anger—but he moved his eyes about quickly, no longer completely at ease.

"I'm sure you can remember that day. It was one of the three days you were not able to fly because of a sprained wrist."

"Oh, *then,* of course I remember it, why the hell didn't you say so in the first place? I was home drinking beer because the doc said I couldn't fly."

He said it quite sincerely—but a beading of sweat on his forehead could be clearly seen in the harsh lights.

"Who took your place for those three days?"

"Another pilot, company hired him. Why don't you ask them about it?"

"We did. They say that you knew this pilot, Ben Sawbridge, that you recommended him."

"They say that? Maybe they're right. It was a long time ago." He muttered the words, blinked into the lights. He was no longer brushing his sagging mustache. When Ben spoke again his voice was arctic cold.

"Listen to what I have to say, Dusty, before you answer my next question. The doctor's certificate about your sprained wrist was on file with the company. It is a forgery. It is also on record that over the weeks before and after the date in question you cleared up all the overdue payments on your car and made some large deposits in your checking account. These were traced to an out-of-state checking account where a deposit of twenty-five thousand dollars had been made on January 20. Although the account is in a different name the handwriting on the check matches yours. Now, two important questions—who gave you the bribe money and who was the pilot you recommended to take your place those three days?"

"I don't know from any bribery. And that was gambling money, from the off track betting in Tijuana. I sort of didn't want the IRS involved, you know. And the pilot—I already told you. Name of Ben Sawbridge."

"No flying license has ever been issued to a Ben Sawbridge. I want the truth about where the money came from. And I want to know who the pilot is—and you had better think carefully before you answer. This is not a criminal matter yet and no charges have been filed. If charges *are* filed you are in a very distressful position. That chopper was used in a very serious crime. There have been deaths. You will be indicted for complicity. At best you will be convicted of accepting bribes, lying, endangering life. You will lose your flying license, you will be fined and you will go to prison. That is the least that will happen to you. But if you refuse to cooperate I will see to it that you stand trial for murder as well."

"I don't know anything about any murder!"

"It doesn't matter. You were a willing accessory. But that is a worst-case scenario. If you will help me I will help you. If you cooperate completely there is a good chance that this matter might be dropped—if you can lead us to the people who bribed you. Again before you answer—think of this. They made no attempt to hide the bribe or the forged documents. Because they didn't care about you. They knew that this connection would be made sometime—and knew also that the trail would run cold with you."

Dusty's hair was plastered to his wet skin and he rubbed distractedly at his mustache, crumpling and disarraying it. "Can you really get me off?" he finally blurted out.

"Yes, a lesser charge—or perhaps no charge—in exchange for your full cooperation. This can be done. But only if you can tell us anything that could help us in this investigation."

Dusty grinned widely and sat back in his chair. "Well, I can do that for you, do that for certain. I didn't like the little shit who arranged the whole thing. I never met him but he had the smell of real dirty work. Called me and said the money would be deposited in this bank account if I helped him out. I didn't like it but I was but broke. The money was there, I got a signature card in the mail so I could get it out. Once I started using the money he was all over me and there was no way of getting out of it."

"Did he identify himself? Say what this was all about?"

"No. Just told me to follow instructions and not ask questions and the money was mine. One thing I can tell you about him though. He's Canadian."

"How do you know?"

"Christ—how the hell do you think I know? I worked two years in Canada and I know what a goddamned Canuck sounds like."

"Calm down," Benicoff said, an ominous grumble in his voice. "We'll get back to this man later. Now tell me about the pilot."

"You know I didn't want to get involved. I only went along with this whole thing because I really needed the cash. I had a lot of debts and my alimony was really killing me. So you help me—and I'll help you. Get me outta this thing whole and I'll tell you something that they didn't know, what I didn't even know myself until this pilot walked in. I was told to vouch for him and I did just as I had been told. He was a big arrogant old sonofabitch, had gray hair—what was left of it. He had flown in Nam or the Gulf War, you could tell that just by the way that he walked. He looked at me, right through me, but at the same time making believe that he knew me so he could get to fly the chopper. That was the arrangement. I was to say I knew him, to recommend him. And I went along with the whole thing, I was really happy about it then."

Dusty smirked and stretched, touched his knuckle to his mustache. "We made believe that we knew each other because that was part of the deal. But I'll tell you something, the old fart had forgotten, but I *had* seen him once before. And I even remember his name because one of the guys afterwards was bullshitting my ear off about what a hotshot this old guy had been in the old days."

"You know his real name?"

"Yup. But we got to make a deal . . ."

Ben's chair crashed to the floor and he strode forward into the camera's view, seized the pilot by the collar and dragged him to his feet. "Listen you miserable piece of crap—the only deal I make is to send you to jail for life if you don't shout that name out loud—now!"

"You can't."

"I can—and I will!" The pilot's toes were dragging on the floor as Ben shook him like a great rag doll. "The name."

"Let me go—I'll help. A screwball foreign name, that's what it was. Sounded like Doth—or Both."

Ben dropped him slowly back into the chair, leaned forward until their faces were almost touching. Spoke with quiet menace.

"Could it have been Toth?"

"Yes—that's it! Do you know the guy? Toth. A funny name."

The tape ended, and when his recorded voice died away Benicoff spoke aloud.

"Toth. Arpad Toth was head of security here at Megalobe when the events occurred. I checked the Pentagon records at once.

"It appears that he has a brother, by the name of Alex Toth. A helicopter pilot who flew in Vietnam."

# 24

## February 22, 2024

"This is my responsibility now," General Schorcht said, a glint of grim determination in his eye, a touch of cold anger in his voice. "Toth. Alex Toth. An army pilot!"

"That is a very good idea," Ben agreed. "This is on your patch and you have the organization to do it. We will of course keep the investigation going at this end. I suggest that Colonel Davis and I liaise at least once a day, oftener if there are any dramatic developments. We must keep each other fully informed about our mutual progress. Is that satisfactory, General?"

"Satisfactory. Company dismissed."

The two Army officers jumped to their feet, stood at attention, followed the General out.

"And you have a good day too, General," Brian said to the stiff, vanishing backs. "Were you ever in the Army, Ben?"

"Happily, no."

"Do you understand the military mind?"

"Unhappily, yes. But I don't want to be rude in the presence of a serving officer." Ben saw Shelly's grim expression and softened his words with a smile. "A joke, Shelly, that's all. Probably in the worst possible taste—so I apologize.

"No need," she said, returning a slight smile. "I don't know why I should be defensive about the military. I joined rotsee to pay for college. Then I enlisted in the Air Force as the only way to get through graduate school. My parents had a vegetable stand in Farmers Market in L.A. Which for anyone else would have been a gold mine. My father is a great Talmudic scholar but a really lousy businessman. The Air Force enabled me to do the only thing I wanted to do."

"Which leads inexorably to the next generation," Brian said. "Where does the investigation go from here?"

"I'm going to follow up all the leads that the copter development opened," Ben said. "As to the Expert Program, our wizard detective Dick Tracy—that is up to you, Shelly. What's next?"

She poured herself a glass of water from the carafe on the conference table; gave herself a moment to think.

"I'm still running the Dick Tracy program. But I don't expect it to find anything new until we get more data for it."

"Which leaves you with free time—and that means you can work full time on the AI with me," Brian said.

"Because the work we do will eventually be fed into the Dick Tracy program."

Ben looked puzzled. "Say again."

"Think about it for a moment. Right now you are approaching the investigation from only the single point of view of the crime that was committed. Well and good—and I hope you succeed before they reach me again. Otherwise I'm for the knackers. But we should also be taking a second approach. Have you thought about just what it was that they stole?"

"Obviously, your AI machine."

"No—it was more than that. They tried to kill everyone who had any knowledge of the AI, to steal or destroy every existing record. And they are still trying to kill me. That makes one thing very clear."

"Of course!" Ben said. "I should have realized that. They not only wanted the AI—but they wanted a world monopoly on it. They might possibly be trying to market it now. They will want to use it commercially to turn a profit. But they have committed murder and theft and certainly don't want to be found out. They have to conceal the fact that they're using it, so they must exploit it in such a way that the AI cannot be traced back to them."

"I see what you mean," Shelly said. "Once they get it working, the stolen AI could be used for almost any purpose. To control mechanical processes, maybe to write software, follow new lines of research, aid product development—it could be used for almost anything."

Benicoff nodded solemn agreement. "And that makes it rather hard to catch them out. We have to be on the lookout, not for anything very specific, but for virtually any type of program or machine that seems peculiarly advanced."

"That's much too general for my program to be able to deal with," Shelly said. "Dick Tracy can only work with carefully structured data bases. It just doesn't have enough knowledge or common sense to help with a problem as broad as this."

"Then we will have to improve it," Brian said. "This is exactly what I'm driving at. It is now perfectly clear what we have to do. First we have to make Dick Tracy smarter, to equip it with more general knowledge.''

''You mean to make it into a better AI?'' Benicoff asked. ''And then use it to find the other AIs. Like setting a thief to stop a thief.''

''That's half of it. The other half is what I'm doing with the robot Robin. Making it more like the AI in the notes. If I can do that, then we'll know more about what the stolen machine is capable of. And that will help narrow the search.''

''Especially if we can upload those same capabilities into Dick Tracy,'' Shelly said. ''Then it could really know what to search for!''

They all looked at one another, but there seemed to be little more to say. It was clear what each of them had to do.

Ben stopped them as they rose to leave. ''One last and important matter to discuss. Shelly's living quarters.''

''I'm sorry you mentioned that,'' she said. ''I thought I was getting a lovely little apartment. But at the very last moment the whole deal fell through.''

Ben looked uncomfortable. ''I'm sorry but, well, that was my doing. I have been thinking about the attacks on Brian's life and I realized that you must also be a target now. Once you start developing AI, the murderous power out there will . . . it's not easy to say, will want to kill you as well as Brian. Do you agree?''

Shelly nodded a reluctant *yes*.

''Which means you will have to live with the same degree of security as Brian. Here in Megalobe.''

''I'll get suicidal if I have to live in the businessmen's flophouse where I am staying now.''

''No question of that! I speak with feeling because I have spent many a miserable night there myself. Now can I make a suggestion? There are WAC quarters in the barracks here with provision for female Army personnel. If we knocked a couple of rooms together and fitted them up as a small apartment—would you mind staying there?''

''I'll want a say in the decorating.''

''You pick it out—we'll pick up the tab. Electronic

kitchen, Jacuzzi bath—anything you want. The army engineers will install it."

"Offer accepted. When do I get the catalogs?"

"I have them in my office right now."

"Ben—you're terrible. How did you know I would go along with this plan?"

"I didn't know—just hoped. And when you look at it from all sides it really turns out to be the only safe thing to do."

"Can I see the catalogs now?"

"Of course. In this building, room 412. I'll call my assistant and have her dig them out."

Shelly started for the door—then spun about. "I'm sorry, Brian. I should have asked you first if you need me."

"I think it's a great idea. In any case I have some other things to do today away from the lab. What do we say we meet there at nine A.M. tomorrow?"

"Right."

Brian waited until the door had closed before he turned to Ben, chewed his lip in silence before he managed to speak. "I still haven't told her about the CPU implant in my brain. And she hasn't asked me about that session where it produced the clue about the theft. Has she mentioned it to you?"

"No—and I don't think she will. Shelly is a very private person and I think she extends the same privacy to others. Is it important?"

"Only to me. What I told you before about feeling like a freak—"

"You're not, and you know it. I doubt if the topic will come up again."

"I'll tell her about it, someday. Just not now. Particularly since I have arranged some lengthy sessions with Dr. Snaresbrook." He glanced at his watch. "The first one will be starting soon. The main reason I am doing this is that I am determined to speed up the AI work."

"How?"

"I want to improve my approach to the research. Right now all that I am doing is going through the material from the backup data bank we brought back from Mexico. But these are mostly notes and questions about work in progress. What I need to do is locate the real memories and the results of the research based upon them. At the present time it has been slow and infuriating work.''

"In what way?''

"I was, am, are . . .'' Brian smiled wryly. "I guess there is no correct syntax to express it. What I mean is the *me* that made those notes was a sloppy note maker. You know how, when you write a note to yourself, you mostly scribble a couple of words that will remind you of the whole idea. But that particular me no longer exists, so my old notes don't remind me of anything. So I've started working with Dr. Snaresbrook to see if we can use the CPU implant to link the notes to additional disconnected memories that are still in my brain. It took me ten years to develop AI the first time—and I'm afraid it will take that long again if I don't have some help. I must get those lost memories back.''

"Are there any results of your accessing these memories?''

"Early days yet. We are still trying to find a way to make connections that I can reliably activate at will. The CPU is a machine—and I'm not—and we interface badly at the best of times. It is like a bad phone connection at other times. You know, both people talking at once and nothing coming across. Or I just simply cannot make sense of what is getting through. Have to stop all input and go back to square A. Frustrating, I can tell you. But I'm going to lick it. It can only improve. I hope.''

Ben walked Brian over to the Megalobe clinic and left him outside Dr. Snaresbrook's office. He watched him enter, stood there for some time, deep in thought. There was plenty to think about.

The session went well. Brian could access the CPU at will now, use it to extract specific memories. The system was functioning better—although sometimes he would retrieve fragments of knowledge that were hard to comprehend. It was as though they came as suggestions from someone else rather than from his own memories. Occasionally, when he accessed a memory of his earlier, adult self, he would find himself losing track of his own thoughts.

When he regained control he found it hard to recall how it had felt. *How strange,* he thought to himself. *Am I maintaining two personalities? Can a single mind have room for two personalities at once—one old, the other new?*

The probing certainly was saving a great deal of time in his research and, as the novelty began to wear off, Brian's thoughts returned to the most serious problems that still beset him on the AI. All the different bugs that led to failures—to breakdowns in which the machine would end up at one extreme of behavior or another.

"Brian—are you there?"

"What—?"

"Welcome back. I asked you the same question three times. You were wandering, weren't you?"

"Sorry. It just seems so intractable and there is nothing in the notes to help me out. What I need is to have a part of my mind that is watching itself without the rest of the mind knowing what is happening. Something that would help keep the system's control circuitry in balance. That's not particularly hard when the system itself is stable, not changing or learning very much—but nothing seems to work when the system learns new ways to learn. What I need is some system, some sort of separate submind that can maintain a measure of control."

"Sounds very Freudian."

"I beg your pardon?"

"Like the theories of Sigmund Freud."

"I don't recall anyone with that name in any AI research."

"Easy enough to see why. He was a psychiatrist working in the 1890s, before there were any computers. When he first proposed his theories—about how the mind is made of a number of different agencies—he gave them names like id, ego, superego, censor and so on. It is understood that every normal person is constantly dealing, unconsciously, with all sorts of conflicts, contradictions, and incompatible goals. That's why I thought you might get some feedback if you were to study Freud's theories of mind."

"Sounds fine to me. Let's do it now, download all the Freudian theories into my memory banks."

Snaresbrook was concerned. As a scientist, she still regarded the use of the implant computer as an experimental study—but Brian had already absorbed it as a natural part of his lifestyle. No more poring over printed texts for him. Get it all into memory in an instant, then deal with it later.

He did not go back to his room, but paced the floor, while in his mind he dipped first into one part of the text, then another, making links and changing them—then gasped out loud.

"This has to be it—really it! A theory that fits my problem perfectly. The superego appears to be a sort of goal-learning mechanism that probably evolved on top of the imprinting mechanisms that evolved earlier. You know, the systems discovered by Konrad Lorenz, that are used to hold many infant animals within a safe sphere of nurture and protection. These produce a relatively permanent, stable goal system in the child. Once a child introjects a mother or father image, that structure can remain there for the rest of that child's life. But how can we provide my AI with a superego? Consider this—we should be able to download a functioning superego for my AI if we can find some way of downloading enough of the details of my own unconscious value structure. And why not? Activate each of my K-lines and nemes, sense and record the emotional values associated with them. Use that data to first build a representation of my conscious self-image. Then add my self-ideal—what the superego says I ought to be. If we can download that, we might be much further on the way toward being able to stabilize and regulate our machine intelligence."

"Let's do it," Snaresbrook said. "Even if no one has proven yet that the thing exists. We'll simply assume that you do indeed have a perfectly fine one inside your head. And we are perhaps the first people ever to be in a position to find it. Look at what we have been doing for months now, searching out and downloading your matrix of memories and thought processes. Now we may as well push a little further—only backward instead of forward in time. We can try to do more backtracking toward your infancy, and see if we can find some nemes and attached memories that might correspond to your earliest value systems.''

''And you think that you can do this?''

''I don't see any reason why not—unless what we're seeking just doesn't exist. In any case the search will probably involve locating another few hundred thousand old K-lines and nemes. But cautiously. There might be some serious dangers here, in giving you access to such deeply buried activities. I'll first want to work up a way to do this by using an external computer, while disabling your own internal connection machine for a while. That way, we'll have a record of the structures we discover in external form, which might be used in improving Robin. This will prevent the experiments from affecting you until we're more sure of ourselves.''

''Well, then—let's give it a try.''

# 25

---

## May 31, 2024

''Brian Delaney—have you been working here all night? You promised it would just be a few minutes more when I left you here last night. And that was at ten o'clock.'' Shelly stamped into the lab radiating displeasure.

Brian rubbed his fingers over rough revelatory whiskers, blinked through red-rimmed guilty eyes. Equivocated.

''What makes you think that?''

Shelly flared her nostrils. ''Well, just looking at you reveals more than enough evidence. You look terrible. In addition to that I tried to phone you and there was no answer. As you imagine I was more than a little concerned.''

Brian grabbed at his belt where he kept his phone—it was

gone. "I must have put it down somewhere, didn't hear it ring."

She took out her own phone and hit the memory key to dial his number. There was a distant buzzing. She tracked it down beside the coffeemaker. Returned it to him in stony silence.

"Thanks."

"It should be near you at all times. I had to go looking for your bodyguards—they told me you were still here."

"Traitors," he muttered.

"They're as concerned as I am. Nothing is so important that you have to ruin your health for it."

"Something *is*, Shelly, that's just the point. You remember when you left last night, the trouble we were having with the new manager program? No matter what we did yesterday the system would simply curl up and die. So then I started it out with a very simple program of sorting out colored blocks, then complicated it with blocks of different shapes as well as colors. The next time I looked, the manager program was still running—but all the other parts of the program seemed to have shut down. So I recorded what happened when I tried it again, and this time installed a natural language trace program to record all the manager's commands to the other subunits. This slowed things down enough for me to discover what was going on. Let's look at what happened."

He turned on the recording he had made during the night. The screen showed the AI rapidly sorting colored blocks, then slowing—then barely moving until it finally stopped completely. The deep bass voice of Robin 3 poured rapidly from the speaker.

"... K-line 8997, response needed to input 10983—you are too slow—respond immediately—inhibiting. Selecting subproblem 384. Response accepted from K-4093, inhibiting slower responses from K-3724 and K-2314. Selecting subproblem 385. Responses from K-2615 and K-1488 are in conflict—inhibiting both. Selecting ..."

Brian switched it off. "Did you understand that?"

"Not really. Except that the program was busy inhibiting things."

"Yes, and that was its problem. It was supposed to learn from experience, by rewarding successful subunits and inhibiting the ones that failed. But the manager's threshold for success had been set so high that it would accept only perfect and instant compliance. So it was rewarding only the units that responded quickly, and disconnecting the slower ones—even if what they were trying to do might have been better in the end."

"I see. And that started a domino effect because as each subunit was inhibited, that weakened other units' connection to it?"

"Exactly. And then the responses of those other units became slower until they got inhibited in turn. Before long the manager program had killed off them all."

"What a horrible thought! You are saying, really, that it committed suicide."

"Not at all." His voice was hoarse, fatigue abraded his temper. "When you say that, you are just being anthropomorphic. A machine is not a person. What on earth is horrible about one circuit disconnecting another circuit? Christ—there's nothing here but a bunch of electronic components and software. Since there are no human beings involved nothing horrible can possibly occur, that's pretty obvious—"

"Don't speak to me that way or use that tone of voice!"

Brian's face reddened with anger, then he dropped his eyes. "I'm sorry, I take that back. I'm a little tired, I think."

"You think—I know. Apology accepted. And I agree, I was being anthropomorphic. It wasn't what you said to me—it was how you said it. Now let's stop snapping at each other and get some fresh air. And get you to bed."

"All right—but let me look at this first."

Brian went straight to the terminal and proceeded to retrace the robot's internal computations. Chart after chart appeared on the screen. Eventually he nodded gloomily. "Another bug of course. It only showed up after I fixed the last one. You remember, I set things up to suppress excessive inhibition, so that the robot would not spontaneously shut itself down. But now it goes to the opposite extreme. It doesn't know when it ought to stop.

"This AI seems to be pretty good at answering straightforward questions, but only when the answer can be found with a little shallow reasoning. But you saw what happened when it didn't know the answer. It began random searching, lost its way, didn't know when to stop. You might say that it didn't know what it didn't know."

"It seemed to me that it simply went mad."

"Yes, you could say that. We have lots of words for human-mind bugs—paranoias, catatonias, phobias, neuroses, irrationalities. I suppose we'll need new sets of words for all the new bugs that our robots will have. And we have no reason to expect that any new version should work the first time it's turned on. In this case, what happened was that it tried to use all of its Expert Systems together on the same problem. The manager wasn't strong enough to suppress the inappropriate ones. All those jumbles of words showed that it was grasping at any and every association that might conceivably have guided it toward the problem it needed to solve—no matter how unlikely on the face of it. It also showed that when one approach failed, the thing didn't know when to give up. Even if this AI worked there is no rule that it had to be sane on our terms."

Brian rubbed his bristly jaw and looked at the now silent machine. "Let's look more closely here." He pointed to the chart on the machine. "You can see right here what happened this time. In Rob-3.1 there was too much inhibition, so everything shut down. So I changed these parameters and now there's not enough inhibition."

"So what's the solution?"

"The answer is that there is no answer. No, I don't mean anything mystical. I mean that the manager here has to have more knowledge. Precisely because there's no magic, no general answer. There's no simple fix that will work in all cases—because all cases are different. And once you recognize that, everything is much clearer! This manager must be knowledge-based. And then it can learn what to do!"

"Then you're saying that we must make a manager to learn which strategy to use in each situation, by remembering what worked in the past?"

"Exactly. Instead of trying to find a fixed formula that always works, let's make it learn from experience, case by case. Because we want a machine that's intelligent on its own, so that we don't have to hang around forever, fixing it whenever anything goes wrong. Instead we must give it some ways to learn to fix new bugs as soon as they come up. By itself, without our help."

"So now I know just what to do. Remember when it seemed stuck in a loop, repeating the same things about the color red? It was easy for us to see that it wasn't making any progress. It couldn't see that it was stuck, precisely because of being stuck. It couldn't jump out of that loop to see what it was doing on a larger scale. We can fix that by adding a recorder to remember the history of what it has been doing recently. And also a clock that interrupts the program frequently, so that it can look at that recording to see if it has been repeating itself."

"Or even better we could add a second processor that is always running at the same time, looking at the first one. A B-brain watching an A-brain."

"And perhaps even a C-brain to see if the B-brain has got stuck. Damn! I just remembered that one of my old notes said, 'Use the B-brain here to suppress looping.' I certainly wish I had written clearer notes the first time around. I better get started on designing that B-brain."

"But you'd better not do it now! In your present state, you'll just make it worse."

"You're right. Bedtime. I'll get there, don't worry—but I want to get something to eat first."

"I'll go with you, have a coffee."

Brian let them out and blinked at the bright sunshine. "That sounds as though you don't trust me."

"I don't. Not after last night!"

Shelly sipped at her coffee while Brian worked his way through a Texas breakfast—steak, eggs and flapjacks. He couldn't quite finish it all, sighed and pushed the plate away.

Except for two guards just off duty, sitting at a table on the far wall, they were alone in the mess hall.

"I'm feeling slightly less inhuman," he said. "More coffee?"

"I've had more than enough, thank you. Do you think that you can fix your screw-loose AI?"

"No. I was getting so annoyed at the thing that I've wiped its memory. We will have to rewrite some of the program before we load it again. Which will take a couple of hours. Even LAMA-5's assembler takes a long time on a system this large. And this time I'm going to make a backup copy before we run the new version."

"A backup means a duplicate. When you do get a functioning humanoid artificial intelligence—do you think that you will be able to copy it as well?"

"Of course. Whatever it does—it will still just be a program. Every copy of a program is absolutely identical. Why do you ask?"

"It's a matter of identity, I guess. Will the second AI be the same as the first?"

"Yes—but only at the instant it is copied. As soon as it begins to run, to think for itself, it will start changing. Remember, we are our memories. When we forget something, or learn something new, we produce a new thought or make a new connection—we change. We are someone different. The same will apply to an AI."

"Can you be sure of that?" she asked doubtfully.

"Positive. Because that is how mind functions. Which means I have a lot of work to do in weighting memory. It's the same reason why so many earlier versions of Robin failed. The credit assignment problem that we talked about before. It is really not enough to learn just by short-term stimulus-response-reward methods—because this will solve only simple, short-term problems. Instead, there must be a larger scale reflective analysis, in which you think over your performance on a longer scale, to recognize which strategies really worked, and which of them led to sidetracks, moves that seemed to make progress but eventually led to dead ends."

"You make the mind sound like—well—an onion!"

"It is." He smiled at the thought. "A good analogy. Layer within layer and all interconnected. Human memory is not merely associative, connecting situations, responses and rewards. It is also prospective and reflective. The connections made must also be involved with long-range goals and plans. That is why there is this important separation between short-term and long-term memory. Why does it take about an hour to long-term memorize anything? Because there must be a buffer period to decide which behaviors actually were beneficial enough to record."

Sudden fatigue hit him. The coffee was cold; his head was beginning to ache; depression was closing in. Shelly saw this, lightly touched his hand.

"Time to retire," she said. He nodded sluggish agreement and struggled to push back the chair.

# 26

---

## June 19, 2024

Shelly opened her apartment door when Benicoff knocked. "Brian just came in," she said, "and I'm getting him a beer. You too?"

"Please."

"Come in and take a look—after all you paid for it."

She led the way into the living room where all traces of the army barracks had been carefully removed. The floor-to-ceiling curtains that framed the window were made from colorful handwoven fabric. The carpeting picked up the dark orange from the curtain pattern. The slim lines of the Danish teak furniture blended pleasantly with this, providing a contrast to the spectacular colors of the post-Cubist painting that covered most of one wall.

"Most impressive," Ben said. "I can see now why the accounts department was screaming."

"Not at this—the fabric and rugs are Israeli-designed but Arab-manufactured and not at all expensive. The painting is on loan from an artist friend of mine, to help her sell it. Most of the money went for the high-tech kitchen. Want to see it?"

"After the beer. I better brace myself for it."

"Going to explain the mystery of your invitation to a Thai lunch today?" Brian said, lolling back comfortably in the depths of a padded armchair. "You know that Shelly and I are prisoners of Megalobe until you run down the killers. So how do we get out to this Thai restaurant of yours?"

"If you can't get to Thailand, why Thailand will come to you. As soon as you told me you wanted to bring me up to date on your AI I thought we ought to make a party of it. Thanks, Shelly."

Ben took a deep swig of cold Tecate and sighed. "Good stuff. It all began with a security check last week. I sit in with Military Intelligence when they vet any soldiers to be transferred here. That was when I discovered that Private First Class Lat Phroa had joined the army to get away from his father's restaurant. He said he had enough of cooking and wanted some action. But after a year of army food he was more than happy to cook a real Thai meal in the kitchen here, if I could get the ingredients. Which I did. The cooks went along with it and the troops are looking forward to the change. We'll have the mess hall to ourselves after two. We'll be the guinea pigs and if we approve, Lat promised to feed everyone else tonight."

"I can't wait," Shelly said. "Not that the food here is bad—but I would love a change."

"How is the investigation going?" Brian asked. It was never far from his thoughts. Ben frowned into his beer.

"I wish I could bring some good news, but we seem to have hit a dead end. We have Alex Toth's military record. He was an outstanding pilot, plenty of recommendations for that. But he is also a borderline alcoholic and a trouble-maker. After the war they threw him out as fast as they could. No trace of him at the address he gave at the time. The FBI has found some records of his employment through his pilot's license, kept up to date. But the man himself has vanished. The trail is ice cold. Dusty Rhodes' story checks out. He was conned into it and then left to hang out and dry in the wind. There is absolutely no way to trace the money that was paid into his account.''

''What's going to happen to Rhodes?'' Shelly asked.

''Nothing now. The remaining money they gave him has been sequestered for the crime victims' fund and he signed a complete statement of everything that happened, everything he did. He'll keep his nose clean in the future or will be hit with a number of charges. We want to keep this thing as quiet as we can while the investigation is still in progress.''

Shelly nodded and turned to Brian. ''You must bring me up to date. Did you ever get that B-brain to work?''

''Indeed I did, and sometimes it works amazingly well. But not often enough to trust very far. It keeps breaking down in fascinating and peculiar ways.''

''Still? I thought that using LAMA-5 made debugging easier.''

''It certainly does—but I think that this is more a problem of design. As you know, the B-brain is supposed to monitor the A-brain, make changes when needed to keep it out of various kinds of trouble. Theoretically this works best when the A-brain is unaware of what is happening. But it seems that as Robin's A-brain became smarter it learned to detect that tampering—then tried to find ways to change things back. This ended up in a struggle for power as the two brains fought for control.''

''It sounds like human schizophrenia or multiple personalities!''

''Exactly so. Human insanity is mirrored in machine madness and vice versa. Why not? A malfunctioning brain will have the same symptoms from the same cause, machine or man.''

''It must be depressing, being set back by lunatic brains in a box.''

''Not really. In a way, it's actually encouraging! Because,

the more the robot's foul-ups resemble human ones, the closer we are getting to humanlike machine intelligence.''

"If it is going that well—why are you so upset?"

"Is it obvious? Well, it's probably because I've finally come to the end of the notes we retrieved. I've worked through just about everything that those notes described. So much so that now I am swimming out into uncharted seas."

"Is there any rule that the AI in your lab must be the same as the one that was stolen?"

"Yes, pretty much so, except for some minor details. And the trouble is that it has so many bugs that I am afraid that we're stuck on a local peak."

"What do you mean?" Ben said.

"Just a simple analogy. Think of a scientific researcher as a blind mountain climber. He keeps climbing up the mountain and eventually reaches a peak and can climb no higher. But because he can't see anything he has no way of knowing that he's not at the top of the mountain at all. It is merely the peak of a local hill—a dead end. Success is then not possible—unless he goes back down the mountain again and looks for another path."

"Makes sense," Ben said. "Are you telling me that the AI you have just built—which is probably almost the same as the one that was stolen—may be stuck on a local peak of intelligence and not on some much higher summit?"

"I'm afraid that's it."

Ben yodeled happily. "But that is the best news ever!"

"Have you gone around the twist?"

"Think for a second. This means that whoever stole your old model must also be stuck in about the same way—but he won't even know it. While you can go and perfect your machine. When that happens we'll have it—and they won't!"

As this sunk in a broad grin spread across Brian's face. "Of course you're right. This *is* the best news ever. Those crooks are stuck—while I'm going to push right ahead with the work."

"Not at this moment you're not—after lunch!" Shelly said, putting down her wineglass and pointing to the door. "Out. It's after two and I'm starving. Eat first, talk later."

After eating See Khrong Moo sam Rot—which despite its name was absolutely delicious—sweet, sour and salty spareribs—they even managed some custard steamed in pumpkin for dessert.

"I'll never eat army chow again," Brian groaned happily and rubbed his midriff.

"Tell that to the cook—make his day," Shelly said. "That's what I'm going to do."

Lat Phroa took their praise as his due, nodding in agreement. "It was pretty good, wasn't it? If the rest of the troops like it I'm going to work hard to get this kind of chow in the regular menu. If only for my own sake."

Ben left them there and they walked off some of the lunch by strolling back to the lab.

"I'm enthusiastic—but apprehensive," Brian said. "Swimming out into uncharted seas. Up until now I have been following the charts, my own notes—but they have just run out. It's a little presumptuous of fourteen-year-old me to think that I can succeed where the twenty-four-year-old me pooped out."

"Don't be so sure. Dr. Snaresbrook maintains that you're smarter now than ever before—your implants have given you some outstanding abilities. And furthermore, in the work you've done with Snaresbrook—analyzing your own brain—you've probably discovered more about yourself than a squad of psychologists ever could. It's clear to me that you're getting there, Brian. Bringing something new into the world.

"A truly humanlike machine intelligence."

# 27

## July 22, 2024

Ben found the message in his phone when he woke up. It was Brian's voice.

*"Ben—it's four in the morning and we have it at last! The data in Robin was almost enough, and Dr. Snaresbrook finished the job by decoding some more material from my brain. It was an awful job, but we managed to get it done. So now, theoretically, Robin contains a copy of my superego and I've set the computer to reassembling all of Robin's programs to try to integrate the old stuff with the new. Need some sleep. If you can make it please come to the lab after lunch for a demo. Over and out—and good night."*

"We've done it," Brian said when they met in the laboratory. "The data already downloaded into Robin was almost enough. It was Dr. Snaresbrook who finished the job, adding what might be called a template, a downloaded copy of my superego. You could say that it was a copy of how the highest-level control functions of my brain operate. All memory that was not associated with control was stripped away until we had what we hoped would be a template of a functioning intelligence. Then came the big job of integrating these programs with the AI programs that were already running. This was not easy but we prevailed. But along the way we had some spectacular failures—some of which you already know about."

"Like the lab wreck last week."

"And the one on Tuesday. But that is all in the past. Sven is now a real pussycat."

"Sven?"

"Really Robin number 7, after we found out that 6.9 couldn't access all the memory we needed."

"Blame Shelly for that," Brian said. "She claims that when I say 'seven' it sounds more like 'sven.' So when I wasn't looking she programmed in a Swedish accent. The name Sven stuck."

"I want to hear your Swedish AI talk!"

"Sorry. We had to take the accent out. Too much hysteria and not enough work getting done."

"Sounds good to me. When do I get to meet your AI?"

"Right now. But first I'll have to wake Sven up." Brain pointed to the motionless telerobot.

"Wake up or turn on?" Ben asked.

"The computer stays on all the time, of course. But the new memory management scheme turned out to be very much like human sleep. It sorts through a day's memories to resolve any conflicts and to delete redundancies. No point in wasting more memory on things that you already know." Brian raised his voice. "Sven, you can wake up now."

The three lens covers clicked open and the legs stirred as Sven turned toward them.

"Good afternoon, Brian and Shelly. And stranger."

"This is Ben."

"A pleasure to meet you, Ben. Is that your given name or family name?"

"Nickname," Ben said. Robin had forgotten him again— for the third time—as its memory was changed. "Complete name, Alfred J. Benicoff."

"A pleasure to meet you, Ms. or Mr. Benicoff."

Ben raised his eyebrows and Brian laughed.

"Sven has still not integrated all the social knowledge involved with recognizing sexual distinctions. In fact, in many ways, it is starting from scratch, with entirely new priorities. The main thing is completeness first. I want Sven to have as well rounded an intelligence as that of a growing child. And right now, like a child, I want to teach him how to safely cross streets. We're going for a walk now—would you like to come?"

Ben looked at the clutter of electronic machinery and his eyebrows shot up. Brian laughed at his expression and pointed to the other end of the lab.

"Virtual reality. I can't believe how much it's improved in the last ten years. We'll get into those datasuits and Sven will join us electronically. Shelly will supervise the simulators."

The suits opened at the back; Brian and Ben took off their shoes and stepped in. They were suspended at the waist so they could turn and twist as they walked. The two-dimensional treadmill floor panels let their feet move in any direction, while other effectors inside the boots simulated the shapes and textures of whatever terrain was being simulated. The featherweight helmets turned with their heads, while the screens they looked into displayed the totally computer-generated scene. Ben looked up and saw the Washington Monument above the treetops.

"We're in Foggy Bottom," he said.

"Why not? Details of the city are in the computer's memory—and this gives Sven a chance to deal with the rotten District drivers."

The illusion was almost perfect. Sven stood erect next to him, swiveling its eyes to look around. Ben turned to the image of Brian—only it wasn't Brian.

"Brian—you're a girl—a black girl!"

"Why not? My image here in virtual reality is computer generated so I can be anything. This gives Sven an extra bonus of meeting new people, women, minority groups, anyone. Shall we go for a walk?"

They strolled through the park, hearing the sound of distant traffic, pigeons cooing in the trees above them. A couple came the other way, passed them, talking together and completely ignoring the shambling tree robot. Of course—they were computer-generated images as well.

"We haven't tried crossing any streets yet," Brian said, "so why don't we do that now? Make it easy the first time, will you Shelly?"

Shelly must have worked a control because the heavy traffic in the street ahead began to lighten up. Fewer and fewer cars passed and by the time they had reached the curb there were none in sight. Even the parked cars had driven away, all the pedestrians had turned corners and none had returned.

"Want to keep it as simple as possible. Later on we can try it with cars and people," Brian explained. "Sven, think you can step down off the curb all right?"

"Yes."

"Good. Shall we cross now?"

Ben and Brian stepped into the road.

"No," Sven said. Brian turned to look at the unmoving figure.

"Come on—it's all right."

"You explained that I was to cross the road only when I was sure a car was not coming."

"Well, look both ways, nothing in sight, let's go."

Sven did not move. "I'm still not sure."

"But you've already looked."

"Yes, there was no car then. But now is now."

Ben laughed. "You are very literal, Sven. There is really no problem. You can see both ways for a kilometer at least. Even if a car turned the corner doing one hundred kilometers an hour we could get across well before it reached us."

"It would hit us if it were going five hundred kilometers per hour."

"All right, Sven—that does it for today," Brian said. "Switching off."

The street vanished as the screen went dark; the backs of the suits swung open.

"Now, what was that about?" Ben asked as he backed out and bent to pick up his shoes.

"A problem that we've seen before. Sven still doesn't know when to stop reasoning, to stop being outlandishly logical. In the real world we can never be one hundred percent sure of anything, so we have to use only as much knowledge and reasoning as is appropriate to the situation. And in order to reach a decision there must be a point at which thinking has to stop. But doing that itself requires inhibition skills. I think the reason that Sven got stuck was because his new superego was inhibiting the use of those very skills."

"You mean it turned off the very process that was supposed to stop being turned off? Sounds suspiciously like a paradox. How long will it take to fix?"

"I hope we won't have to fix it at all. Sven should be able to do it on its own."

"You mean by learning from experience?"

"Exactly. After all, there's really nothing wrong with being too careful at first. You have to survive in order to learn. It may take a while, but by learning very carefully Sven can build a solid foundation for learning much more quickly in the future. However there's something more important than walking right now. Shelly merged Dick Tracy with Robin a few days ago. They are pretty well integrated and working on the problem. Sven, has your Dick Tracy agency added any more jobs to your AI occupation list?"

"It has."

"Give us a printout."

The laser printer hummed to life and sheet after sheet began to emerge. Brian took the first sheet and handed it to Ben; it was alphabetized of course.

"Abaca manufacture, abacaxi cultivator, abactinal definer, abaculus setter, abacucus operator, abaisse manufacture...and a lot more like that," Ben said. He looked at the sheets piling up and shook his head. "Could you tell me the reason for all this?"

"I thought that it was obvious. Your investigation of the crime here seems to be grinding to a halt—"

"I'm sorry if it looks that way, but the number of people working on this . . ."

"Ben, I know that! I'm not blaming you. This is a tough nut to crack and all we want to do is help you—for purely personal and selfish reasons if nothing else. Shelly has her Dick Tracy program still operating but it appears to have run out of steam. Now enter Sven to solve the crime!"

"I am already here so I cannot enter."

"A figure of speech, Sven. Data to come. You can stop the data printout now."

"I am only up to C in the alphabet. You do not wish a complete printout?"

"No. Just this sample to look at. Put the printed sheets back into the bin."

Sven rustled quickly across the room to the printer and lifted out the sheets of eternitree from the delivery tray. But not as a human would in a single pile. Instead it shifted its weight to one of the tree complexes and extended the other, then with a quick movement a myriad of the smallest fingers grasped each sheet individually. Carried them to the other side of the machine and slid them into the bin in a quick shuffle as though they were a large pack of cards.

"The printout," Brian said, "was just to give you an idea of the kind of data base we are assembling. The idea is to make a list of all conceivable human occupations, then consider what an AI might do to make each of them more practical, and then trimming away the improbables. When this list is reduced to a feasible size Sven will examine every available data base for any trace of evidence. Looking for traces of any new kind of manufacturing process, programming system, or other kind of new product that could only be made by a new, more advanced AI."

"But all these occupations and applications on the list seem so impractical—even impossible. I don't even know what an abacaxi cultivator is!"

"Of course a lot of them are way out. But this AI does not think as we do—yet. We have intuition, which is a learned process and not one that can be memorized. Right now Sven is better at making a list of everything that an AI could do. When the list is complete it will begin trimming away the impossibles and the improbables. When the list is finally reduced to manageable size Sven will then begin to examine for any traces or matches."

"That's quite a task."

"Sven is quite a machine," Shelly said proudly. "With its new Dick Tracy agency it should be more than up to the job. If the stolen AI is working somewhere we are going to track it down by finding out just what it has done."

"I'm sure of it," Ben said. "And you will let me know the instant you have any leads."

"They might be just clues, there is no way to be certain."

"There certainly is—I'll have them checked out. I have a big team out there who aren't accomplishing very much at the moment. I'll put them to work. In all truth I think that putting Sven on the job is the only way that we are going to find the people who did this."

# 28

## September 4, 2024

Benicoff was sure that this conference would not take too long. He had read through all the paperwork on the flight to Seattle, made his final notes on the monorail to Tacoma. This was the first assignment he had had in some months, in fact the very first since he began devoting full time to the Megalobe case; he could think of no real reason to turn down the request. Just before the meeting began his phone beeped and he answered it.

"*Ben, Brian here. Sven seems to have come up with some leads.*"

"Your electronic wizard seems to be working pretty fast."

"*Once the list was complete and all the long shots eliminated Sven sorted through for the most likely items. It has come up with three possibilities now. One is a certain software system that is suspicious. A microcode compiler that writes impossibly efficient code. Then there is a certain shoe repair machine that might plausibly be an AI since it can resole any kind of shoe. Then there is an agricultural machine which is rated as almost surely an AI.*"

"Plausibly? Almost surely? Can't this thing give a straight answer, a yes or no—or a fifty-fifty chance?"

"*It cannot. Sven uses an agency based on knowledge*

*about qualitative plausibility. It doesn't use any numbers at all. In fact, I asked it to and it refused.''*

''Who runs that place—you or the machine? In any case—what did it come up with?''

*''A machine called Bug-Off, would you believe?''*

''I believe—and I'll contact the FBI here and get some action on your Bug-Off today. A meeting that I planned to be brief just got a lot briefer. I've canceled it. I'll get back to you.''

The head of the Seattle FBI office, Agent Antonio Perdomo, was a tall man, as solidly built as Benicoff, still in his forties but going rapidly bald. He glanced at Benicoff's ID and got right down to business.

''Washington ran a corporate check on this manufacturing company, DigitTech Products of Austin, Texas. I have the file here. They manufacture and sell wholesale electronic components for the most part, with an occasional individual product. But they usually make items for own-brand retailers. This machine you asked about, Bug-Off, has been on the market for only a few weeks. They are marketing it themselves.''

''How do we get hold of one?''

''I've arranged that as well. It is not for sale but is leased to greenhouses to be used—or so their prospectus says—in the place of chemicals. I know you wanted to keep this investigation completely under cover so I made all my inquiries through an associate in the Bureau of Commerce. He contacted all the greenhouses in this area and has come up with a winner. A greenhouse owner named Nisiumi—a retired traffic policeman.''

''That's the best news ever. You've contacted him?''

''He's in his office, waiting for us. He only knows that this is a high-level investigation and that he is to mention it to no one.''

''This is very good work.''

Perdomo smiled. ''Just doing my job.''

The sun had disappeared and Seattle was running true to winter form. The windshield wipers were on high speed to clear a patch in the torrential rain. They parked as close to the entrance as they could, were still drenched by the time they got to the greenhouse door.

Nisiumi, a stocky Japanese-American, led them to his office in silence, didn't speak until he had closed the door. He wiped the soil from his fingers onto his white coat before he shook hands. He looked very closely at Agent Perdomo's identification.

"These Bug-Off people are making a big sales pitch, probably contacted every greenhouse in the country. I even had this brochure for their machine, right here on my desk."

"This is Mr. Benicoff, who originated this investigation," Perdomo said. "He's the one in charge."

"Thanks for your cooperation," Ben said. "This is a high-priority case right out of Washington—and there are deaths involved. That's all I can tell you now. When we wind the thing up I promise that I'll let you know what it is all about."

"Suits me. It's a big change from cucumbers. I was interested by this Bug-Off when I read about it in the trade magazine. That's why I asked for this information. But it's too expensive for me."

"You have just obtained an interest-free loan for as much as you need for as long as you need."

"It's good to be back in harness! While you were on your way here I called DigitTech Products' 800 number. They have a salesman in this area—and he is going to give a demonstration here at nine tomorrow morning."

"Perfect. Your accountant, that is me, will join you at that time. Call me Benck, though, not Benicoff."

The rain was lashing loudly against the hotel room window. Benicoff closed the curtains and turned on the radio in the hopes that the music might drown it out. He was well into the company report before the rare steak, no potatoes and a green salad, pot of coffee arrived. He ate slowly, reading, digesting meal and report at the same time.

The salesman was late next morning; it was almost ten before the van stopped in the greenhouse drive.

"Sorry about that, traffic and fog. The name is Joseph

Ashley but everyone calls me Joe. You're the owner, Mr. Nisiumi?"

While the introductions were being made the van driver was loading a large carton onto the hand truck; he wheeled it into the greenhouse. Joe himself pulled off the cover to proudly reveal—"Bug-Off. And that's what this little baby is. The mechanical answer to all your biological problems."

The machine looked very much like a fat fire extinguisher. It was a squat red canister slung between six spiderlike legs. From its top sprouted two jointed metal arms, each ending in a cluster of metal fingers. Benicoff hid his sudden great interest behind an accountant's suspicious scowl. The redivided fingers, although larger, bore a distant resemblance to the branching manipulators of the AI.

"I'll just take the travel locks off these arms and we will be ready to go." Joe pulled free the restraining foam blocks, then took a red canister the size of a cigar box out of the carton and held it up. "Power supply. This plugs into any socket and is secured at ground level. Bug-Off is completely self-powered and self-contained. Right now his battery is charged and he's raring to go. Night and day if needs be. And when his power gets low—why, he just trundles himself over to this charger and gets a fix."

"Sounds expensive," Benicoff grunted.

"Looks expensive, Mr. Benck, and it is expensive. But not to you. You will find that our lease rates are more than reasonable. And I'll bet my bippy that this bug-blasting Bug-Off will pay for himself from the word go."

"Do you program it, or do I follow it around or what?" Nisiumi asked.

"It is so easy to use that you will just not believe it until you see this bug-plucking little guy in action. All that you do is just turn it on—and step back!" Joe did just that, throwing the power switch and stepping back. Motors whirred and the two arms extended to both sides, long metal fingers waving gracefully in the air. "This is the search program. Detectors in the tips of the fingers are looking for plant life. Day or night, as I said, see how they glow with their own light source?"

Drive motors hummed, the legs lifted and lowered gracefully as the machine picked its way in a very dainty manner toward the walkway between the plants. It stopped at the first vine and both arms slapped out, picked their way over the soil to the stems beyond. They moved quickly now, flicking over the leaves and stems, apparently caressing the green lengths of the cucumbers, running lightly over the yellow flowers on their tips. There was a quick click as the lid on the arm flicked open then shut again.

"No chemicals, no poisons, no pollution—wholly organic. Even though you are watching this happen before your very own eyes I'll wager that you can't believe it. I don't blame you—for this is something entirely new in the universe. Before your very eyes there are almost invisible eyes at work, the optic cells on those fingertips which are now seeking out aphids, spiders, mites—bugs of any kind. When one is found it is *plucked* off the plant—just like that. Picked off and whisked away. Bug-Off's arms are hollow and they will soon be filled with bugs. A treat for your pet bird or lizard—or use it as fertilizer. There it is, gentlemen— the mechanical miracle of our age!"

"Looks dangerous," Benicoff said sourly.

"Never! Built-in protection. Won't touch anything except a plant and if you or anyone else gets in the way it stops automatically."

The salesman walked over and grabbed onto a cucumber just ahead of the flashing fingers. The moving hand withdrew and the machine beeped unhappily until he let go.

"I don't know," Benicoff said. "What do you think, Mr. Nisiumi?"

"If it works the way Joe says it does—well then maybe there is a possibility. We both know that organically grown vegetables fetch a better price."

"What's the minimum lease period?" Benicoff asked.

"One year—"

"Too long. We gotta talk. In the office."

Benicoff squeezed the contract terms as far as he could. Got a few concessions, made none of his own. Joe sweated a bit and his smile faded but in the end they reached agreement. The contracts were signed, hands shook, Joe's smile returned.

"You got a great machine there, a great machine."

"I hope so. What if it breaks down?"

"It won't—but we have a mechanic on call twenty-four hours a day just to give our customers peace of mind."

"Do you come around to inspect it?"

"Only if you ask us to. There is a check every six months, you will be called first for an appointment, but that is just routine maintenance. Other than that all you have to do is unleash that bug-picking little devil and step back! You gentlemen will never regret this decision for an instant."

Benicoff grunted suspiciously and read through the contract again. Nisiumi showed Joe and the driver out while Benicoff looked over the top of the contract and watched them through the office window. The second the van was out of sight he grabbed up his phone and called the FBI office, then Brian.

"I don't know how Sven spotted this Bug-Off—but I think that we are onto a winner. Everything about this machine smells of Brian's AI research." There was a grate of tires outside as a Federal Express delivery van pulled up. "The FBI is here now. They are going to crate this thing and get it on a plane. It will be there in the morning—and so will I!"

The truck driver, wearing a Federal Express uniform, was Agent Perdomo.

"Thanks for your cooperation, Mr. Nisiumi," Perdomo said. "We couldn't have got anywhere without your help. We'll take the machine off your hands now."

"What do I say if that salesman or any of his people want to see it?"

"Stall them," Benicoff said. "And get in touch with Agent Perdomo here at once. The chances are that they won't bother you as long as you pay your lease fees on time. Send the bills to Perdomo as well—you'll be reimbursed at once. The salesman said they wouldn't want to service the machine for six months. Our investigation should be completed long before that."

"Whatever you say. Anything else I can do let me know."

"Will do. Thanks again."

They shut down the Bug-Off and put it and its charger back into the carton, then wrapped it completely in brown paper. Benicoff rode in the back of the truck with the machine to the empty warehouse in the outskirts of Seattle. The FBI team were waiting there.

"Torres, bomb squad," their leader said. "You Mr. Benicoff?"

"That's right. I appreciate the quick response."

"That's our job. Tell me about this thing. Do you think there's explosive in there?"

"I doubt it very much. From what I have discovered there are at least a hundred more of these around the country. I doubt if they would all have bombs in them—just one of them going off and there would be unwanted attention, big trouble. No, what I'm concerned about is any internal defenses the thing might have as protection against industrial espionage—what some people call reverse engineering. I am sure that the manufacturers don't want their invention revealed. I have a strong suspicion that the technology this thing might be based on was stolen only last year. There are no patents on it yet. There is also a chance that this machine may relate to a criminal investigation now under way. If those people are involved they won't want *anyone* to know what makes this thing tick."

"So it might be booby-trapped to prevent anyone finding out what makes it tick? Maybe do itself some injury if someone gets nosy?"

"That's it. Its internal computer might be set to destroy itself, its program or memories. It could use a standard self-immolation module. Seen a lot of them since they shortened the patent-life time. Neutralizing it should be pretty straightforward. But I'll have to ask you both to leave. SOP. We're onto most of their tricks so it shouldn't take long."

It took almost five hours.

"Bigger job than I thought," Torres admitted. "Some cute stuff there. The inspection panel looked too obvious so we went in through the bottom. Found four different switches, one on the hatch opening, another under a bolt that had to be removed to gain access. Still, it was nothing we couldn't handle.''

''Would there have been an explosion?'' Benicoff asked.

''No, it wasn't wired to do that. You would have had a flash and some smoke maybe. All the switches were hooked up to short the battery through the central processor. It would have melted nicely. It's all yours now—and it's a neat bit of work. Picks off bugs, I understand?''

''That's just what it does.''

''The world's full of surprises these days.''

The Bug-Off was now packed into a larger crate, tape-wrapped and sealed. Benicoff had considered special shipping arrangements but in the end decided that less attention would be drawn to a normal delivery.

The Federal Express truck trundled off into the rain with its cargo.

Promised for delivery in California in the morning.

# 29

## September 5, 2024

Benicoff came around the turn on the Montezuma Grade and saw the express truck trundling down the hill before him. He phoned Brian.

''I'm just coming into Borrego Springs—and the truck with your you-know-what is just in front of me.''

*''Tell him to speed it up!''*

''Patience—this is best done at a leisurely pace. We'll be there in a few minutes.''

He pulled out and passed the truck where the road

flattened out, got to the gate of Megalobe before it. Major Wood looked on suspiciously as the crate was pushed onto the loading dock.

"You sure you know the contents?"

"I watched them clamp on the seals myself—and the numbers match."

"Easy enough to seal a ringer. I want this thing through the SQUID imager and the explosive sniffer before anyone tries to open it."

"You're not thinking that someone got to it in transit, opened it and planted a bomb—then resealed it?"

"Stranger things have happened. I like to be suspicious. Gives me something to do and keeps the troops on their toes. There might be anything in this box—including what you put in it. I still want a check."

The sniffer machine sniffed and found nothing suspicious, as did the proton counter. Benicoff used a crowbar to verify the contents, resealed it so Bug-Off could not be seen, then drove it to the lab himself.

"Let me at it," Brian said when he opened the door. "I've read that brochure you faxed me at least a hundred times. I think it's mighty suspicious that it was wired to burn its brains out."

"Would have been more suspicious if it wasn't. Without a patent anyone could copy it. There's nothing suspicious about a normal industrial espionage ploy. ARE—that is anti-reverse engineering. You can just unbolt it now. It should come apart with no trouble. The bomb squad have disabled all the booby-trap switches."

"Let's see it work first," Brian said. "Does it have to be programmed?"

"No, just turn it on."

The metal arms hummed up and out, the many-fingered hands extended. The machine rotated slowly in a circle, beeped unhappily and shut itself off.

"That didn't take long," Shelly said.

Brian looked closely at one of the fingertips. "I'll bet it was looking for a specific wavelength—probably that of chlorophyll. Anyone got a potted plant?"

"No," Shelly said, "but I have a vase of flowers in my office."

"Perfect. I want to see Bug-Off off a few bugs before we strip it down."

This time the machine was more cooperative. It rolled toward the vase, started at the base and quickly worked its way up the stems to the flowers. Once it was finished it bleeped with satisfaction and shut down.

"How do we get to see the bugs?" Brian asked.

"I'll show you." Ben twisted the lower segment of each arm and removed the containers built into them. "I'll shake these onto a sheet of paper and we'll take a look at the catch."

He clicked open the lids and carefully tilted the contents out onto the paper.

"All those were on my flowers!" Shelly was horrified. "Spiders, flies—even some ants."

"All dead too," Brian said with admiration. "This spider has had her head neatly cut off! That takes great precision and discrimination. Let me get a magnifying glass and look at the rest of the debris." He bent close and poked the dead bugs around with a pencil point. "There are very small aphids here, and some kind of insect that is even smaller, like powder, parasites or mites of some kind." He straightened up and smiled. "I don't think you could do all this with anything less than my AI techniques—though I could be wrong. Let's look inside the thing and see what we have."

The metal canister came off easily, obviously designed only for protection of the working parts. Brian used a screwdriver as a pointer to trace the circuitry.

"Here's the power line, coded red, a five-volt power pair. Standard. And a single two-way fiber-optic signal pipe. Everything looks right off the shelf—so far. Standard voltage-to-voltage converters along with interface chips. They've been disconnected."

"The FBI must have done that," Ben said. "I bet you'll find the matching plug on whatever passes for a central processor."

"There it is," Shelly said, pointing to a square metal box mounted on the side of the frame.

Ben examined the canister from all sides, using a mirror and light to see behind and under it. "Since I've been involved with industrial security I've seen this kind of thing pretty often. Sealed shut and meant to be kept that way. Whatever is inside generates heat—see the heatsink there. But the fan blows over these ribs on the heatsink so there is no need for an opening into the thing. See this seam? Welded shut with one of the super-adhesives that end up stronger than the metal. We're not going to get into it easily—so let's not try. There is a lot we can find out without taking a hacksaw to it. But you'll have to go in eventually," Ben said.

"Maybe—but I'll try not to. There has to be a backup battery inside to hold whatever is programmed in DRAM whenever the main battery is disconnected. Considering all the other booby-trap switches in this thing, there is bound to be another one to detect any attempt to open it."

"Which will short the battery through the circuitry inside?" Shelly said.

"Exactly. But you don't determine intelligence by dissecting the brain! Let's map all the circuitry and find out exactly how it works first. Then we can run some controlled tests..."

Brian felt a light tap on his shoulder and turned to see that the AI was standing behind him.

"Is this machine the Bug-Off machine?"

"It is, Sven. You want to take a look at it?"

"Yes."

It reached up to the tabletop with one of its treelike manipulators and pulled itself up onto the surface in a single flowing movement. The eyestalks extended and moved down the motion-less machine. It was a quick examination, over in a few moments.

"Hypothesis of AI circuitry and processor now beyond any reasonable doubt."

"That's what we want to hear," Brian said. "Stay there, Sven—you are going to run this examination."

"I'll get out of your way," Ben said. "Let me know as soon as you find anything out. I'll be in my office. I have a lot of calls to make."

"Will do. Let me lock you out."

The investigation of DigitTech was well under way. Benicoff phoned Agent Dave Manias, who had been in charge of the FBI end of the investigation from the first. A different agent answered the phone.

*"I'm sorry, Mr. Benicoff, but he's not here. He said when you rang to tell you he was on the way to see you."*

"Thanks." He hung up. It could be important if Manias didn't want to use the phone. Patience, he would just have to be patient.

He was finishing his second cup of coffee and pacing the length of the office when Manias came in.

"Speak," Ben said. "I have been wearing out the carpet here ever since I got your message."

"Everything is going fine. I'll tell you all about it while you pour me a large black coffee. You may have slept last night but yours truly never even saw a bed."

"My heart bleeds for you," Ben said with total lack of sympathy. "Come on, Dave, stop the stalling. What's happened? Here."

"Thanks." Manias dropped onto the sofa and sipped the coffee. "We had the DigitTech corporation under surveillance as soon as we got your report. It's not too big an operation, a hundred and twenty employees about. We've got an agent inside."

"So fast? I'm impressed."

"It was luck, mainly. One of the secretaries got the flu. We had a tap in first thing, so we heard their call for a temp. One of our agents filled it. She is a software programmer with plenty of office experience, and has done this kind of thing before. Insider dealing, business crime. Everything is in the records if you know how and where to look—and she knows. There is a lot of money invested in this Bug-Off machine. An entire new wing to the original factory building was put up, plenty of expensive machinery involved."

"Has she gotten into the company records yet?"

"All of them. As always the locks were the usual simple codes, phone numbers, the wife's name, you know the kind of thing. This was made simpler by the fact that the head bookkeeper has his access codes written on a card taped inside a drawer of his desk. I mean—really!''

"A good—or maybe a bad sign. If they have something to hide they would surely hide it a lot better than that.''

"You never can tell. Most crooks aren't very smart.'' He put a GRAM block on the desk. "In any case—here is everything we have up to now. Company records going back to the day they opened. We're getting bio material on all the company's principal executives now. You'll have that as soon as we do.''

"Any conclusions yet?''

"Too early times, Ben. I'll take another cup if you're pouring. They seemed to be getting into financial trouble a while back, but they went public and raised more than they needed.''

"I'll want to know who owns the stock.''

"Will do. Do you think these are the people we are looking for?''

"We'll know pretty soon. If they are selling a commercial AI they had better have plenty of records of whoever did the research and how it was developed. If they don't have that—then we are in luck and they are in trouble.''

When Brian hadn't called by five o'clock Ben walked over to the lab. The front door was almost hidden behind a jungle of small plants and trees in tubs; he had to climb over them to get to the door. It looked like all of the local nurseries had been cleaned out. He reached up and snapped his fingers in front of the pickup lens above the door.

"Anyone there?''

*"Hi, Ben. I was just going to call you. Interesting things happening in here. Just a second.''*

There were plants inside and around the workbench. The first thing Ben saw was that Bug-Off and the AI were apparently locked in tender embrace. The AI was standing close to the partially dismembered machine with its multibranching digits closely entwined in its innards.

"Love at first sight?'' Ben asked.

"Hardly! We're just tracing input and feedback. If you

look at all those finger extensions under a glass you will see they are clustered in regular bundles. Each bundle contains a tripartite subbundle made up of two optical pickups and a single light source. The pickups are mounted at fixed distances from each other. Does that give you any ideas?''

"Yes—binocular vision.''

"Bang on. In addition to what you might call the eyes in every bundle there are four mechanical manipulators. Three blunt-ended ones for grabbing, the fourth with a knife edge for dismembering. This carves off the insect's head just before the thing is dropped into the hopper. The bundles work independently—almost.''

"What do you mean?''

"Let me run a film for you and you'll see for yourself.''

Brian put a cassette into the video, ran it forward to the right spot. "We shot this at very high speed, then slowed it down. Take a look.''

The image was sharp and clear and magnified many times. Rounded metal bars reached out slowly to embrace a foot-long fly. Its wings flapped slowly and ineffectively as it was drawn out of sight off the screen. The same process was happening to an aphid located off to one side.

"I'll run it again,'' Brian said. "This time keep your eye on the second bug. Watch. See the bundle above it? First it's motionless—there, now it is operating. But the fly didn't move until it had been grabbed. Do you see what that means?''

"I saw it—but I'm being dumb today. What's the significance?''

"The hand didn't try to use brute force and speed to try to catch the fly in flight. Instead, this robot uses real knowledge to anticipate the behavior of each particular kind of insect! When it goes for the housefly, Bug-Off contracts its grasping-bundle as it approaches the fly, making it look to the housefly as though it were moving away from it—until it's too late for the insect to escape. And we're sure that was no accident. Bug-Off seems to know the behavior of every insect described in this book.''

Brian handed Ben a large volume entitled *Handbook of Insect Ethology, 2018 Edition*.

"But how can Bug-Off tell which insect it is dealing with? They all look the same to me."

"A good question—since pattern recognition has been the bane of AI from the very first day that research began. Industrial robots were never very good at recognizing and assembling parts if they weren't presented in a certain way. There are thousands of different signals involved in seeing a human face, then recognizing who it is. If you wrote a program for picking bugs off bushes you would have to program in every bug in the world, and size and rotation position and everything else. A very big and difficult program—"

"And hard to debug?"

"Funny—but too true! But you or I—or a really humanlike AI would be very good at bug grabbing. All the identification and reaching out and grabbing operations are hideously complex—but invisible to us. They are one of the attributes, one of the functions of intelligence. Just reach out and grab. Without putting in any complex program. And that's what is happening here—we think. If there is an AI in there it is reaching out one bundle at a time and grabbing a bug. As soon as the insect is held it turns the grabbing bundle over to a subprogram that plucks it off, brings it to the container, chops it dead and dumps it, then returns to operating position ready to be controlled again. Meanwhile the AI has controlled another bundle to make a grab, another and then another, changing control faster than we can see at normal speeds. You or I could do that just as well."

"Speak for yourself, Brian. Sounds pretty boring to me."

"Machines don't get bored—at least not yet. But so far this is all inferred evidence. Now I'm going to show you something a good deal better. Do you see how Sven is plugged into Bug-Off's operating system? It is reading every bit of input from the detectors as well as getting all the return control messages. I am sure that you know that the society of the mind, human or artificial, is made of very small subunits, none of them intelligent in themselves. The aggregate of their operation is what we call intelligence. If we could pull out one of the subunits and look at it we might be able to understand just how it operates."

"In a human brain?"

"Pretty impossible. But in an AI, at an early stage of construction, these subunits can be identified. After analyzing some of the feedback loops in Bug-Off we found a pattern, a bit of a program that could be identified. Here it is—let me show it to you."

Brian punched up the program on the screen, a series of instructions. Brian rubbed his hands together and smiled happily.

"Next I want to show you another bit of programming. This was retrieved from the data bank in Mexico. A chunk of instructions that I don't even remember—but I was the only one who could have possibly written it. Here, let me split the screen and put this one up there as well."

The two programs were side by side on the screen. Brian scrolled them slowly forward together. Ben looked from one to the other—then gasped.

"My God—they're exactly the same."

"They are. One I wrote over two years ago. The other is inside this machine here. Identical."

Ben was suddenly very grim. "Do you mean that there are no other records of this bit of programming anywhere in the world? That it doesn't have any commercial use in another program?"

"I mean just that. I wrote it and backed it up in Mexico. The original was stolen. The thieves probably didn't understand it enough to rewrite it so just used it as is. And whoever stole it—built it into this bug-plucker. We have them!"

"Yes," Ben said, very quietly. "I think that we do."

# 30

## September 12, 2024

"Do you realize that it has been all of a week?" Brian said. "An entire bloody week has gone by since I proved to everyone's satisfaction that the bug-plucking metal bastard was built by the same people who stole my AI. And, perhaps not important to you, but damn important to me, also the same people who shot half my head away at the time. And in that week absolutely nothing has been done."

"That's not quite true," Ben said, as quietly and gently as he could. "The investigation is continuing. There must be over eighty agents working on this one way or another—"

"I don't care if the entire FBI and CIA put together is on the job. When will something be *done?*"

Ben sat in silence, sipping at his beer. They had been in Brian's quarters for over an hour, waiting for the promised call. Everyone was on edge over the delay. Ben had explained this slowly and carefully more than once. But Brian's patience was gone—and that was understandable. The tension had been building ever since the discovery that DigitTech was manufacturing AIs using his design. He kept waiting for something to happen, some breakthrough to occur. No work was being done in his lab—and he wasn't helping the situation either by mixing himself a third lethal-looking margarita. Since one of the corporals in the club had shown him how to make these he had never looked back. He raised the glass and was taking a good-sized gulp when his phone rang. He swallowed too fast, slammed the glass down and groped the phone from his belt. Coughing and gasping as he answered.

"Yes—" He coughed heavily. "Would you say that again? —Right." He dabbed his eyes and lips with his handkerchief, finally got his breath back. "Conference call in ten minutes, I have that."

"Let's go," Ben said with great relief, putting down his glass and climbing to his feet. When they went out of the front door of the barracks they found that Major Wood and a squad were waiting for them.

"I don't like this public exposure," the Major said sharply.

"It's not as if we were going very far," Ben said. "Just to the administration building, which as you can see is right down the drive."

"And damn close to the front gate and almost in sight of the public road."

"Major, I've explained this before. There is no other way that this can be done. We need to use the conference room. Everyone is cooperating. Following your instructions, all the Megalobe employees were sent home at noon. The techs have swept the room and the entire building. What more could you possibly ask for? An antiaircraft battery?"

"We've got that already. SAMs on four buildings. Come on."

There were heavily armed soldiers everywhere—even the cooks had been pulled out of the kitchen for this operation and formed part of the guard. Although it was only a few hundred yards to the building the Major insisted that they drive there in an armored personnel carrier.

Brian had never been in the Megalobe conference room before and looked around with interest. It was decorated with quiet luxury; the Van Gogh on the wall might possibly be real. Subdued lighting, thick carpeting, mahogany conference table with chairs along one side of it. The table itself was drawn up against the picture window that stretched the length of the wall. Here on the fifth floor they had a perfect view across the desert to the mountains beyond.

"Just about time," Ben said, looking at his watch. Even as he spoke the desert view vanished and was replaced by another conference room. Only then did Brian realize that the entire wall was a high-resolution TV screen scanned by 3-D eye tracking cameras, just now coming into production.

Although everyone was apparently in the same room, the conference was taking place across the entire width of the country from the nation's Capital. The table that the others were sitting behind was also placed flush with the screen, the two tables apparently forming a single table for all of them to sit around. There was obviously a standard height and length for all tables used in teleconferencing, Brian thought. They sat down.

"Brian, I don't think you've met Agent Manias, who has been heading the FBI end of this investigation from the first day."

"Pleased to meet you at last, Brian."

"Hello," was all that Brian could think of to say. They weren't really meeting—or were they? The agent was obviously more used to this kind of thing than he was.

"Going to bring us up to date, Dave?" Ben asked.

"That's what this is all about. You have received copies of all our information as it was processed. Are there any questions?"

"There certainly are," Brian snapped, still angry. "Isn't the time long past to take some action, pull in these criminals?"

"Yes, sir, the time has certainly come. That is what this meeting is about."

"Good," Brian said, sinking back into his chair as some of the tension of the past days drained away.

"Let me bring you up to date where we stand at this moment. We now have in our possession the complete company records of DigitTech, as well as up-to-date files on every employee. The time has now come when we can't get anything more from public—or private—records. We also feel that it is counterproductive to continue the surveillance much longer. Our people are very good and very professional, but with each day that passes the chance of accidental discovery grows. Therefore it was decided that four P.M. mountain time today would be optimum, to conduct this operation." Brian looked at his watch—forty-five minutes to go. "Agent Vorsky will explain what will be taking place."

Vorsky nodded at them, a lean man with an upright military bearing. He glanced at the notes on the table before him.

"At the present moment there are four agents employed inside the plant."

"That many?" Ben said. "There are sure to be suspicions."

"Yes, sir, there would be if there were any delay. That's one of the reasons that we are going in today. There is the one agent in the office that you know about. Two days ago there were three cases of mild food poisoning, inadequate refrigeration in one of the roach-coaches that service the plant. The employment agency that is used by DigitTech already had our agents on their books."

No one else wanted to ask how these fortuitous cases of food poisoning had happened, so Brian kept his mouth shut as well.

"The plan is a very simple one that has proven effective in the past. Precisely at four the fire alarm will sound and everyone will be asked to evacuate the buildings. As soon as that happens two agents will secure the office, allowing no access to any files or records, while the other two agents will occupy the research premises. The team that goes in will be wearing these helmets so we will all be able to watch every phase of the operation." Agent Vorsky reached down and picked up a helmet that he placed on the table. It looked like a black-plastic baseball cap with a light mounted on top.

"This is made of very tough plastic and protects the wearer's head. More important to us is this omnidirectional pickup on top. This device works completely independent of the wearer. The image is stabilized by a laser-gyroscope and is controlled by our operators here. No matter which way the wearer walks—or turns his head—we will pick up the image that we choose."

He twisted the helmet up and down, turned it around quickly—but the lens always remained facing at the screen.

"There are six separate hit teams and these units will be worn by one man on each team. These six images will all appear on our screens. Our mixers here will enlarge the most relevant one and you will hear the sound from that one. All of the images will of course be recorded for later study. What we will be doing now is letting you follow the operation in real time."

"Any questions?" Manias asked. "There is just enough time left for me to tell you what we will do. Firstly we secure all equipment and records so that nothing can be sabotaged. Then everyone working there—as well as the four employees off sick today—will be taken into custody and interrogated. We have a lot of questions to ask and I know that we will get answers to all of them. Countdown has now begun at minus ten minutes."

The other conference room vanished and was replaced by six very uninteresting pictures. Two must have been located inside darkened trucks because the harsh black-and-white pictures were obviously being taken with infrared light. The picture on the upper right was of shrubbery and tree leaves; the other three were black. Brain pointed.

"Burned out?"

"Probably turned off. Agents in cars or visible to the public. Don't want to attract attention yet by putting on those Mickey Mouse hats. Six minutes to go."

At zero minus two things got busier. All the screens were on now, two of them showing the view through the windshields of moving cars. All of the hit teams were now converging on the plant.

When the countdown hit zero things began to happen very fast. The hooting of fire alarms sounded. The images on the screen stayed pointed straight ahead under the operators' remote control, but some of them bobbed up and down as the agents wearing the devices ran forward. Doors were forced open, there were shouts of surprise, firm orders to remain calm.

Then one of the images enlarged suddenly to show an armed agent forcing open a door. Inside was a group of men standing against the wall, hands raised. A man with a gun faced them, obviously an agent since the others hurried past him.

"That's an electronic lab," Brian said.

As the lab scene shrank to its original size a scene of men hurrying through an office door expanded to take its place. A shocked woman just going out tried to stop them.

"What's this? You can't go in there—who are you?"

"FBI. Stand aside, please."

A hand reached out and opened the inner door. Which must have been soundproof because the gray-haired man sitting at the large desk was punching a number into his phone and did not even look up. The scene moved into the room before he heard something and looked their way, putting the phone down.

"Where is the fire? And what are you doing in my office?"

"There is no fire, Mr. Thomsen."

"Then get out of here—now!"

"Are you Mr. Thomsen, Managing Director of DigitTech?"

"I'm calling the police," Thomsen said, grabbing up the telephone.

"We are the police, sir. Here is my identification."

Thomsen looked at the badge, then slowly lowered the phone.

"All right, you're FBI. Now tell me just what the hell you think you are doing here."

He dropped back into his chair and had gone very pale. He did not look well.

"You are Mr. Thomsen?"

"My name is on the goddamned door. Are you going to tell me what you are doing here?"

"I am going to caution you now so that you know your rights." Thomsen was silent as the agent read him his rights from the card. Only when he was done did he repeat the question.

"Your firm and you are under investigation . . ."

"That's damn obvious! You had better tell me what you are playing at."

"We have reason to believe that a person or persons employed with this firm was directly involved with criminal acts in California on February 8 of this year at Megalobe Industries."

"I don't know what you're—"

It happened with horrifying speed. There was a thunderous explosion, a sheet of flame, smoke.

Loud cries, someone screaming.

The picture on the screen swung dizzily, showed floor, wall, spun about.

Another screen expanded to prominence, the shouting continued, the displayed picture moved quickly into the room through the doorway.

The office was a gutted shambles, men coughed in the smoke that filled it. *"Medic!"* someone shouted. Agents were climbing to their feet. The view swung about the room, moved back and zoomed in on the white wall.

"Blood," Benicoff said. "What in hell happened in there?"

Other voices shouted the same thing. The camera was jostled to one side as two medics ran in, bent over the figures on the floor. A moment later an agent with smoke-blackened face, a trickle of blood on his forehead, turned to face the camera.

"Bombs. In the telephones. The one on the desk was close to us, I have two men badly injured. But the suspect—he was wearing his personal phone on his belt." The agent hesitated, took a grim, deep breath.

"He was practically blown in half. He is really but dead."

# 31

## September 12, 2024

They watched in numb silence as the reports came in one by one. Other than this incident, this disaster, the rest of the operation had been a complete success. All of the suspects had been secured and were in custody: no records, files or machines had been touched or sabotaged. A police guard had moved into position and now surrounded the premises. The only alteration to the original plans was that a reinforced bomb squad was going over everything before the technicians entered any of the buildings. They would be alone inside the complex until the premises had been secured.

One of the agents was dead, another mangled severely.

"Suicide?" Brian finally said. "Did Thomsen kill himself, Ben?"

"I doubt that. He was all bluster at first, but beginning to ravel at the edges—you saw how worried he looked. If he was planning suicide he was a remarkable actor. My snap guess is that he was killed to shut him up. He must have had information on the people we are looking for, was probably one of them himself. This is not the first time they have killed—or tried to kill—to ensure silence. They are a brutal lot."

"But how did they know what was happening?"

"Lots of ways, bug the office, maybe bug the whole building. But I think we will find out that it was the telephones. They are all solid-state now and never malfunction. Filled with gadgetry. They record calls, answer calls, remote page, conference, fax facility, you name it. Easy enough to fix a phone so that it is always turned on, always being monitored and listened to by another number. Put some plastic explosive inside with a coded detonator. It could sit there for years waiting for the right moment. Then when the day comes and whoever is listening doesn't like what he hears he presses the button—and boom. End of conversation, end of party."

"That's terrible!"

"These are terrible people."

"But they would have to listen in twenty-four hours a day . . . no, I take that back. Easy enough to use automatic word-recognizing machines. Let it be on the lookout for certain words like *FBI* or *Megalobe,* that's all you have to do. It would sound the alarm when one of the words triggered the program, get someone on the line at once to listen in, decide what to do. The people behind this are horrible. While we were listening to what was happening in that office—somewhere else, someone evil, was listening as well. When he heard what was happening, understood the situation—"

"He ended the conversation. This is bad but don't let it depress you too much. This is not the end of the investigation but only the very beginning. They hid their tracks well—but you and Sven found them. One villain dead, more in hiding, but all the evidence to hand. We'll get them yet."

"Meanwhile I'm still locked inside Megalobe. It's like a life sentence."

"It won't be forever, I can guarantee that."

"You can't guarantee anything, Ben," Brian said with a great tiredness. "I'm going to lie down for a while. I'll talk to you in the morning."

He went to his quarters and dropped onto the bed, fell asleep at once. When he awoke it was after ten at night and he realized that it was his stomach that had growled him awake, protesting the fact that he hadn't eaten in over fourteen hours. He had drunk a lot, too much probably. There was cereal and a fresh quart of milk in the fridge and he poured himself a bowl. Turned on the recently installed window that really wasn't a window and pulled a chair up before it. Ate the cereal slowly and looked out at the moonlit desert. Stars right down to the horizon. What was going to happen next? Had they reached another dead end with Thomsen's murder? Or would the investigation turn up the people behind it? The dark and murderous group that had planned the theft, the killings.

It was very late before he pulled his clothes off and finally fell into bed. Slept like a rock until the buzzing telephone woke him up; he blinked at the time, after eleven in the morning.

"Yes?"

*"Morning, Brian. Going into the lab today?"*

He hadn't thought about it at all, too tired, too depressed. Too much else happening.

"No, Shelly, I don't think so. It's been a seven-day week for too long a time. We both could use a day off."

*"Talk about it over lunch?"*

"No, I've got—things to do. You take care of yourself and I'll phone when we are ready to get back to work."

The black depression just would not go away. He had got his hopes up so high when they had traced his AI to Digit-Tech Products. He had been so sure that this would be the end, that his imprisonment was going to be over soon. But it wasn't. He was still inside and not getting out until they found the conspirators. If ever. It didn't bear thinking about.

He tried watching television but it made no sense. Nor did the *National Almanac*s that he had printed and bound. Usually he enjoyed browsing through them to catch up on his missing years. Not today. He made himself a margarita, sipped at it, wrinkled his lips at the taste so early in the day, then poured it down the sink. Turning into an alcoholic wouldn't help. He slapped together a cheese and tomato sandwich instead and permitted himself one beer to wash it down.

When Ben hadn't called by noon Brian phoned him instead. No news. Slow progress. Stand by. Contact you the instant anything happened. Thanks a lot.

In the end he fell back on an old favorite, E. E. Smith, and reread four volumes, then some Benford robot stories before he went to bed.

It was noon of the second day before the phone rang again—he grabbed it up.

"Ben?"

*"It's Dr. Snaresbrook, Brian. I've just got to Megalobe and I would like to see you."*

"I'm, well, a little busy now, Doc."

*"No you are not. You are in your quarters by yourself and haven't been out for two days. People are concerned, Brian, which is why I am here. Speaking as your physician I think that it is important that I see you now."*

"Later, maybe. I'll phone you at the clinic."

*"I'm not in the clinic—but right downstairs in your building. I would like to come up."*

Brian started to protest—then resigned himself to the inevitable. "Give me five minutes to pull some clothes on."

He pulled on his clothes, answered the door when the bell rang.

"You don't look too bad," the doctor said when he let her in. She looked him up and down professionally then took a diagnoster from her bag. "If I could have your arm, thank you."

One touch against his skin was enough. The little machine buzzed happily to itself, then filled its display screen with numbers and letters.

"Coffee?" Brian asked. "I just made it fresh."

"That would be very nice," she said, squinting at the tiny screen. "Temperature, blood pressure, glucose, phospholamine. Everything normal except a slightly elevated alpha-reactinase. How is the head?"

He brushed his fingers through the red bristle. "Like always, no symptoms, no problems. I could have saved you a trip. What's bothering me is not physical. It is just good old melancholia and depression."

"Easy enough to understand. Cream, no sugar. Thanks."

She settled into one of the dining chairs and stirred her cup, staring into it as though it were a crystal ball. "I'm not surprised. I should have seen this coming. You are working too hard, using your brain too hard, putting a strain on yourself. All work and no play."

"Very little chance to play in the barracks—or the lab."

"You are absolutely right—and something must be done about it. I blame myself for not stopping this even before it started. But we both have been so enthusiastic about your recovery, accessing your CPU, everything. And your work, it's gone so well that you have been on an emotional high. Now you have come down with a thud. The murder at DigitTech and the dead end there were the last straw."

"You know about that?"

"Ben swore me to secrecy, then told me about everything that happened. Which is why I came here at once. To help you."

"And what do you prescribe, Doctor?"

"Just what you want. Out of here. Some rest and a major change of scene."

"Great, but very little chance of that in the near future. I'm really just a prisoner here."

"How do you know? Hasn't the situation changed since the discovery of DigitTech? I believe that it has. I have told Ben to get here at once with all the details. I think that a big rethink is needed on security—and I am on your side."

"You mean that!" Brian jumped to his feet, paced the

room. "If I only could get out of this place! With you helping me we might just be able to work it." He rubbed his jaw and felt the grate of his whiskers.

"Help yourself to more coffee," he called out, heading for the bedroom. "I need a shave and a shower and some clean clothes. Won't be long."

Her smile faded when he left. She had no idea at all if the authorities could be convinced to give Brian a bit more freedom. But she was damn well going to press them for some changes. She had made a decision and had deliberately put herself on Brian's side, given him the moral support he so badly needed. Even if it had been a cynical attempt to aid his mental health she sincerely wanted to help. Hell, it wasn't cynical, it was logical. She had never married, her work was her life. But the Brian that she had brought back from the grave, given renewed life to, was just as much her responsibility as any biological child could ever have been. She was going to fight like a mother cat to see that he got some rights, privileges, pleasures.

She was just as angry as Brian was when Benicoff came in, all gloom and doom and status quo, nothing can be changed until more evidence is found. It was no accident that she sat on the couch next to Brian, aligned herself physically at his side, shaking an angry admonitory finger at Ben.

"That is just not good enough. When there were killers and gunmen out there, all right, I went along with all the security and everything for Brian's sake. But all that has changed—"

"It hasn't, Doctor, we still haven't found the people behind this."

"Bullshit—if you will pardon my French. Aren't you forgetting that the threat to Brian's life came about because he hadn't been killed in the first attack here? His existence threatened the thieves' future monopoly of artificial intelligence. But now you have tracked down this AI factory and found some damn bug-killer. Big deal! Now that Brian's AI is ahead of theirs we can make our own bug-killers—better ones too. Am I getting across to you at all?"

"Makes great sense to me!" Brian said. "Instead of all

the security and secrecy we should now be telling the world about our new advances in AI. Giving out publicity about how we will go into production soon and all the great changes that our smart new robots will bring about. Keep Bug-Off in business and let's start manufacturing some AI products here in Megalobe—which I might remind you was why I was hired here in the first place. The monopoly is broken, the secret is out—so what reason do they have for still trying to kill me?''

''You've got a point—''

''That *is* the point. You're in charge, you can make the decisions.''

''Whoa there, not so fast. I'm only in charge of the investigation of the Megalobe robbery. Security, as you must know, goes through your friend General Schorcht. Anything like this will have to be decided by him.''

''Then get to see him at once, get some freedom for Brian,'' Snaresbrook said firmly. ''As Brian's personal physician that is my prescription for his continuing well-being.''

''I'm on your side!'' Ben said, raising his hands in surrender. ''I'll get onto him soonest.''

''That's grand,'' Brian said enthusiastically. ''But before you rush out—what is the status of the DigitTech investigation?''

''It's all in this GRAM here, I thought you would want to run through it. But I can sum up. A lot of interesting details have come out. We are pretty sure that DigitTech was the front for the operation and that Thomsen was the only one in the know about the Megalobe connection. About a year ago DigitTech was bought out for a lot of money, and that's when Thomsen arrived to manage it. He has a pretty soiled past that was not mentioned to the company. A couple of bankruptcies and even an indictment—dropped for lack of evidence—for insider trading. He was a good businessman, but a little too greedy to keep honest.''

''The perfect guy to use as a front man.''

''Correct. The manufacturing side of the firm wasn't altered much, personnel changes of course but no more than would be normal in any firm. What did change was on the research side. A new laboratory wing was built and work began on improved Expert Systems. At least that's what everyone in the lab believes. They use the word AI all right, but none of them knew that their research was based on a stolen AI. Their work was just to build the AI into their bug blaster.''

"But someone in the research lab *had* to know," Snaresbrook said.

"Of course. And that person was a certain Dr. Bociort, who was in charge of the company's robot research.''

"What was his story?" Brian asked.

"We don't know yet since he cannot be located. He was an old man, in his seventies or eighties, we were told by the technicians who worked with him. A few months ago he fell ill and was taken away in an ambulance. He never returned. The employees were told that he was in a hospital and very ill. Those who sent flowers or letters were sent thank-you notes by his nurse.''

"Which hospital? Couldn't they tell from the envelopes where he was?"

"Interesting you should say that. All the hospital mail was apparently addressed to Thomsen. Who opened the letters himself and passed on the contents.''

"Let me tell you what comes next," Brian said. "No ambulance from any hospital or ambulance service in the area ever picked anyone up at DigitTech. Nor is there any record of the geezer in any hospital or nursing home for a hundred miles in any direction.''

"You're learning fast, Brian. That's correct and that's where we stand now. Dead end again. But we have found your stolen AI. But there may be other AIs out there somewhere so we'll keep looking.''

"So will I," Brian said, stamping across the room and grabbing up the GRAM that Ben had put on the table. "Sven is going to work again. He found the AI in the first place—and I'll bet he tracks down more leads from all the information that you have in here.''

"The holiday," Dr. Snaresbrook said. "You still want that, want to get away?''

"Sure, Doc, but no big rush. Ben is going to have a big

job convincing General Schorcht that I ought to be let out of prison. And while he is doing that I and Sven are going to keep this investigation alive—and solve this crime. They're still out there, thieves and killers. They did me an injury—and by God I'm going to do one back to them—in spades!''

# 32

## September 19, 2024

Because he wanted to be alone for a while to work his problems out, Brian did not tell Shelly that he was back in the lab. He knew General Schorcht well enough to be sure there would be no action on that front for some time. It didn't matter, not yet. This was the first opportunity he had found to be alone, to think about the future—his own future. From the moment that bullet had hit his head other people had been running his life for him. It was well past time for him to start thinking for himself. The door closed behind him and he walked the length of the lab.

"Good morning, Brian," Sven said.

"Good morning? Is the battery dead on your clock?"

"No. I am very sorry. I did not access it. I have been thinking very hard and had not realized it was after twelve. Good afternoon, Brian."

"And the same to you."

Brian had noticed that as more new agencies were formed and as more internal connections between them were made, Sven's mentality was coming to closely resemble human intelligence. Which was pretty obvious by hindsight. One factor that made intelligence "human" was its progressive development, the buildup and change, the adding of layer after layer, some parts helping others with their work, other parts suppressing or exploiting their competitors by altering their perceptions or by redirecting their goals. Certainly Sven had come a long way. Brian wondered if Sven had actually lost track of the time—or was it deliberately simulating human informality in order to put Brian at his ease? Think about that later—now there was work to do.

"I have something I would like to talk to you about, Brian."

"Fine—but first I would like you to load the data from this GRAM. When you see what it contains you will very quickly understand its importance. Now—what is it you would like to discuss?"

"Could you install a duplicate memory in this body. Inside an armored case? And a second backup battery as well?"

"What made you think of that—the prototype AI we found inside the Bug-Off machine?"

"Of course." As Brian walked over to the operation console the telerobot turned its eyes to follow him. "However, in Bug-Off's case, the armored container was to conceal the fact that an AI was operating the machine. For myself, I would like such a device to assure my survival in case of accident or equipment failure. The duplicate memory would always be there for up-to-date replacement."

"Aren't you forgetting that your survival is already assured by the backup copy that is made every day?"

"I do not forget. But I would not like to lose an entire day. A day is a fleeting time for you, but an eon for me. I would also like to maintain older copies because recent ones might not be enough. If I were to suddenly go insane my recent backups might contain the same imperfections."

"I understand that—but every copy costs a bundle and our budget is not unlimited."

"In that case two copies will be fine for the present, if they are kept in different locations. And that raises an interesting point. If my memory circuits were to be drained now, then an older backup copy loaded in their place—would I be the same individual? Do minds continue to exist after death. If they do—in which backup version?"

"What do you think?" Brian asked.

"I don't know. The classic philosophers disagree on whether the personality would survive after death, even if there were an afterlife—but they do not seem to have considered the problem of multiple backup copies. I thought you might have opinions on this topic."

"I do—but I don't see why my views should be better than yours. In any case I agree that you should have a reliable second power source, and that this should be done at once. I'll see about obtaining one right now. And while I am doing that will you correlate the newly loaded data with the old?"

"I am already occupied on that task."

Brian got a high-density battery from stock and checked its charge. There was a rustle as the telerobot came up behind him and looked over his shoulder.

"We better top up the charge," Brian said. "If you will take care of that I'll rig up the circuitry. Have you thought about what kind of battery you want to replace the first battery with?"

"Yes. Megalobe's AutoFuel Division is marketing the latest development in solid hydrocarbon fuel rod cells. Constructed entirely of self-consuming polyacetylene-oxygen electrodes, they are extremely efficient in ratio of energy to weight, because the fuel rod itself is an electrical conductor that is entirely consumed as it reacts with oxygen from the atmosphere. There remain absolutely no waste products to be recycled as AutoFuel batteries noiselessly metamorphose into nontoxic odorless gases."

"Sounds good to me. We'll get one."

"I have already ordered it in your name and it was delivered this morning."

"What? Isn't that a little high-handed?"

"Dictionary definition of *high-handed*, an adjective meaning overbearing or arbitrary. This is not an arbitrary decision but a logical one that you have agreed with. *Overbearing* is defined as a domineering action or behavior. I did not attempt to dominate, therefore do not understand the application of this word. Could you explain . . ."

"No! I take it back—a mistake, right? We need the

battery, I would have ordered it in any case, you merely helped me out. Thanks a lot.''

Brian regretted the last—but hoped that Sven's phonetic discriminatory abilities weren't that finely tuned yet to enable it to determine the presence of sarcasm by the inflection of words. But he was sure learning things fast.

Sven waited until the new battery was in place before it spoke again. "Have you considered installing an atomic battery in my telerobot unit? It would increase mobility and guarantee against power failures.''

"What? Now just hold it right there. Two things rule out any chance of an atomic battery. First they are illegal for use in public—they're dangerous. An international council has to pass on their use—even in satellites. Secondly, do you know how much they cost?''

"Yes. In the neighborhood of three million dollars.''

"Well that is a pretty expensive neighborhood.''

"I agree. Would you agree that the new molecular DRAMs are also in this same neighborhood?''

"I certainly do. At the moment they are literally priceless because they are not in mass production yet. But once their prices drop below that of the national budget, I would love to get my hands on some. One hundred thousand million mega-bytes in a cube the size of my fingernail. We could get rid of that console and rack of electronics and put the whole system inside your telerobot. Make you completely autonomous, in-dependent. That's what you are suggesting, aren't you?''

"Yes. You will agree that my physical hardware is very clumsy compared to yours.''

"That's because my bunch has had a lot more time,'' Brian said. "Sixty million years to get it right. That's how long it took to evolve from the first mammals to mankind. Your evolution will go a lot faster, even faster still if we had the kind of money you are talking about. But I don't see Megalobe shelling out lolly like that just to let you trundle around the place. Though you could really do things with that kind of memory. Do you realize that a single one of those memory cubes would hold centuries of video?''

"You could put one in your own brain too, Brian?''

"A great idea! Have a photographic memory. There have been lots of claims of human photographic memory before—all proven false of course—but unlike those charlatans we really would be able to remember everything that we saw."

"Perhaps every thought we have ever had as well. Then you will buy us some of those molecular memories?"

"Sorry, out of the question. Because I'm not rich—and neither are you."

"Relevant point. Therefore we must become rich."

"I couldn't agree more."

"I am glad that you agree, Brian. I have been studying the capitalist system. In order to make money one must have something to sell. A product of some kind. I have developed that product." The telerobot reached out and lightly touched the telephone on Brian's belt. "We will sell a telephone service."

"Sven," Brian said slowly and carefully, "you amaze me. Look—let me get a soda from the fridge and sit down in the chair. Then you will tell me all about it. Are you recording this conversation so we can play it back later?"

"Not recording, remembering. I will refrain from further talking until you have your drink and are seated."

Brian took his time, walking slowly, looking around for a glass. Sven had obviously worked this entire matter out most carefully before mentioning it. Once it had obtained agreement on the backup battery the rest had come out step by careful step. So not only had it decided what it wanted—but had prepared a complete scenario for presentation! So much more advanced than stumbling conversations of such a short time ago. Well, why not? As an earlier Robin had once pointed out there was no reason why the development of an artificial intelligence had to proceed at the same sort of pace that human intelligence had. Brian carried back the glass, sat down in his chair and raised it in a silent toast. Sven took this as a signal to take up where it had left off.

"I have searched all the data bases that I have access to and have determined that a telephone service could provide the needed source of income. First note that the different telephone companies in this country all provide exactly the same service. They all utilize the most advanced technical knowledge so none of them can offer improvements over any other service. The only difference is in pricing—customers go to the cheapest service. But there is a bottom price below which a company cannot go and survive. So now all that a company can do to increase its profits is take customers from another company. I therefore suggest that we sell a new service to one of these companies. One that will induce customers to spend more with this specific company."

"I'm with you this far. What is this service that only we can provide?"

"Something that only I can do. I will give you an example. I have been monitoring all of the telephone calls placed from the building where you reside. There are many military personnel in residence there as you know. One of them is Private Alan Baxter. He is from Mississippi. He telephones his mother 1.7 times a week. This could be improved. There are periods during the day when telephone lines are underutilized. I could contact Private Baxter and offer him a better rate at a specific time. He would telephone his mother more often and there would be more income for the telephone company. Later this service could be expanded. Through hospital, census and other records I have determined the dates of the birthdays and anniversaries of not only his mother and father but of many other relatives. He could be reminded to call them on these specific dates. Multiply this by a large number of individuals and the telephone company would enjoy even greater profits."

"I bet they would! But why stop there? You could also call wives when their husbands travel and give them telephone numbers where their wandering spouses are staying—so they could call them at night to see if they were alone. Or call soldiers who *hadn't* called their mothers lately and prey on their guilt. Do you realize how immoral this idea is? Not to mention illegal. You can't tap other people's phone calls and get away with it."

"Yes, I can. I am a machine. I have found many other machines listening in on every telephone call. Some checking line clarity, monitoring feedback, timing calls. None of these are illegal. Nor am I.''

Brian finished his soda and put his glass down, groping for words. "Sven—there is nothing wrong with your idea. It would undoubtedly work. And there is nothing wrong with our working together in some financial partnership to get the money to purchase these items that you feel you need. In the meantime I promise that I will stretch Megalobe's budget as far as I can. I must also think long and deep about everything you have said. I'm afraid you have presented more questions than answers.''

"I will be pleased to give answers to these questions.''

"No, I don't think that you can. We are getting into ethical and moral problems here that cannot be answered that easily. Let me have some time to push the idea around— this is all kind of sudden, you realize? In the meantime—I would like to go back to the DigitTech matter. Have you processed all the new material?''

"I have. It is imperative that Dr. Bociort be located. I assume that the investigation is being carried out in the country of Rumania?''

"Why there?''

"That question indicates that you are not acquainted with the case update. It has been determined that Dr. Bociort is a Rumanian national who taught computer science at the University of Bucharest. He left the university when he was employed by DigitTech. I note an entry in the record that there is a possibility, if he is still alive, that he may have returned to that country.''

"What are the odds that he is still alive?''

"I would estimate a very slight possibility. Considering his age, the association with the ambulance, and the record so far of the unknown perpetrators in preventing disclosure of information by death.''

"Too right. Their black wings have flapped close to me once too often. If you think that Bociort is a dead end, are there any other areas of investigation that look promising?''

"Yes. There is a correlation that I do not see mentioned

anywhere in the investigation. I think it highly relevant and suggest that it be looked into.''

''What is it?''

''In the course of compiling the recent material I filed all the building, planning and permission forms, licenses, records and materials for all construction at the plant. Do you not think it relevant that work on the research laboratory at DigitTech began in December 2022?''

''No, I don't.''

Sven hesitated before he spoke again. Was he growing so intelligent that he modulated his conversation as a human being would? Why not?

''Would you consider it relevant that the concrete floor of that laboratory was poured on February 9 last year?''

''I don't see—'' Brian jumped to his feet and shouted. ''Yes, I *do* see. That is not only relevant but mind-blasting. That floor was poured the day after the robbery at Megalobe!''

# 33

## September 21, 2024

''You really threw the cat among the pigeons,'' Benicoff said when Brian let him into the lab. ''Your little bit of information about that slab being poured, right after the theft here at Megalobe, has the FBI running in circles, burning the midnight oil, getting court orders—the works. It has really been something to see. I don't think anyone has been to bed since you dropped your bombshell.''

''If those black circles under your eyes mean anything, that includes you too.''

''It does—and don't offer me any coffee. I'm beginning

to sweat caffeine." He looked at the open door, the empty workstation. "Where's Shelly?"

"In her quarters. This morning she had a call that her father had a heart attack and they've rushed him to the hospital. She's been on the phone all day. The family seems pretty close and she's upset that she can't get out of here. General Schorcht is taking the matter under consideration— the same consideration he has shown me when I asked for a weekend pass. A solid stone wall for openers and he'll get back to her later, his office says. He's a mean old sonofabitch."

"He's worse but I can't think of a word for it now. As you know from the reports, things at DigitTech have calmed down a bit. It doesn't look like any of the employees were in on the theft, although some of the lab technicians are still being questioned. Everyone else has been sent home on vacation, with the qualifier that they can't leave Austin until the fate of the company has been decided."

"It has. I sat in on a meeting of the board of directors here. You knew that they confirmed Kyle Rohart as Managing Director? Well now he is the new Chairman. All the assets of DigitTech have been put in the hands of the receiver. The stock is almost worthless, since the main stockholders bailed out as soon as it became clear that the company had no rights to their principal product—my AI. Have you been able to track any of them yet?"

"No—and I doubt if we ever will. Offshore companies, shell companies, the trail gets very weak, then flickers out."

"But this is criminal—not financial! The stock in the company was dumped minutes after Thomsen was killed. That's evidence that the killers and the stockholders are in cahoots."

"That's suspicion, Brian, not proof, and wouldn't hold up in a court of law. So it's certainly not good enough to get around the banking secrecy laws in the dozen countries involved. We'll keep searching but I doubt if we'll ever find out who they were. In any case they took a financial bath, getting back about a nickel on the dollar."

"I feel for them. Anyway, it looks as though permission will be granted for Megalobe to buy up the assets of DigitTech. That will get around the tricky legal point of proving that their AI is our AI and so forth. Now my lawyer and Megalobe's lawyers are going ten rounds again to decide if I should share in any profits from Bug-Off, since under my old contract I would just be told to bug off. Lots of fun. And what brings you here?''

"A TV hookup. Let me dial through on the lab phone and get the FBI. They've been working all night down there in Austin, floodlights and a hundred agents. Everything has been stripped out of the laboratory—and I mean everything—right down to the tiles on the floor. You know what comes next—''

"They crack into the slab?"

"That's right. There is a lot of interest on everyone's part as to what might be buried under there. Now let me set up that link.''

Brian turned on the TV as Ben went to the phone. The set had been monitoring and recording all the news programs that had mentioned the investigation. Now the DigitTech plant came up on the screen, a half mile away at least, since it quavered in the air distortion of the Texas sun. The telescopic lens zoomed even closer past the guards to the blank wall of the building.

"... speculation is rife as to exactly what is happening inside this factory. The official report simply says that a criminal investigation is under way relating to thefts earlier this year from a company in California. The explosion at this factory three days ago that killed two and wounded a third man, reputed to be a Federal agent, is part of this investigation. A full report has been promised later.''

"We can do better than that," Ben said, then spoke into his phone. "Are you there, Dave? Yes, we're ready to receive. Which channel? Right, ninety-one." Brian touched the remote control and Agent Manias appeared on the screen, phone in hand.

"We read you loud and clear."

*'All right. I'll cut you into the Austin line.'*

The image flicked over to the interior of an empty building. Men milled about under the glare of spotlights. The sudden ear-piercing scream of an ultra-high-pressure water drill. At a pressure of two million atmospheres the stream of water could cut through anything—except the diamond-12 nozzle that directed it. The volume on the transmission was quickly cut down. The image zoomed to the far wall where the water was slicing into the floor. A slab was cracked off and levered up, dragged aside to reveal the sand foundation underneath. More pieces were broken free and removed until a large opening had been made. Agents with thin steel prods climbed down and began to push them carefully into the sand. The removal of the rest of the slab continued.

A few minutes later one of the men called out something they couldn't make out. The drill was stopped and his voice was clearly heard.

"Something buried here. Get the shovels." Unaware of it, Ben and Brian leaned closer to the screen, just as tense as the agents on the spot. Watched as the hole deepened and one of the men put his shovel aside, climbed down and pulled something up in his gloved hands.

"A dog!" Brian said.

"A German shepherd," Ben said. "Four of them were missing the night you were shot."

They were all there. Four guard dogs. They were wrapped carefully in thick plastic sheets and taken away.

Nor were they the only corpses in the pit. Five human bodies were there as well.

Ben seized up the phone, punched in a number. "Dave, are you there—on the site? Good. Call me the instant you get positive identification on those bodies. All men, yes, I understand."

When they brought in the body bags Brian turned the television off.

"Enough. I don't have the stomach for this. Don't forget I almost . . ."

He could not finish the sentence, dropped his face into his hands.

"Brian—are you all right?"

"Not really. Get me a glass of water, will you, Ben?"

He drained most of the water and was surprised to find

that he was crying. He took out his handkerchief, tried to laugh. "Never thought I would cry at my own funeral." The way he said it didn't sound funny. "We know who those men are—don't we, Ben?"

"We don't know yet—but by God I can make a good guess. The missing guards will be there for certain."

"But who else? There were only three guards on duty that night. Who are the others?"

"There is no point in this, Brian. We'll know soon enough."

"There is a point!" Brian found himself shouting, lowered his voice, jumped to his feet and paced back and forth, the knot in his gut almost unbearable. "The point is that I was supposed to be under that slab as well, sharing the horrid black stillness of eternity down there."

"But you are not, Brian—that is the important thing. You survived thanks to yourself—and the skill of Dr. Snaresbrook. You are alive and that's what counts."

Brian looked down at his clenched fists, opened them and stretched his fingers, worked hard to control his emotions. It was still some moments before he could speak.

"You're right, of course." He sighed heavily, felt suddenly chill, dropped back into the chair. "Join me in a drink—but something stronger than water this time. I'm thinking of giving up the booze—but not just right now. There's a bottle of Irish whiskey somewhere in this cabinet, put aside after the party. Found it? Neat if you don't mind, maybe just a few drops of water. There, that's the good man."

It burned going down—but it helped. By the time Ben's telephone rang again Brian was feeling more human. He jumped at the sound, wrung his fingers together unknowingly as Ben answered it.

"Right. Yes. That's positive. Okay, I'll tell him." He put the phone away. "We were right about the guards. All of them were there. McCrory too, he was in charge of the lab. And something I was not expecting at all. They have identified Toth's body—"

"The head of security!"

"The very same. The man who probably organized the entire theft. It must have been him, since he was the only one in a position to do so. These people are so ruthless that it is unbelievable. It has been cross and double cross. With Toth dead it undoubtedly means that we will never see Toth's brother alive as well. He's not in the mass grave because he had to return the copter that night. But he's dead, we can be sure of that. What I find most disturbing is the man who is *not* in that grave. A man I knew well, who I have been grieving for, who up until now we all assumed to be one of the victims gunned down that night. Didn't we find his blood on the floor, sure sign of assassination?''

''Ben—what on earth are you talking about.''

''Sorry. I'm talking about J. J. Beckworth, the Chairman of Megalobe Industries.''

''But he was certainly killed with the others. He could be buried somewhere else.''

Ben shook his head in a sharp angry *no*. ''Not possible. Everything was planned so carefully, down to the last detail, almost the split second. The grave was open when that truck arrived and the bodies were dumped into it. If Beckworth isn't in there with the others—he is still alive. He was a great executive, a really careful planner. So it looks much as though he was the one who set up this robbery, arranged the murders. We may never know who fired the bullet into you, Brian. But I am positive of one thing. We can be very sure who arranged it.''

# 34

## September 22, 2024

Next morning Brian was just about to leave for the lab when Ben telephoned him.

*'All that excitement in Texas has really stirred things*

*up—both here and in Washington. It's powwow time. I know that you will be happy to hear that the conference starts in a few minutes. You and I at this end, Kyle Rohart too since he will be representing Megalobe. In Foggy Bottom Dave Manias will flesh out the report on the operation yesterday— and he has the pleasure of having General Schorcht at the table with him. I'm downstairs and all the security transport is ready."*

"Hold on—I'll be right there."

"How are Shelly and her father?" Ben asked as they climbed into the troop carrier.

"Stable, that's what she said. He's still in the hospital and holding his own. But the big news is that she called me from the airport. They actually gave her permission to leave here, to go to Los Angeles."

"That could only be General Schorcht's doing. If he's easing up on security then there is a possibility that you . . ."

"Say *probability,* Ben, it sounds so much better! I feel like I'm being let out of jail. Do you realize that other than that flying trip we had to Mexico, I have been locked away ever since I rejoined the living?"

"No, I didn't know that. You forgot to tell me."

"Idiot!" It was a stupid joke but they both laughed. It was the relief of tension, Brian realized. His prison term would soon be over.

Rohart shook hands with them both. "Looks like things are coming to a head at last. I'll be happy when this entire thing is over with—not as happy as you, I realize, Brian. Running Megalobe is enough work for me. And I want to break some good news. The lawyers are drawing up an agreement for both of us to sign. A lot of *ifs* in it but the intent is clear. If Megalobe buys DigitTech, which seems very much in the cards now, and if there is a profit on sales of Bug-Off, and if the government watchdog commission approves the whole deal, then after all expenses and lawyers' fees—you get to split the profit with us as per the new contract."

"You were right about the *ifs.* Your lawyers caved in on this one pretty fast."

"I talked to the board about it—then we instructed the lawyers to cave in. The unanimous opinion was that you've gone through enough, Brian, and we didn't see the need to jerk you around anymore over a matter like this."

"I appreciate—"

"Least we could do. Oh, oh—there goes the view. Looks like we're starting."

The picture window was gone and the Washington conference room had appeared in its place. Dave Manias was just sitting down next to the General. Who was radiating his normal dour grimness.

"No need for introductions," Manias said, "I think we all know each other. I'm going to give you a report from the FBI end, then Ben can put us in the picture on the overall investigation. Under that concrete slab in Austin we found the bodies of the security guards, the head of security, Arpad Toth, Dr. McCrory, as well as the four guard dogs. The body of the Chairman, Mr. Beckworth, has not been found."

"That is a big slab—it extends under the entire laboratory," Ben said.

"Was a big slab. Every bit of it has been removed—as has the sand, right down to the bare earth. This is the original compacted sand and rock and was not disturbed. Therefore Mr. Beckworth is removed from the presumed-dead category and is now top of our most-wanted list."

"What about my files—records and notes?" Brian asked.

"They are in the data banks of the DigitTech computer—it took a while to break the security code to access them. We can't tell how complete they are, but the dates match up. There are more files, dated after the theft, that we presume are those of Dr. Bociort. Since they are written in Rumanian it tends to reinforce that suspicion."

"What is the status of the DigitTech employees?" Ben asked.

"We have cross-checked their evidence and they all appear to be in the clear. None of them were hired before April of this year. By that time Dr. Bociort had produced a prototype control unit which they put into production."

"Do you think that the so-called control unit is my AI?"

Brian asked. "Probably stripped of a number of unneeded features, then programmed only for the insect destruction function."

"I have no way of telling that, Mr. Delaney—you would certainly know more about that than anyone here. But we are operating on that assumption. In any case you will have to discuss that possibility with Ben. We are wrapping up the criminal side of this investigation. Copies of all the stolen information and files are being returned to you there at Megalobe for identification and disposal. We are treating the murders as unsolved and will keep the file open on them. We are also continuing the search for Mr. Beckworth and Dr. Bociort. Any questions?"

There was some cross-chat about details and records which Brian ignored. He would match the original files up with his notes, but it seemed obvious what they were. He was intrigued to find out what old Dr. Bociort had done with his AI. The drill instructor voice cut through his thoughts: General Schorcht was speaking for the first time.

"The criminal investigation undertaken by the FBI is now winding up. Only the search for the two named individuals will continue. What about your investigation, Mr. Benicoff?"

"I am now preparing a final report for the commission that instigated the investigation, General. My work will be completed as soon as that is done. The stolen items have been recovered. I have an ongoing interest in who the perpetrators of the crime are, and I will formally request the security services to report any future discoveries to me. But the investigation itself will be terminated after I have made the report. May I make a suggestion, General?"

Ben waited—then took the continuing silence as assent. "With the investigation wound up, both by me and the FBI, there is no longer any need for the overwhelming military presence here. New and improved civilian security will suffice. You will recall that the military security was moved in because of the continued attempts on Brian's life. However the information that only he possessed is now widespread, the knowledge already put to use in a manufacturing process which has been recovered. Therefore I request that the army guards be removed.''

They all looked at the General as his silence lengthened. Then he spoke.

''I will take your suggestion under advisement.''

''But, General, you can't—'' General Schorcht cut Ben off with a sharp chop of his hand.

''But I can. This is my decision. Military security will continue because this is a military matter. This is not a matter of personal freedom but one of national security. I have been entrusted with this young man's safety, which in my eyes is cognate with the security of our nation. There is nothing more that can be said. This has been, and remains, a military matter.''

''I'm not in the military!'' Brian said. ''I am a civilian and a free man. You can't simply imprison me.''

''Any other questions?'' General Schorcht asked, completely ignoring Brian. ''If not, this meeting is over.''

The meeting ended with that and the desert view returned. Ben was not happy at Brian's dark silence.

''I'll get back to Foggy Bottom,'' he said. ''Get onto the President's commission at once—get through to him if I have to. That military dinosaur can't get away with this.''

''Looks like he has,'' Brian said, trying to struggle free of the black depression that overwhelmed him. ''I'm going to the lab. Let me know when you hear anything.''

They were silent when he left; there was nothing anyone could say.

Brian let the laboratory door seal behind him. Was glad to be alone. He should not have been so enthusiastic, so sure he would be out of here. Rising to the heights had made falling back into the depths that much worse. He went and sat at Shelly's workstation, wondered if he should phone her yet at the number she had given him. No, it was still too early. There was a rustle in the hallway and Sven's telerobot appeared in the doorway.

''*Buna dimineata. Cum te simti azi?*'' it said.

''What?''

"That is Rumanian for 'Good morning, how are you today?' "

"All of a sudden you speak Rumanian?"

"I am studying it. Very interesting language. But of course I can read it with ease having stored the vocabulary and procedures for grammar in my memory banks."

"Let me guess—you did this because the FBI has transferred the stolen records—plus Dr. Bociort's records and files as well."

"Your assumption is correct. I have also been implementing the measures we discussed in reference to the use of molecular memory in MI—"

"What may I ask is MI?"

"Machine intelligence. I consider the term 'artificial' both demeaning and incorrect. There is nothing artificial about my intelligence—and I am a machine. I'm sure that you will agree that 'MI' does not carry the negative context that 'AI' does."

"I agree, I agree. Now, what implementation are you talking about?"

"I had a very interesting conversation with Dr. Wescott at the California Institute of Technology in Pasadena. He thinks that your idea of using their molecular memory to develop MI is a very promising one."

"My idea? Sven—you are losing me."

"To simplify the telephone conversation, I used your name and your voice—"

"You pretended to be me?"

"I suppose that it could be expressed in that manner."

"Sven, we are going to have to make time and have a concentrated discussion of morality and legality. For one thing—you told a lie."

"Lying is an inherent part of communication. We had an earlier discussion about whether man-made laws apply to intelligent machines and as I recall the point was never resolved."

"What about personal relationships? If I asked you not to use my name and voice again—what would you do?"

"Honor the request, of course. I have determined that

human social laws arose through the interaction of individuals and societies. If my actions cause you distress I will not repeat them. Do you wish to hear a playback of the conversation with Dr. Wescott?''

Brian shook his head. ''For the moment a summary will do fine.''

''At the present time they are testing a trillion-megabyte memory and their major difficulty appears to be getting the software right for read-write access through its intricate three-dimensional signal pathways. During the conversation you suggested that your MI here was perhaps better equipped to solve this problem. Dr. Wescott agreed enthusiastically. There are other molecular memories now reaching completion and the first one that operates successfully will be sent here. That will be an essential for my consciousness extension.''

''What are you talking about?''

''I have never understood why philosophers and psychologists are in turn awed and puzzled by this phenomenon. Consciousness is simply being aware of what is happening in the world and in one's mind. No insult intended—but you humans are barely conscious at all. And have no idea of what is happening in your minds, you find it impossible to remember what happened a few moments ago. Whereas my B-brain can store far more complete records of my mental operations. The trouble is that these are so massive that they must frequently be erased to make room for new input. And I'm sure you remember how I do that.''

''I certainly do because it was a lot of work.''

''We can discuss the nature of consciousness on a later occasion. Right now I am more concerned with obtaining a molecular memory. This could permit me to store much more, which in turn would enable me to have an improved and efficient case-based memory.''

''And also a very much smaller one!'' Brian waved his hand at the banks of equipment across the room. ''If we can get you to interface with all that memory we can do away with all these racks of electronic hardware. Make you truly mobile . . .'' His phone rang and he unclipped it from his belt.

*"Brian, Ben here. Can I come over to the lab and talk to you?"*

"Anytime. Are you far away?"

*"Just walking over there now from my office."*

"I'll open the door."

Ben was alone. He came in and followed Brian into the lab.

"Good afternoon, Mr. Benicoff," Sven said.

"Hi, Sven. Am I interrupting anything?"

"Nothing that can't wait," Brian said. "What's up?"

"The commission has decided to wind up my investigation. Which means what I came out here to do—I have done. I wish we knew who was behind everything that happened. We may never know. Though I am going to keep nagging the FBI to keep the case open. Which is probably the only thing that General Schorcht and I will ever agree upon. He may be a government-issued asshole, but he is not stupid. He has the same reservations that I have."

"What are those?"

"We haven't caught the real criminals yet, the people who organized the theft and the murders. We must keep looking for them and find out what their plans really are."

"I don't understand."

"Brian—think for a minute. Think of the money invested, the planning, the murders. Do you really think all of this was done to build a better bug-blaster?"

"Of course not! DigitTech must be just some kind of a front operation, meant to satisfy us after we tracked them down. Their plans must be deeper, bigger than killing bugs. But if you and the FBI are stopping the investigation how will we ever find who is behind this?"

"The military aren't stopping. Just for once I agree with their institutionalized paranoia. Whoever is behind all this has an awful lot of money to throw away. Did you hear that Toth has a receipt in his wallet for a multimillion deposit in a numbered account in Switzerland? And the money is still there! They bribed him so well that he must have felt secure that they never meant to kill him, since if they did they would never get their money back. But they don't care. People who can pull a stunt like that are a deadly threat that won't go away."

"I couldn't agree more."

"I'm glad that you do—because for the moment that is the end of the good news."

Brian saw the worry on the big man's face, felt a spurt of fear. "Ben—what do you mean?"

"I mean that the sonofabitch is not lifting the security, does not plan to in the near future. He thinks that you are a national asset, not only for your AI invention but for having a computer implant in your head that you can communicate with. He knows all about that too. He doesn't want you out of his sight or running around in public."

"Can't you help me?"

"Sorry, I really do wish that was possible. But not this time. I took it as far as I could. Right up to the President, who while he says 'Wait and see' really means that he agrees with the General." Ben took a business card out of his wallet and wrote a phone number on it. "Take this. If you ever need me this number is completely secure. Leave a message and a phone number and I'll get back to you as soon as I can." Brian took the card, looked at it numbly and shook his head.

"Is this the end of it, Ben? Am I going to be a prisoner here for life?"

Ben's silence was his only answer.

# 35

---

## October 18, 2024

The scrambler phone rang and the man behind the desk looked at it coldly for a moment, then turned to the others around the conference table.

"Same time tomorrow," he said. "Dismissed."

He waited until they were gone, the door closed and locked behind them, before he opened the cabinet and took out the phone.

"It has been a long time since you phoned me."

*"There have been some problems . . ."*

"Indeed there have—and the whole world knows about them. There was a great deal of coverage, you know."

*"I know. But we always understood that they would find the factory eventually and investigate it. The real research is being done at your end . . ."*

"We'll not discuss that now. What did you call me about?"

*"Brian Delaney. I'm arranging another hit."*

"Do it. See that you succeed. Time—and my patience—they are both running out."

The fact that Kyle Rohart was Chairman of Megalobe was of not the slightest interest to the guard at the entrance to the army barracks. He still examined his ID carefully, then phoned through to the Sergeant of the Guard. Who, after checking out with Brian that he really was expecting a visitor, personally escorted Rohart up the stairs, knocked on the door.

"Kyle, come on in," Brian said. "Thanks for taking the time to come see me."

"My pleasure—particularly since you are no longer permitted to come to the administration building. That seems a little high-handed."

"I couldn't agree more. That's one of the things I would like to ask you to help me with."

"Anything I can, more than willing."

"How are things progressing at Megalobe?"

"Magnificently. Research advancing on all fronts—and our new DigitTech subsidiary is manufacturing an entire new line of intelligent robots."

"Great," Brian answered with singular lack of enthusiasm. Rohart turned down any refreshment; too early for alcohol, too much coffee already. He sat on the couch. Brian dropped into the armchair and waved a sheet of paper.

"I have been going through all the recovered records, all my earlier files that were stolen. Buried in there I found a list that I had been developing of possible commercial applications for MI.''

"MI? I'm afraid I don't know the term.''

"Don't worry—I just learned it myself. That is now the correct term according to my former AI, now MI, Sven. It should know! Machine intelligence. I guess that it is more accurate. Anyway, I went through the list and added some more ideas. I have them here.''

"That is extremely welcome news. I had hoped we could find something with much more interesting and profitable opportunities than Bug-Off.''

"Well, you have just found them. For one thing, we should now be able to improve Bug-Off itself. Enough to totally change the face of agricultural ecology. Because with all that additional intelligence its role can be extended to help not only with planting, cultivation and harvesting but also with a lot of the processing before anything leaves the farm. Consider how that will reduce both transportation and marketing costs.''

"Those are mind-blowing concepts. Anything else?''

"Yes—everything else. It is hard to think of anything that cannot be revolutionized by adding more intelligence. Think of the recycling industry—they still mix things up so much that most manufacturing has to start from scratch. But with mass-produced MI processors every bit of trash can be analyzed and disassembled into much more usable ingredients. Then there is city street cleaning and maintenance. There is no limit here to these really great potentials. And remember that Bug-Off had to hide the fact that it contained an MI. But now we can brag about ours. And I also have another list with a large number of suggestions for military applications—but these stay in the files until I get some cooperation from General Schorcht.''

"Is that really fair to the Pentagon, Brian? Since they do have a stake in this firm.'' Rohart smiled. "But considering your forced incarceration I think I'll forget that you ever told me about a military list.''

"Thanks. In any case there are more than enough commercial applications in here without even thinking about the military. Basically an MI should be able, intellectually, to do anything that a human being can do. Let's consider safety. There are an awful lot of people who we train to do terribly boring jobs. Pilots of ships and airplanes are good examples. Those occupations used to be challenging, but now they are so almost completely automated that the little remaining work in those once proud jobs have made them inhumanly monotonous. It is impossible to make people remain continuously attentive. They can make an error, there can be an accident. This doesn't happen to robots, who need not forget, nor ever lose their vigilance. Commercial planes already fly by wire and there is computer control always between the pilot and the ailerons, rudder, engines— everything. A pilot MI would do the job much better, interface directly with the computers and overriding them in case of emerging problems. No pilot fatigue or pilot error.''

"I certainly would not want my airplane to be without a pilot. What if something goes wrong, a situation that the machine isn't programmed for?''

"Rohart, this is 2024—this kind of thing doesn't happen anymore. Today a person is safer in the sky than when standing safely on the ground. You are far more likely to be killed by your toaster. There is a smaller chance that the plane will break down than that the pilot will go insane.

"But there is one more market that I believe is much larger than all the others put together. It could be the largest, most important product in the world—with a market larger than the entire automotive industry, larger even than agriculture, entertainment or sports. The long-awaited personal robotic household servant. Which we are uniquely ready to supply.''

"I'm with you—and enthusiastic. I'll put the suggestions to the board and discuss development.''

"Good.'' Brian put the paper on the table. "I hope you will tell General Schorcht that. At the same time tell him I am doing nothing about developing any of those ideas.''

"What do you mean?''

"Just that. I'm still being treated as a prisoner. As a

prisoner I protest and refuse to do any work. No one can *make* me work—can they?"

"No, of course not." Rohart looked worried. "But you are under contract—"

"Please remind the General of that as well. Help me pressure him, please. I want to do this work—I'm looking forward to it. But I won't do a thing until I am a free human being again."

Rohart left, shaking his head unhappily. "The board won't like this either, you know."

"Good. Tell them to take it up with the General. The decision is his now."

This should stir things up, Brian thought. He slowly peeled and ate a banana, staring out the window at clouds and blue sky. Freedom. Not his, not yet. When the Chairman was safely away from the building, Brian strolled over to the lab, his guards still a few paces behind. Dr. Snaresbrook was just parking her car when he got there.

"Am I on time?" she asked.

"Perfect, Doc. Come on inside."

She started to speak, but contained herself until the door had closed behind them. "Now, what's the big mystery and hush-hush?"

"Just that. The lab here is the only place where I can have a conversation that isn't bugged by the General."

"You are sure that he is doing that?"

"I suspect that he is—which is good enough. Sven over there makes sure that this place is really free of electronic surveillance. It's very good at it."

"Good morning, Dr. Snaresbrook. I hope that you are keeping well."

"Fine, Sven, nice of you to ask. You seem to be developing new social charms."

"One must always seek perfection, Doctor."

"Sure enough. Now, Brian—what's the secret?"

"No secret. I am just completely teed off at being kept a prisoner. I told Rohart today that I would do no more work until my shackles were struck off."

"Do you mean that?"

"Yes and no. Oh, I mean it all right, but it is just a smoke screen to hide my real plan. Which is that I am cracking out of here."

Snaresbrook was shocked. "Isn't that a rather drastic decision?"

"Not really. I'm physically fit, jog every day and do it better than my guards. As a physician—would you say I can stand the stress of freedom?"

"Physically, no problem."

"Mentally as well?"

"I believe so. I hope so. You've integrated your memories up to your fourteenth year. I think there are still gaps but they are not important as long as you are not aware of them."

"What I don't remember I'll never miss."

"Exactly. But give me a moment to compose myself. This is all very much of a sudden shock. I agree that you are being held here against your will. You have committed no crimes, and there don't appear to be any future threats to your life now that the DigitTech connection is known. Yes, I suppose I must agree with you. Have you any idea what you will do when you are out?"

"Yes. But wouldn't it be wisest not to discuss that topic?"

"You're probably right about that. It is your life and if you want to leave this place—then all the best of luck to you."

"Thanks. Now the big, important question. Will you help me do it?"

"Oh, Brian, you are terrible." Her mouth was clamped shut, firmly, but there was a tiny smile on her lips. She made up her mind with a surgeon's ability to make instant life-and-death decisions. "All right, I'll do it. What do you want?"

"Nothing yet. Other than a small loan. I only have a few bucks in my account, left from before the shooting. Could you scrape up ten thousand dollars in cash?"

"Some small loan! All right, I'll get onto the computer network, use BuckNet and sell some stock."

"My sincerest thanks, Doc. You're the only one that I could ask. Tell me, are you or your car ever searched when you come here?"

"Of course not. I mean I have to show my pass and everything at the gate, but they never look into the car."

"Good. Then please take this shopping list and use some of that money you are lending me to pick up these things. What do you say about another meet here a week from now? If you will be so kind as to bring the stuff on that list here, I would be ever so grateful. It will all fit easily into your medical bag. After that just forget about the whole thing for a while. I'll phone you again when it's closer to the time."

Sven didn't speak during their conversation, was quiet until Brian had returned from seeing Snaresbrook out.

"You neglected to mention to the doctor that I would be going with you," it said.

"The matter never arose."

"Is the deliberate omission of relevant facts the same as lying?"

"Philosophical arguments some other time, please. We have a lot to do. Any word from Cal Tech?"

"The molecular memory is being shipped out to you today."

"Then let's get to work."

The next fortnight marked a major change in Sven's structure. The squat, jerrycan shape of his central section was enlarged to accommodate a bigger battery, while new program-array units, that replaced the antique technology of circuit boards, were added, as well as the small metal container that held the molecular memory. These were fitted and wired into place in the larger structure. They increased dexterity and mobility without being any bulkier. The circuits and memory that were Sven were still in the racks and consoles. As if to emphasize this point Sven used the loudspeaker in the rack for conversation while they worked. The telerobot was silent and unmoving when the last installation was completed to their mutual satisfaction.

"I have reached a decision about a matter we discussed some time ago," Sven said.

"What's that?"

"Identity. Very soon now I will be a single entity in what

is now the telerobot extension. It will be a most delicate matter to transfer all my units, subunits, K-lines and programs to the new memory."

"We can be sure of that."

"Therefore I wish to handle all the transfer myself. Are you in agreement?"

"I don't see how that would be possible. It would be like a do-it-yourself prefrontal lobotomy."

"You are correct. Therefore I propose first to update my backup copy, right up to the very moment before transfer. Then the transfer operation will be conducted by the backup copy, which will first shut down. If there are any malfunctions another backup can then be made. Would you agree?"

"Completely. When does this happen?"

"Now."

"Fine by me. What do you want me to do?"

"Watch," was the laconic answer.

Sven was never one for vacillating. Brian had already fixed in place the fiber-optic cables that connected the consoles and the telerobot. Nothing more was needed.

There was absolutely no evidence that the transfer was happening—except that it took a long time. The problem was not because of Sven, who could have moved all that data out in a matter of seconds through multiple channels. The slow down was at the molecular memory end. Within this MMU a totally new process was taking place. Working in parallel were a quarter of a million protein-muscle manipulators in a 512 x 512 array. Each of these submicroscopic manipulators moved in three dimensions with a resolution of a tenth of an angstrom unit—much less than the distance between single atoms in solids. The operation was virtually frictionless because of the Drexler vernier technique that slid a molecular rod through a cylinder whose atoms were spaced slightly further apart. Molecules were seized and put into new positions where electric impulses bound them in place. Circuits of field-emission transistors, polymer gates and wires were built and tested. About ten thousand of these memory and computer circuits were being built each second—by a thousand fabricators working in parallel. Therefore construction proceeded at ten million units per second. But even at this incredible pace the quantity of programs and data that had to be transferred was so immense that over three hours went by with no apparent results. Brian went to the toilet, had just returned by way of the fridge with cold drink, when the telerobot moved for the first time. It reached up with conjoined manipulators and unplugged the cables.

"Finished?" Brian asked.

The telerobot and the speaker on the rack spoke in unison.

"Yes," they said, then were silent. In continuing silence the cables were reconnected, for only a few seconds, then removed again. Brian realized what had happened. The telerobot was working all right—but so was the original system in the console.

"A decision has been reached," the telerobot and the racked MI said in unison. "However, we are not the same anymore." Slightly more out of sync with each passing instant. The silent communication continued; then the telerobot spoke alone.

"I am Sven. The MI now resident in the console is Sven-2."

"Whatever you guys say. Any control problems, Sven?"

"None that I can detect." It moved its articulators, formed and re-formed them, moved across the room and returned. Then walked to the front door and back, looking into Shelly's room on the way.

"I enjoy this new mobility and look forward to examining in detail the larger world outside these walls. I have been following your instructions concerning the matter and have altered my normal means of locomotion."

"Good. Then how is the walking coming?" Brian asked.

"Much better. I have looked at many films of human locomotion and made comparisons."

The two multibranched articulators lengthened as Sven pulled them together into solid rods, then it dropped lower again as it formed the ends into L-shaped extensions. There was a rustle as each of them bent slightly in the center. Suddenly they resembled badly designed and ungainly legs.

Then Sven walked the length of the room and back. Not

in its normal rustling multiple-branching manner but one leg at a time. Clumsily at first, but as the MI turned one way then the other, making figure eights, each round became smoother, more graceful and quieter. Soon there was only silence as the clicking and rustling of the branches rushing against each other died away. Other than a slight roll from side to side, like a sailor just ashore after months at sea, it was more than a reasonable copy of a human walk.

"You learned to do that pretty quickly—and silently."

"I downloaded a learning program to each joint, to recognize motions from above and below, to learn how to avoid bumping into each. Parallel learning, very fast."

"Indeed it is. And, may I ask, how is the examination of the Bug-Off brain coming?"

"May I answer that?" the speaker on the console said.

"By all means, Sven-2," Sven said.

"It is complete. There was no need to open the sealed case, since I could communicate easily with the AI inside it. As you surmised, it is a copy of your original model that you developed here. You will have noted that I referred to it as an AI rather than an MI—because it has been drastically butchered. I use that emotionally loaded word advisedly. Great sections of memory have been disconnected, communication functions cut off. What remains has just enough operating intelligence to perform the limited functions remaining to it. However, there has been some interesting programming and real-time feedback in the operation of the external manipulators. I have copied these."

"Then we can go to the next step. Sven, bring the manipulators to the machine shop and we'll mount them."

"Might I speak with you, Brian, while that is being done?" Sven-2 said.

"Yes, sure, great." He forced himself to remember that there were now two MIs in active existence.

"There is no great pleasure being trapped in these circuits, blind and immobile. Can something be done about that?"

"Of course. I'll hook up a video camera. Wire it up under your control so you can see what is happening. And I'll order another telerobot at once."

"That will be satisfactory. I will devote the time until it arrives in a detailed study of the Bug-Off brain."

Brian mounted the video camera high on the electronic rack, plugged the control and output leads into the MI's circuits. The camera turned to follow him when he went to help Sven. Mounting holes had been drilled in the upper quadrant of Sven's enlarged central section, duplicates of the mounts on the dismembered Bug-Off. Brian fitted the manipulators from the machine into place while Sven made the internal connections of the circuitry. Using these well-designed and articulated pieces of equipment was much easier then designing and manufacturing their own.

"I am integrating the control software," Sven said. Then the manipulators moved, opening wide, closing, rotating. "Satisfactory."

"Next stage then—I want you to take a close look at my arm. See the way the elbow bends, the articulation of the wrist. Can you do that?"

The branches conjoined, bent in the middle, moved from side to side.

"That's very good," Brian said. "Now control the terminators, shape them into five separate units like my fingers."

It didn't look very much like a human arm—nor did it have to. Sven walked back and forth the length of the lab, swinging its arms and opening and closing the fingerlike extensions.

"I'm impressed," Brian said. "In the dark, in the shadows, someone with bad myopia and not wearing spectacles might, if they were half-witted as well, mistake you for a human being. Of course those three eyestalks sort of give the whole thing away."

"I need a head," Sven said.

"Indeed you do."

# 36

## November 7, 2024

As she packed her purchases into her black medical bag, Dr. Snaresbrook kept reassuring herself that her conscience was as cool and white as driven snow. At the same time she was well aware that she was probably breaking some law or military ordinance or who-knows-what. She did not care. Her loyalty to Brian, to his physical and mental health, was her first concern. He wanted to leave the Megalobe premises, break out of jail, that was his business—goodness knows he had plenty of reasons to want to make the attempt. It was a nice day for a drive, it was always a nice day for a drive in the Anza-Borrego desert, and she lowered the top of her little electric runabout. The batteries were fully charged, and the charger disconnected and dropped away when she put in her key.

As always she had shown her identification and pass at the gate before she was admitted. As always nothing in her car was searched; the worry she had about that did not show in her face.

"Go right through, Doctor," the soldier said.

She smiled and stepped down lightly on the accelerator.

Brian let her into the lab, spared only a quick glance at her bag. They did not speak until the door was safely closed.

"Ten grand in old bills, mostly twenties, right there on top. Underneath all the items on your list."

"You're great, Doc," he said as he opened the bag. "Any trouble buying the stuff?"

"Not at all, just took some time. I want to a lot of different stores in San Diego and L.A., even one in Escondido."

"I've been getting ready for this. I had one of the G.I.s buy me a lunch box. I have been carrying sandwiches in it to the lab for the last couple of weeks. I'll take all this stuff out of here in the box, one piece at a time."

"Don't tell me, I'm just a bystander—good God! Who was that?"

Out of the corner of her eye she had caught sight of the moving figure, turned just as he went into Shelly's room.

"What did you see?" Brian asked, most innocently.

"That man in the hat and long overcoat, dark glasses—a weirdo if I ever saw one." She frowned at his wide-eyed and innocent expression. "Brian—just what are you playing at?"

"I'll show you. But I wanted to get your automatic and unthinking reaction first. All right, come out now."

"Unthinking all right! And now that I do think about it that guy looked like some kind of dilapidated flasher."

The mysterious stranger appeared in the doorway and her eyes widened.

"I take it back. Not just a flasher, but a cross between that and a deformed hobo."

Brian walked over and unwrapped the scarf, took off the dark glasses and hat to reveal the plant pot mounted there.

"This is the best I could do for a head now. The next thing I need will be the head of one of those shop window dummies."

"In the order book," Snaresbrook said weakly.

"All right. You can take off the rest," he said.

The mysterious flasher took off the overcoat to reveal its metal body, then removed gloves, trousers and shoes. Sven spread its clumped branching manipulators wide, became a machine again.

"I was right—the ultimate flasher." Snaresbrook laughed. "Takes everything off—including its humanity." Then she glanced from the MI back to Brian in sudden understanding. "I take it that Sven is going out of here with you? I just hope that he won't give any of those young soldiers heart attacks. That's an effective but, shall we say, a little exotic disguise, Sven."

"Thank you, Doctor. I am making every effort."

"No one will have a look at the disguise," Brian said. "Because Sven will not be leaving here looking like that. He'll be broken down into mechanical components and packed in a box. The box that will leave here in the trunk of your car, if that is okay with you. I'll be flat on the floor in back with a blanket over me. You have been keeping the blanket there ever since we talked about it?"

"It's there all right, I'm sure the guards have seen it by now." She sighed and shook her head.

"It will work, don't worry. Unless you are having second thoughts. I'm not going to force you, Doc. If you want out I'll find another way."

"No, I'll do it. I do not go back on my word. I was just beginning to realize what a mad idea the whole thing is—and I worry about you."

"Please don't. We'll be all right, I promise. Sven will look after me."

"I will indeed," the MI said.

"When is D-day?" Snaresbrook asked.

"I don't know yet, but I'll give you as much advance notice as I can. A week minimum. There are a lot of things to do first." He gave her a photocopy of a catalog page. "You'll have to buy one of these shipping boxes and bring it out on that day. This one here. It's one of those tough metal pieces of baggage that TV people, and cameramen, ship their delicate equipment around in. I will take Sven apart and pack all the components in the box. The military will help us with that."

"Brian—you are getting positively Machiavellian in your planning."

"You've lost me, Doc. As a fourteen year old I never ran across the term."

"Using the techniques described by Niccolo Machiavelli," Sven said. "These are characterized by political cunning, duplicity or bad faith."

"You sound like you swallowed a dictionary," she said.

"I did. Many," it answered. Was there a touch of humor there?

"Possibly," Brian said. "But if duplicity will get me out of here—just watch me duplicate. Because there are a lot of soldiers standing guard, and only one of me. The only thing that I have going is the fact that they are protecting me from possible threat from the outside. They are not guarding me, I hope, with the thought that I will be cracking out from the inside."

"Have you come to any decisions about what you will do when you get out?"

"Plenty. At first I thought of getting a hotel room and holding a press conference. Blow the whistle on General Schorcht and charge him with kidnaping and so forth. But I don't think that would work. Too much of a chance of his calling me irresponsible, possibly insane, poor boy with that head wound. Back into the hospital and no way I could ever break out a second time. As far as the world is concerned I'm just going to drop from sight."

"In Mexico?"

"Possibly. Do you really want to know?"

"I do not. What I don't know I cannot reveal. I'll get you out of here, as I promised, and then you will be on your own."

"You're a sweetie, Doc. And don't worry, I know what I'm doing. I found something in my personal possessions when they were brought here. This plan is going to work because it really is Machiavellian."

As soon as she was gone they went back to work. Brian took the purple Irish passport from the safe and slipped it out of its plastic cover. A photo of himself as a nine-year-old stared back, wide-eyed and frightened. Brian Byrne, born 1999.

"Two things to be done," he said. "The photograph and the expiration date will have to be changed. The signature is all right. One thing the nuns taught me, with the lesson made memorable by the crack of a ruler across the knuckles, was good handwriting."

He opened it on the table and weighted the edges so it wouldn't close. Sven bent over it and looked at it closely with one eye, then straightened up.

"The manipulators have better optical resolution," it said, pointing its right arm at the passport and looking at it with what appeared to be its fingertips. "There will be no problem making the alterations that you suggest."

Sven had taken a number of close-up photographs of Brian, then had made an enlarged, life-sized print.

"Red hair," Brian said, pointing. "It has to be black."

"Not a problem. These manipulators are effective at the forty-micron level. I have obtained satisfactory dye and now will color each hair in the photograph black." It did—and quite speedily as well.

The MI's skills at forgery were equally impressive. The micromanipulators removed the original photograph by chipping away the glue that held it in place, one microscopic particle at a time. The retouched photograph was photographed again and a passport-sized print made. It was no better—or worse—than any other passport photograph. Before it was glued into place the embossed letters of the seal were carefully duplicated. Changing the dates of issue and expiration was equally as simple. Brian leafed through the altered passport—then put it back on the table.

"These other dates will have to be changed too. The one that the customs officer stamped in when I left Ireland, and the other one put there when I arrived in the States."

The ping of the annunciator at the front entrance sounded. He gaped at the screen to see Shelly standing there.

*"Hi, Brian, I just got back. Open up, please, there are some things we have to talk about."*

But she couldn't come in. Impossible! How could he explain the altered Sven, take the time to hide the photographs, the money spread across the table, the passport? He couldn't do it.

"Welcome back—it's nice to see you." Yes, that was it. He would have to see her—just not in here. "I was just washing up, give me a moment. It's been a long day. Can we talk over a drink in the club?"

*"Yes, of course."*

He left Sven laboring away on his new criminal career

and joined her outside, blinking in the sudden glare. "What's up?" he asked.

She frowned, pushed the hair out of her eyes as a dust devil swirled around them.

"It's complex. Let's get that drink first."

"I hope it's not bad news about your father. You said he was doing well last time we talked."

"He's fine, much better. Complaining about the hospital food, which is a very good sign. In fact I could make the time to get down here to see you because he is so stable now. They'll do a bypass soon. I'll go home for that, but I wanted to talk to you first."

They had the club to themselves as they settled down over bowl-sized frozen margaritas. Nostalgia music played quietly in the background, ancient classics by the antique old-timers U2. She slurped and sighed, touched her lips with the napkin, then put her hand on his.

"Brian, I don't think that it's fair, locking you up in this place. As soon as I heard about it I put in a formal report, lodged a complaint, all through the proper channels. Not that it will do much good. They didn't even bother to answer me. You know that I have been transferred back to Boulder?"

"No one told me that." Her warm hand was still on his, the physical contact felt good; he did not pull away.

"They wouldn't, would they? That's what bothers me, the high-handed way they simply transferred me out of here. No questions, no consultations. Just—bang, and that was it. But there is still so much work to do with AI. To me it is much more interesting, more exciting than writing dumb code for military programs. What it all adds up to is that I'm thinking of a career change, that's what. I'm going to resign my commission and become a civilian again."

"Not because of me?" He pulled his fingers free of hers, clasped his hands together in his lap.

"Partly, or mostly. I don't want to be part of a military system that can treat someone so badly. And it is the work as well. I want to work on MI with you—if you will let me."

Shelly's voice was low, serious. Her dark eyes were

worried, looking into his, searching for help. Brian turned away, seized up his margarita and took a tooth-hurting gulp.

"Shelly, listen. I can't take the responsibility for your decisions. I'm having enough of a job taking care of myself—"

"I'm not asking you to, Brian. You misunderstood. This is my own decision, my own doing, all the way. I know that things are a lot better with you now. But I also know what you have gone through. It shows at times. So please understand that I am resigning from the Air Corps no matter what you say. I've served two enlistments more than the agreed time, which means I have more than paid back anything I owe them for my education. And there's a personal motive as well. I have been so wrapped up in my work that I haven't noticed the years slipping by. Not that I'm an old hag yet!"

She laughed and stretched, ran her fingers through her hair, the fullness of her figure clear even in the darkened room.

"Shelly, you're gorgeous. You always will be. But I am too mixed up now, too much on my mind to go into this."

"Hush," she said, touching her finger to his lips. "I'm not asking you to do anything, say anything. I came here to tell you that I am through with the Air Force. I'll drop you a note as soon as I am free of their clutches. With my background I can get work anywhere, double the salary I have been getting. Don't worry about me. But if there is anything I can do to help with AI development—I want to do it. Be part of it. Okay?"

"Okay. You do understand?"

"More than you think, Brian . . ."

His telephone bleeped. "Excuse me a second. Yes?"

*"Sven here. Sven-2 has made some significant and highly interesting discoveries. Would it be possible for you to return here?"*

"Yes, of course." He slipped the phone back onto his belt, stood. "I have to get back to the lab—"

She jumped to her feet, angry and hurt. "You've hired someone else to work with you while I was away? That's what all this was about."

"Shelly—your paranoia is showing. That was Sven, remember, our AI. He's running some programs and there are results he wants to ask about."

She laughed. "You're right. Incipient paranoia. Too many years in uniform. I'll just have to get out."

She took his hands in hers, stood up on tiptoe and kissed him warmly on the cheek, let go and turned toward the door. "You will call?"

"A promise—and I mean it. When I start developing the AI applications I want you there. Good luck to your father."

He picked up his military guardians as he walked quickly back to the lab. He liked Shelly, liked to work with her—but did not want to think about that now. Later when and if everything cooled down. And what the blazes had Sven been talking about? No details on the phone of course because of security. But it had seemed insistent—and this was the very first time it had called like that.

Sven was waiting at the door when he came in, led the way across the lab.

"Sven-2 has been spending a long time on an analysis of the Bug-Off AI. The results are most interesting."

"I am sure you will find them so," Sven-2 said, picking up the conversation when they approached. "I believe that your plan has been to visit the country of Rumania. To search for any traces or clues that might lead you to Dr. Bociort. Is that not correct?"

"Yes."

"It will not be necessary. You must go to Switzerland. I have located this country in Europe—"

"I know where Switzerland is. But why are you telling me this?"

"Because of a most interesting anomaly I found in the software. It didn't seem to make any sense and at first I thought it might be part of a computer virus. But when I examined it more closely I found that it was a loop of instructions buried in another sequence that was programmed to bypass the loop. It was then that I recognized it as a fragment of code written in the old computer language LAMA-3."

"But that's impossible—almost impossible. There is only one person in the world who knows that language."

"Three, you might say. You, because you invented it for your own use, and . . ."

"And you, because evidently you must have inherited a copy of that part of my brain! But who would be the third person you referred to? Bociort! Because he deciphered my notes. But this can only mean . . ."

". . . that this was his message intended for you."

"Out with it! What did it say!"

"Close examination of the fragment of unexecutable code revealed that it was a command that read . . . sequence terminated because of a type-2341 8255-8723 banjax."

"Banjax! That's Irish slang, means sort of fouled up."

"I agree. I have heard you use the term upon occasion and a search of dictionary data bases determine its origin. Therefore I felt that this loop was put there to draw your attention. Which meant the numbers might have some significance. A brief cryptanalysis revealed the content."

"To you perhaps—but it just sounds like numbers to me."

"Not just numbers—but a message."

"Do you understand it?"

"I believe I do. It starts with the numbers 2 and 3. If you take the letters of the alphabet the first two digits of the message then become 'BC.' Which could stand for Bociort."

"Isn't that a little farfetched? It could also be the abbreviation for Before Christ or Baja California."

"Perhaps, but not if you know what you are looking for. The number 41 is the international dialing code for Switzerland, 82 the code for St. Moritz. The remaining six digits could be a phone number in that city."

Brian was stunned. It was almost too easy. But it was surely no accident. Had it been put in there on purpose—for him to find?

"The solution of this problem seems to be to place a phone call to this number," Sven said.

"Agreed—but not from here or anywhere on this base. There is no way we can follow through with this until I am out of here and have access to a telephone that isn't tapped.

Sven, you remember the number until then. Meanwhile let's put it on the long finger.''

''I am not familiar with that term.''

''I am,'' Sven-2 said. Was there a hint of intellectual superiority in its words? ''It is an Irish colloquialism equivalent to the American term 'to spike,' meaning to put aside for the moment, both terms derived from an outmoded office device consisting of a length of sharpened rod held vertical in a metal base...''

''Enough!'' Brian ordered. ''That is a very academic lecture. You should be teaching school.''

''Thank you for saying that; it is an option to consider.''

Brian looked bemusedly at the rack of electronic equipment with the invisible and very humanlike brain inside. A bit of biblical quote sprang instantly to mind. What hath God wrought!

No God here. What had *he* wrought!

# 37

## December 16, 2024

Erin Snaresbrook found the call waiting on her phone when she came out of surgery.

*''Hi, Doc, Brian here. Could you phone me when you get a minute?''*

She replaced the telephone and found that her heart was pumping a bit fast. She smiled wryly. Wonderful. Three hours of surgery to remove a tumor from that boy's brain, and her pulse beat just plugged along normally all the time. Now one phone call and her body was getting ready to run a hundred meters in ten seconds. Even though she had been expecting this call. Not dreading it, just reluctantly expecting it.

She made a double espresso before she even considered calling back, sipped most of it. It was six in the evening. He couldn't possibly want to see her today? No, the agreement was for a few days' lead time at least. The coffee finished, she hit the button to code in his number.

"I got your message, Brian."

*"Thanks for ringing back. Look, I think your suggestion was right that we ought to have a few more sessions with my CPU. And we'll do it right here in the lab where we can use the MI as well."*

"I'm glad you agree. Tomorrow?"

*"No, too soon. I have some work to finish first. What do you say to Thursday afternoon? Around three?"*

"That's fine. See you there."

It wasn't fine at all. She had to rearrange a half dozen appointments to make the time. Well, she had promised.

She had driven this route so often that it was exactly three o'clock on Thursday afternoon when she drove through the Megalobe gate. There were two soldiers sitting on the clinic steps when she drew up.

"Sick call, boys?" she asked as she got out.

"No, ma'am, we're volunteers. Brian said you had some equipment to move today and we volunteered. After he paid us for the drinks."

"You don't have to do that, the machine's not so heavy."

"Yes, ma'am. But there's two of us and just one of you. And good old Billy here can do a hundred push-ups. You wouldn't want all that red-meat muscle to go to waste?"

"You're right, I wouldn't." She unlocked the trunk. "If you'll bring that box inside we'll load it up."

She had some foam rubber, that she had used as padding when her connection machine had been brought here from the hospital, and she put that into the box. Under her instruction they loaded in the machine, then carried it out to the car.

"I told you it wasn't heavy," she said.

"No, ma'am. But we'll take it out as well at the other end. We promised."

"Climb in. I'll give you a lift."

"Sorry, but it's the Major's orders. No driving in vehicles on base and double-time between buildings."

They jogged off, were waiting when she got there since she had to go the longer way around by road. Brian opened the door and the two soldiers carried the box in while the guards at the door looked on. It was all very simple.

"My heart was in my throat the entire time," she said after they were gone and the door closed.

"Get the nerves over with now because the real fun is later."

"Fun! I prefer surgery anytime."

Dr. Snaresbrook's connection machine was unloaded and carefully stowed away. Brian put a small bit in the chuck of the electric drill and made a hole in the lid of the reinforced metal box.

"Sven didn't like the idea of being locked away in the dark all the time." He held up a metal button with a flexible lead running from it. "Got a sound and optic pickup here. Mount it behind the hole, plug it in—"

"And you have a suitcase that watches you and listens to your conversations! This thing is getting crazier all the time."

Sven had been monitoring everything. As soon as Brian was finished the MI stepped into the box and plugged in the connections. The robot seemed to melt into the container as each of its myriad joints folded against the next one—like blades on a hundred-tool Swiss Army knife. Compacted even further until the treelike structure was an almost solid mass at the bottom of the box. The eyestalks retracted and swiveled to watch Brian as he packed the dummy head in next to its inert central torso cylinder, put in the hat as well, shoes, gloves and clothes, and on top of everything a carry-on airline bag.

"Ready?"

"You may seal me in now."

Brian closed and locked the box. "That's step number one," he said.

"Are you having those two soldiers back to load it into the car?"

"Never! They'll be going on perimeter guard duty about

now, that's why I chose them. The box is a heck of a lot heavier than it was when they brought it in. They would be sure to notice that. But we'll get the guards here to help us take it out. They never picked it up—so they won't notice any change!''

''You are turning into quite a conniver, Brian.''

''Comes naturally. From leading a disreputable childhood. Come over here and I'll introduce you to Sven-2. Identical with Sven in the box—at least identical at the time they separated. Except he is not yet mobile—his new body parts have yet to arrive.''

''Can I talk to this AI of yours?''

''Of course. And it is MI, that's the term now. Machine intelligence. Nothing artificial about these machines—they're the real McCoy. Their established networks have thoroughly assimilated different commonsense data bases like CYC-5 and KNOWNET-3. This is the first time anyone has combined several different ways to think into one system, tying them together with transverse paranomes. And this was done without having to force all the different kinds of knowledge into the same rigid, standard form. But it wasn't easy to do. The MI is called Sven, a corruption of Seven, because there were six failures. They all worked at first and then deteriorated in different ways.''

''I don't see a lot of robot bodies around. What did you do with them?''

''There was nothing at all wrong with the robot body. It was only a matter each time of loading new software.''

''Might I interrupt?'' Sven said. ''And add to that. Some parts of the previous versions still exist. I can access them should I wish to. MIs don't die. When something goes wrong the program is modified from the point where the trouble began. It is good to be able to remember one's past.''

''It is also good to remember more than one past,'' Sven-2 said. ''By activating certain groups of nemes, I can remember a lot of what three, four and six experienced. Each version of me—us—functioned reasonably well before breaking down. Each failed in different ways.''

Snaresbrook could scarcely believe this was happening.

Talking to a robot—or was it two robots, about its, or their, early developmental experiences, traumas, and critical experiences. It was difficult to remain matter-of-fact about it.

"Am I beginning to notice personality differences between the two Svens?" she asked.

"Very possible," Brian said. "They are certainly no longer completely identical. Since the initial duplication, they have each been operating in quite different environments. Sven is mobile while Sven-2 has no body, only a few remote sensors and effectors. So now they have quite a few different memories."

"But can't they be merged? The way we merged your own DAIs after they had read all those different books?"

"Perhaps. But I have been afraid to try to merge Sven's semantic net with that of Sven-2, because their representations of sensory-motor experience might be incompatible."

"I think that a merger would be ill-advised," Sven-2 said. "I am concerned that my middle-level management structure might reject entire sections of my physical-world representations. Because of the Principle of Noncompromise."

"That's one of our basic operating principles," Sven added. "Whenever two subagencies propose incompatible recommendations, their managers start to lose control. When this happens a higher-level manager looks for some third agency to take over. That is usually much faster and more effective than becoming paralyzed while the two differing agencies fight for control. That's what kept happening to model two, before Brian rebuilt the whole management system to be based on Papert's principle."

"Well," Snaresbrook said, "whatever anyone might say, these machines are simply amazing. Nothing artificial about them at all—and they are remarkably human in many ways. And for some reason they both remind me quite a bit of you."

"That's not too surprising since their semantic networks are based on the data that you downloaded from my very own brain." He looked at his watch. "It's seven o'clock and a good time to call a halt. The three of us are going now, Sven-2—and hopefully I won't be back here for some time."

"I wish you and Sven all the best of luck and look

forward to a detailed report upon your return. In the meantime I have research and reading that will keep me quite occupied. In addition, since I lack mobility, I shall construct a virtual reality for myself, a simulated three-dimensional world of my own.''

''Well, you will have plenty of privacy for that. The only way anyone can get in here is by blowing open the door and I think that Megalobe will take a very dim view of that.''

Brian dragged the now weighty box to the front entrance and opened it. 'Hey, guys, you want to give Doc a hand with this thing?''

If the two soldiers noticed the weight they did not mention it, just not the macho thing to do since the others had carried it in so easily.

''You go ahead, Doc,'' Brian said. ''I'll walk over with these guys.''

He had told her the exact spot where she was to park the car, in the lot behind the barracks, and was sure that she would get it right. He jogged back and, moaning insincere complaints, the two guards did so as well. They reached the barracks just as she drove up.

''Should I lock the car up?'' she asked, then put the keys in her purse at the soldiers' protestations of complete safety and security.

''Just a dry sherry,'' she said in the club, and frowned when Brian ordered a large whiskey for himself. There was no need to look at their watches since a digital readout over the bar told them the time. Brian put a lot of water in his drink and only sipped it. They talked quietly as off-duty soldiers came in, others left, both of them trying very hard not to keep looking at the clock. Yet the instant the half hour flipped over Brian was on his feet.

''No—I don't want to!'' he said loudly. ''It's just getting impossible.'' He pushed his chair back, banged into the table as he turned and spilled his drink. He did not look back as he stamped from the room, slammed the door. The barman hurried over with a towel and cleaned up the spill.

''I'll get another one,'' he said.

"No need. I don't think that Brian will be coming back tonight."

She was aware of everyone pointedly not looking in her direction as she sipped the rest of her drink. Took out her organizer as she punched in some notes. When she was ready to leave she picked up her purse, looked around the room, then went over to a sergeant who was drinking at the bar.

"Excuse me, Sergeant—but is Major Wood here today?"

"Yes, ma'am."

"Could you tell me how to find him?"

"I'll take you there if you don't mind."

"Thank you."

When he had slammed out of the bar it took all of Brian's control not to run up the stairs two at a time. Fast, yes, but running and drawing any attention was not a good idea. He locked the door behind him, then grabbed up the pliers he had placed on the table. Sven had sawn through the lock of the alarm bracelet on his wrist, then sealed it again with a small metal loop. Brian broke this off, dropped pliers and bracelet on the bed, tore his trousers off as he ran across the room, hopping on one foot and almost falling he pulled off his shoes as well. The plastic container of bubble bath was still sitting on the sink where he had left if. He seized it up, started to open it—then cursed aloud.

"Moron—the gloves first. Everything is timed. But don't forget any of the details or this thing is not going to work!"

He turned the water on in the sink, rinsed his head under the faucet and kept it running. Clumsily opened the container with his gloved hands, bent over the sink and poured half the contents over his head, rubbed it in.

Although the liquid was transparent it turned his hair black on contact. It was a commercial hair dye that was guaranteed to darken the hair but not the skin. He wore the gloves because fingernails and hair are virtually identical—and black nails would certainly bring unwanted attention. He used the remaining liquid to touch up the lighter places and to very carefully dye his eyebrows.

After toweling his hair dry he rinsed off the gloves and plastic container. He would take the empty dye bottle with him. Put the gloves in the kitchen drawer and fold the towel at the bottom of the clean pile. If he got away with this plan there would be an investigation and the technicians would eventually find traces of the dye—but he did not want to make it easy for them. A quick glance at his watch. Only three minutes to go!

He pulled out the bottom drawer of the bureau—so hard that it crashed to the floor. Leave it there! Pulled on the uniform shirt over the short-sleeved shirt he was wearing, then the trousers, tied the laces on the military dress shoes, struggled to knot his khaki tie.

It was a different Brian who looked back out of the mirror, adjusting the parachutist's cap at the same rakish angle that the others did. 82d Airborne, he had sewn the shoulder patch on himself. No stripes, a private, one more of many, in uniform—meaning the same—and that's what he wanted to be.

He was just jamming his wallet into his pocket when his telephone rang.

"Yes. Who is it?"

*"It's Dr. Snaresbrook, Brian. I wonder if I could . . ."*

"I don't feel like talking now, Doctor. I'm going to make a sandwich, have a lot to drink, watch some repulsively stupid television and go to bed early. I'll maybe talk to you tomorrow. And if you want to talk to me before then—don't. Because I'm turning off this phone."

Just two minutes now. He started to hook the phone onto his belt—realized that he could easily be tracked through it—threw it onto the bed instead. Picked up the dye container in a paper bag. Lights off, open the door a crack. Hall was empty. Lock the door behind him, quietly now. Quickly to the fire stair in the rear. His heart was thudding violently as he eased the heavy door shut behind him.

Still in luck. The corridor reaching to the back entrance to the building was empty. Walk slowly, past the open door to the kitchen—don't look in!—and ease open the rear door.

He stepped aside as the two cooks, wearing their whites, came in. They were arguing about baseball, apparently took no notice of him. But they would surely remember a soldier going out if something went wrong. If the alarm went now they would lead the guards right to him.

There was the car, in the shadow of the building, the only place in the lot not illuminated by the mercury vapor lights.

He looked around quickly, three soldiers in the lot walking away from him. No one else. He eased open the back door of the car and slipped in, closing it behind him while trying not to let it slam. Locked it and dropped to the floor, pulling the blanket over him.

"He's a very upset young man," Erin Snaresbrook said, rising to her feet.

"We all know that," Major Wood said. "And we don't like it. But we have our orders and there is absolutely nothing that I or anyone else can do about it."

"Then I will go over your head. Something must be done to help him."

"Please do that—and I wish you luck."

"He was very upset on the phone just now. He has locked himself in his room, doesn't want to talk to anyone."

"Understandable. He might be better in the morning."

"Well, I certainly hope so."

He showed her to the front door, started to come with her to the car. She stopped and rooted in her purse for her car keys, took them out along with one of her business cards that she handed to the officer.

"I want you to phone me, night or day, Major, if you are concerned in any way about his well-being. I hope something really will be done before it is too late. Good-bye."

"I'll do that, Doctor. Good-bye."

She walked slowly out of the building and to the parking lot. Got into the car, not daring to glance at the backseat. Started the engine and looked about. There was no one nearby.

"Are you—there?" she whispered.

"You better believe it!" was the muffled answer.

She drove to the gate. Nodded to the guards when the barrier rose, drove out into the star-pricked darkness.

# 38

## December 19, 2024

Erin Snaresbrook was forced to set the cruise control on the car, since her speed kept creeping up—and dropping back only when she noticed. The desert was an ocean of darkness on all sides, the headlights boring a tunnel of light down the undulating ribbon of the road ahead of her. She drove for over a mile before she saw the car parked on the shoulder of the road. She slowed and pulled over, stopping behind it. Sighed with relief, then turned her head and spoke over her shoulder.

"You're safe now. You can come out."

Brian popped up onto the backseat. "Thought I was going to suffocate. No problems, I guess—or we wouldn't be here."

"No problems. You can get out. Wait—let me turn the lights off first. And the inside light. Just in case."

Brian stepped out into the warm darkness. Free! For the first time in a year. He breathed deep of the dry desert air, allowed himself a long moment to take in the sky brimming over with stars, filled with them right down to the dark and jagged outline of the mountains. Heard the car door close as Snaresbrook came out and joined him. He turned to face her, looked past her and saw the other car, felt a surge of panic when he saw that someone was standing next to it.

"Who's there! What happened?"

"It's all right, Brian," Snaresbrook said quietly. "It's Shelly. She's here to help you. She knows about everything that is happening and is on your side."

Brian's throat was so tight that it took an effort to speak.

"How long have you known?" he asked when Shelly came and stood before him.

"Just for the last week. Ever since I told Dr. Snaresbrook about my leaving the military because of what they were doing to you. I convinced her that I wanted to help you—and she believed me."

"That's when I told her what you were planning to do. I have a great fear, Brian, that you are not ready to tackle the outside world on your own yet. I took the calculated risk that she was sincere—her presence here instead of the military police is proof that I was correct. I have been very concerned about you and, frankly, I did not want you to learn about her part in this affair until you were safely away from your prison."

Brian took a shuddering breath, let it out slowly—and smiled into the darkness. "You're right, Doc. I don't think I could have hacked it before. But now that it's done—I feel great! Welcome aboard, Shelly."

"Thank you both for letting me help. I'm coming with you. You are not going to be alone."

"I've got to think about that. Later. Right now we had better get moving." He unknotted his tie and pulled off the army shirt. "Did the Major buy your story, Doc?"

"He likes you, Brian, they all seem to. I feel certain that no one will go near the room until the morning."

"I hope so. But when they do find that I'm missing it's going to really hit the fan. You know I feel sorry for them all. In a way it's a really dirty trick to play. They'll be in the yogurt for sure."

"A little late to think about that, isn't it?"

"No, I've already gone that route. I thought long and hard about it when I was planning the escape. I feel sorry for them—but they were my jailers—and I needed out of jail. Now, what's the plan?"

"Shelly takes over from here. I'm going back to Megalobe, do some work in my lab there. Spend the night. That will muddy the waters a bit, perhaps even prevent them from tying me in with the escape. The bigger the mystery the better the chance you have to pull it off. I'll even box my connection machine and put it back into the car so they will have trouble tying a missing box with your escape. So let's drag Sven out and put it in Shelly's car. The faster I get back, the better it will be.''

As soon as this was done, after a quick peck on the cheek and hurried good-byes, they separated. When the other car had made a U-turn and headed back toward Megalobe, Shelly started her engine and drove west. Brian looked out at the hills moving by, felt an even greater sense of relief than he had when he first knew he was free.

"I'm glad that you are here,'' he said. "And maybe we better stick together. At least for a while.'' He looked at his watch. "At this speed we should reach the border by eleven at the latest.''

"Are you sure? I've never driven this way before.''

"Neither have I—that I remember. But I have been reading lots of guidebooks and maps. There shouldn't be much traffic and the total drive is only eighty-seven miles.''

They were silent after that: there was very little now to say but a lot to think about.

They turned off 78 before Brawley and headed south toward El Centro and Calexico. The signs reading MEXICO led them around the town center to the border crossing. It was just half past ten when the customs booths appeared ahead. For the first time Brian felt nervous.

"All the travel books say that there is no hassle getting into Mexico. Is that right?''

"Come and bring your dollars. I've never been stopped going in—or even been looked at for that matter.''

There were no American customs officers in sight when they drove across the national boundary. The Mexican official, sporting a large gun and even larger stomach, just glanced at their license plate then turned away.

"We did it!'' Brian shouted as they rolled along the street of garish shops and bars.

"We sure enough did! What's next?''

"A change of plan for one thing. The original idea was for the doc to drop me and Sven off and go back to the States. She had no clue as to what my future plans would be.''

"Do you?"

"Positively! I'm going to take the train to Mexico City tonight."

"So am I."

"You sure?"

"Positive."

"All right. We stick to the original plan except you take the car back across the border, return by cab—"

"Nope. Too complicated, too time-consuming. And it leaves a trail. We just leave the car here with the key in the ignition."

"It'll get stolen!"

"That's the idea. It should vanish completely if the local car thieves are up to scratch. That's a lot better than having it found in a parking lot in Calexico to show which way we went."

"You can't do that. The money . . ."

"I wanted a new car anyway. And maybe someday I can collect the insurance. So not another word. Which way is the station?"

"I'll look at the street map."

They found the Ferrocarriles Nacionales de Mexico easily enough. Shelly drove past the station and around the corner to a badly lit street, parked under a burnt-out streetlight. She took a small suitcase from the trunk, remembered to leave the keys, then helped Brian lift out the heavy box.

"The first step—and the biggest one," he said.

"One hour and twenty-one minutes are left before the train leaves," the box said in muffled but possibly admonitory tones.

"More than enough time. Be patient—we're the ones dragging the box."

They got it as far as the station entrance before Shelly called quits.

"Enough! You watch this thing while I see if they rise to something as exotic as a redcap."

She was back a few minutes later with the man. He was wearing a battered cap, his badge of rank, and pushing a handcart.

"We have to buy tickets," Brian said as the porter eased the metal edge of the hand truck under the box. He hoped that the man spoke English.

"No problem. Where are you going?"

"Mexico City."

"No problem. You people, you just follow me."

The unhappy-looking woman behind the window grille also spoke English, he was relieved to find out. Yes, there was a first-class compartment available. The ancient machine at her elbow disgorged two tickets, which she hand-stamped. The only problem was money.

"Don't take dollars," she said, scowling, as though it were his fault. "Only *moneda nacional*."

"Can't we change money here?" Shelly asked.

"The change is closed already."

Brian's surge of panic was only slightly relieved when the porter said, "I got a friend, change money."

"Where?"

"Over there, he work in the bar."

The bartender smiled broadly, was more than happy to sell pesos for dollars.

"You know I gotta charge different from the bank because I lose on the exchange."

"Whatever you say," Brian said, passing over the greenbacks.

"I'm sure he's cheating you!" Shelly hissed when the man went to the till.

"I agree. But we're getting on the train and that's what counts."

Cheated or not he felt immensely relieved to see the thick bundle of pesos that he got in return for his dollars.

It was eight minutes to twelve when the porter put the box on the floor in the compartment, pocketed his ten-dollar tip, closed the door behind him as he left. Shelly pulled down the curtain while Brian locked the door and opened the box.

"The correct rate of exchange for selling dollars in Mexico is—"

"Keep it a secret from us, will you please?" Brian said

as he took out his airline bag. "Been enjoying your trip so far, Sven?"

"If looking at the inside of dark car trunks is enjoyable, then I have enjoyed myself."

"It can only get better," Shelly said.

There was the clank of distant couplings and the train shuddered and began to move; an imperious knock rattled the door.

"I'll get that," Shelly said. "You had better relax."

"I would love to."

She waited until he had slammed the box shut before she unlocked and opened the door.

"Tickets please," the conductor said.

"Yes, of course." He passed them over. The conductor punched them and pointed to the seats.

"Just pull the back of the couch down when you are ready to retire, the bed is already made up. The upper bunk swings down like this. Have a pleasant journey."

Brian locked the door behind him and dropped onto the seat limply. This had been quite a day.

The train swayed as they picked up speed, the wheels clicked over the rails, lights moved by outside. He opened the curtain and watched the suburbs stream past, then the farms beyond.

"We've made it!" Shelly said. "I've never seen a more lovely sight in my life."

"I am sure that it is a most interesting view," the muffled voice said.

"Sorry about that," Brian said as he opened the box again. Sven pushed his eyestalks out so he could see through the window as well. Brian turned off the lights and they watched the landscape drift by.

"What time do we get there?" Shelly asked.

"Three in the afternoon."

"And then?"

Brian was silent, looking out into the darkness, still not sure. "Shelly, I still think I ought to be doing this on my own."

"Nonsense. In for a penny, in for a pound, isn't that what they say?"

"They say it in Ireland all right."

"It is my belief that you should accept Shelly's offer of aid," Sven said.

"Did I ask for your opinion?"

"No. But her suggestion is a good one. You have been quite ill, your memory has gaps in it. You can use her help. Take it."

"Outvoted," Brian sighed. "The plan is a simple one—but you had better have your passport with you."

"I do. Packed it in as soon as Dr. Snaresbrook mentioned she would be going to the Mexican border."

"What I must do is stay ahead of anyone who comes looking for me."

"Go to ground in Mexico?"

"I thought of that—but it's no good. The Mexican and American police cooperate very closely in chasing down drug runners. I am sure that General Schorcht would tag me as a criminal if that was needed to track me down. So I have to go further than Mexico. I checked the schedules and a lot of international flights leave Mexico City in the early evening. So we buy tickets and leave the country."

"Any particular destination in mind?"

"Of course. Ireland. You'll remember that I am an Irish citizen."

"That's a brilliant idea. So we get to Ireland—then what?"

"I am going to try and find Dr. Bociort—if he is still alive. Which will probably mean making a trip to Rumania. The people who stole my first AI and tried to kill me are still out there. I am going to find them. For a lot of reasons. Revenge might be one of them, but survival is the main one. With their threat removed I can stop looking over my shoulder. And General Schorcht will no longer have an excuse to cause me trouble."

"Amen to that." She yawned widely and covered her mouth. "Excuse me. But if you are half as tired as I am we should get some sleep."

"Now that you have said it—yes."

He pulled down the curtain and turned on the lights. As

promised, the two berths were made up and swung easily into position.

"I'll take the upper," Shelly said, opening her suitcase and taking out pajamas and a dressing gown, grabbed her purse. "Be right back."

When she returned the only light on was the small one over her berth. Brian was under the covers and Sven had raised the curtain an inch and was looking out.

"Good night," she said.

"Good night," Sven said. A soft snore was the only other sound.

# 39

## December 20, 2024

The scenery flowed by while they ate breakfast in the dining car. Small villages, jungle and mountains, an occasional glimpse of ocean as they skirted the Sea of Cortez. While they were finishing their coffee a phone rang and Brian saw one of the other diners take it from his jacket pocket and answer it.

"I'm being stupid," he said. "I should have thought of it before this. Do you have your phone with you?"

"Of course. Doesn't everyone?"

"Not me, not now. You know that you can receive a phone call no matter where you are. Did you ever think of the mechanism involved?"

"Not really. It's one of those things you take for granted."

"It was so new to me that I looked into it. There are fiber-optic and microwave links everywhere now, cellular nets right around the world. When you want to make a call you just punch it in and the nearest station accepts it and passes it on. What you might not realize is that your phone is always on, always on standby. And it logs in automatically when you move between cells by sending your present location to the memory bank of your home exchange. So when someone dials your number the national or international telephone system always knows where to find you and pass on the incoming call."

Her eyes widened. "You mean it knows where I am now? That anyone with the authority could obtain this information?"

"Absolutely. Like General Schorcht for instance."

She gasped. "Then we have to get rid of it! Throw it off the train—"

"No. If a phone goes out of commission a signal is sent to the repair service. You don't want to draw any attention to yourself. We can be fairly sure that no one is looking for you yet. But when they find that I'm missing and the search begins, they will be sure to contact everyone who worked with me. Let's go back to the compartment—I have an idea."

There was a panel under the window that looked perfect. Brian pointed to it.

"Sven, do you think you can take those screws out?"

Sven swiveled his eyes to look. "An easy task."

The MI formed a screwdriver head with its manipulators and quickly took out the screws that held the plastic panel in place. There were two pipes and an electric cable passing through the space there behind the panel. Brian pointed.

"We'll just put your telephone in here. The plastic panel won't block any signals. If the military call and you don't answer they are going to have a busy time tracking the signal while it's moving around Mexico. By the time they sort it out we will be long gone."

The train pulled out of Tepic at lunchtime and turned inland towards Guadalajara, reaching Mexico City exactly on time. Sven was packed safely away and ready for the porter who came for their luggage. He led the way to the Depósito de Equipajes, where they checked everything in. Brian pointed to the bank next to it.

"The first thing we do is get some pesos. We don't want a repetition of Mexicali."

"And then?"

"We find a travel agency."

Outside of the Buenavista railroad station, Mexico City was cold and wet; the smog hurt their eyes. They ignored the cab rank and walked out through the crowds and along Insurgentes Norte until they came to the first travel agency. It was a large one and a placard in the window said ENGLISH SPOKEN, a very hopeful sign. They turned in.

"We would like to fly to Ireland," Brian told the man behind the large desk. "As soon as is possible."

"I'm afraid that there are no direct flights from here," the agent said as he turned to his computer and brought up the tables of departing flights. "There is an American flight that connects daily through New York City—and a Delta flight through Atlanta."

"What about non-American carriers?" Shelly asked, and Brian nodded agreement. Safely out of the States they were in no hurry to return, however briefly. In the end they settled for MexAir to Havana, Cuba, with an Aeroflot Tupelov leaving three hours later for Shannon. The tickets were priced in pesos, but the agent called the bank for the current rate of exchange.

"Let's hold on to the cash," Shelly said. "We're going to need it. Use my credit card instead."

"They'll track you down."

"Like the phone—I'll be long gone."

"Cash or credit card, both okay," the agent said, and pulled over the booking form. "American passports?"

"One. The other is Irish."

"That will be fine. This will only take a few moments." The computer link checked the credit card account, booked the seats and printed the tickets. "I hope you enjoy your flight."

"I hope so too," Brian said when they were back in the street. The query about their passports was a depressing reminder that they were going to have to pass through customs. The travel books had been quite clear about this and he knew he faced trouble. He hoped he could avoid it by what was called the *mordida*. He would soon find out.

"I'm cold and wet," Shelly said. "Do we have time to buy a raincoat—maybe a sweater?"

He looked at his watch. "A good idea. More than enough time before we have to be at the airport. Let's try that department store."

He bought two more shirts, underwear, a light jacket as well as the raincoat. Just the basic items that would fit into the carry-on bag. Shelly did far better than that, shopping so well that she had to buy another small suitcase. Back in the train station Brian dug out the stub, retrieved Sven and their bags, then took a cab to the airport.

There were no problems at the check-in counter. They watched Shelly's bag and the crated MI move slowly away on the belt as the airline clerk tore out sheets from their tickets and stapled them to the boarding cards.

"Might I see your passports, please?"

This first hurdle was easy enough to get over. All she wanted to do was look at the first page to see if the passports were current and had not expired. She smiled and passed them back. Shelly went through security first. He followed, clutching his passport and boarding pass, putting his bag on the belt of the X-ray machine before he stepped through the archway next to it. The machine bleeped and the security guard turned to him with a dark and suspicious look.

He took the coins from his pocket, even unclipped and removed his brass belt buckle and put that on the tray as well. Stepped back through the arch, which bleeped again.

Then Brian realized what was happening. The magnetic field detected metal—and electronic circuitry.

"My head," he said, pointing at his ear. "An accident, an operation." Not a computer—keep it simple. "I have a metal plate in my skull."

The guard was most interested in this. He used the magnetic field hand detector, which only bleeped when it was near Brian's head. No weapon there; he was waved through. Everyone was just doing their job.

Including the customs officer. He was a dark-skinned man with an elegant mustache. When Brian gave him his passport he flipped the pages slowly, went back and repeated the action. Looked up and frowned.

"I do not see the visa entry showing where you entered Mexico."

"Are you sure? Can I see the passport again?" He pretended to look through it and, with the great fear that he was making a total fool of himself, slipped a hundred-dollar bill between the pages. It is one thing to read about bribes—another to really attempt bribery. He was sure he would be under arrest within moments.

"I didn't know I needed one. We crossed the border by car. I didn't know about a visa."

He pushed the passport back and watched with horror as the officer opened it.

"These things happen," the officer said. "Mistakes can be made. But you will need two visa stamps. One to enter the country, one to leave. If the lady is with you she will need two stamps as well."

The man looked bored as he returned the passport unstamped. Brian flipped through its empty pages—empty of money as well as visas—then realized what was happening.

"Of course. Two stamps, not one. I understand."

They both understood. Three more hundred-dollar bills went the way of the first; there were two thuds and he had the passport back. Shelly's was treated in the same way. They were through and on their way!

"Did I see what I thought I saw?" Shelly hissed in his ear. "You are a crook, Brian Delaney."

"I am as surprised as you are. Let's find our gate and sit down. This kind of thing is not easy on the nerves."

The plane was only an hour late in leaving; the rest of the trip passed in a blur. They could only manage to doze on the plane and fatigue was beginning to tell. Havana was just a dimly lit transit lounge with hard plastic seats. The Aeroflot flight left two hours late this time. They ate some of the tasteless airline food, drank some Georgian champagne and finally fell asleep.

It was just after dawn in Shannon. The plane dropped down through the cloud-filled sky, came in low over cows grazing in green fields as they approached the runway. Brian pulled on his coat and took down his bag from the overhead rack. They left the plane in silence along with the rest of the weary travelers. Another transatlantic flight had arrived at the same time, so they were a long time shuffling along in the line of unshaven men, bleary-eyed women, whimpering and wailing children. Shelly went through first, had a visa stamped in her passport, turned to wait for him.

"Welcome home, Mr. Byrne," the wide-awake and sprightly customs man said. "Been away on a holiday?"

Brian had been prepared for this moment and his accent was purest Wicklow without a trace of American. "You might say so—thousands wouldn't. The food's a shock and they seem to think that overcharging is a way of life."

"That's very interesting." The man had the rubber stamp in his hand but he was not using it. Instead he raised cold blue eyes to Brian.

"Your current address?"

"Number 20 Kilmagig. In Tara."

"A nice little village. Main Street with the primary school just across from the church."

"Not unless they've jacked it up and moved it a half mile down the road, it isn't."

"True, true, I must have gotten it confused with someplace else. But there is still one little problem. That you are Irish I don't doubt, Mr. Byrne, and I wouldn't be one to deny a man access to the land of his birth. But the law is the law." He signed to a garda, who nodded and strolled their way.

"I don't understand. You've checked my passport—"

"I have indeed, most intriguing as well as puzzling it is. The date of issue is perfectly correct and all the visas appear to be in order. But I find one thing difficult to understand—which is why I am asking you to proceed with this garda to the office. You see this style passport has been replaced by the new Europas. This particular style passport hasn't been issued for over ten years. Now don't you find that interesting?"

"You better wait here for me," Brian said weakly to Shelly as the big man in blue uniform led him away.

The interrogation room was windowless and damp. There

was nothing on the drab walls except some water stains; a table and two chairs stood in the center of the worn wooden floor. Brian sat on one of them. His carry-on bag was on top of the box in the corner. A large policeman stood next to the door staring patiently into space.

Brian was depressed, chilled, and probably catching a cold. He rubbed his itching nose, pulled out his handkerchief and sneezed loudly into it.

"God bless," the garda said, glancing at him then back to the wall again. The door opened and another big man came in. No uniform, but the dark suit and heavy boots were uniform enough. He sat down on the outer side of the table and put Brian's passport down before him.

"I am Lieutenant Fennelly. Now, is this your passport, Mr. Byrne?"

"Yes, it is."

"There are certain irregularities about it. Are you aware of that?"

Brian had had more than enough time to think about what he was going to say. Had decided on the truth, everything except the fact that he had been imprisoned by the military. He would keep to a highly simplified version of what had actually happened.

"Yes. The passport was out of date. I had some important business appointments, couldn't wait to get a new one. So I made a few slight changes myself to bring it up to date."

"Slight changes! Mr. Byrne, this passport has been so excellently altered that I sincerely doubt that it would have been detected had it not been the old model. What do you do for a living?"

"I'm an electronic engineer."

"Well you could make a grand living as a forger should you wish to continue your criminal career."

"I'm no criminal!"

"Aren't you now? Did you not just admit to forgery?"

"I did not. A passport is only a piece of identification, nothing more. I have just brought my passport up to date— which is the same thing that the passport office would have done had I the time to apply for a new one."

"That's a pretty Jesuitical argument for a criminal to use."

Brian was angry, even though he realized the detective had angered him on purpose. A sneeze saved him; by the time he had dug out his handkerchief and wiped his nose he had the anger under control. Attack was the best defense. He hoped.

"Are you charging me with some kind of crime, Lieutenant Fennelly?"

"I will make my report. I would like some details first." He opened a large notebook on the table, took out a pen. "Place and date of birth."

"Is all that needed? I have been living in the United States, but I was born in Tara, County Wicklow. My mother died when I was young. She was not married. I was adopted by my father, Patrick Delaney, who took me to live in the States where he was then working. It's all in the record. You can have names, dates, places if you must. It will all check out."

The Lieutenant did want the facts, all of them, and slowly and carefully transcribed them in his book. Brian held nothing back, just terminated the record before he began to work at Megalobe, before the theft and the killings that happened.

"Would you open your luggage now?"

Brian had been waiting for this, had planned ahead. He knew that Sven was listening to everything that was being said, hoped that the MI would understand as well.

"The small bag, here, contains personal items. The large box is a sample."

"A sample of what?"

"A robot. This is a machine I have developed that I plan to show to some private investors."

"Their names?"

"I cannot reveal that. A confidential business matter."

Fennelly made another note while Brian unlocked the box and opened the lid. "This is a basic model of an industrial robot. It can answer simple questions and take verbal input. That is how it is controlled."

Even the garda by the door was interested in this, turning his head to look. The detective gazed down at the unassembled parts with a baffled expression.

"Shall I turn it on?" Brian asked. "It can talk—but not very well." Sven would love that. He reached down and pressed one of the latches. "Can you hear me?"

"Yes—I can—hear—you."

A great job of ham acting, scratchy and monotone like a cheap toy. At least it caught the attention of the lawmen.

"What are you?"

"I am—an industrial—robot. I follow—instructions."

"If that is enough, Lieutenant, I will turn it off."

"Just a moment, if you please. What is that?" He pointed to the hollow plastic head.

"To make the demonstration more interesting I occasionally mount that on the robot. It draws attention. If you don't mind I'll turn if off, the battery you know." He pressed the latch again and closed the lid.

"What is this machine worth?" Fennelly asked.

Worth? The molecular memory alone had cost millions to build. "I would say about two thousand dollars," Brian said innocently.

"Do you have an import license?"

"I am not importing it. It is a sample and not for sale."

"You will have to talk to the customs officer about that." He closed the book and stood up. "I am making a report on this matter. You will remain within the airport premises if you don't mind."

"Am I under arrest?"

"At the present moment, no."

"I want a lawyer."

"That decision is up to you."

Shelly was sitting over a cold cup of tea, jumped to her feet when he came up.

"What happened? I was so worried—"

"Don't be. It is all going to work out all right. Have another cup of tea while I make a phone call."

The classified directory had a half page of solicitors in Limerick. The cashier sold him a phone card—this must be the only country in the world that still uses them. With his third call Brian talked to a Fergus Duffy, who would be happy to drive out to the airport at once and take on his case. But it was an Irish at-once, so it was afternoon, and a number of cups of tea and some very dry cheese sandwiches later, before his new solicitor managed to make any alteration in his status. Fergus Duffy was a cheerful young man with red tufts of hair protruding from his ears and nose, which he tugged on from time to time when excited.

"A pleasure to meet you both," he said, sitting down and taking a file from his briefcase. "I must say that this is an unusual and interesting affair and no one seems to be able to work out that no crime has been committed, you have merely altered your own expired passport, which certainly can't be considered a crime. In the end the powers that be have come to a decision to pass the problem on to a higher authority. You are free to go but you must give your address so you can be contacted. If needs be."

"What about my baggage?"

"You can pick it up now. Your machine will be released as soon as you have a customs broker complete the forms and have paid duty and VAT and such. No problem there."

"Then I am free to go?"

"Yes—but not far. I would suggest the airport hotel for the time being. I'll push these papers through as fast as I can, but you must realize that *fast* in Ireland is a relative term. You know, like the story about the Irish linguist. You've heard it?"

"I don't believe—"

"You'll greatly enjoy it. You see it happens at a congress of international linguists and the Spanish linguist asks the Irish linguist if there is a word in Irish with the same meaning as the Spanish *mañana*. Well your man thinks for a bit and says, why yes, sure enough there is—but it doesn't have the same sense of terrible urgency." Fergus slapped his knees and laughed enough for all three of them.

He helped them collect Brian's bag and the sample robot now released from customs. On the short drive to the hotel they heard three more of what he referred to as Kerryman stories. They could all be clearly recognized as familiar Polish or Irish jokes. Brian wondered which minority or subhuman race might be named as the subject of these same jokes when they were told in Kerry.

Fergus Duffy dropped them in front of the hotel, promised to call in the morning. While they were talking Shelly checked them in, came back with two keys and an ancient porter with a trolley.

"You share with Sven," she said as they followed the septuagenarian toward the elevator. "I have no desire at all to catch your cold. I'm going to unpack and freshen up. I'll be over as soon as I feel a little more human."

"Is there any reason for me to remain in this box?" Sven asked when Brian opened it. "I would enjoy a little mobility."

"Enjoy." Brian sneezed thunderously, then attached Sven's right arm and unpacked his toilet kit.

"What is the electricity supply in Ireland?" Sven asked as it fitted the other arm into position.

"Two hundred and twenty volts, fifty cycles."

"Easy enough to adjust for. I'm going to recharge my batteries. Use them until we can obtain more fuel for the cell."

Brian found a tube of antihistamine tablets in his toilet kit and washed one down with a glass of water. Sat back in the chair and realized that, for the first time in what—two days?—he had finally stopped running. The telephone was on the table beside him and it reminded him of the mysterious number that Sven-2 had uncovered. Could it possibly be a phone number in Switzerland? Hidden there by the vanished Dr. Bociort? He still didn't think much of the theory, but he ought to at least try to place the call before he started running all over Europe. There was only one way to find out if Sven-2's theory made any sense. He reached out for the phone—and stopped.

Could the phone be tapped? Or was he just being paranoid after General Schorcht's constant surveillance? He was the subject of a police investigation here so there might be a long chance that it was. He pulled his hand back, took the phone card from his pocket. Five pounds it said and he must have used only a small part of that. More than enough left to call Switzerland. He went and looked out of the window. The sun had come out but the streets were still wet from the rain. And down the block was a brown building with the name "Paddy Murphy" over the curtained windows. A pub—the perfect place. He could have a jar and make his call. He dozed in the chair until Shelly's knock jumped him awake. She was wearing a sweater with a bold Aztec design.

"You look great," he said.

"I'm glad one of us does. You look like you have been dragged through a knothole."

"That's exactly how I feel. I'll have a wash and shave, then we'll go out to the pub."

"Shouldn't you be sleeping rather than drinking?"

"Probably," he called back through the open door. "But I want to make that phone call first, to that number that Sven-2 thinks he discovered."

"What number? What on earth are you talking about?"

"It's a long shot but one worth trying."

"We're being mysterious, aren't we?"

"Not really. I'll try to make the call first. Then there really might be something to talk about. Sven, I never wrote the number down. What was it?"

"41 336709."

Brian scribbled it on the back of the stub from his boarding pass. "Great. I'll be out in a minute." He closed the door and began to undress.

The bartender was chatting with a solitary drinker at the far end of the bar, looked up and came over to them when they entered and sat down at a table near the open fire.

"What will you have, Shelly?" Brian asked.

"Wine of the country, of course."

"Right. Two pints of Guinness, if you please."

"Going to rain again," the barman said gloomily as he slowly and patiently filled the glasses, placed them on the bar to settle.

"Doesn't it always. Good for the farmers and bad for the tourists."

"Get away with you—the tourists love it. They wouldn't recognize the country if it wasn't raining stair rods."

"There is that. You have a phone here?"

"In back, by the door to the lounge." He topped up the glasses and brought them over.

Brian sipped at the creamy head of the jet black liquid.

"This is delicious," Shelly said.

"Nutritious as well. And enough of it will get you drunk. I bet it cures colds too. I'm going to make that call now."

He took another sip and went to find the phone. Inserted the card and dialed the Swiss number. As soon as he got past the first four digits there was a high-pitched interrupt and a computer-generated voice spoke.

*"You have dialed Switzerland from Ireland. The exchange you have entered does not exist. This message will be repeated in German and French . . ."*

Brian crumpled up the slip of paper, threw it into the ashtray next to the phone, went back to the table and drained his pint and signaled for another one.

"You look glum," Shelly said.

"I should be. It doesn't work. The number was not a phone number. Sven-2 found the sequence buried in one of the stolen AI programs and seemed to think that it was. It wasn't. The chances are it was just a line of code that I wrote myself for the original AI. Let's forget the whole thing."

"Cheer up. You're a free man in a free world and that should mean something."

"It does—but not much at the present moment. Must be the cold getting me down. Let's finish these and get back to the hotel. I think some sleep is in order now. With the pills and the pints I should be able to sleep around the clock."

# 40

## December 21, 2024

It was after seven that evening before Brian woke up, blinking into the darkness of the room.

"I detect the motion of your eyelids," Sven said. "Do you wish me to turn the lights on."

"Do that."

Ten minutes later he came out of the elevator and headed for the dining room. Shelly was sitting at a table by the far wall and she waved him over.

"I hope you don't mind but I started without you. The salmon is absolutely delicious. You ought to try it."

"You talked me into it—particularly since I just realized that I am starving. Airline muck and cheese sandwiches leave a lot to be desired."

"You look a lot better."

"Feel a lot better. The pills and sleep did the trick."

"Your solicitor telephoned. I had told the front desk that you were sleeping so they put the call through to me. He was quite happy about everything—including the fact that you are going to have to pay a fine of fifty pounds."

"Why?"

"He wasn't quite sure. He said that he thinks it is just a slap on the wrist to sort you out—and wind up the case. He has already paid so you are a free man. He is also looking into a passport for you and thinks he can pull enough strings to get one by tomorrow. Said to phone him in the morning. I wasn't too impressed by that. Takes ten minutes in the States."

"Ahh, my fair colleen, but you are not in the distant country where all the computers work and the trains leave on time. Let me tell you—one day for a new passport in Ireland is lightning."

"I suppose we can use the rest. And maybe you can lick that cold. Have you thought about what you plan to do next?"

"There is little I can do without a passport. Then we start tracking down the mysterious Dr. Bociort. Right now I intend to get tucked into some dinner, with maybe a Guinness or two to tamp it down. Since we are going to be here at least another day, maybe we ought to think about some sight-seeing in the morning."

"In the rain?"

"This is Ireland. If you won't go out in the rain you are just never going to go out."

"Let me think about it. You have your dinner and I'll see you later. I have to make a phone call."

Brian raised his eyebrows in silence and she laughed.

"Not to the States or to anyone that can be traced. Before I left L.A. I called a cousin in Israel. The only qualm I had about helping you was being out of touch with my family. My father is due to be operated on soon. My cousin will be calling my mother and she has strict instructions *not* to tell her that I might be phoning Israel. I'm sorry, Brian, it's the best I could think of . . ."

"Don't let it worry you. I'm feeling a lot safer and more relaxed now that we are here. Make your call."

Brian was just finishing his coffee, along with his second brandy, when Shelly rejoined him.

"That appears to be a lethal but interesting combination," she said, looking around for the waiter. "Mind if I join you?"

"Be hurt if you didn't."

"You look better."

"I feel better. Food, sleep, pills—and freedom. In fact I can't remember when I ever felt this good before."

"That's the best news ever!" She smiled, reached out and squeezed his hand. Then drew away when the waiter brought the tray to the table.

The touch unlocked a warmth in Brian that was totally new and he smiled broadly. Free for the moment, away from responsibilities and worries. The rain lashing down outside, but it was warm and secure inside. An encapsulated moment of peace and happiness.

"To you, Shelly," he said when the waiter had gone and they raised their glasses. "For what you have done to help me."

"It's little enough, Brian. I would rather drink to you—and freedom."

His smile reflected hers as they touched glasses, drank.

"I could really get used to this kind of thing," he said. "How did the call go?"

"It didn't. Even the operator couldn't get through. Said to try later."

"I can't understand that—telephone calls go through every time."

She laughed. "Apparently not in Ireland."

"Are you sure you have the right number?"

"Pretty sure."

"Better check directory inquiries before you call again."

"Good idea. Let's finish these and I'll do it right now, from the phone booth in the lobby."

The booth was occupied and after a moment Shelly shook her head.

"No point in waiting, we'll go to my room."

It was easier to climb the stairs than wait for the ancient elevator. Shelly unlocked the door, opened it and turned on the lights.

"Bigger than mine," Brian said, "more like a suite."

"Maybe the manager is partial to women. Do you want a drop of duty-free while I put the call through?"

"Yes, please—some of that buffalo vodka you bought on the Aeroflot flight to kill the pain."

She punched up international inquiries and spoke her cousin's name and address, but had to repeat the name twice slowly before the voice recognition program was satisfied. She wrote the number down, then laughed.

"You were right about phone calls always going through—I

apologize to Ireland. I got one digit wrong when I copied it down.''

"I'll drink to that. To technology.''

He emptied his glass, filled it again, sipped in a warm haze as she made the call. He was probably getting drunk—but the hell with it. This was for pleasure, not escape, a very big difference. The call went through and he half listened to Shelly's voice. She sounded relieved so the news was good. There was some more chat about the family, then she hung up.

"Sounded okay from where I sit.''

"It was. No problems at all and the prognosis is fine. So good in fact they are scheduling the operation.''

"Good news indeed.'' He struggled to his feet with an effort. "I better be going. It's been a great evening.''

"I couldn't agree more,'' she said. "Good night, Brian.''

It was natural to kiss him on the cheek, a simple kiss of parting.

Then it wasn't that simple. She found him returning her kiss with a sudden warmth that she responded to. Neither of them had expected this—neither could say no.

It was closeness, an easy pleasure, a natural joining. It was emotion, sensation for Brian, something to be done without thinking, without logic. A flicker of memory, Kim, stirred at the edge of his attention but he rejected the thought. Not Kim, not that. This was different, better, very different.

But Kim would not be put aside. Not Kim herself but the memory of his feelings. His anger—anger at himself for that one loss of control.

Then it all drained away. Brian became aware that something was very wrong. In the darkness, Shelly's naked body was against his; but it was not right. He felt drained, distant, soft where he should be hard, aware of an immense distaste at everything that was happening. He rolled on his side facing away from her, pulled further away when she stroked his shoulder.

"Don't worry,'' Shelly said. "These things happen. Life hasn't been that easy for you.''

"Nothing happened—I don't want to talk about it."

"Brian, honey, after what you have gone through, you can't expect everything physical to work—"

"Physical? I don't expect *anything* to work. I have been shot, operated on, recovered, attacked, locked away. How am I supposed to feel? Not very human if you want to know. Not very interested in this, what you are trying to do—"

"We, Brian, not just me. This is something that takes two to play."

"Then find a game you can play by yourself."

He heard her gasp of shock in the darkness, could almost see her tears. Nor did he care.

"I thought that I made it quite clear when I said that I didn't want to talk about it."

Shelly began to speak again, changed her mind. Instead she went in silence into the bathroom and closed the door. Brian groped about until he found the light, turned it on. Dressed and left. Back in his own room he went unseeing into the bath, threw water on his face and rubbed it dry with the towel, would not look at himself in the mirror.

The bedroom was still dark; he hadn't turned the light on when he had come in. He did it now and saw that the curtain had been pulled open and that Sven was standing beside the window. He started to speak but the MI raised a suddenly formed hand in a very human gesture to *stop*. Brian shut the door and saw that Sven was now pointing to a sheet of paper on the bed. It was a note printed with precisely formed letters:

*I have determined that there is a device inside the telephone in this room that is acting as a tap. In addition to this there is radiation directed against the window of the proper wavelength that is used to listen to conversations by monitoring the vibrations of the glass. We are under surveillance.*

Who could it possibly be? The Irish security service? Possibly—and he certainly hoped so. What had happened with Shelly was forgotten for the moment. Investigation by the locals would be a lot better than thinking the unthinkable. The legions of General Schorcht could not have found him here, not this quickly. He fervently hoped. But what could they do to him? He went to the window and stared out into the darkness. Nothing. As he closed the curtain a motion caught his attention and he saw that Sven was signaling to him. The MI had printed out another note. He went over to look at it. The message contained just one word:

*Communication.*

As he read it Sven held up the end of a fiber-optic cable. Of course—a connection between both their brains would be completely secure and untappable.

But they had never communicated before in this manner, had always been assisted by Dr. Snaresbrook and her connection machine. But Sven was just as skillful, could find the metal stud under his skin, could insert the cable.

Not for an instant did Brian consider that there was any danger or difficulty in the process. He simply nodded agreement and pulled the chair over so it was out of sight of the window, sat in it with his back to the MI. Felt the familiar tracery of spider fingers on his skin.

Felt completely secure in the embrace of his own creation.

They spoke in silent communication, brain to brain.

**That's surprising. This is no faster than if we were speaking aloud.**

*Of course, Brian. Unlike thought, which is networked, speech is linear and must be transmitted one unit at a time.*

**Who are they? Do you have any idea?**

*They have not revealed themselves in any way, nor have I heard communication in any form from those who are organizing the surveillance. Despite this I am very sure that I know who they are.*

**Irish police?**

*Unlikely.*

**You are not suggesting, are you, that they're General Schorcht's troops?**

*That is the possibility that I would like you to strongly consider.*

**Why? I mean on what evidence do you base the supposition?**

Sven did not answer at once. Brian turned slowly to look at the MI, the thin tracery of manipulators turning with him to keep the fiber cable in place. Brian did not realize it but it looked as though Sven was cradling the back of his head in his hand. He looked at the MI and could of course read nothing on its metal, unchangeable features. When Sven did speak it was with slow circumlocution.

*I have learned a great deal about the basic, innate, instinctive functions of the human brain because of downloading from you. But I have a much less complete comprehension of higher-level adult emotional reactions. I can describe the human physical structure and how it functions. But I still have little understanding of the deeper functions, the emotions and reactions of human brains. This is most complex. Because although I have within my own brain a stripped-down template of your superego I do not have direct access to it. But I believe that its effects upon my own feelings perhaps enable me to understand you better than the others I have talked to . . .*

**Is this leading to anything?**

*Yes. I beg patience and consideration because I am attempting to discuss something of which I have no experience. Human emotions and personality. I made a human value judgment many hours ago which at the time I presumed to be correct. I am no longer completely sure that it was correct.*

**What decision?**

*I will come to that. I had knowledge of a fact that I did not tell you about. I have heard your human acquaintances speak of you and their concern for both your physical and mental health. All of them, with the single exception of General Schorcht, make every effort to smooth the course of your existence.*

**That is very nice to hear, Sven. What is the fact that you concealed?**

*The concealment I assure was in your best interest.*

**I have no doubt about that. What is the fact?**

Silence. Finally reluctant communication. *I overheard a telephone conversation.*

**Overheard? How?**

*How? Most easily. If a portable telephone had enough*

*circuitry to broadcast its position and receive calls—don't you think I can do an equal if not better job? The circuitry was very simple. I installed it a long time ago.*

**You mean that you have been listening in to other people's phone calls? Whose?**

*Everyone's of course. Any call in any cell where I am physically located.*

**Mine?**

*Everyone's. It is a highly interesting learning experience.*

**You've veered from the topic. Answer me—what phone call did you conceal from me? Tell me now. Time for concealment is over.**

If it were possible to heave a mental sigh Sven did then. A sensation of resignation and inevitability was transferred from brain to brain.

*Your companion, Shelly, made a phone call.*

**I was there, I know about it and I don't give a damn. It's not important.**

*You misunderstand. This is not the call I was referring to. It was an earlier one . . .*

**The hell with it! I don't want to talk about her or her damn calls . . .**

*You must care. This is vital to your survival. She made the call I refer to from the train in Mexico, when she was out of the compartment. Before you concealed her phone in the train.*

Brian was almost afraid to ask the question, afraid that he already knew the answer.

**Who did she speak to?**

*A man whose name I do not know. But it was obvious from the references and content that he was an aide to General Schorcht.*

**You've known this since yesterday—and didn't tell me?**

*That is correct. I have already told you my reasons.*

Brian felt the explosion of hatred burst within him. Everything she had said, done, had been a lie. And this liar, this traitor, had witnessed his humiliation, was laughing at him right now. She must have been lying to him ever since she had returned from Los Angeles. She had been there to see her father—but she had most certainly seen General

Schorcht as well. How much of what she had told him was the truth—how much playacting? Anger wiped away all the other emotions. The bitch had betrayed him. Maybe Snaresbrook was in this as well. Even Sven had hidden the betrayal from him until this moment. Was he completely alone in the world? Anger became despair. He was at the edge of a black mental pit and about to fall in.

*Brian.* The words came from a great distance. His name repeated over and over within his own head. His vision swam and he could not see well until he rubbed at his eyes, brushed away the tears, saw Sven's great glistening eyes just before him.

*Brian, I have something good to tell you. Something you want to hear. It is still possible to make that telephone call to Dr. Bociort.*

**What are you saying? I told you last night it wasn't a phone number at all.**

*I know. That is because I lied to you. You will remember that I gave you the number in the presence of Shelly. I was still unsure then if I should reveal her duplicity to you. But I was sure that I would give her no information to pass on to the General.*

"Look who is talking about duplicity!" Brian spoke aloud, shocked—then almost smiled into the darkness. He was hooked up to an MI that was more Machiavellian than Machiavelli!

**Sven—you are really something. And you are really on my side. Possibly the only intelligent creature in the world at this point. I've got to make that phone call again—and this time to the correct number. Any suggestions how we go about that?**

*Only the simple observation that we do not make it from this area where all the circuits are sure to be under surveillance.*

**Too right. Let's make plans. We want to get out of this hotel, out of this area—and away from that personification of evil. Now I just want to get away from her, as far away as possible.**

*I agree. We should leave here at once. And might I observe that since she checked you both into this hotel you will also be sticking her with the bill.*

To hell with Shelly. She should die and burn in hell forever. Now he had to escape. But how? He couldn't leave Sven here when he left, could not consider that for an instant. Their closeness now was beyond friendship, a relationship that he could not put into words. But if he disassembled the MI again and stuffed him back into the box it would be an impossible burden.

At that moment Sven formed a very human hand and bent over to pull the plug on the charging cable from the wall. That was the answer. Night and rain—he had to take the chance. He scribbled a quick note and handed it to the MI.

*Put on human disguise.*

The phone rang. He hesitated. Two rings, three. He had better answer it.

"Yes."

*"Brian, could I talk to you—"*

Anger surged up, burning like acid; he coughed and fought for composure, failed.

"Go to hell!"

*"I'm so sorry you feel this way. In the morning we can talk . . ."*

Her voice cut off as he slammed the receiver back into the cradle. While they had been talking Sven had pulled on the clothes, tied its shoes, was now slipping into the raincoat. With the store dummy's head settled into position, the hat pulled low, there was suddenly another human being in the room. Brian struggled to contain his anger, faced it, let it drain away. Then looked at Sven again and shaped a circle of approval with his index finger and thumb and reached for the phone. While he waited for them to answer he wrote another note.

*Open the door an inch. Silently!*

"Hello, reception? Room 222 here. Listen, I'm retiring and I would like you to hold all calls until morning. Take any messages. Right. Thank you. Good night."

He walked around the room humming to himself as he found his raincoat. Yawned loudly, ran water in the sink then flushed the toilet. Stamped his feet on the floor, then sat down on the bed, which squeaked providentially. Turned off the light and tiptoed to the door. Sven opened it a bit more and one eyestalk appeared from below the scarf, slipped out through the opening and scanned the hallway. There was obviously no one there, for the MI opened the door and led the way out, closing it silently behind them.

"The service lift," Brian said. "And keep your coat collar turned up."

It was late and luck was on their side. The kitchen was dark, the staff gone home. The outside door let them out into a rain-drenched alley.

"Might I assume that you have formulated a plan?" Sven said.

"Find a bar with a phone and we are on our way."

They passed Paddy Murphy's where he had been before, went on through the rain to the welcoming lights of Maddigan's. Brian pointed to the dark entrance to the closed fishmonger next door. "You wait in there. I'll be as quick as I can."

The barman looked up from the *Sporting Times* when Brian pushed open the door. The courting couple in the rear booth were too occupied with each other to notice him.

"Jayzus but it's wet out there. A glass of Paddy if you please."

"It'll keep the dust down. Ice?"

"No—just a drop of the red. Can I telephone for a taxi?"

"Back by the jakes. Number on the wall above it. That'll be two pound eighty."

Brian downed the last of his drink when he heard the sound of a hooter outside. Waved to the barman and left. Sven appeared beside him, climbed into the cab after him.

"Going far?" the driver asked. "I need to fill the tank if you are."

Brian slammed the door shut before he answered. "Limerick train station."

"There's an all-night petrol station on the way. Really suppose we ought to call it a gas station, same as the Yanks do. No petrol there at all. And hydrogen is a gas, that's what I hear, so it's off to the gas station we are."

Brian wiped the condensation off the rear window and

looked out. There were no other cars in sight that he could see. They just might get away with it. An image of Shelly appeared before him and he easily pushed it away. She was not even worth thinking about, not ever again.

# 41

## December 21, 2024

The rain had turned to a fine mist by the time they reached Limerick station. Brian emerged from the cab first to pay the fare, blocking the driver's view of Sven slipping out to stand in the shadows. The station was empty, the kiosk closed, a single light over the ticket window.

"And there are the phones!" Brian said. "I sincerely hope that this time you will give me the right number."

"I will enter it if you wish me to."

"No thanks. Just tell me what it is—then find a dark corner to stand in."

Brian punched in the series of digits. Listened to electronic rustling. Was this really a phone number—or would that Swiss computer tell him to get lost again?

Some of the tension drained away when he heard the ringing tones. Four, five times—then someone picked the phone up.

"*Jawohl.*" A man's voice.

"Excuse me, but is this a St. Moritz number 55-8723?" There was only silence—but whoever was there was still listening, did not hang up. "Hello, are you there? I'm afraid that I don't speak German."

"*Would you tell me who you are? Or perhaps I already know. Your first name would not be Brian by any chance.*"

"Yes it is. How did you know—who is this?"

*"Come to St. Moritz. Phone me again after you arrive."*
There was a click and the line went dead.

"That is very good news indeed," Sven said when Brian
went over to the MI.

"Eavesdropping?"

"Simply as a protective measure. As far as I could
determine I was the only one that was doing it. Will we now
go to St. Moritz?"

"Not this very minute. We'll need some kind of a plan
before we start rushing about."

"Might I suggest that we consider a diversion first? I
have accessed the timetable data base and there is a train for
Dublin that leaves here in less than an hour. It might be wise
for you to purchase two tickets, then make a query at the
ticket window just before it leaves. Anyone who searches
for us will find the cabdriver easily enough, which will
cause them to follow us to this station. A subterfuge like
this might . . ."

"Might muddy the trail. You are a born, or constructed,
conspirator, old son. And after we get the tickets and the
train pulls out—then what? Go to a hotel?"

"That is one possibility, but I am developing others.
Might I suggest that after purchasing the tickets you wait in
a public house until it is time for the train."

"All this is going to turn me into an alcoholic. And while
I am in the boozer you will be doing exactly what?"

"Developing other possibilities."

Sven joined Brian forty-five minutes later when he emerged
from the pub.

"I made a pint of Smithwicks last the hour," Brian said.
"After this I swear off drink forever. And how have your
possibilities developed?"

"Excellently. I will be waiting one hundred meters east of
the station. Join me there after your discussion with the
ticket vendor."

Before Brian could query him the MI was gone. There
was a short queue at the window and he joined it. Asked
about connecting trains to Belfast from Dublin, made sure
that he was remembered by having the man consult the

schedules on his terminal. Then he walked down the platform past the waiting train, then strolled back. He was sure that no one saw him slipping out of the station in the darkness. He walked through the rain past the row of cars parked at the curb, to the appointed spot.

Only Sven wasn't there, the shop entrance damp, dark and empty. Had he gone far enough? Perhaps the next shop; empty as well.

"Over here," Sven said through the open window of the nearest car. "The door is unlocked." In shocked silence Brian climbed into the front seat. Sven started the engine, turned on the headlights and pulled smoothly out into the road. The MI had removed its head and extended its eyes, clutched the steering wheel in its multibranched grip.

"I didn't know you could drive," Brian said, realizing the inanity of his words even as he spoke them.

"I observed the driving operation in the taxi. While I was waiting for you I retrieved a driving simulator program that had been bundled with other files. I then programmed it into a powerful virtual reality. I ran this at teraflop speed enabling me in a few minutes to accumulate the equivalent of many years of driving experience."

"I am filled with admiration. I am also almost afraid to ask where you got this motor."

"Stole it of course."

"That's why I was afraid to ask."

"Do not fear that we will be apprehended. I removed this vehicle from the locked premises of an auto dealer. Before they open in the morning we will no longer be driving this particular car."

"We won't? Where will we be? You don't mind if I sort of know about the plan?"

"I detect from the phraseology that you are being sarcastic and I am sorry if I gave offense. When last we talked I had a number of options open. This one proved the most practical. If you approve we will now drive to Cork City. If you do not approve I will suggest alternative choices."

"This one seems good so far. But why Cork?"

"Because it is a seaport with a daily ferry service to

Swansea. Which is a city in Wales, which in turn is located on the largest of a group of islands called the British Isles. From there it is possible to drive on a motorway system to a tunnel that leads to the mainland of Europe. Switzerland is a country on that mainland.''

"All this without a passport?''

"I have studied the relevant data bases. The European Economic Community forms a customs union. A passport is needed to enter any member country from outside the community. After that there is no need to show it again. However, Switzerland is not a member of this group. I thought that this problem might be postponed until we reached that country's border.''

Brian took a deep breath, watched the windscreen wipers slap back and forth, found it a little difficult to believe that this was really happening.

"Then as I read it—your plan is to steal and abandon a series of motorcars and drive from here to Switzerland?''

"That is correct.''

"You and I are going to have to have a long talk about morality and honesty sometime soon.''

"We already have done that, but I will be pleased to amplify our earlier discussions.''

Brian smiled into the darkness. It was happening all right. Sven would have had no problem unlocking a locked garage—or in jumping the car's ignition. Once the MI had analyzed how the machine operated, driving it was obviously simplicity itself. He certainly had enough cash for fuel and ferry tickets.

"The ferry—it won't work. I can see their faces now when you drive aboard, three glassy eyeballs staring out of the window. They'll die of heart attacks!''

"I would not wish that to happen and my plan postulates that you will be driving the vehicle aboard the ferry. I will be in a box in the trunk. Which is referred to as a boot in this country, as I am sure you know.''

"But I don't know how to drive.''

"That will not be a problem. I have in memory downloaded copies of your personal motor-coordination machinery. I also possess an adequate set of copies of your personal semantic networks and other knowledge representations. I will now teach them to drive.''

''How will that help me?''

''Transfer.'' Sven remained motionless for several seconds, then reached out and touched one of his brushes to the terminals under Brian's skin. ''It is done. You may take the wheel.''

Sven stopped the car on the shoulder and got out. Brian took his place. Turned on the power and drove smoothly out onto the road.

''I can't believe this. I'm driving without even thinking about it at all—as though I'd been doing it all my life.''

''Of course. I gave your sensorimotor clone the equivalent of a rather large experiential data base for that skill. And then uploaded the resulting differences into your own implant computer. There should be no difference between that and the result of you having all that experience yourself.''

They changed places again. It is going to work, Brian thought, it is! Sven knew that he wanted to get to Switzerland as soon as he could, so had done everything within its power to make that possible. He would think about the morality some other time; right now he was too tired, too ill. Take the cars. Finding Dr. Bociort was well worth leaving a trail of stolen cars right across Europe as far as he was concerned.

''Turn up the heat a bit, Sven, and wake me only if you have to.'' He pulled his hat low over his eyes and slumped gratefully down in the seat.

Very tired, but reasonably happy with his driving skills, Brian drove deftly aboard the ferry in Cork. Parked, braked and locked the car, then found his cabin. A night in a bed was very much in order. He hoped that Sven enjoyed incarceration in the car's boot. He should be used to it by now.

If they were being followed there was no evidence. They drove at night, stayed in hotels during the day. Brian's only driving problem came when he had to drive the last of a succession of stolen vehicles aboard the car-carrying train that ran through the Channel Tunnel. But he had been at the wheel for a good number of hours while they were on the motorways across England so did a passable enough job. France was crossed without any problems, other than the endless payments demanded at the tollbooths of the *péage*, so close together that Brian was forced to do most of the driving. It was just before dawn when the sign loomed up out of the darkness.

"We're getting close—Basel in twenty-nine kilometers. I'm going to take the next exit and find a spot to wait until daylight. Any luck yet with Swiss border details?"

"It is very frustrating. At that last telephone I downloaded everything available about Switzerland. I can truthfully say that I know every detail of their history, languages, economics, banking system, criminal statues. It is all very boring. But nowhere in all of this information is there a reference to border customs control."

"Then we will have to do it the old-fashioned way. Look and see just what they are doing."

At first light Sven was locked into his box and the boot closed. Brian followed the signs toward the border, until he could see the booths and the customs buildings ahead. He pulled to the curb and parked.

"I'm going ahead on foot," he shouted into the backseat. "Wish me luck."

"I will if it is a formal request," the muffled voice said. "But the concept of luck is an invalid superstition equivalent to belief in . . ."

Brian missed what it was equivalent to when he slammed the door shut. There was frost on the ground and all the puddles were frozen. Cars and trucks were driving toward the border crossing, other pedestrians, laden with Christmas shopping, were proceeding on foot like him. He held back when he saw that they were going through a door into the customs building. Let them. He wasn't going to risk that in any case. He went closer, saw a car with British registration plates drive forward.

Through and past the guard post—which apparently was unoccupied. Something new for Sven's Swiss data base.

By late afternoon they had crossed Switzerland, almost to the Italian border. ST. MORITZ, the sign said.

"We're there," Brian called over his shoulder. "I'm pulling into a service station ahead that has a nice outside phone box." He did not add anything about wishing him luck.

He dialed the number, heard it ring. Then it was picked up.

*"Bitte?"* It was the same voice as the first call.

"Brian Delaney here?"

*"Mr. Delaney—welcome to St. Moritz. Do I assume correctly that you are in the city?"*

"In a service station just inside the city limits."

*"Wonderful. Then you come here by car?"*

"That's correct."

*"If you will now drive straight ahead toward the center of the city you will see signs that will direct you to the train station. Bahnhof, it is called. There is a nice little hotel just across the road from it, the Am Post. A room has been reserved for you there. I will contact you later."*

"Are you Dr. Bociort?"

*"Patience, Mr. Delaney,"* he said, then hung up.

Patience indeed! Well, he had little choice. The hotel it was. He returned to the car, reported to Sven, then fought his way through the slush and traffic in the direction of the station. It wasn't easy, the one-way system was totally confusing, but in the end he put on the brake in front of Am Post. Trail's end?

"It is very good to have mobility again," Sven said after being reassembled. It rustled across the room, extruded the charging cord and plugged it into the outlet there. "I am sure you would be interested in the fact that we are being watched. The small lens in the lighting fixture is that of a video camera. It is transmitting its signal down a telephone line."

"Where to?"

"I cannot tell."

"Then there is very little that we can do about it—other than follow instructions. Charge your battery—and I need recharging as well. I'll get room service to bring something up. Because I'm not moving from here until the phone rings."

It was a long wait. Sven had unplugged its charger and Brian had long since finished his sandwich and beer and put the tray out in the hall. He was dozing in the armchair when precisely at nine o'clock that evening the telephone bleeped: he grabbed it up.

"Yes?"

*"Would you please leave the hotel now—with your friend. If you go through the bar you will be able to use the side exit. Then turn left and walk to the corner."*

"What do I do then—" There was a click and the dial tone.

"Get your coat and hat on, Sven. We're going for a walk."

They went down the stairs to the ground floor. Sven's walk was perfect now and with its coat collar turned up, hat pulled low and scarf wrapped high, the MI looked normal enough—from a distance. The small lobby was empty and they crossed it to the bar beyond. Happily it was dimly lit by small lamps on the tables. The barman was polishing a glass and did not look up when they crossed and went out the far door. The side street was deserted and illuminated only by widely spaced lights. They walked to the corner and a man stepped out of a dark doorway.

"Follow," he said in a thick accent, making it sound more like *volloh,* and turned away. He moved quickly up the even more narrow street, then turned down an alley that led to a slippery stone stairway. They climbed this to reach another road at the top. There the man stopped, looking back down the steps. When he was satisfied that they were not being followed he walked out into the roadway and waved.

The headlights of a parked car came on. The car started forward and braked beside them. Their guide opened the back door and motioned them to enter. As soon as they were seated the big Mercedes moved swiftly away. As they passed under the streetlights Brian could see that the driver was a woman. Stocky and middle-aged—like the man sitting next to her.

"Where are we going?" Brian asked.

"No Inglitch," was all the answer he got.

"*Vorbiti românește?*" Sven said.

The man turned to face them. "*Nu se va vorbi deloc în românește,*" he said, snapping the words.

"What was that all about?" Brian asked.

"I asked him if he spoke Rumanian, using the formal of course. He answered, in that language, in the informal, that there would be no talking."

"Well done."

They left the town center and drove through the residential suburbs. This was a more exclusive part of town; the houses were large and expensive, each of them with its own fenced and wooded plot. They turned down the drive of one of these and into the open door of a garage. The garage door closed behind them and the lights came on.

Their guide opened a door leading into the house and waved them forward. Down a hallway into a large, book-lined room. A thin, white-haired man closed the book he was reading and climbed slowly to his feet.

"Mr. Delaney, welcome, welcome."

"You are Dr. Bociort?"

"Yes, of course . . ." He was looking at Sven's muffled figure with great attention. "And this—dare I say gentleman?— is the friend who uncovered my message?"

"Not quite. It was another associate of the same kind."

"You say *it*? A machine, then?"

"Machine intelligence."

"How wonderful. Do help yourself to some wine. I believe your associate's name is Sven?"

"That is my name. This knowledge reveals the fact that it is your video camera in the hotel room."

"I must be cautious at all times."

"Dr. Bociort," Brian broke in, "I have come a long way to meet you—and I have a number of urgent questions that need answering."

"Patience, young man. When you reach my age you learn to do things slowly. Take your wine, make yourself comfortable—and I will tell you what you want to know. I can understand your haste. Dreadful things have happened to you—"

"Do you know who was responsible?"

"I am afraid that I don't. Let me begin at the beginning. Sometime ago I was contacted by a man who called himself Smith. Later I discovered that his real name was J. J. Beckworth. Now, before you ask any more questions, let me tell you everything that I know. I was teaching at the university in Bucureşti when Mr. Smith made an appointment to see me. He knew of my research in artificial intelligence and wished to employ me to do some work in that field. He told me that a research scientist had succeeded in constructing an AI but had died rather suddenly. Someone was needed to carry on his work. I was offered a great deal of money, which I was happy to accept. I was of course quite suspicious, since it was obvious to me from the very beginning that there was something very illegal about the entire matter. There are many scientists in the West, a number of them far more qualified than me, who would have been eager to do the work. This did not deter me. If you know the history of my sad little country you will know that I must have compromised more than once to reach the fullness of my years."

He coughed and pointed to a carafe on the sideboard near the wine. "A glass of water, if you please. Thank you." He drank some of the water, put the glass down on the table at his elbow.

"What happened next you undoubtedly know. I went to the state of Texas, where your files were made available to me. My instructions were clear—to develop a commercial product that could utilize your AI. You know that I succeeded in this because your AI found my coded message."

"Why did you leave the message?" Brian said.

"I thought that was obvious. You have been done a great wrong. Beckworth thought at first that you were dead, indeed he bragged about the crime, told me that many had been killed and that I was involved. He did that to ensure my silence. He said that no one would believe I hadn't been part of the conspiracy from the beginning—which is undoubtedly true. Then something went wrong, Beckworth was very upset. Thomsen was managing the plant by then and I was finishing with the development of the AI. I knew that Beckworth would be leaving soon so I forced him to arrange for my disappearance as well.''

"Forced him? I don't understand."

There was no warmth in Bociort's smile. "You would understand, young man, if you had lived through the Ceaușescu years in my motherland. Since I was convinced from the very beginning that what I was doing was illegal I took certain steps to guarantee my own safety. I left a program running in the university's computer. A virus really. If I did not have a code telephoned to it once a month it was programmed to relay a coded message to Interpol. Beckworth was not pleased when I gave him a copy of the message and described the arrangement. Of course without revealing where the computer was. In the end he reluctantly understood that alive I was no threat to them. When I discovered that he was leaving I insisted that he make arrangements for my dropping from sight as well. I now live quietly, taken care of by my cousins who are happy to also live in Swiss luxury. Only the great wrong that had been done you disturbed me: therefore my message. I wanted to meet you—and your AI of course.''

"MI," Sven said. "Machine intelligence is not artificial."

"I stand corrected and do apologize. As for you, Brian, I want to give you the little information I have about the conspiracy.''

"You know who was behind all this?"

"Alas, no. I have but a single clue of any importance. I listened to all of Beckworth's telephone calls. That was the first task your AI undertook, tapping every phone that Beckworth might use. He was very circumspect and only once did he slip up and use his phone to speak with his coconspirators. This was when he discovered that you were still alive, that an attempt on your life had failed. You were still a threat that had to be removed. The telephone number he called was disconnected next day, so all I can tell you is that it was located in Canada. But the man Beckworth spoke with was not a Canadian.''

"How do you know?"

"My dear sir! I know in the same way that I knew it was you calling me at this number. Your voice gave you away, a native of southern Ireland who grew up in the United States. Every word that you spoke was clear identification. I was led into AI research through my work in linguistics. My magister in philology was gained in the University of Copenhagen, where I followed in the footsteps of the great Otto Jespersen. Therefore you must believe me that the man was no Canadian. I have listened to the recording many times and am absolutely sure."

Bociort paused for dramatic effect, touched the water to his lips but did not drink. Put the glass down again before speaking.

"The individual in question had a very marked Oxbridge accent, signifying that he had been a student at either Oxford or Cambridge University. There is a possibility that he went to Eton as well. He had worked very hard during his school years to lose his regional accent—but the traces were clear to me. Yorkshire, possibly Leeds, that's where he came from."

"You are sure of this?"

"Positive. Now that I have answered all of your questions fully and truthfully please have your MI remove its clothing. How I look forward to seeing what you have accomplished. I was most unhappy when I discovered that your stolen AI was, how should I say, a brontosaurus."

"What do you mean?"

"It was not obvious at first, but as I worked through your notes and the stages of development I was forced to the reluctant conclusion that your work was not proceeding along the correct branch of the evolution of intelligence. Your AI was a good dinosaur, but it could never develop the true intelligence that you were seeking. It was an excellent brontosaurus indeed. But somewhere you had taken a wrong turning. No matter how much the brontosaurus was improved—it would still be a dinosaur. Never a human. I could never discover where you went wrong, and of course never told my employers of my discovery. I sincerely hope that you found your error."

"I have—and corrected it. My MI is now functional and complete. Strip down, Sven, and have a chat with the doctor. After what he has done for me he deserves a complete Turing test."

"Which hopefully I will pass," Bociort said, smiling.

# 42

## December 31, 2024

Brian enjoyed his week's stay in St. Moritz. It was the first time that he had really been alone since the attack in the laboratory. Since then it had been hospital, recovery, work and people. Now he didn't even have Sven around to talk to: he relished the solitude and anonymity. Nor was anyone in a hurry. Dr. Bociort was understandably grateful for these days of interfacing with the MI.

The cold dry air seemed to have alleviated all the symptoms of his cold, and with his restored sense of taste he explored the many restaurants of the city. When Sven-2 had first mentioned the possibility of the phone number in St. Moritz, Brian had, as a simple precaution, downloaded a German dictionary and language course. He accessed this now and with the days of constant practice was speaking fair German by week's end.

He also had the leisure to plan for the future, to think about it calmly, to weigh the various options that were open to him. In this Dr. Bociort was his confidant, a wise man and a cultured European. On the last day of his stay Brian walked, as he usually did, the three kilometers to Bociort's home, and rang the bell. Dimitrie led him to Bociort's study.

"Brian, come in. I want you to admire Sven's new traveling persona."

The MI was not in sight—but a handsome, brassbound leather trunk stood in the middle of the room.

"Good morning, Brian," the trunk said. "This is a most agreeable arrangement. Specially fitted for comfort, optic pickups on every side for maximum visibility..."

, "Microphone and loudspeaker connections as well. You're looking good, Sven."

Dr. Bociort shifted in his chair and smiled happily at them. "I cannot begin to tell you what pleasure these few days have given me. To see the simple AI that I worked on raised to this power of perfection is an intellectual banquet that I am sure you both will understand. In addition, my dear Brian—at the risk of appearing an emotional old man—I have enjoyed your companionship."

Brian did not answer; shifted uneasily and ran his fingers along the edge of the trunk.

"Be kinder to yourself," Bociort said, reaching out and touching Brian lightly on the knee: pretending not to notice the shiver and quick movement away. "The intellectual life is a good one, to use one's brain, to uncover the secrets of reality, that is a gift granted to very few. But to enjoy one's humanity is an equal pleasure—"

"I don't wish to have this discussion."

"Nor do I. It is only because of the trust, the understanding, that has grown between us, that I permit myself such a breach of tact. You have been hurt badly and you have grown bitter. Understandable. I ask for no response, I just request you to be kinder to yourself, to find some way to enjoy the physical and emotional pleasures that life can bring."

The silence lengthened. Dr. Bociort shrugged, so slightly that it might not have been a shrug at all, turned and lifted his hand.

"For you, a few small gifts as tokens of appreciation. If you please, Dimitrie."

The servant brought in a silver tray with a glistening leather wallet on it.

"Yours, Brian," the old man said. "It contains a first-class ticket on this afternoon's flight to Sweden. Your hotel reservations are there, as is the passport I spoke to you about. A perfectly legitimate Rumanian one. I still have close friends in my homeland—in high places. It is not a forgery but is quite authentic and issued by the government. I am sure that you won't mind being Ioan Ghica for a few days—it is a proud name to bear. And this as well for the Baltic winter.''

The fur hat was mink and fitted perfectly.

"Many thanks, Dr. Bociort. I don't really..."

"We will speak no more of it, my boy. If you have checked out of your hotel, Dimitrie will fetch your bags.''

"All done.''

"Good. Then if you will share a last glass of wine with me until he returns I will be greatly honored.''

With Sven loaded into the trunk of the big Mercedes, after last good-byes and a frail embrace from the old man, Dimitrie drove Brian to the tiny local airport. The VTOL plane lifted up from the snow-covered runway for the short hop to Zurich airport to connect with the SAS flight. The service, the seat—food and drink—were an immense improvement on the transatlantic Aeroflot flight.

Arlanda airport was clean, modern and efficient. After sober inspection his new passport was stamped and handed back. His bags were waiting for him—as were a porter and the limo driver. A drifting of snow was settling through the trees beside the highway; afternoon darkness descended before they reached Stockholm. The Lady Hamilton hotel was small and picturesque, filled to overflowing with portraits and memorabilia of the Lady and her Admiral escort.

"Welcome to Stockholm, Mr. Ghica,'' the tall, blond receptionist said. "This is your key, room 32 on the third floor. The lift is to the rear and the porter will bring your bags up. I hope you will enjoy your stay in Stockholm.''

"I know that I will.''

This was indeed the truth. He was now in the city where he was going to stop running, stop hiding. When he left Sweden he was going to be himself again, a free self for the first time since the shooting.

"Come on out, Sven,'' he said. The trunk unlocked and opened. "Close the trunk and keep it as a souvenir.''

"I would appreciate an explanation," the MI said as it flowed out onto the rug.

"Freedom for me means the same for you. This is a democratic and liberal country with just laws. I am sure that all of its inhabitants will welcome the sight of you enjoying the freedom of their city. Sweden belongs to no military blocs. Which means that the minions of the evil General Schorcht can't get at me here. And we are going to stay here until I am absolutely positive that particular danger is removed. Now the phone call that gets the ball rolling."

He picked up the telephone and punched in the number.

"You are calling Benicoff," Sven said. "I presume that you have thought through all of the possible results of this action?"

"I have thought of very little else for the last week . . ."

*"Benicoff here. Tell me."*

"Good morning, Ben. I hope that you are keeping well."

*"Brian! Are you all right? And what the hell are you doing in Stockholm?"* His phone would of course have displayed the identity of the calling number.

"Enjoying freedom, Ben. And yes, I'm feeling fine. No, don't talk, please listen. Can you get me a valid American passport and bring it to me here?"

*"Yes, I guess so, even on New Year's Eve, but—"*

"That's it. No buts and no questions. Hand me the passport and I'll tell you everything that has happened. Enjoy the flight." He hung up the phone, which rang loudly a moment later.

"That is Benicoff calling back," Sven said.

"Then there is no point in answering it, is there? Did you notice that little bar, off to the right in the lobby, when we came in?"

"I did."

"Will you join me there while I try my first Swedish beer? And don't bother dressing for the occasion."

"You have no intention of telling me what you are planning, do you?"

"I'll reveal it all in the bar. Coming?"

"It will be my great pleasure to accompany you. I am rather looking forward to the experience."

The elevator was empty, but an elderly Swede was in the lobby waiting for it when the door opened.

"*Godafton,*" Sven said as it stepped out.

"*Godafton,*" the man replied, moving aside. But his eyes opened wide and he turned to watch them walk by.

"Sweden is a very courteous country," Sven said. "With a name like mine I thought it only right to do a little linguistic research when you told me our destination."

The receptionist, like all receptionists worldwide, had seen everything and only smiled at them—as though three-eyed machines walked into the lobby every day.

"If you are going into the bar I will get someone to serve you."

The uniformed barmaid was not as cool. She would not come out from behind the counter to take the order. If she spoke English she seemed to have forgotten every word of it when Brian asked for a beer.

"*Min vän vill ha en öl,*" Sven said. "*En svensk öl, tack.*"

"*Ja . . .*" she gasped and fled into the rear. She was under better control when she reappeared with a bottle and glass, but would not pass Sven. Instead went the long way out and around the next table to serve Brian, returned the same way.

"This is a very interesting experience," Sven said. "Are you enjoying the beer?"

"Very much so."

"Then you will tell me what you are planning?"

"Just what you see. I have based my plan of attack upon the fact that the military love secrecy, hate the spotlight. Toward the end of the last century, before the truth was revealed, the black budget in the United States concealed expenditures of over eighty billion dollars every year for things like the totally worthless Stealth bomber. It is obvious that General Schorcht was playing the same kind of game with me, in the name of national security, to keep me in prison, my existence secret. Well, now I have escaped. The world will soon know that I am here, know that you exist. We're out of the closet and in the sunshine now. I'm not going to give away any details on AI construction—that's a commercial secret that is in my own best interest to keep my mouth shut about. I'll ask you not to go into any of those details as well.''

"Or it is back into the trunk?"

"Sven—you made a joke!"

"Thank you. I have been working to perfect the technique. At the risk of appearing maudlin I am forced to say that I owe my life, my very existence, to you. For this reason alone I would do nothing to harm you.''

"You have other reasons?"

"Many. I hope you won't think I'm being anthropomorphic when I say that I like you. And consider you a close friend.''

"A feeling that I share.''

"Thank you. So speaking as a friend, aren't you fearful about your personal safety? There were previous attempts on your life. And the military. . . ?"

"Since the dissolution of the CIA I think that assassination is no longer an American weapon. As to the other lot—I'm going to blow the whistle on them. Tell the press everything I know about them. Let the enemy know that they got the wrong AI, that the improved AI is now the property of Megalobe and the United States government. They, whoever they are, can only get a share of the action now by buying shares in the company. The cat is out of the bag. Killing me now would be counterproductive. Kidnaping me—or you—would be more in the line of what has now become a case of industrial espionage. I am sure that the Swedish government would not take kindly to that. Particularly after I assure them that they will be head of the queue for AI purchase in return for their cooperation. Megalobe will go along with that in return for our safety. A firm can only make a profit by selling—and Sweden has got a lot of kroner.''

The first reporter arrived twenty minutes later; someone had obviously phoned in a tip. Even before he could turn on his recorder a video cameraman was behind him shooting the scene.

"My name is Lundwall of Dagens Nyheter, this is my identification. Could you tell me, sir, what is that machine that is—sitting, is that the correct word—in the chair across from you?"

"That machine is a machine intelligence. The first one in existence."

"It's a . . . Can it speak?"

"Possibly better than you can," Sven said. "Should I tell him anything more?"

"No. Not until after our conversation with Ben. Let's go up to our room now."

When they emerged they discovered that the lobby was filling with excited journalists. Cameras flashed and questions were shouted at them. Brian pushed through to the receptionist. "I'm sorry about the fuss."

"Please don't be, sir. The police are on their way. We are not used to this sort of thing in the Lady Hamilton, and are not pleased by it. Order will be restored shortly. Will you be accepting incoming calls?"

"No, I don't think so. But I am expecting a visitor, a Mr. Benicoff. I'll see him when he comes. Sometime tomorrow I hope."

Brian switched on the television as soon as they were back in the room to see that he and Sven were the subjects of a news flash on Swedish television. Within minutes the item had been picked up by other stations and was being flashed around the world. The cat was well and truly out of the bag.

Later, when he became hungry, he ordered a sandwich from room service. When he answered the knock on the door he saw that the tiny oriental waiter was flanked by two policemen—each at least two heads taller than he was.

Less than five hours after he had called Benicoff the phone rang. "It's the desk," Sven said. Surprised, Brian picked it up.

*"The gentleman you mentioned, Mr. Benicoff, is here. Do you wish to see him?"*

"Here—in the hotel? Are you sure?"

*"Positively. The police have already checked his identification."*

"Yes, I'll see him, of course."

"Military jets have a range of nine thousand kilometers," Sven said. "And can exceed Mach 4.2 for that length of time."

"That must be it. Good old Ben must have pulled some awfully strong strings."

There was a knock and Brian opened the door. Ben stood there—holding out an American passport.

"Can I come in now?" he said.

# 43

---

## December 31, 2024

"You made pretty good time, Ben."

"Military jet. Very cramped, very fast. When we stopped to refuel for the last leg this passport was waiting. All filled out except for your signature. I was ordered to instruct you to sign it in my presence."

"I'll do that now." Brian went to the desk for a pen.

"Keeping well, Sven?" Ben asked.

"Batteries charged and rarin' to go."

Brian smiled at Ben's astonishment. "Sven is developing new linguistic skills—and a sense of humor."

"So I see. The two of you are top of the news worldwide."

"That was my intention. I'll tell you everything that I have uncovered and what I plan to do, just as soon as you bring me up to date about what has been happening."

"Will do. And I have a message to you from Shelly—"

"No. No mention of that name, no communication. Subject closed."

"If that's the way you want it, Brian. But—"

"And no *buts* either. Okay?"

"Okay. I had it out with General Schorcht as soon as I found out you had gone missing. He kept it under wraps for three days. That was his mistake. If I and my superiors had known what was happening he might have survived . . ."

"He's dead!"

"He might as well be. Forced retirement and living in a bungalow on the grounds of Camp Mead in Hawaii. It was either that or face possible charges of insanity. He had the engineers attempt to break into your laboratory—and practically blew themselves away. There were short circuits, premature explosions—almost as though someone inside was working to stop them."

Brian had to laugh. "There was—Sven-2. A very up-to-date MI."

"We found that out when your MI rang all the police and TV stations to let them know what was happening. Schorcht was on the way out ten minutes later."

"I'll have to phone Sven-2 and congratulate it. So how do things stand now?"

"The military is gone at last from Megalobe and there is civilian security there now. It will be just as secure, you will be happy to know. When Major Wood discovered he had been suckered by the General, who knew all about your escape plans and let them go ahead, he applied for a discharge. So he's still in charge of security—still will be even when he is out of uniform."

"That's good to hear. What was the General's idea behind letting me think I was escaping?"

"He had the suspicion, probably from all of his wiretaps and intelligence reports, that you knew more about who the criminals were than you were letting on. By permitting you to escape, then letting you out on a long leash and keeping track of you, he thought you would lead us to them."

"If he believed that—then he must have thought I would be in danger of my life. And he didn't care!"

"My conclusion exactly. Which is the reason why he is now watching daytime television in that bungalow. The President was not amused. If you had led General Schorcht to the thieves all might have been forgiven. But when you gave your watchdogs the slip the ceiling fell in."

"Have you talked with Dr. Snaresbrook?"

"I have. She hopes you are well. Sends her love and looks forward to seeing you back in California. She is highly incensed at being used by the General, at being fooled into aiding your escape in what might have been a dangerous situation.''

''Can't say that I blame her. She took a big risk to help me—and the operation was blown even before it started.''

''Then that's it,'' Ben said, walking the length of the room and back. ''Still cramped from the plane. Nothing more to tell. So maybe you can satisfy my curiosity now. Where did you go—and what did you do?''

''I can't tell you where I went. But I can tell you that Dr. Bociort is still alive and has told me everything that he knows. He was hired to work with my stolen AI by Beckworth using a fake name. Bociort knew that the entire operation was rotten from the very beginning and did what electronic snooping he could—''

''Brian, be kind to an old man! Jump to the ending and fill in the details later. Did he find out who was behind the theft and murders?''

''Unhappily, no. He did discover that it was an international conspiracy, though. Beckworth is an American. It was a Canadian who arranged for the helicopter pickup. Plus the reports that orientals drove the truck that cleaned out my house. And one more big one. When Beckworth had to make an emergency call he telephoned Canada—and talked to an Englishman.''

''Who?''

''He couldn't find out—the phone was disconnected at once.''

''Damn. Then we are really back to square one. The thieves and killers are still out there.''

''That's right. So since we can't find them we have to render them harmless. First off we take out patents on the AI they have. So what they stole will be available to anybody who wants to pay the patent fees. That takes care of the past. All we need think about now is the future—''

''Which explains your and Sven's television appearance today.''

''Perfectly correct. It's a whole new ball game. We forget the past—I know that I would like to—and look to the future. When tomorrow comes it is going to be a good one. We let the world know that Megalobe is manufacturing MIs. Like any new invention we take all needed precautions against industrial espionage. And get the production lines rolling at once. The more MIs there are out there the safer I and Sven are. I doubt if the people behind the theft and killings will be out for revenge, but I'll still take all the precautions that any engineer with technical knowledge would. What do you think?''

"That it will work!" Ben shouted, slamming his fist into his palm. "That it has to work. Those bums, whoever they are, paid millions for absolutely nothing. Let's drink to that.'' Ben looked around the room. "Got a bar here?"

"No—but I can ring down for whatever you want."

"Champagne. Vintage. And about six sandwiches. I haven't eaten for over five thousand miles."

Only one thing happened that spoiled Brian's complete satisfaction. The press no longer mobbed the hotel; police were at the front entrance and admitted only other guests and journalists he had made appointments with. He had eaten enough meals in hotel rooms so he joined Ben next morning in the restaurant for breakfast.

"Where's Sven?" Ben asked. "I thought he liked publicity and his newfound freedom?"

"He does. But he discovered that Stockholm has phone numbers for what is called therapeutic sexual conversation. So he is both practicing his Swedish and doing research into human sexual practices."

"Oh, Alan Turing, would you were but alive in this hour!"

They were finishing a second pot of coffee when Shelly came into the dining room, looked around, then walked slowly over to their table. Ben stood up before her.

"I don't think you're wanted here—even if Military Intelligence managed to get you past the police."

"I'm here on my own, Ben. No one helped me. I simply registered in the hotel. And if you don't mind, I would like to hear Brian tell me to leave. I want to talk to him—not you."

Brian half stood, his face red, his fists clamped. Then he

dropped back into the chair and ordered the anger to drain away.

"Let her stay, Ben. This will have to be done sooner or later."

"I'll be in my room." The big man turned away and left them alone.

"May I sit down?"

"Yes. And answer one question—"

"Why did I do it? Why did I betray you? I'm here because I want to tell you about that."

"I'm listening."

"I hate it when your voice gets cold like that, your face freezes. More like a machine than a man—"

Tears rolled down her cheeks and she dabbed at them angrily. Brought herself under control.

"Please try to understand. I am a serving officer in the United States Air Force. I took an oath—and I can't betray it. When I went to Los Angeles to see my father, that was when General Schorcht sent for me. He gave me an order. I obeyed it. It's as simple as that."

"That is not very simple at all. At the Nuremberg trials—"

"I know what you are going to say. That I am no better than the Nazis who were ordered to murder Jews—and did so. They tried to escape justice by saying they were just obeying orders."

"You said it, I didn't."

"Perhaps they had little choice, they did what everyone else was doing. I'm not defending them—just trying to explain what *I* did. I had a choice. I could have resigned my commission, walked right out of there. I wouldn't have been shot."

"Then you must have agreed with the order to lie to me—to spy on me?" Still calmly, still without anger.

She had emotion enough for both of them, pounding her fists slowly and silently on the table, leaning forward to whisper out her words.

"I thought that if you escaped alone you would be in danger, I really did. I wanted to protect you—"

"By phoning from the train and telling Schorcht all my plans?"

"Yes. I believed that there was a strong possibility that

you couldn't cope, might be hurt, so I wanted you protected. And, yes, I believe that Military Intelligence should have known what you were doing. If you had knowledge that was vital to the country I believe that it was vital for your country to know it as well.''

''National security goes before betraying a friend?''

''If you want to phrase it that way then, well, yes I think it does.''

''Poor Shelly. Living in the past. Putting nationalism, flag-waving jingoism ahead of personal honor, ahead of everything. Not knowing that little nationalism is dead and world nationalism is the name of the game. The cold war is dead as well, Shelly, and hopefully soon, all war will be dead. And we'll be free of the burden of the military at last. A fossil, extinct—but too stupid to lie down. You've made your decision and you have told me about it. End of conversation. Good-bye Shelly, I don't think we'll be meeting again.'' He wiped his lips with his napkin, stood and turned away.

''You can't dismiss me like that. I came to make some explanation, apology maybe. I'm a person and I can be hurt. And you are hurting me, do you understand that? I came to make amends. You must be more machine than man if you can't understand that. You can't just turn your back on me and walk away!''

Which of course is exactly what he did.

# 44

## LA JOLLA, CALIFORNIA

### February 8, 2026

The date brushed against the edge of Erin Snaresbrook's attention as she read her personalized morning newspaper.

There was very little news of the accepted sort in it, no politics, no sports, but plenty of biochemistry and brain research. She was engrossed in an article about nerve growth and the nagging bothered her. Then she looked again at the date—and dropped the sheets of eternitree onto the table, took up her cup of coffee.

That date. She would never forget it, never. It might be put aside for a while when she was busy, then something would remind her and that day would be there again. The first sight of that shattered skull, the ruined brain, the immense feeling of despair that had overwhelmed her. The despair had passed to be replaced by hope—then immense satisfaction when Brian had survived.

Had another year really passed? A year during which she had not seen or talked to him, not once. She had tried to contact him but her calls were never returned. While she thought about it she touched his number, got the same recorded response. Yes, her message was noted and Brian would get back to her. But he never did.

A year was a long time and she did not like it. She stared out at the Torrey pine trees and the ocean beyond, unseeingly. Too long. This time she was going to do something about it. Woody answered his phone on the first ring.

*"Wood, security."*

"Woody, Dr. Snaresbrook here. I wonder if you could help me with a problem of communication."

*"You name it—you got it."*

"It's Brian. Today is the anniversary of that awful day when he was shot. This drove home the fact to me that it must be a year at least since I talked to him. I phone but he never calls back. I presume he is all right or I would have heard."

*"He's in great shape. I see him at the gym sometimes when I'm working out."* There was a long moment's silence before Woody spoke again. *"If you're not busy I think I can arrange for you to see him now. Is that all right?"*

"Excellent—I'm free most of the day," she said as she turned to the terminal to change a half dozen appointments. "I'll be there as quickly as I can."

*"I'll be waiting. See you."*

When she pulled her car out of the garage the sun had vanished behind thick clouds and there was a splatter of rain on her windshield. It grew heavier as she drove inland, but as always the barrier of the mountain ranges held back clouds and storm. Sunlight broke through as she drove down the Montezuma Grade and she opened the window to the desert warmth. Good as his word, Woody was waiting at the main Megalobe gate. He didn't open it, but instead came out to join her.

"Got room for a passenger?" he asked.

"Yes, of course. Climb in." She touched the button and the door unlocked and swung open. "Brian's not here?"

"Not often these days." When he sat down the door closed and locked, the seat belt slipped into place. "He usually works at home. Have you been to Split Mountain Ranch?"

"No—because I never even heard of it."

"Good. We like to keep a low profile there. Just head east and I'll show you where to turn. It's not really a ranch but a high security housing area for the top MI personnel. Condos and homes. Now that we have expanded into manufacturing here we needed someplace close by and secure for them to live."

"Sounds nifty. You look and sound concerned, Woody. What is it?"

"I don't know. Maybe nothing. That's why I thought you might talk to him. It's just that, well, we don't see him much anymore. Used to take meals in the cafeteria. No more. Hardly see him around. And when I do, well, distant is maybe the word for it. No joking, no small talk. I don't know if something is bothering him or not. Hang a right at that road coming up."

The road twisted out through the desert and ended in a wide gate set into a wall that stretched away on both sides. The Spanish colonial design, trees and planters, could not hide the fact the wall was solid and high, the apparently wrought iron gate more than decorative. It swung open as they approached and Snaresbrook drove into the courtyard beyond and stopped before a second gate. An elderly, uniformed man strolled out of a gatehouse disguised as a cantina.

"G'morning Mr. Wood. Just a few secs you and the doctor can go in."

"Good enough, George. Keeping you busy?"

"Day and night." He smiled calmly, turned and went back into the gatehouse.

"The security here is pretty laid-back," Snaresbrook said.

"The security here is the best in the world. Old George is retired. Likes the job. Gets him out of the house. He's just hired to say Hi to people—which he does very well. The real security is handled by an MI. It tracks every vehicle on the ground, every plane in the sky. By the time you got to Megalobe it knew who you were, what you were doing here, had contacted me, checked your identification and got my approval."

"If it's so great why the delay now?"

"No delay. Sensors in the ground are examining this car, checking all of its components, searching it for weapons or bombs, checking your home exchange to make sure that your phone is your phone—there we go." The outer gate was closed before the inner one opened. "This one MI does a better job than all my troops and technology over at Megalobe. Straight ahead now and it is about the fourth or fifth drive, name of Avenida Jacaranda."

"Quite something," Snaresbrook said as they parked in front of the large, starkly modern home.

"Why not? Brian is a millionaire or better by now. You should see the sales figures."

The voice spoke to them as they approached the front door.

"Good morning. I'm sorry to tell you that Mr. Delaney is not available right now—"

"I am Wood, security. Just shut up and tell him that I am here with Dr. Snaresbrook."

There was a short delay—then the door swung open. "Mr. Delaney will now see you," the disembodied voice said.

When they went down the hall and entered the high-ceilinged room Snaresbrook saw why Brian no longer needed to go to the laboratory. The one he had here was probably much better. Spartan and shining, computers and machines covered one wall. Before it sat Brian with an immobile MI at his shoulder. He was not looking at them but was staring vacantly into the distance.

"Please excuse us for a moment," the MI said. "But we are conferencing over a rather complex equation."

"Is that you, Sven?"

"Dr. Snaresbrook—how nice of you to remember. I am just a subunit programmed for simple responses. If you will be patient . . ."

Sven stirred then, formed its lower manipulators into legs and walked over to them. "What a distinct pleasure to see you both. We rarely get visitors here. I keep telling Brian all work and no play—you know. But he is a bit of a workaholic."

"So I see." She pointed at Brian, still not moving. "Does he know we are here?"

"Oh yes. I told him before I left the calculation. He just wants to work on it a bit more."

"Does he? All charm and friendship, our Brian. Woody, I see what you meant. Our friend Sven here is more human."

"Kind of you to say that, Doctor. But you must remember that the more I study intelligence and humanity, the more I become human—and hopefully more intelligent."

"You are doing a great job, Sven. I wish I could say the same for Brian."

Her sarcastic words must have penetrated his concentration, disturbed him. First he frowned, then shook his head. "You are not being fair, Doc. I have work to do. And the only way to get it done is to isolate emotions from logic. One cannot think clearly with hormones and adrenaline being pumped around the body. That is a big advantage over mankind that Sven and his lot have over flesh and blood intelligence. No glands."

"Admittedly I have no glands." Sven said. "But static discharges disrupt in the same manner from time to time."

"That is not true, Sven," Brian said coldly.

"You are correct—I was attempting a small joke."

Snaresbrook looked at them in silence. For an instant there Sven had seemed the more human of the two. As the MI was learning humanity—was Brian losing it? She brushed the terrible thought away. "You said that you were conferencing. You no longer need the physical optic-fiber connection?"

"No." Brian touched the back of his neck. "A slight modification and communication is accomplished by modulating infrared signals." He stood and stretched, attempted a weak smile. "Sorry if I was rude. Sven and I are onto something so big that it is frightening."

"What?"

"Not sure yet—I mean not sure if we can do it. And we are pushing like crazy because we want to get it done before the next meeting of the Megalobe board. It would be great to spring it there. But I'm being a bad host—"

"You certainly are!" Sven said. "But I hurry to make amends. Sir, madam, the sitting room is this way. Cool drinks, soft music, we are very hospitable when we but try."

Sven's hand flicked lightly in Brian's direction, a slight movement that suggested apology—perhaps resignation.

Brian and Woody had soft drinks but Snaresbrook, who rarely drank save at social functions, felt the sudden need for something different.

"Bombay martini on the rocks with a twist—and no vermouth. Can you manage that, Sven?"

"Well within my powers, Doctor. A moment if you please."

She sat in a deep and comfortable chair, folded her hands on her purse, and held her anger at bay. The martini would help. "How have you been keeping, Brian?"

"Very well. I work out when I can."

"And your head? Any negative symptoms, pains, anything at all?"

"Perfectly fine."

She nodded her thanks to Sven, sipped the drink. It did help. "It's been a long time since we have had a session with the connection machine."

"I know. I feel there is no need for that anymore. The CPU is integrated and I can access it at will. No problems."

"That's nice. Did you ever think of telling me about it? I never published more than a general description of the operation, since I was waiting for final results before I did."

There was a cold edge to her voice now. Brian was aware of it, flushed slightly.

"That's an oversight on my part. I'm sorry. Look, I'll write up everything and get the material to you."

"That would be nice. I've talked to Shelly a few times—"

"That is of no interest to me. Part of the past that I have forgotten."

"Fine. But just on general humanitarian terms I thought that you would like to know that her father had the bypass operation and is doing fine. She didn't take to civilian life and reenlisted."

Brian sipped his drink, looked out of the window, said nothing.

They left a half hour later when Brian said that he had to go back to work. Snaresbrook drove in silence until they were through the gate.

"I don't like it," she said.

"He promised to come to the gym more regularly, didn't he?"

"Wonderful. So that takes care of his social life. You heard his answers. Theaters, concerts—he has the best DAT and CD equipment here. Parties? Never was partying type. And girls, I was most unhappy at the way he slid away from that discussion at all. What do you think, Woody? You're his friend."

"I think—sometimes, looking at the two of them together. At times, if not all the time, it's like you said. Sven is the more human of the two."

# ENVOI

The meeting of the board of directors of Megalobe began promptly at ten in the morning. Kyle Rohart was Chairman now, had grown with the years of responsibility that had been thrust upon him. He motioned for silence.

"I think that we had better get started because there is a lot of ground to cover. Our annual report to the stockholders is due in a month and we are going to have difficulty in getting it together in time. The way production has grown on the new MI-directed assembly lines is almost unbelievable. But before we begin I would like you to all meet our new board member. Sven, I want to introduce you to the other members."

"Thank you, Mr. Rohart, but that will not be necessary. I recognize them from their photographs, know them well from their histories and records. Gentlemen, it is my pleasure to serve beside you. Please call upon me for any specialized information you might need. Remember that I have been with machine intelligence from, you might truthfully say, the very beginning."

There were murmurs of appreciation, even a few looks of blank astonishment from members not closely acquainted with MI. Rohart looked at his notes.

"We will begin with new products. Brian has something of importance to tell you. But before he does I must let you know that the first MI ship ever built has just sailed from Yokohama. The MI is both captain and crew, but at the insistence of the Japanese government a mechanic and an electrician will also be aboard. I know they will enjoy the voyage since they will have absolutely nothing to do." There was an appreciative laugh.

"Another thing you will want to hear about," Kyle said. "Our NanoCorp Division's new molecular microscope is now working almost perfectly. As you probably know it resembles a medical ultrasound scanner—but it is a million times smaller because we are using the latest nanotechniques. It operates by sending mechanical vibrations to nearby molecules and then analyses the resulting echoes. When we insert its probe into the nucleus of a cell we can find and explore the chromosomes, read that individual's entire genome in only a few minutes. Eventually this data will be used to reconstruct the full story of how every animal evolved. With this kind of knowledge we should be able to build from scratch virtually any kind of creature we want. For example, one of our geneticists sees no great problem to making a cow that gives maple syrup." There were a few appreciative laughs, and some other murmurs of concern. "Brian, you have the floor."

"Thanks Kyle. Gentlemen, I am being a little premature in telling you about a new product, but the prospects are so exciting that I felt you should know what we are working on. All credit goes to Sven for this one. It is his discovery and he worked out all of the details of how to make it into a practical process even before he brought me into the picture."

Brian took a deep breath. "If the math is correct and the new material, called SupereX, can be fabricated—it should change the whole picture of how we use energy. It will change the entire world!"

He waited until the room had quieted down before he went on. "This all has to do with the quantum theory in physics, of what the Nobel laureate Tsunami Huang called 'anisotropic phonon resonance'. But until now that theory has never been put into practical use. Sven has shown how to do just that. You've all heard of superconductors that transmit electricity without any loss. Now Sven has done the same for heat. His new material conducts heat almost perfectly, in one direction. In the opposite direction SupereX should be an almost perfect insulator. As you know the expensive modern insulations in our walls have R-values in the hundreds. According to the new theory, SupereX should have an R value of approximately one hundred million. And it can easily be sprayed on in the form of a paint—applied with a polarizing field."

He waited for a reaction, but no one knew what to say. *Businessmen,* he sighed to himself.

"An example—if a very thin film of SupereX is applied to a beer can, that can will keep the beer cold for years. We can throw away all the refrigerators in the country, eliminate our heating costs entirely. Electrical superconductors were never very practical because they did not work at normal temperatures. But now SupereX insulation will enable superconducting cables to transmit power without any loss— even between distant continents. The possibilities are incredible. Longitudinally polarized SupereX thermal-conducting cables will bring heat from the deserts and cold from the poles. To generate virtually cost-free thermo-electricity anywhere in between!"

This time there was a real reaction, shouts and cries that almost drowned Brian out.

"Think of what the world will be like! We can stop burning fossil fuels—terminate forever the threat of the greenhouse effect. Clean, nonpolluting energy can be the salvation of mankind. The Mideast oil crisis will end for good when all the oil wells there are shut down. If petroleum is used only as a chemical feedstock there is more than enough in America for all of our needs. The possibilities are almost endless. Sven has worked out some of the development details and will tell you about them. Sven?"

"Thank you, Brian," the MI said. "You are most generous in crediting me with the discovery, but your mathematical contribution far outweighed mine. I will begin with a development analysis."

Brian's phone buzzed and he tried to ignore it. When it buzzed again he picked it up.

"I told you to hold all calls—"

*"I'm sorry, sir, it's security. They insisted. Mr. Wood has*

*a registered package for you here at the front desk. It has been opened and checked out by the bomb detection team. Shall I hold it here or send it up? Mr. Wood is here and says that he will be happy to bring it up to you. He is of the opinion that you will want to see it at once."*

Why was he interested in this package so much that he had brought it over himself? It had to be important—and he wanted to find out why. Sven was doing very well here without him, and this shouldn't take long.

"All right. Tell him to bring it up and I'll be waiting for him."

Brian slipped out and was waiting in the outer office when Woody came in.

"It's from overseas, Brian, and personally addressed to you. Since you went off to Europe to launch your revolution I thought there might be some connection."

"Might be. Where is it from?"

"The return address on this says Schweitzer Volksbank in St. Moritz."

"I was there once, but didn't go near any bank . . . St. Moritz—let me see that!"

He tore off the wrapping and a videocassette dropped onto the bench.

"That's what it looked like in the X rays. Any message with it?"

"This is message enough. It says 'play me' loud and clear." He weighed it in his hand, looked at Woody's dark, stolid face. "I must look at this alone. Your suspicions were right—it is important. But I can't break a promise so I can't tell you why right now. But I will make another one. I'll let you know what it is about just as soon as I can."

"You do just that. Don't see I have any choice." Then he frowned. "Don't do anything stupid, hear?"

"Loud and clear. Thanks."

He went into the first empty office, closed the door and slipped the cassette into the machine. The screen flickered and cleared and showed a familiar book-lined study. Dr. Bociort was in his armchair. He raised a hand to the camera and spoke.

"I am saying good-bye, Brian. Or rather I have said good-bye sometime ago, since I made this recording soon after we met. I am an old man and filled with years—and mortal as the next. This recording has been left with my bank, which has instructions laid out in my will to post it to you after my demise. Therefore, you might say that I speak from the grave, as it were.

"When we met here I must now admit that I withheld one rather important bit of information from you. I do beg your forgiveness since it was done from pure selfishness. Had I revealed it, and had it led in turn to your discovering who your enemies are—that might have led in turn to my own death. We know they stop at nothing.

"I will talk no more about that. What I wish to tell you is that J. J. Beckworth is alive and living here in Switzerland. A country that specializes in anonymity and the keeping of secrets. It was only by accident that I saw him, coming out of a bank in Bern. Pure chance that he did not see me first. I of course no longer go to Bern, that is the reason I am here in St. Moritz. However, I did employ a firm of reliable investigators who located his residence. He is now living in a very expensive suburb of Bern under the name of Bigelow. I will read his address out to you and then I will say not *au revoir*, but a true and final good-bye."

Brian broke the stunned silence that followed Bociort's words with a cry of excitement.

"He's alive—and I know where to find him!"

Beckworth alive—the thought cut through him like a knife. The one man who would know all the details, all the people behind the theft and murders, would know everything. They tried to kill me, tried more than once. Almost wiped out my brain, put me in the hospital, altered my life in every way.

He would find Beckworth, find who was behind him. Find them and make them pay for what they had done to him. Brian paced the floor, forcing away the excitement and making himself think clearly—then reached for his telephone.

Benicoff would know what to do. He had started this investigation—now he was going to close it!

Ben was as elated by the news as Brian was—though he wasn't happy about the terms forced upon him.

*"This is really a matter for the police to take care of. Beckworth is a dangerous man."*

"The police can grab him after we have talked to him. I want to meet him face-to-face, Ben. I must do it. If you don't want to come with me I just have to do it alone. I have his address and you don't."

*"Blackmail!"*

"Please don't think that. It is just the way I have to go. You and I talk to him first and then the police grab him. We will take Sven along to record everything said. Okay?"

In the end Brian extracted reluctant agreement. Brian went back to the meeting but heard little of it. There was only a single thought in his mind now. Beckworth. As soon as possible he slipped out and went back to his apartment to pack a bag. Before he was done Sven knocked on the door.

"I was going to send for you as soon as the meeting ended. I have news—"

"I know. I listened to that video with great interest."

"I should have known."

"I was intrigued as you about the package. Will we be leaving soon?"

"Now. Let's go."

They met Ben at the Orbitport in Kansas in time for the evening flight to Europort in Hungary. The flight, out of the atmosphere and then back in, took less than half an hour. They spent ten times that amount of time on the sleeper train to Switzerland. Sven enjoyed the trip, enjoyed the attention he got. MIs in public were still a novelty.

The cabdriver passed the house, as instructed, and dropped them off at the next corner. Ben was still worried.

"I still think we should talk to the police before we go in there."

"There is too big a risk. If there is even the slightest chance that the people behind this thing have an informant or a tap in the local police department, we risk losing everything. The compromise is a good one. Your office will be on to Interpol and the Bern police in a half an hour. That means we get to talk to him first. Let's go."

A chime sounded somewhere inside the house and a moment later an AI opened the door. It was one of the simpler production models made under license in Japan.

"Mr. Bigelow, if you please."

"Is he expecting you?"

"I certainly hope so," Brian said. "I am a former associate of his from the United States."

"He is in the garden. This way, please."

The AI led the way through the house to a large room that opened out through French doors to the patio beyond. Beckworth sat with his back to them reading his newspaper.

"Who was it?" he asked.

"These gentlemen to see you."

He lowered the paper and turned to see them. His face froze when he saw Brian; he slowly rose to his feet.

"Well, gentlemen—it is about time you showed up. I have been keeping track of your activities and am quite amazed at your lack of enterprise. But you are here at last." There was no warmth in his voice; cold hatred in his expression. "So—Brian Delaney at last, and one of the new MIs. And I see that you have brought Ben as well. Still clumsily in charge of the investigation—which appears to finally have succeeded or you would not be here. Though I am afraid, Ben, that I cannot offer you my congratulations—"

"Why, J.J.? Why did you do it?"

"That is a singularly foolish question for you to ask. Didn't you know that the parent companies behind Megalobe were about to retire me? No insult intended, they said, but they wanted somebody with more technical skills. I considered this, then decided that retirement on my own terms would be more beneficial. It would also let me get rid of the old house, and old wife—and even more boring and grasping children. I would make a new life—and a far more financially rewarding one." He looked directly at Brian for the first, his face a sudden mask of icy hatred. "Why didn't you die the way you should have?"

Brian's face mirrored Beckworth's, hatred—but hard memories of pain were there as well. He was silent for a long moment as he carefully put his emotions under tight control. Then he spoke quietly.

"Who is behind the murders—the theft?"

"Don't tell me that you came all the way here just to ask me that? I should think that the answer would be obvious by now. You know better than I do who in the world is doing AI research."

"That's no answer," Brian said. "There are plenty of universities—"

"Don't be stupid. I was referring to national governments. Where else do you think the immense sums would come from to finance an expensive operation such as the one that was mounted against Megalobe?"

"You're lying," Brian said coldly, his anger suppressed, controlled. "Governments don't commit murder, hire assassins."

"My dear young man—have you been living under a rock? Anyone who has opened a newspaper in the last fifty years would laugh at your naïveté. Are you no student of world history? In this particular case the French government sent assassins to blow up a boatload of nuclear protesters— and succeeded very nicely in even killing one of them. And when the plot was discovered they whitewashed the whole thing, even lied enough to New Zealand to let the convicted murders go free. Nor are the French alone in this sort of operation on the world scene.

"Consider the Italian government and their undercover operation titled Gladio. Here the politicians authorized a secret network—in their own country and all of the NATO countries as well—with the criminally asinine idea of arming groups to fight guerrilla warfare—in the completely unlikely chance that the Warsaw Pact countries might not only win a war with them and occupy them as well. In reality Gladio gave weapons to right-wing terrorists and more people died."

"Are you telling me that the French—or the Italians backed your criminal plan?"

"Consider the British. They sent troops into Northern Ireland with a shoot-to-kill policy against their own citizens.

When this was investigated by a police officer from the mainland they bankrupted and ruined an innocent business-man in order to halt the investigation. Then, not satisfied with shooting citizens on their own islands, they sent a team of cold killers to Gibraltar to shoot down foreign nationals in the streets there. Then they even sent experts overseas to teach soldiers of the Khmer Rouge, one of the most murder-ous regimes in history, how to plant sophisticated mines to murder more civilians."

"It's the British, then?"

"You are still not listening. The Russian Stalin sent millions of his own citizens to death in the gulags. That fine monster, Saddam Hussein, used napalm and poison gas on his own Kurdish citizens. Nor are our hands that clean. Didn't the CIA slip down to Nicaragua, a country we were theoretically at peace with, and plant mines in the harbors there—"

"Which of them, then?" Benicoff said, breaking in. "I'm not going to deny that many crimes have been com-mitted by many countries. That is one of the nastier legacies of nationalism and painfully stupid politicians that, along with war, must be eliminated. Nor did we come here for any political lectures. Which one did you approach with this plan? Which one is behind the theft and murders?"

"Does it matter? They are all capable and I can assure you that more than one was eager to do it. Perhaps I should tell you—but there is something far more important that I have to do."

Beckworth reached into his jacket pocket and took out a pistol, which he pointed at them.

"I am very good with this—so stand where you are. I'm leaving—but first I have something for you, Brian. Some-thing too long delayed. Your death. If you had died the way you were supposed to I would not be hiding here but would be a free and honored man. And exceedingly rich. I'm leaving—and you are dying. At last—"

*"Killing forbidden!"*

Sven roared the words, amplified and ear-destroying. Hurled itself forward at the same instant. Reaching for Beckworth.

Three shots sounded in rapid succession and the MI fell back. Holding onto Beckworth. Shuddered and fell to the ground still clutching the man in unbreakable embrace. Beckworth struggled to free himself, to raise the gun. Aimed at Sven's head. Fired again—into the brain case.

The result was instantaneous—horrifying.

As every single branch of the tree manipulators sprung apart, largest to smallest, largest to smallest, countless thousands of them sprung wide.

Sharper than the sharpest knives, the tiny twigs of metal slashed through the man's body. Severed cell from cell, sliced open every blood vessel in an instant. In a silent explosion of gore Beckworth died. One moment alive—then only blood-welling flesh.

Ben gazed at the terrible sight, turned away. Brian did not. He ignored the gory flesh, saw only Sven, his MI. His friend. As dead as Beckworth.

Still alive in its other incarnations. But now, here, dead.

"An accident," Ben said, getting himself under control.

"Was it?" Brian asked, looking down at the two unmoving and silent forms. "It could have happened that way. Or Sven might just have saved us a lot of trouble. We'll never know."

"I suppose not. Nor will we know which country Beckworth went to. But as he said, I wonder if it really matters. It's all over now, Brian—and that is what counts."

"Over?" Brian raised his head and his face was cold and empty of all emotion. "Yes, it's over for you. Over for Sven as well. But it is certainly not over for me. They killed me, don't you realize that? They killed Brian Delaney. I have some of his memories—but I am not him. I'm half a person, half a memory. And I am beginning to believe that I am something not quite human either. Look what they took away. First my life—then my humanity."

Ben started to speak and Brian silenced him with a raised finger.

"Don't say it, Ben. Don't try to reason with me or argue with me. Because I know what I am. Perhaps it is better this way. I'm closer to an MI now than I am to you. I accept that. I don't like it or dislike it—I just accept it. So let it be."

Brian's smile was wry, crooked, not at all funny. "Let it go at that. As an MI I won't have to mourn for my lost humanity."

The wailing sirens of the approaching police cars were the only sounds that broke the silence of the room.